THE HUNT FOR THE RED BANNERS

PAUL ALLEN

PAUL ALLEN BOOK

ISBN 9780645220827
Published by PaulAllenBooks.online

❀ Created with Vellum

CHAPTER 1
CHARACTERS

Abu Ahmed, Older Brother, Bagdad
Abu Sarek, Younger Brother, Bagdad
Alan James, MI5 IT Counter-Terrorism
Bratva Xasin, Nuclear Specialist Russian
Brian Clinton, ASIS London Embassy
Carol Gorstren, Coroner Stockholm
Carol Lapel, U.K. Home Secretary
Chief Alvald, Vardo Police
Darko Gusev, Russian Mafia
David Hallgren, R.P.S. Sweden
Denya Driminov, Russian President
Dr John Moody, ASIS Agent Australia
Emma Smirnov, ASIS Agent Oslo Station
Erik Hakansson, Police officer Sweden
Frank Warren, ASIS Statopn Chief Stockholm
Franz Zhukov, Russian Oligarch
George Philips, Dept. Energy Melbourne
Gideon Downer, D.I.D. Director Canberra
Greg Arnfinn, NRPA Inspector
Hunter Whyatt, ASIS Agent Sydney

Hussain Humid, Terrorist
Igor Medkov, Security Council Russia
Isaakovic Apresyan, Russian Mafia
Ivan Bely, S.V.R. Russia Foreign Intelligence
Jayanbalan, Detective Kaula Lumpur
Jessica Von Berg, ASIS Chief Oslo
John Lewis, HQJOC IT Canberra
John Porter, PM Australia.
John Quilliam, MI5 Boss
Karen Richards, ASIS Assistant Director
Laura Ruby, E.L.B. Builders
Leonid Prokhor, Police Murmansk
Liv Wei, Dept Intelligence Bureau China
Mitch Burleigh, Counter-Terrorism London
Nicolai Maskim, ASIS IT Sydney
Noel Adams, MI5 IT Counter-Terrorism
Paul the Apostle, MI5 Agent KL
Peter Jonas, ASIS IT Sydney
Rachel Stewart, Embarkment Police
Sergi Moghailov, Russian Mafia
Sir Brain Jackson, MI5 Retired Agent
Sir Robert Allen, MI5 Boss.
Steve Joel, UK Immigration Officer
Vegard, FSK Team Leander Norway
Vlad, Russian Mafia
Vlad Drovopsky, Russian Mafia

CHAPTER 2

MOVIE STUDIOS, GOLD COAST AUSTRALIA

"Get out of here now!" shouted Hunter.

The Pilot of the US CX-22A Osprey was now stationary, hovering thirty feet off the ground on the sandy outskirts of the western Iraqi city of Fallujah. Like the bird, these aircraft tilt their propellers upwards, becoming a helicopter. Directly behind the Osprey were apartments either shot away or burnt out and now home to some trigger-happy jihadists.

"You're in the wrong location!" Hunter had stumbled over three wounded U.S. soldiers while stalking a Syrian gun supplier. He was six feet six inches and weighed 260 pounds of solid muscle, including his battle scars. His fists were bricks, and his face turned to leather from the Iraq sun. Hunter's olive skin and a three-month-long beard helped him fit right in with the locals, except for his bright blue eyes.

ASIS agent Hunter threw his satellite phone to the soldier slumped in the front seat, semi-conscious, "Order an extraction, now! Hey, wake up, mate! Warn them that the extraction site will be in hostile territory. You know how to contact them?"

The tilt-rotor plane was blowing walls of blinding dust, flicking sunburnt rubbish everywhere, and getting the wrong attention. The Osprey was in the wrong place.

"Get out of there!" shouted Hunter.

Three dark silhouettes stood near a burnt-out building. One of them had a man-portable surface-to-air missile. "Who sold you that?" cried Hunter. He saw the missile flash of light and the whisper of smoke ascending—the pilot powered up the two Rolls-Royce turboshaft engines. Countermeasures were shot out of the body of the Osprey, tempting the missile to go away. It reminded Hunter of a New Year's Eve fireworks over the Sydney Harbour bridge.

"Too late! Get out of there!" he shouted again.

Even the Osprey gunner, seeing the same flash and smoke on his LCD screen, fired 50 rounds per second from the six-barrel belly-mounted Gatling gun. The three dark silhouettes retreated from the Gatling gun and watched.

It was too little and too late.

The missile destroyed one turboshaft engine, and shrapnel punched the neighbouring buildings like bayonets. One graphite-fibre rotor blade passed through the surviving engine at full power, causing all the rotor blades to become uncontrolled projectiles. The $73 million Osprey flipped over, crashed, and exploded into a rising ball of red and yellow flames.

Hunter dropped his binoculars as the wind pushed the burning smoke towards his position. He planted his foot, shouting, "Get out of that hornet's nest!"

The V8 came to life, and the belts rumbled. The turbocharger forced compressed air into the motor, and the fuel burnt faster. Gravel flew as the tyres spun hard and gripped, launching the truck forward.

Walking through the smoke towards the Osprey, three insurgents fired their AK 47s into the now-dying carcass of the burning Osprey. Like a soccer team, they wore black clothing and utilities with Kevlar vests. They held weapons gangster style, shouting and whooping, giving high fives to each other. He looked sideways at the two semi-conscious soldiers. One was in his thirties, aboriginal, skinny and six foot six; in lousy shape, injuries extensive but still awake but bleeding. The other bloke had suffered blood loss, a broken arm and a leg. He had that look of a mournful undertaker face.

"Why were you blokes out here in the badlands?" shouted Hunter.

His passengers didn't reply. "Hold these Berettas. Point and shoot whatever moves! Don't blackout on me!" shouted Hunter. He checked the soldier in the back.

"Hey, don't give up, mate!" The guy might survive the next sixty minutes. "Hold tight; this will get ugly." The truck launched forward as Hunter drove directly into the path of insurgents. The truck was bringing death and a swirling dust storm. Jihadists were dragging the injured pilot out of the wreckage.

"Three hundred meters to go, boys, get ready!" Hunter was eleven seconds away. He knew what these jihadists' next step was. They wasted precious seconds turning on their cell phones, opening photo or video apps, and not focusing on what was coming their way. "No time to waste, boys. Start shooting now!" screamed Hunter. This plane carries up to twenty-five soldiers. 'How would that work out?'

One soldier had survived the tumble roll of the Osprey and was crawling out of the wreckage, firing his weapon and wounding two insurgents. That left one insurgent unscathed. Hunter saw the gunner retreat behind the burning plane. The uninjured insurgent dropped the pilot onto the hard, sun-baked gravel and moved forward, firing his A.K. 47s at the new target. The insurgents saw the approaching truck barrelling towards them but were not fast enough. Hunter thought of 10-pin bowling. "No more fighting for you blokes," said Hunter. He got out of his truck and removed their weapons, knowing more insurgents were on their way.

The soldiers in Hunter's truck cabin were firing at a new group of Jihadists attracted by the sound of gunfire. Hunter grabbed two insurgents' A.K. 47s and gave them to both the pilot and the gunner. He checked his six, grabbed both men's collars and dragged them back to his truck.

"Can you walk? Any others in that plane?" asked Hunter.

The pilot's blood was spilling onto the ground. Bullets had blown through one shoulder and shattered both ankles. "No, my ankles are broken. Just three of us," said the pilot.

"Only three, not twenty-five?" asked Hunter.

"Yes, us two and one more," groaned the pilot, now spitting out blood.

"Keep firing those AK.s until they are empty. I don't care for your pain; keep firing!"

Hunter then took a bullet in his leg. The Osprey exploded again, and the insurgents retreated, giving Hunter a few more seconds. Hunter lifted and threw them into the back of the truck, giving them the third AK 49 as a reserve. "Give me cover now!" shouted Hunter, limping back from the last marine.

The insurgents retreated to safety. Hunter found the last wounded soldier on fire, scattered among the wreckage of charred metal and burning rubber. He dragged him to the truck and threw him in the back. Hunter hobbled to the truck cab, got in and shouted, "Keep firing!" but the two in the front passenger seats were both unconscious.

He grabbed both Berettas and fired. Then he threw his truck into reverse and punched the accelerator hard. His desert tyres were spinning, causing vast plumes of dust, making the vehicle invisible. Hunter dropped the Berettas in his lap and threw the fire extinguisher, which hit the pilot.

He shouted to one bloke, "Put that guy out!" He lifted his Beretta gun and kept shooting. The V8 engine turbocharger screamed, burning gasoline as Hunter did a fast reverse handbrake turn, then powered off, heading to the closest forward operating base of Camp Bah-aria in Fallujah, in the Al Anbar province.

There was no response. The pilot asked, "Who are you? You look local, but your accent, you're American, no Australian?"

"Doesn't matter, mate," replied Hunter.

Everybody in the truck clapped and smiled. The people outside the 4WD truck clapped, with some heading off to get coffee and morning tea.

"I think this script can work as an opener. Are you happy with those scenes?" asked George Gibson, the movie director. George graduated from Bond University School of Media on the Gold Coast.

"I'm worried about the truck running over the insurgents like a bowling ball in an alley," said Kedesh, assistant to the director. "G.G., it may push the movie classification rating M15+ to 18+, you know, strong violence. Guns are okay, but ploughing into people."

"Okay, the script needs adjusting," said G.G. "What do you think, Hunter?"

"Make the collision implied," Hunter said. I'm sorry, G.G.; my boss needs me."

"When will you be back?" asked G.G.

"Beats me, mate!" replied Hunter.

CHAPTER 3

ASIS -AUSTRALIA SECRET INTELLIGENCE SERVICE

Mr Nicolae Maksim, a key operative of a division within ASIS, was tasked with intercepting and recording all digital communications. His expertise in Cybersecurity, honed through his doctoral studies at Sydney University, made him the perfect candidate for this mission. He was fluent in Russian, a skill that proved invaluable when he overheard a mobile phone conversation between an unknown S.V.R. agent and a Russian oligarch, Franz Zhukov.

Franz Zhukov, the subject of Mr Maksim's surveillance, was a man of immense wealth and power. His involvement in shipping and communications had earned him a fortune of twelve billion U.S. dollars. However, his excessive lifestyle, marked by his weight, baldness, and violent tendencies, painted a different picture. ASIS had meticulously documented his actions, revealing a man who, despite his public support for the president, was not as he seemed.

The mobile phone conversation was brief. "Confirm W.J. got 77. Confirm R.B." The code made Mr Maksim suspicious.

The S.V.R. agent replied, "Confirmed."

Maksim recorded the conversation, typed Franz Zhukov, and tagged the following searchable words: W.J., 70, R.B., S.V.R. He then coded an alert when and if either Franz Zhukov or the S.V.R. agent made contact again with each other or someone else. He recorded the burner phone numbers, adding keywords and phrases with other Russian oligarchs on his list.

Maksim wondered if anyone had read his reports.

CHAPTER 4

BAGDAD IRAQ

"The breeze contained contaminants for sure," said Abu.

It was suffocating. Small stones were falling to the ground like pellets of rain. They could taste the smoky metallic ash in their mouths. The blinding particles had an electric charge but were molten pieces of falling metal, burning people's clothing and skin as they ran. Abu squinted at the vanishing sunlight. It kept reappearing through the clouds of coloured, distorted smoke, causing bouts of coughing. He had to cover his eyes and rub his stinging eyes several times. Few people could recognize Abu. The drastic weight and hair loss changed his features but not his spirit.

He thought standing on a battered U.S. military prison sign was symbolic. Tasting freedom, hundreds of prisoners ran, shouting in the chaos and smiling. Abu took a deep breath and followed. Although some explosions continued, nothing would stop them from seeking freedom.

Most of the prison population ran through the open spaces between the prison buildings and the breached perimeter wall of what used to be called Abu Ghraib. Built by British contractors in the 1950s, expanded by Hussein, abandoned and vandalized, rebuilt by the US-led coalition, then closed in 2014 and was now a burning inferno. Ten minutes ago, 120 mortar rounds flew directly into the prison. Extremists, future ISIS terrorists, hardened al-Qaeda militants and suspected rebels ran to freedom through a wall of gunfire.

Iraq correctional officers abandoned their posts first when the mortars started exploding. Contractors replaced them, but as the one hundred and twenty RPG mortars kept coming like an endless flock of birds heading south for the winter, they, too, retreated to a hardened section of the prison.

Four vehicles, loaded with C-4 explosives, had driven up to different parts of the perimeter wall. Drivers left the engines on and ran for cover. Released energy from the C-4 created light, heat and a devastating shock wave, killing insurgents, obliterating vehicles and destroying the prison wall.

Even the ground heaved and shook. In one sense, it was an impressive statement. Then the RPG mortars did their job, followed by one hundred and twenty-five armed men and women pushing through the dust, putrid smoke and falling debris, ready to fight. The return fire was brutal for the first thirty seconds, and then it stopped as the contractors retreated. Two thousand prisoners emerged from the prison building, shouting and celebrating their good fortune. There were recognizable bomb makers, jihadist leaders and terrorist tacticians. Chosen fighters were escorted to vehicles and escaped; other drivers abandoned the damaged cars and ran for their lives.

Abu smiled when he saw Ahmed. "I'm covered in dust, almost deaf, and I'm bleeding," shouted Abu.

"But you are okay?" asked Ahmed.

"Yes, I am more than okay. I am good," replied Abu, hugging his brother.

"We must go now. You need food, clothes and a haircut, and you smell," said Ahmed. They both laughed. Abu Ahmed and Abu Sarek were brothers. Both were the same height, dark olive skin tones, but with distinct personalities. Ahmed was the planner, thick-skinned, a trader in stolen military goods, and his older brother, Abu, was more emotionally outgoing and friendly.

CHAPTER 5

QUEENSLAND AUSTRALIA

Dr John Moody lived on a cattle property in Western Queensland. He was familiar with handguns but preferred sniper rifles. At 12, his father had imported a McMillan TAC-50 calibre sniper rifle. Every day, his father gave him one bullet. Before using the McMillan T.A.C. 50, his father wanted him to calculate the barometric pressure, the range, wind direction, gravity, humidity and even the Coriolis effect act upon the bullet by observing his environment. Only then was he given the ammunition. Bullets move in a curve, not a straight line. Over long distances, a shot will drift right when shooting in the northern hemisphere and left in the southern hemisphere.

John's dad trained him to consider everything before firing. He fired one bullet a day for ten years, and his dad extended the target each week.

The cattle industry collapsed and bankrupted his dad's company. John left home, completed his medical studies at Sydney University, and joined the Australian Army in Timor. He was tall, intelligent, muscular, with sandy blonde-red hair, a warm, friendly personality, and religious.

Sniper skills are perishable, so John joined sniper training teams every six months. He had to apply, and often, his credentials opened doors. He flew to New Zealand to train with their elite special forces team. On the battlefield, snipers are the most feared, creating psychological nightmares for soldiers. For John, this skill was not for war but for sport. When the final day of training arrived, the supervisor announced, "A Canadian sniper had shot an insurgent in Iraq at a distance of two miles or 3,540 meters."

"Here is the challenge. I will set up three targets, 1,500 meters, 2,500 meters, and 3,540 meters," said the trainer. He took the team to a high-rise building on the isolated property and said, "Everybody listens. I have a few questions about the target at 3,540 meters. How much will your bullet drop?"

John closed his eyes, converting from meters, and said, "6,705 inches, two inches per foot or 940 feet per second."

John opened his eyes and saw the trainer looking at him. "How many foot-pounds of energy does it have when it hits the target?"

It took a minute, and John said, "1,472 foot-pounds of energy."

CHAPTER 6

BAGDAD ABU GHRAIB.

"Ahmed, was this you?" asked Abu. Ahmed smiled. "Thank you for rescuing the parents. I got your message."

The C-4 used had a unique metallic code that could be traced. The tagging agent produces a distinctive vapour signature to aid detection. A bomb technician from the U.S. State Department identified the C-4 as stolen or sold from its ammunition bunker.

Ahmed looked at the fires consuming the prison. "Brother, are you ready to fight again?"

He wiped soot and dust from his face. His eyes were red. "I need time to recover, Ahmed. Look at the prison; what a glorious sight!" said Abu. The fires were consuming the place of death and torture. For Abu, he could close that chapter of his life.

Ahmed waited a few minutes and said, "Abu. I need to explain something to you. I must keep your identity secret. I have a plan."

Abu didn't understand. Years later, the meaning of that simple sentence would become apparent. It would cause a division between them, a betrayal of trust.

CHAPTER 7

DARLING POINT, SYDNEY

Eric Miller is a businessman who imports low-cost Chinese security camera systems and sells them online. He also runs a more profitable business from his single-bedroom apartment in Darling Point, Sydney. He sells shell companies worldwide, despite the tightening of Australian Government regulations. Although Miller's trade is not illegal, his shell companies have links to criminal networks.

He provides nominee directors who appear on the directorship in exchange for a fee, often his drinking friends. Nominee directors mask those who work in shell companies and criminals can hide their identities. Most people use shell companies to open bank accounts anywhere in the world. The banks take their profits, the criminals move their laundered money, and nominees get paid. Miller has no direct connection to any shell company. On a Friday afternoon, Miller was ready to go to Double Bay for a drink and meal. He had one final shell company called Sarek Industries to set up for two offshore Chinese Government men.

CHAPTER 8

raq Police and the Contractors will be rounding up whoever they can catch. We need to move indoors. I posted a burner cell phone for our parents. Use this one to call them. Keep it short," asked Ahmed.

"Thanks," replied Abu.

Ahmed leaned over the bench and grabbed his emergency military first-aid package. "Here, use this," said Ahmed. He injected himself, washed, and then stapled an open wound with the phone wedged between his shoulders and head. "Nobody is answering. I'll try later."

"Do you recall when we fought in Fallujah?" asked Ahmed.

"Yes, in the spring of 2007. It's an ugly place west of Baghdad. I became injured, caught, then sent to prison," replied Abu.

"They messed up your identity," suggested Ahmed.

"Oh," said Abu. "When did those coalition troops go home?" asked Abu.

"2011. Embassy employees under the State Department and independent military contractors are still here," replied Ahmed.

"Those contractors were in charge of the prison. They play by other rules," said Abu. "What have you been doing?'

"I kept fighting," replied Ahmed. "I continued as an insurgent for years." He hasn't told Abu yet that he has changed tactics. He created a fake profile for Abu as a victorious al-Qaeda mastermind, leader and tactician. When ISIL's relationship with al-Qaeda changed, Ahmed saw his opportunity.

He launched a collection of crusades of strategic bomb strikes in Government Buildings at night, avoiding civilian casualties. His militia torched several empty Chaldean Churches and liberated militants from Bagdad's westernmost suburban Police station with no human fatalities. In the Sinjar region in Northern Iraq, the motherland of Iraq's Yazidi religious minority, Ahmed convinced entire villages of an imminent attack. Using several tractor-trailers, they packed trailers with people from all the Yazidi villages. They drove them up to the Kurdish forces using Yazidi drivers, declaring they required a safe passageway from violent radicals.

But in Bagdad, armed with pictures of empty Yazidi villages, Ahmed posted Abu's glorious victory over this religious minority group that many viewed as pagans on social media. Each post inferred genocides and atrocities.

Ahmed turned to Abu. "Are you hungry?"

"You mean, am I ready to eat actual food," said Abu.

Ahmed documented each campaign on a jihadist blog and attributed it to 'Abu the Islamic Scholar and Fighter.' Whispers, rumours, and gossip proved that Ahmed's profile of Abu was working. Lebanese Shiite militia claimed Abu would inspire fighters on a Livestream channel.

They only heard his voice as he shared his vision. He would slip past you the next day, leaving money with instructions for the next battle. No one saw him. He was a mystery. It amazed people that he could swap languages from Lebanese to German, Syrian to English to Arabic. Ahmed laughed at such nonsense. Abu became more powerful and mysterious by the day.

He fuelled talk of Abu with the title of Caliph. It was complete utter nonsense but served Ahmed's purpose.

Ahmed made himself the contact for Abu. It was a dangerous arrangement for both hostile and friendly actors, especially the emerging Dash.

CHAPTER 9

LONDON COUNTERTERRORISM

Mitch Burleigh was in charge of all the U.K. Counterterrorism units with a central London headquarters. He was a tall and confident leader who expressed intimidation by wearing black army-style clothing with a double-shoulder gun holster instead of a suit and tie. He had wiry black hair with lots of grey showing through, robust facial features, heavy eyebrows, and a short temper.

His contempt for PowerPoint presentations with coloured sketches and spinal-bound notebooks with policies, strategies, and processes was well known.

He was a bully and a street-smart guy. Burleigh had recruited various skilled individuals: ex-cops, ex-soldiers, ex-MI6, computer operators, and wiretap experts. These units were competent and clandestine, and politicians never challenged his budget or techniques. There were no out-of-shape people on his team. He discriminated, ignoring P.C.'s complaints thrown his way.

Currency and certification were crucial to Burleigh. Today was a suburban sniper and arrest certification training day. Each team member will train using a Remington 750 rifle with a Leupold Mark 5.9 tactical scope with live ammunition.

The location is a former WWII airfield converted to a fake suburb with cardboard people. He was proud of his team, loved the action and hated politics and the office.

Office workers were time-wasters and paper pushers. Burleigh stood with his hands on his hips, shouting and giving orders all day. He loved power.

He also had a secret.

CHAPTER 10

STREETS OF BAGDAD.

Ahmed was expecting vehicular roadblocks and even hostile ambushes. Insurgents trained Ahmed in tactical driving, a technique used to capture car occupants. You hit your target vehicle at speed and extract your target while the occupants are still in shock. Ahmed then taught fighters the skill of ramming a blockade without stopping.

The stolen U.S. army S.U.V. could easily smash through any blockade except a tank. The airbags were disabled as an exploding airbag stopped the fuel pump. Then you were dead in the water.

"Did they answer?" asked Ahmed

"They are happy that I am okay. Dad said, thanks for saving their lives and paying for their new accommodation," said Abu. He stopped talking as Ahmed was scanning for any aggressively approaching vehicles.

Abu asked, "Why did the Americans target our parents?"

"They didn't know you were in prison," said Ahmed, distracted

"What do you mean?" asked Abu.

"They thought you were living with our parents," said Ahmed.

"I don't understand," responded Abu. "Why target me?"

"While in prison, you became a hero," declared Ahmed.

Abu shouted, "Roadblock!"

The vehicle ahead straddled the road. It was a large sedan similar to a Police vehicle V8, maybe a mercenary vehicle. It is heavy with the engine up front and lighter at the trunk. Mercenaries use 4X4 cars, but not today.

"Any shooters?" asked Ahmed.

"Not sure! There is only one person behind the vehicle," shouted Abu.

Ahmed knew this S.U.V. was a body-on-frame vehicle with good rigidity using high-strength steel.

Abu shouted, "Shotgun. He sees us."

Ahmed put the vehicle into a lower gear with only seconds left before impact to increase torque and accelerate hard. The motor screamed. He aimed his left frame rail at the rear wheel axle of the obstructing vehicle to create the bump. The impact was hard. The roadblock vehicle spun like a top, flicking the shooter and Shotgun into the air.

Ahmed looked in the rear-view mirror. "Did he use his cell or radio?"

Abu spun around in his seat, "He's out to it." Ahmed slowed and elected a substitute route to his factory. He changed his mind.

"We have no time for a surveillance detection run. The drones will be flying. Wipe your prints," added Ahmed. He swung into a laneway, "We're getting rid of this vehicle," declared Ahmed.

"Torch it?" asked Abu.

"No, burning. It will invite scrutiny," replied Ahmed. He parked the SUV in a side alley and left the keys in the ignition. As they returned to Ahmed's factory, he asked Abu, "Are you interested?"

"Maybe," said Abu.

Ahmed said, "It will put us both on a terrorist list."

"I'm already on it; I've been busy while in prison, remember?" said Abu

They both laughed. Ahmed said imagine, "An independent Islamic state handed to us. Imagine that!"

Abu looked at him and thought Ahmed was dreaming. 'What a

stupid idea.' Just surviving in this city without getting yourself killed was a daily achievement. Ahmed stopped walking and said, "If this mission is successful, we will control the region west of Baghdad, either by demand or civil war. Topple the Shiite-dominated central government, and then we create an independent Islamic state. Remove the Yazidi mob, empty the Nineveh Plains, and throw out contractors and westerners."

Abu raised his eyebrows and said, "Just the two of us?"

"Yes. Just the two of us!" replied Ahmed.

"You're mad," said Abu.

"Maybe, if we do this right, you will inspire a new generation of Islamic fighters," said Ahmed.

Abu replied, "Ahmed, you're dreaming and mad." They walked past his factory and home, turning left into a vehicle boneyard on the other side of the lane.

"We stay in this shadow. We watch and wait," said Ahmed. He got out his phone, opened his video surveillance app, and scrolled backwards. "No one entered the street in the last few hours. Keep to the shadows, okay? There are drones."

"Drones, Ahmed? Do you think they are watching us?" asked Abu. They saw no movement in the lane or the nearby factories. Entry into Ahmed's factory was from the back of the building.

"Look, a slither of paper dropped from the door seal," said Ahmed. We're safe. Come, are you hungry?" Abu showered and shaved, and then they ate together. "While you were in prison, I selected empty enemy buildings to bomb. I was pretending to be you," said Ahmed.

"Why did you pretend to be me?" asked Abu.

"Everybody wants an independent Islamic state. I needed a mysterious leader to inspire the insurgents, and it worked," said Ahmed. "Our people have a hero, Abu. You are inspiring an uprising," said Ahmed. "People are giving money to the cause."

'And I am the fall guy,' Abu thought, unhappy. Where is all the money coming from?'

Ahmed continued to make a fresh cup of coffee and said, "I don't know. It is a serious amount of money."

Abu was troubled over Ahmed's negligence to the source of the money, saying, "It could be those Syrian jihadists."

"Why do you say that, Abu?" replied Ahmed.

"They are a treacherous mob, Ahmed. They manufacture Captagon. The police arrested some of them in Spain," said Abu. "The street price for Captagon on the last seizure was USD 1.6 billion. They were selling it to bankroll their missions."

"Drug money is still money," answered Ahmed.

"But you're contracting with savage people," replied Abu.

"How do you know this?" asked Ahmed.

"How do I know? They were in my cell block, boasting of their wealth, soliciting to recruit me and others. When the explosions started, they were running in front of me. I thought those savages targeted Abu Ghraib to get their workers. I accompanied them until I looked at you. It could be those boys who are backing you," said Abu.

It disturbed him that Ahmed had implicated him in his mad project, notably with the Syrians.

Ahmed added, "$1.6 billion? This is drug money. It could be those guys. I don't know."

"They will kill you if you look at them the wrong way!" Abu was pacing the room. "Do they know where you live?" Abu's concern was straightforward. "Taking cash from the Syrians is no different from getting money from the Italian mafia."

"What is it called?" asked Ahmed.

"Captagon is the brand name. It's an amphetamine drug, fenethylline hydrochloride, used for depression and hyperactivity. It's a nasty stimulant drug," replied Abu. "They will turn on you, Ahmed. They will demand something in return."

"Okay, Abu, settle down; I get it," replied Ahmed, now exasperated by his younger brother lecturing him. "Look, I can't pinpoint who is giving me the cash. There have been no conditions to any preceding missions except this last one."

"What are the conditions?" asked Abu.

"Abu, sit down. Just cool off for a minute. Let me clarify. After a few successful missions, a stranger greeted me in a café," answered Ahmed. I was dining in a café. This man entered, scanned the room, recognized me, came, and sat down. He said nothing at first. I ordered fruit, some rice pudding, and Coffee. The guy whispered in a low voice as he gazed at the exits."

Abu asked, "Who was he a Kurd, Iranian, Syrian, C.I.A., ASIS, MI6, what?"

"He spoke Arabic," replied Ahmed. "I politely inquired of his name in Kurdish, then suggested tea instead of Coffee in the Turkoman dialect. He realized what I was doing and said, stop. He said he was just a courier. His contact was offering to finance all of Abu's missions. It was up to you to say yes or no. The guy gave me a box of money as goodwill regardless of your decision."

"Did the courier identify himself or his contact?" asked Abu.

"No. If I disagreed, I could keep the money in the shoebox, and the meeting never happened," explained Ahmed.

"Do you believe he wasn't working with those Syrians?" asked Abu.

"No," replied Ahmed. "He gave me a burner phone and said we would never meet again. The burner phone is the only communication tool. I receive a text saying, 'Any plans?' I'd respond by typing in a mission target. If they agree, they say yes or No. They have never said no. Every time I sent a text with a target, they sent the money."

"How?" asked Abu.

"I'd receive G.P.S. coordinates plus the money pickup date, time and location," replied Ahmed. "I've used a Faraday Cage to stop any Americans listening. I had one concern. The courier recognized me and knew I was in that café."

"When he left, did you follow him?" asked Abu

"Yes. The courier's vehicle was old, considering the money we're dealing with," said Ahmed.

"How much money?" asked Abu.

"Lots. In the Shoebox was USD 50,000," said Ahmed. For three years now, they have backed these missions with no conditions attached. I outline the target, and then the money arrives. There were no time frames, reports, feedback, nothing."

"How many missions?" asked Abu.

"Twelve," said Ahed.

"All attributed to me," said Abu.

He nodded. "We have one last mission; it's risky and big," said Ahmed.

Abu sensed a minor shift in Ahmed's tone. They picked at their food and drained a pot of fresh tea, and Ahmed appeared to loosen up. Abu asked Ahmed a question that had plagued him.

"I don't understand the connection," said Abu. "Is the money connected to an independent Islamic State? If they were residents, that vision would make sense, plus their desire to remain anonymous. They are wealthy. If they are not residents, what is their agenda?"

Abu stood and crossed his arms and said, "Ahmed, what is the big deal about an Islamic State? I don't wish to humiliate you. Why do you crave a thousand square miles of desert? Have you thought this through?"

Ahmed was fuming at the insult but didn't reveal it. "Six months ago, something changed. Perhaps it was a security issue. Something happened. I received a text. But this time, it was a hyperlink to a blog about gardening."

Abu gave a surprised look.

"Yes, that's right, gardening. It didn't make sense to me either. I read the articles and thought the link was incorrect. I was searching for the business contact details at the bottom of the site. Then I found it. It was in the comments area, the final mission details," replied Ahmed.

"What is the last mission?" asked Abu.

CHAPTER 11

MI5 BASEMENT, LONDON

In the MI5 basement in London, Noel and Driscoll stood discussing their plan of action. Noel's doubts were evident as he asked, "Will this plan work?"

Driscoll's response was confident and reassuring, "She just recognized you, didn't she? That's the idea, it will take time."

Although Noel still seemed hesitant, Driscoll knew that the key to success was to have faith in their team.

"Joyce is the best, I know her skills," he said, with an air of certainty. Noel left to go upstairs, and Driscoll was left alone with his thoughts. He turned his attention to the new A.I. supercomputer he had built, and he couldn't help but feel excited about its potential.

"Joyce, you are going to be magnificent," he said with enthusiasm. Driscoll knew that with hard work and determination, their plan would succeed.

CHAPTER 12

USA STATE DEPARTMENT, BAGDAD

The police waited for Hans, the Norwegian forensic contractor, to process the mangled U.S. Army S.U.V.

"The vehicle damage is at the front. The paint residue matches the police vehicle. It is the vehicle stolen from the State Department car lot three days ago," said Hans. "I'll call in a tow," said Hans to the police officer.

As Hans returned to his vehicle to retrieve his gloves and briefcase, he was taken aback by a startling discovery. 'The S.U.V. is unlocked. The key is still in the ignition. It's a wonder no one made off with it,' he pondered. The tow truck arrived, reversing in and parking. The driver stepped out to introduce himself.

"Hi, here is the tow address. I need a few minutes to take finger-prints," replied Hans. "I'll have to eliminate the other drivers,"

"It's not a pool car," the observant tow driver reassured. "See that sticker! Only one person drove it."

"Just one person," Hans confirmed. He meticulously dusted for latent prints, first from the rearview mirror and then from both internal and external door handles. It was a laborious and time-consuming process. "I want to dust the key? Is that okay?" asked Hans. "You will need it?"

"I don't need a key. I will drag it onto the tilt tray," replied the driver, demonstrating his understanding of the situation. "This level of damage should have triggered the airbags. They didn't. Your thief disabled them. In a crash, these S.U.V.s halt the fuel pump for safety reasons. Your thief was aware of this and disabled the airbags," the driver reported, revealing the thief's intricate knowledge of the vehicle's safety features.

"So his prints will be on the fuse box?" said Hans.

CHAPTER 13

AHMED'S FACTORY BAGDAD

"What is the mission, Ahmed?"

"If I tell you straight away, you might back out!" replied Ahmed. "It requires detailed planning. We have to hire people. We have a primary target and a secondary one if anything goes sideways. Our timeframe ranges from five to eight years."

"Why can't the money people do it?" asked Abu.

"They're probably office employees," said Ahmed. They both chuckled. "It will take one year to plan and two to get everything into place without drawing attention. Then we let it cool off and wait. It involves a lot of money for it to succeed."

"You already have the money?" asked Abu.

"I followed the G.P.S. coordinates to the money dump," said Ahmed. "USD 75 million in various currencies."

"$75 million?" whispered Abu, lifting his eyebrows. This smells like the Syrian drug cartel idiots."

"I doubt it because of the particular process," replied Ahmed. "We must travel, offer bribes, hire individuals, buy equipment, and lease long-term accommodation. The money came in three currencies: USD,

Euros and U.K. pounds. If this were my cash, I would demand detailed proposals, development timetables and receipts. The mission has been left up to us to plan and execute," replied Ahmed.

"Someone trusts you, Ahmed. Tell me about the money dump," asked Abu. He stood, checked the windows, and looked up and down the dark lane. Ahmed spoke without watching Abu.

"I've installed motion sensors outside and several cameras at either edge of the lane and inside here. I've been dumping putrid rubbish at both ends of the footpath daily. I want to provide the impression this is a dumpsite, disused and abandoned," said Ahmed.

"Yeah, I smelt it," laughed Abu.

"I have infrared security at either end of the lane. Those microwave motion sensors offer intelligent detection security. Plus, I have passive infrared sensors on the front, back and top of this building," added Ahmed.

"Right, so we live in Fort Knox, and you're paranoid," replied Abu.

"I am not. I'm cautious. The sensors will detect temperature contrasts between the person with the gun moving through the detection pattern and the environment. Any movement will trigger an alarm on my phone, and the cameras come to life. If an intruder triggers an alarm, we each have a go-bag. I cleared a drain that runs under the factory floor. The drain exits beside a fence one block south," said Ahmed.

"Have you tested it?" asked Abu.

"It takes three minutes to the exit," replied Ahmed. "Three minutes of running."

"The money isn't here, is it?" asked Abu.

"No, the money is safe. It is not here. I have cabled C-4 throughout the factory and am ready to burn it down. The trigger is near the wall at the end of the drain," replied Ahmed.

"Why are you going to all this trouble?" asked Abu.

"The courier identified me in the café. My fingerprints will be all over this factory," replied Ahmed. "I've been trading, stealing and selling military things for years. I have crates of guns, ammunition, RPGs, plastic explosives, and Kevlar jackets hidden inside the factory.

From here, I've coordinated each mission but recruited militia off-site. It only takes one person to connect me to this factory," said Ahmed.

"Then it is all over," replied Abu.

CHAPTER 14

DOG AND RED LION PUB LONDON

Sir Brian Jackson enjoyed a lamb shank on potatoes and carrots and washed it with a jug of Guinness with his friend Robert Allen. Brian Jackson was the retired and former head of MI5. At six feet tall, sixty years of age, with abundant orange-grey hair and blue eyes, Jackson displayed confidence in his dress code. Sir Robert Allen, a former lawyer, had replaced Brian Jackson when he retired last year.

"Robert, any new secrets?" asked Sir Jackson.

"Plenty of secrets,' replied Sir Robert Allen

"You seem troubled, old boy," asked Sir Jackson.

"We're hiring youngsters to fight online terrorism," said Robert. "These kids sit in their parents' garage tapping away, changing their school results. The Home Secretary wants me to hire them to fight cyber-terrorism. I will need to buy them acne treatment cream to be presentable!"

"They are rather brazen, my dear fellow," said Jackson. Sir Brian Jackson enjoyed a lamb shank served with potatoes and carrots and washed it down with a jug of Guinness while dining with his friend Robert Allen at the Dog and Red Lion pub in London. Sir Brian

Jackson was a retired and former head of MI5, standing at six feet tall, sixty years of age, with abundant orange-grey hair and blue eyes. He exuded confidence in his dress code. On the other hand, Sir Robert Allen, a former lawyer, had replaced Sir Jackson when he retired last year.

During their conversation, Sir Jackson asked Sir Robert Allen if he had any new secrets. Sir Robert replied that he had plenty of secrets and seemed troubled. He then explained that they were hiring youngsters to combat online terrorism. These young professionals work from their parents' garages, changing their school results, and the Home Secretary wants them to fight cyber-terrorism. Sir Robert even joked that they would need to buy them acne treatment cream to make them presentable.

Sir Jackson remarked that these youngsters are rather brazen and cited an incident where they had closed down an airport while drinking Cachaca on a Brazilian waterfront. Sir Robert added another example of them tampering with an election while drinking a Caipirinha or Caju Amigo on a surf beach. They both laughed.

Sir Robert then went on to explain that they had a group of youthful I.T. professionals working for them, who dressed appallingly. He even suspected that one of them had not bathed in a month. Despite this, they were extremely intelligent and capable, with one young man even developing his own A.I. software and calling it 'Joyce.'

Sir Jackson concluded that it's the wild digital west and lifted his glass of Guinness, toasting to Joyce. They were closing down an airport while drinking Cachaca on a Brazilian waterfront.

"Or tampering with an election while drinking a Caipirinha or Caju Amigo on a surf beach," said Robert. They both laughed.

"We have this group of youthful I.T. chaps. They dress appallingly," replied Robert. "I am convinced one chap has not bathed in a month. The problem is they are extremely intelligent gits. One young fellow has developed his own A.I. software and called it 'Joyce.'"

"It is the wild digital west, my friend," declared Jackson. He lifted his glass of Guinness and said, "To Joyce!"

CHAPTER 15

"Walk me through that initial contact with the courier at the café. How many people were in the café? Take it slow, describe it," asked Abu.

"Maybe a dozen individuals. A few older guys were in groups playing backgammon. One or two other people may have been sitting at tables by themselves. A few were in the kitchen, and one waiter," said Ahmed.

Abu asked, "Did anyone watch you?"

"Nobody followed me out the door. I watched, then followed the courier. Nobody followed me," replied Ahmed.

"Have you checked your car for a wiretap?" asked Abu.

"No. I use stolen cars," said Ahmed.

"Let's return to the people in the café. Was anyone sitting alone?" Abu asked.

Ahmed closed his eyes and ran the scene through his mind. "A lady sat near the door. A man sat in the back corner."

Abu asked, "Apart from your contact, did anyone else enter the café after him?"

"No," said Ahmed.

"Did anyone see or observe the courier scan the room?" asked Abu.

Ahmed thought, "Abu, people do it all the time. You scan a room when you look for a friend."

"The guy in the corner, could he hear the conversation with the contact?" asked Abu.

"I doubt it," replied Ahmed. "The café is noisy."

"Can you describe the guy?" asked Abu.

"He had olive skin, a dark reddish beard, and normal clothing. He was drinking coffee. He was maybe sixty years old. I think he gave something to the waiter."

Abu asked, "Money, a tip, or a piece of paper?"

"I recall he gave the waiter too much money," said Ahmed.

"Why do you say that?" asked Abu.

"There was no food on the table, just coffee," replied Ahmed.

Abu said, "Your waiter is an informant. You may need to pay him cash and ask a few questions."

Ahmed realized his mistake.

"Describe the person at the door?" asked Abu.

"She was twelve feet from me and reading a book. She never raised her head," replied Ahmed.

"She was nobody?" asked Abu.

CHAPTER 16

CAFÉ BAGDAD

Grant Potts was an ASIS agent whose job was to blend in with the locals and gather intelligence. He was of mixed Pakistani and British heritage, with olive skin, a reddish beard, and fluency in several languages. After 45 years of service, he was assigned to a paramilitary unit whose sole purpose was to gather information.

Potts spent his days observing people and recording their conversations, using cash to pay his contacts. He frequented cafes, shops, and taxi drivers to gather information discreetly. One day, while eating at his favourite cafe, his contact failed to show up. Potts paid for his meal and was about to leave when the waiter handed him the bill with a note on the back. The note contained the name and location of an ISIS leader.

As Potts sat there sipping his coffee, a well-dressed stranger entered the cafe and sat at the table in front of him. Potts ordered a pot of coffee in Mesopotamian Arabic and watched as the stranger pushed a shoebox across the table to the man he was meeting. Potts wondered what was in the box and if it contained drugs or a bomb.

To record the conversation, Potts placed his usual plate under his coffee cup, tapped his watch with his left hand, and rested his wrist on the table. The stranger and the man exchanged only three sentences before the stranger left. Potts followed the man with the shoebox, observing him as he paid his bill and left the cafe.

Outside the cafe, the man scanned the street without moving his head. Potts continued to follow him, wondering what kind of offer the stranger had made and why the man with the shoebox looked so troubled.

CHAPTER 17

THE NEXT DAY.

"Describe the cash pickup," asked Abu.

"I purchased a truck, dressed as a beggar, and parked nearby. I wandered into the square and watched until 2 am. Nothing happened, so I brought the truck in and loaded the boxes."

"You expected an ambush?" replied Abu.

"Nobody showed up," replied Ahmed.

"There was no surveillance?" asked Abu.

"I had infrared binoculars. I watched for hours. There was nobody," said Ahmed. "The money was in nine large cardboard cartons, the size of commercial washing appliances. I opened one crate. There were plastic sacks on top filled with rotting food scraps. It stank."

Abu asked, "Smart."

"I brought the money here and purchased packing crates. The money is now in long-term storage in Moscow, London, and Amsterdam," said Ahmed.

Ahmed didn't mention that he used Abu's name on the leases. "I have one concern. The Euros were five hundred euro notes, brand new," said Ahmed. European Police agencies are demanding they be withdrawn."

"Why?" asked Ahmed.

"Previously, you filled suitcases with enough money," said Ahmed. "Now, the same amount of money fits in a backpack."

Abu smiled and then asked, "Are they genuine?"

He had one in his pocket and handed it to Abu. "Hold it up against the light. You should observe a ribbon or thread as a dark ribbon. There are tiny letters on the thread. Can you identify two words?" asked Ahmed.

"EURO and 500," replied Abu. "Seems genuine. Any other money concerns?"

"The Bagdad Commercial Bank," said Ahmed. "It arrived digitally, then cashed."

"Do you think the bank staff would have been suspicious?" Abu asked. You may recall that the U.S. military flew pallets of American dollars in. I assume some Banks held some of that money."

Ahmed looked troubled. He stood and paced the room.

"Ahmed, the bank took a percentage. The manager kept it tight. He chose and paid a trusted person to pack and deliver the cash," replied Abu.

CHINA

Wang Li Jun is an agent in the J.S.D. Intelligence Bureau. You would never pick him out of a crowd. He was of average height, single and wore boring suits.

Jun received information from his undercover operative in Iraq. He left his office for lunch and went to a coffee shop on Gulou Road, Andingmen subdistrict. Jun ordered a green tea and sat outside under an awning. When he finished, he inverted the cup, stood and left.

Liu Wei from the Joint Staff Department Intelligence Bureau watched from the shop's back corner. Liu Wei waited, stood, placed his suit jacket over his arm, and scanned the room as he walked to the entrance. He removed the slip of paper from inside the cup and kept walking.

The message read, 'It has begun."

A hidden CCTV camera under the shop awning captured the sloppy spycraft.

CHAPTER 18

AMMAN

Ahmed bought hundreds of second-hand books and used a laser cutter to extract exact sections of pages to fit each currency. After vacuum-sealing each book in transparent plastic wrap, he packed them into nine wooden transport crates. Four crates were destined for storage facilities in Moscow, London, Amsterdam, and Paris.

At the airport, Ahmed watched as the freight handlers loaded the crates into the plane under the ramp agent's direction. After the inspector signed off on a form and gave a copy to the ramp agent, Ahmed bid farewell and returned to his truck. On his way to downtown Amman, he enjoyed the sunny afternoon and hummed a song, relieved that everything went as planned.

As the market streets of Amman lit up with the exotic aroma of spicy food at sunset, Ahmed found a cheap hotel room, paid cash and parked his truck two blocks away. Before returning to the food market, he performed counter-surveillance to indulge in some deep-fried goat with flatbread. He wandered the market, purchasing food before retiring to his hotel room.

As he settled down for the night, he whispered, "It has begun."

CHAPTER 19

BAGDAD, FACTORY

"Why did you make me the leader and not yourself?" asked Abu.

Ahmed had already considered this question and he wanted to appeal to Abu's ego. "I knew that we needed a hero to make this work, someone who could help us create our own Islamic State. I didn't want just any soldier, contractor, or corrupt Iraqi police to shoot the hero before we even got started. With you in prison, it worked. Plus, I needed a mysterious figure to lead each mission, someone who couldn't be captured or killed," Ahmed explained.

"That strategy worked when I was in prison, but what about now?" asked Abu.

"You will be able to get the world to demand an Islamic Independent State," declared Ahmed.

Abu couldn't help but think to himself, "You're dreaming."

CHAPTER 20

CAFE BAGDAD

ASIS agent Grant Potts had followed the man out of the café and decided to call him Mr Shoebox. Shoebox tried to follow the other person but was unsuccessful. After that epic failure, Potts watched Shoebox perform a surveillance detection run.

"Well, that's interesting," said Potts. He followed Shoebox for twenty minutes, around several back roads and an alley to a factory. It was a rundown location, even abandoned, with rubbish scattered everywhere. Shoebox either lived or worked in an old factory.

Later that night, Potts returned to set up his video camera with Wi-Fi feeding back to his phone.

'When Shoebox leaves, I will break in and have a look,' thought Potts.

CHAPTER 21

KL MALAYSIA

Abu Sarek was born as Abu Ibrahim to a clerical family in Samarra, Iraq. Ahmed used social media to claim that Abu was a descendant of the Prophet Muhammad. He knew that illiteracy and rumours were his allies.

Their family moved to Kuala Lumpur in Malaysia from Iraq. After having heated arguments with his father, Ahmed ignored his father's pleadings and returned to Iraq.

Years later, Abu became tired of the humidity. His friends urged him to come back to Iraq and fight with ISIL. Abu's parents were devastated. But there was another reason for Abu to leave.

Ahmed joined them at the physical training site at the University of Diyala near the capital of Baqubah, in the east of Iraq. The weather was pleasant, with a slight breeze heading towards winter. Students, faculty, and staff were on vacation for five weeks, providing Ahmed uninterrupted access to their facilities and media department.

Abu sipped his coffee and said to Ahmed, "When I watch them train, it reminds me of a soccer team?" Finishing his cup, Abu turned and grinned at Ahmed.

"Next week," Ahmed said, "we will start weapons and combat

training indoors in that sports building. Will you join them for a run now?"

"Are you?" asked Abu with a mischievous smile. "I am in better shape than you, brother."

Ahmed had struggled with his conscience when it came to using Abu. He knew he was putting his brother's life at risk without his consent and full disclosure of the mission. But his conscience and heart had died in Iraq after a life-altering event. After that day, everything became cancer for Ahmed. He cared only about revenge. He watched the team of men doing their early morning 10 km run. Ahmed needed Abu's reputation to reach the U.S. State Department's wanted list.

Ahmed had a plan.

CHAPTER 22

BAGDAD

Abu's leadership fell apart after one brutal four-hour street battle in Bagdad with U.S. coalition troops. There were losses on both sides. Abu knew reinforcements were coming along with their total defeat and his humiliation. They withdrew, carrying the injured and the dying using a pre-determined escape route. Coalition troops regrouped and searched for them, street by street, alley by alley. Abu and his team hid in a decrepit, empty, safe house miles away from their failure. Many friends had died because of Abu's inexperience.

He never said it, but he felt manipulated by Ahmed. It had happened before, many times when they were young.

Ahmed arrived around 2 am. He had food, bottles of water, tea, coffee, a gas burner, candles, and bottles of alcohol. Ahmed saw each man's injuries. He left the safe house and returned with gloves, vials of midazolam and fentanyl, blankets, first aid kits, various saline drips, dressing packs, and sterile surgery equipment.

All were stolen from a private hospital.

Ahmed attended to the injured. One jihadist had two leg fractures that could wait for an hour. Three had contaminated haemorrhaging wounds, and another needed an amputation. Ahmed inserted cannulas into each patient and started pushing in fluids.

'Do I gag them to stop the coming pain?' thought Ahmed. He changed his mind. Men screaming in pain at 2 am was not ideal. He removed the cloth gags, calculated each man's weight, and inserted the correct dosage of midazolam and fentanyl into the saline drips. Their breathing needed monitoring. Ahmed could not do endotracheal intubation, so he injected 2-3ccs of lidocaine. They waited for two minutes, then started cleaning the wounds.

To one soldier, Ahmed said, "I want you two to copy what I do." He applied a sterile tourniquet control with washed hands and gloves, cleaning the wounds with soap and sterilized water. Ahmed glanced at the soldier and said, "Your friend here is not well. Get me that syringe with 2-3cc's of that there, lidocaine."

The bleeding had stopped, and Ahmed showed how to do a debridement. Using disposable scalpels, they cut away dead and dying tissue. "Cut away the injured tissue. It is dead. Don't cut the live tissue." Ahmed knew they were soldiers, so he checked their work as they removed the necrotic material around the dead tissue.

"If you leave any dead tissue, that will cause infection and inflammation. Before you go ahead, check for any contamination between tissue layers obscured by dried blood," said Ahmed.

"Contamination?" asked one soldier.

"Check for any sand, mud or bugs that may cause sepsis," replied Ahmed.

The second soldier said, "I can see dirt hidden here."

Ahmed took forceps, punctured a small hole in the top of a water bottle, lifted the tissue and squeezed the bottle to form a jet of water to flush the contaminants out.

"If you are confident that the wound is clean. We stitch the wound and put glue over the top. Understand? Then bandage the wound," said Ahmed.

'The amputation will be last,' thought Ahmed. He removed the dead tissue and the crushed bones below the knee, then filed the bone smooth. He cut and shaped the muscles after sealing the blood vessels and nerves. There was significant blood loss. Ahmed knew this soldier might die in the next few hours of anaemia. He administered 2 litres of isotonic sodium chloride solution and waited for stabilization. Ahmed guessed where to apply the plaster bandages based on swelling, but no C.T. scans or ultrasound guidance were available. He could do nothing if there were any internal bleeding. At dawn, the house was silent.

"Are you exhausted?" asked Abu.

Ahmed ignores the question and asks, "Abu, what went wrong?"

Abu is silent, staring. "I'm not cut out for this."

"Abu, defeat is always devastating. Then you question yourself and lose faith in yourself and they in you," replied Ahmed.

"Before you showed up, they were bracing to execute me. I am useless as a leader. Don't you get it? I failed them. This is my fault," answered Abu.

"Yeah, I get it. We could talk about the mistakes that happened yesterday. Now is not the time. They need coffee and food, and you pat them on the back. Okay? These brothers will be awake soon. You have a job," replied Ahmed. He stood to return to the safe-house, stopped and turned around, "You can do this, Abu."

Abu watched Ahmed walk to the safe house. Abu made his decision.

The U.S. Coalition had dozens of squads and mercenaries out hunting in Humvees and Toyota 4X4s. Retribution was on their minds. They were hunting for those responsible for yesterday's bloody battle.

It was a dragnet.

Anyone who looked suspicious got arrested. Abu's blood-saturated clothes were a dead giveaway. He got thrown into jail with many others.

When the U.S. State Department realized Abu Sarek was the leader behind the street battle, they launched a media blitz with a million-dollar bounty. Posters appeared across the city. The photo they used was a poor hand-drawn sketch from the Malaysian police. It was a worthless exercise. They were unaware Abu Sarek was in jail due to incompetence or identity confusion, but Ahmed now had his idea.

Abu kept blaming himself for the death of so many of his brave friends. His admiration for terrorists like Yemen's al-Qaeda teams with their technical schemes faded. Prison life dictated survival. His spirit, along with his energy, died daily.

Ahmed paid a boy USD 10 to deliver a sealed envelope addressed to the fortified U.S. Embassy in Baghdad office at 8:40 am.

"Do not enter the compound," said Ahmed. Just hand the guard the envelope. Then, walk away. Do you understand?"

"Yeah, I get it. If I go inside the U.S. compound, someone will torture and waterboard me, cut out my fingernails, one by one, until I give you up," replied the youth.

"You watch too many movies," replied Ahmed.

"Yes, so! That's what they do to spies," answered the boy.

"Deliver the envelope by 8:40 am tomorrow. When you have done that, I will give you another $10," said Ahmed. He handed him the envelope.

"You're wearing a plastic glove. My fingerprints will be on the envelope. That will be an extra $10," replied the boy

"No," said Ahmed.

"What's in it, an explosive?" declared the boy.

"It's not a bomb. It is an envelope with a message, and it is none of your business," replied Ahmed impatiently, checking that no one was observing their exchange.

"Okay, I won't open it. But that will be another $10," replied the boy.

"Don't get captured," replied Ahmed.

The envelope enclosed a burner phone. The CIA will dismantle it but to no avail. At 7:20 pm that night, Ahmed would send a text with Abu Sarek's location. He included a picture of a man who looked like Abu in the envelope, except the height, weight, hair, and eye colour were incorrect. Ahmed hoped the CIA would distribute the false image with Abu's details to international law enforcement bureaus. He wanted that image on terrorist lists and passport databases. Also, in the envelope were details about Abu that could be validated.

'The bait is in the water,' thought Ahmed.

The reward had to be settled into a Cayman Islands bank account by 7:00 pm local Iraq time. Then Ahmed would send a text identifying Abu's location, a one-hour drive from Bagdad. He knew the State

Department was exercising more authority with the departure of coalition troops. 'They have no alternative but to investigate. The money will be the sticking point,' thought Ahmed.

At 7:00 pm, the USD one million landed in the Cayman Islands account. At 7:03 pm, Ahmed transferred the money to a bank in Vanuatu. He had instructed the Bank of Vanuatu to deposit the funds into twelve separate accounts in Paris, France.

Ahmed paid the twelve jihadists to show up at this house at 8:00 pm. One jihadist, dressed in formal Western clothes, would be the only one to enter the home.

CHAPTER 23

LOBAL HAWK DRONE

G Five thousand private security contractors replaced the U.S.-led coalition forces. For safety purposes, contractors accompanied U.S. Embassy staff on any trip outside the Green Zone. There were twelve thousand Embassy personnel, and many over-booked the Global Hawks for minor shopping excursions. Iraqi leaders suspected this practice wasn't for protection but for surveillance. The local tabloid summed up the emotion: "Our sky is our sky, not the USA's sky."

The CIA cared little about Iraqi personal offences. For the next thirty-six hours, they overruled State Department Global Hawk book-ings, causing furious outbursts from Embassy staff. Alongside the Hawk was the new Scan Vulture MQZ1D with artificial intelligence.

Today, the Global Hawk had been flying for 34 hours, with 4 hours remaining. It loitered at 58,000 feet, twice the height of commercial planes, scanning 35,000 square miles of the city and surrounding region. The CI. reduced that scope to five square miles. Joining the Hawk was the Scan Vulture, which incorporated artificial intelligence. If a roadside bomb exploded in Iraq, analysts reversed the Global Hawk video feed to identify the person responsibly.

It was tiring work counting cars and following many clusters of people. You had to watch what a person did and where they went. At times, it came down to examining a single video frame. Shades of light and darkness hampered visual clarity. Skilled analysts took days to verify individuals from complex video scenes. In contrast, Scan Vulture's UHD cameras use artificial intelligence to compare video with facial recognition databases.

The Global Hawk operator identified the three vehicles at 8:41 pm approaching an agriculture community along the Euphrates River at Al Diwaniyah of Qadisiyah Province, southern Iraq. The Scan Vulture, nicknamed 'Bob', took over, coming to a lower altitude to identify the vehicles and passengers.

Bob had been recording all day. It had already tracked the three vehicles backwards to a location.

"The three vehicles have arrived at the destination," reported the engineer over the I.T. network. "I am counting nine jihadists. They are standing guard. They have formed a perimeter in front of the home. One person is standing at the back of the house."

CIA team leader John Gillan saw the heat signatures of each of these guards as they left their cars. "Turn off the heat signature. The guards are armed and are scanning for targets. Let Bob do his thing."

Gillan's administration had hundreds of jihadists' pictures in their digital databank, incorporating today's image delivered to the Embassy.

"Vulture is recording each guard's height, stride, arm and leg length," replied the engineer. "Scarves and caps are stopping facial recognition. Vulture is analyzing the passenger from the middle vehicle."

"Good," replied Gillan.

"The drivers are remaining in the cars," said the engineer. "They have not switched off the engines."

"A quick visit or a quick getaway," replied Gillan.

"The target is leaving the middle vehicle and walking towards the house entrance," said the engineer. Gillan didn't correct the engineer for what was obvious. The AI software compared images and measured his height, weight, gait, and facial dimensions to form a complete profile.

"Who is it? Give me the threshold?" asked Gillan.

The operator said, "I have an 80% match to the photo of Abu Sarek."

"I want that threshold higher," demanded Gillan. The Scan Vulture had a wingspan of 57 feet. It was bigger than you would anticipate, silent, and fast. As it decreased altitude, the Scan Vulture captured higher-definition images and videos, processing them within milliseconds. It came back within 3.56 seconds with a 93% confirmation that the person who had just entered the single building was Abu Sarek.

John Gillan asked, "Are those vehicle heat signatures the same?"

The operator replied, "The three vehicles are showing consistent heat signature. Their engines are running. They are not cooling."

Gillan said, "Okay, it's a brief visit with a fast exit. Is the Global Hawk ready?"

"Yes," replied the operator.

"The house is the target. Get Bob back away," John declared, looking at the screen and smiling. 'We have you,' John thought.

Gillan announced, "I am satisfied the person is Abu Sarek. Go ahead."

The Global Hawk fired its missile. The three vehicles, jihadists Abu and his family, died in 9.3 seconds. Ahmed witnessed the explosion from the other side of the river. He delivered USD 5000 to each of the twelve jihadist families. Ahmed knew Abu might find out but gave it two days before texting a paid correctional officer. The officer handed the message to the prisoner in cell D178a.

It read, "Parents are okay. A." Ahmed wanted Abu to have revenge in his heart towards those who bombed an innocent family. Ahmed's plan relied on Abu staying the course alone for several years.

CHAPTER 24

STREETS OF BAGDAD

ASIS agent Grant Potts visited the alley where Shoebox lived for several months, reviewing camera footage to discover any co-conspirators visiting Shoebox. The Shoebox video file was worthless. There was nothing. Potts decided it was time to have a look inside Shoebox's building.

He would take pictures and gather intelligence on Shoebox's home or business. If there was nothing of value, the file was to be closed. Potts walked into the rotting rubbish-filled alley, settling into a blind spot to watch. Potts checked his CCTV camera recordings. They were motion-triggered and recorded for only ten seconds.

"The same dog wanders over to sniff the trash," said Potts. The next ten-second video showed a woman wandering through the alley, but that was it. 'I wasted my time. The video displayed an upstairs light coming on each night. There must be a back entrance,' thought Potts.

The foul aroma washed over Potts. 'This bloke puts waste here on purpose.'

He deleted the videos and reset the CCTV. He looked up. 'The light was off,' thought Potts. He poked his head around and saw a shadow move across the end of the alley. "Yes, definitely a back entrance. Time to have a glance," mumbling to himself. Potts entered the back door of the factory using his picks.

The place was a working factory with tools and machinery here and there, stacked wooden crates, fuel cells in steel cages, and a pile of spare parts. A factory bin had books with the guts ripped out. The walk up the stairwell was simple. There is an office, a kitchen and two beds.

He checked the bins for envelopes with names, but nothing. "No computer," said Potts. In the dish sink were dirty plates and drinking glasses. 'Two plates and two glasses, two individuals. Shoebox and a woman?' wondered Potts. "A woman would refuse to live in this dump," said Potts. 'No washing machine, perhaps he hand washes his clothes? Only a few clothes are in a single dressing closet. There is no woman's attire. Shoebox must have a partner.' He snapped photographs. Food scraps were on both plates, "Still soft, not even hardened, and the electric kettle was warm. They ate and left minutes."

Potts pocketed the two drinking glasses for possible prints. Ten minutes they had expired. 'Oh no, you blind old fool!' mumbled Potts.

Three surveillance cameras pointed towards him on top of the other buildings. He swore, spun around and glanced up. "Dumb mistake," Potts mumbled. Then he looked up and saw small cameras hidden in the corners of the kitchen. 'Time to leave. Why so many damn cameras?' wondered Potts.

CHAPTER 25

MOSCOW

Katarina Agapov was born in Moscow and raised by her military parents. Her career started as a soldier, then she was trained as an assassin. She joined the Russian SVR/RF foreign intelligence. The pay was low, and she grew tired of her drunken boss and his unwanted advances. Her career with the SVR/RF ended with a single punch. Others wanted to do the same but feared the repercussions. Agapov didn't care anymore.

At 39 years of age, she was now an independent contractor. She had USD one million in a French Bank and realized she should have left earlier. At 5 feet, 9 inches, she was slim, blonde, and athletic. Agapov knew an agent was unlike a soldier. Soldiers had friends when surrounded by enemies. As an agent, she was still determining the friendly people of her nationality. She knew all she had was her alertness, initiative and observation. Agapov had been in London for two weeks and had contracted to collect intelligence on a US Democrat congressional representative. There was plenty of dirt, so it was easy work.

She received a contract from her French broker to immediately go to Bagdad to protect an asset. There were no further details. The dirty

Democrat congressional representative could wait. Agapov knew the new SVR boss had summoned her through her broker. She never liked him either; he was untrustworthy, played three sides of the game, and you never knew the complete picture, but he paid. Katarina preferred London to Bagdad. Bagdad was a simple job, way below her skill set, but she needed the money for a renovated unit in London.

Agapov was bored after two months of surveillance in Bagdad. When she first arrived, she wore a full Burka and wandered through an alley where the asset Ahmed was living, or squatting was the better word, according to Agapov. She observed his infrared security and the CCTV on either end of the narrow alley. 'Such overkill for this nobody,' she thought.

The disused building opposite the factory became her observation post and temporary accommodation. Ahmed's routine was predictable. Every day, he would leave on foot carrying canvas bags. He would return to driving different vehicles until she realized they were stolen and dumped at the end of the block. Kids waited for new cars to steal. Ahmed would return carrying his canvas bags. When he left, the bag appeared empty. When Ahmed returned, it was packed, most likely with guns. She followed him and knew he was trying to lead some down-and-out jihadists. They blew things up and then went home to watch TV.

Her protectee, Ahmed, ate at the Historical Café daily. It was a predictable and dangerous habit. Agapov went to the cafe before the factory owner arrived, but not always. She arrived early one morning and observed an exchange. A stranger gave her protectee a shoebox.

A significant development occurred in Bagdad during her stay. She watched Ahmed lead a group of fighters to blow up the jail. Now, an ex-prisoner was staying in Ahmed's filthy factory.

Agapov entered the factory through a back lane and unlocked the back door using a hairpin and nail file. She extracted the username and password for the factory CCTV and planted tracking devices on clothing and an audio-listening device.

Months into her now boring routine, Ahmed returned with a truck. He unloaded boxes the size of washing machines. When she checked the factory CCTV, she saw the contents were money. For weeks,

Ahmed cut the guts out of books, inserted money, and sealed each book.

She identified the prisoner as the infamous Jihadist Abu Sarek. She tuned in to their boring discussions about one last mission. To her ears, she felt that Ahmed, the factory owner, was trying to convince Abu to head up his mission. Ahmed rambled on about some pipe dream of an Islamic State. Agapov knew Ahmed was lying to Abu about millions of dollars he found dumped in an alley. She was certain Ahmed was setting up Abu to be the fall guy for his stupid plan. Each week, she sent an encrypted report summarizing their conversations. The reply was to watch and protect. She knew she was missing something but couldn't see it.

'An independent Islamic state comprised of various sects engaging in constant infighting. Why do these two men need protecting, and from what? What is it that makes these two so important?' thought Agapov.

About eight weeks into her now boring assignment, she saw a local man enter the alley. He spent a few moments watching, and then he left. When he came back the second time, she took note. He would find a blind spot, stay and observe Ahmed's factory. She examined him more intently when he came back at night. The alley was dark, and his face lit up when he turned his mobile phone on. With binoculars, she concentrated on his hands. He looked at his mobile phone or tablet, flicking through video after video. She assumed it was of the factory.

'He might have me on that video,' thought Agapov. She saw him open another app through the binoculars but couldn't determine what it was. Then he looked up to check something. Agapov also shifted her head and followed where he was facing. He was checking Ahmed's shop window reflection. Then she caught it, a red dot.

'The Mystery man is watching Abu and Ahmed. I missed his camera,' thought Agapov. The following day, he entered the alley and took his picture. Her contact sent her the information. Her mystery person was Australian ASIS agent Grant Potts.

'Great, another surveillance operation, and I'm missing something here?' thought Agapov. She knew her two assets were not in the factory that evening and had left through the back gate. She also knew what Potts was going to do, so she did the same. After ten minutes, Potts entered the factory and came back out in a panic.

"Potts saw the cameras. Smile! The amateur is reporting in, time to stop the show," said Agapov. Potts stood outside the factory. He took a final few pictures of the factory. He opened his email and attached the photos and final report on the two men with excessive CCTV.

'Why so many CCTVs? There's nothing to steal. I am missing something here,' thought Potts. He didn't care. The email wasn't working. Potts tried to send his report again, but it kept failing.

Ahmed had installed six portable mobile phone isolators with Wi-Fi interceptors but excluded the cameras. It blocked all mobile phone signals inside the alley.

Grant knew his reports were lightweight, often disregarded by his direct boss, and Potts was treading water, ready to return home and retire. 'I'm in a Wi-Fi blind spot. The nearest café will have Wi-Fi reception,' thought Potts. He returned the mobile phone to his lower leg pocket and left before Shoebox returned.

A blaring grinding noise then jolted Potts. His words were slurring, and now he could not recall his name. His thinking was blurring. There was a loud screeching sound in his ears. Potts put his hand up against a wall to steady himself, but nausea overwhelmed him, falling to the ground in agony. Katarina Agapov continued to point her sonic device towards Potts as she removed Potts's tablet, personal items, and two drinking glasses.

Then, the factory exploded.

CHAPTER 26

L ONDON MONTHS LATER
Abu handed over his passport to Gatwick Airport's UK Border Force official. He smiled and waited. He owned two passports, one from the Gulf State of Bahrain and the other from the UK. The forger reassured Abu that the numbers and codes were original. Each passport and a UK birth certificate cost €10,000. But the real cost was the constant juggling of his two identities, a secret he hid from Ahmed.

One of Abu's favourite movies was The U.S. Marshall Service. He chuckled every time he watched it. The guy in charge shouted a dozen commands at everybody in one breath. But what struck him more was their witness protection program. The Marshall service relocated the witness to a new city, job, home and identity, a drastic change that left Abu contemplating the profound impact such programs can have on a person's life.

'Imagine experiencing your entire life change in a single day. There was no farewell to friends. You can never return or make contact with your family,' wondered Abu. 'I also will need time to adjust.' Another colleague of Abu, a master of deception, created two digital social lives years ago. The Bahrain passport was his only option if he needed to leave the UK in an emergency. However, that did not concern him. What worried Abu was how he would fit into a new culture.

Abu waited calmly in line for his passport to be processed. He was casually scanning faces. Habits die hard. He was not drawing any undue scrutiny, except for a few ladies. He wore sunglasses, dark blue jeans, a stone-washed white shirt with a blue blazer, leather shoes, a three-day manicured manly stubble beard, and a styled haircut. He was marginally less formal than business casual or professional business style and wanted to give the impression of casual confidence and wealth. He achieved it.

Having flown in from Barcelona on the early flight, he anticipated resting for a few days in Brighton. Then he would catch a train to Euston Station and walk out the side entrance. The Central London Great Holiday Stay was a five-minute walk. He would pay for a month's accommodation then find something more permanent. Google informed him of several Islamic cafés and a Mosque near his rented room.

As an overseas investor, Abu can register a UK corporation. He proposed to employ a contract lawyer, plus an architect specialising in Grade 1 listed building renovations. All the work would be subcontracted. But before any of that could happen, he needed dozens of banking accounts with different banks to wash the money in storage. The process would take months. Only then would the money be electronically moved to his business account, ELB or Elite Renovation Builders.

Ahmed purchased two cell phones from a business called 'WAS'– 'We Are Secure'. Each cell phone cost him USD 2,500, consisting of a 72-month subscription to 'WAS' data service. Ahmed or Abu could renew their subscription if needed for a further USD 50 each. There was no other cost like monthly bills, receipts and no contact from WAS. The phones had the microphones and camera removed and could not send emails, make calls or search the internet. The WAS system was a private independent messaging system with military-grade encryption. Ahmed and Abu agreed this would be their only form of communication.

CHAPTER 27

Abu waited calmly in line for his passport to be processed. He was casually scanning faces. Habits die hard. He was not drawing any undue scrutiny except for a few ladies. He wore sunglasses, dark blue jeans, a stone-washed white shirt with a blue blazer, leather shoes, a three-day manicured manly stubble beard, and a styled haircut. He was marginally less formal than a casual or professional business style and wanted to give the impression of casual confidence and wealth. He achieved it.

Having flown in from Barcelona on the early flight, he anticipated resting for a few days in Brighton. Then, he would catch a train to Euston Station and walk out the side entrance. The Central London Great Holiday Stay was a five-minute walk. He would pay for a month's accommodation and then find something more permanent. Google informed him of several Islamic cafés and a Mosque near his rented room.

As an overseas investor, Abu can register a UK corporation. He proposed to employ a contract lawyer and an architect specialising in Grade 1 listed building renovations. All the work would be subcontracted. But before that could happen, he needed dozens of banking accounts with different banks to wash the money in storage. The process would take months. The money would be electronically moved to his business account, ELB or Elite Renovation Builders.

Ahmed purchased two cell phones from a 'WAS'–'We Are Secure' business. Each cell phone cost him USD 2,500, comprising a 72-month subscription to 'WAS' data service. Ahmed or Abu could renew their subscription for a further USD 50 each if needed. There were no other costs, such as monthly bills and receipts, and no contact from WAS. The phones had microphones and cameras removed, and they could not send emails, make calls, or search the internet. The WAS system was a private independent messaging system with military-grade encryption. Ahmed and Abu agreed this would be their only form of communication.

CHAPTER 28

CANBERRA AUSTRALIA

Wayne Scott is a 20-year-old IT hacker who runs a criminal organization on the dark web under his handle, Black Roo. The Federal Police arrested him on charges he didn't know existed. Scott had a choice: twelve months in prison or work for HQJOC. He accepted the job. Scot was a self-trained IT professional with a high IQ. He had scraggy long blonde hair and a friendly temperament, and his boss suspected him to be on the spectrum. His wardrobe consisted of three identical sets of jeans, boots and shirts. Wayne worked full-time in Australia's defence headquarters, HQJOC or Joint Operations Command. It was a thirty-five miles drive east from Canberra, and he was running late for his night shift. Travis Jones shook his head as Scott's old, smoky, paint-peeling Hyundai Excel approached the exterior security gate.

"Hi Wayne, how is it going, mate?" asked Jones.

"I'm late, Travis. Can we hurry this up, please," asked Wayne.

"Mate, you earn adequate money here to buy something better than this heap of junk," replied Wayne, shaking his head in disgust.

"So, you're into insults tonight, mate?" replied Wayne.

"I'm surprised you make it here every night, mate," replied Jones as he processed Wayne's access code.

"Nothing wrong with my car?" asked Wayne.

Jones asked, "What do you spend your money on, Wayne?" Travis continued around the car, running an automobile inspection mirror.

"Computers, mate. I'm coding something that my employer might use one day," replied Wayne.

"Mate, your ride is leaking oil over my road. Move on, see you later," said Jones.

"See you later, mate. Have a good one, hey," replied Wayne, waving at his friend Travis Jones.

"Yeah, right, stop chatting and get lost," replied Jones.

HQJOC was a brand-new expanded headquarters on 300 acres of land with a functioning capacity of 1400 personnel. It is the home for Australia's most senior defence leadership and supports their domestic and international complex multi-domain operations, including cyber and space operations. It is now 2 am. Wayne shouted to his manager, "Hey John, we're getting hacked!" The small team of five raised their heads.

Wayne Scott's team manager, John Lewis, asked, "What's happening, Wayne?"

"Chinese hackers are struggling to penetrate the Sydney-based IT contractor's web server. The blokes who developed our IT and security for this place," replied Wayne.

"Show me. The hackers could be Russian or your neighbours?" suggested John.

"John, please! I have been trailing them for weeks," said Wayne with a gigantic smile.

"You have? It would help if you had told me. How come you're monitoring the IT contractors?" asked John.

"They want to access our systems. They are going through the IT contractor's server to discover a way to our servers. They are reading documents about our VPN's wiring, our software source code, some personal data, trade secrets, and intellectual property," replied Wayne.

"Can you stop it?" inquired John

"I have stopped them dead in their tracks. I've given them my virus bomb! Our IT contractor had two-factor authentication. I added two more to all our stuff months ago. It's unbreakable. But anybody who tries is delivered to another website I developed. It looks like our stuff, but it's not," replied Wayne, now grinning.

"Okay, Wayne. What's taking place now?" inquired John.

"I got the alert ten minutes ago, and I observed them. They've gone to the bogus site. They are not going to get anything. Okay, I gave them some fake VPN credentials to give them access to Orlando University's Digital Library. Anyway, their computers are now compromised. When I hacked their server, I stole the RSV Secure ID software token and used a valid code to enter permanently. I can now watch what they are doing."

"So, they didn't take anything?" asked John.

"They got my bomb, John. That's what they got," replied Wayne.

"They got nothing?" asked John again.

"They got nothing. Oh, by the way, these blokes are with the JSD Intelligence Bureau. They are your local Chinese spies. Anyway, a bloke called Wang Li Jun stole USD 75 million from a Bank in the USA; brash, hey? I tagged the money and watched it go around the world a few times, stopping in Bagdad."

"Bagdad?" said John.

"Some bank called 'Iraq Total Business Trading Bank' got USD 75 million. The bank bloke turned it into cash," said Wayne. "The Bank's fee was USD 1 million. I mean, talk about dodgy."

"Who collected it?" asked John.

"I hacked into the Bank video and have a photo of some bloke loading a truck. As expected, there are no matches on the bloke's face in any of our databases," replied Wayne.

"So what is this, cash for jihadists sponsored by the Chinese Government? How does that serve China?" asked John.

"Beats me, mate. But it is extremely questionable," replied Wayne.

"No, kidding. Email me everything. I'll take it upstairs," ordered John.

"You mean now? Nobody is upstairs. It's 2:30 am, and it's my lunch break," Wayne replied.

"Now. Hey, and good job, buddy," stated John. "Email me every-thing, thank you."

"You want me to keep my eye on Jung?" asked Wayne.

"Yes," replied John.

"What about the USA Bank?" asked Wayne.

"Leave that with me. I doubt that the bank knows who hacked them. When they do, some accountant will rework it as bad debt," answered John.

"At least the new IT guys the bank brought in are better than the last mob," added Wayne.

"Wayne, quit telling me stuff," replied John, "Send me the stuff, okay?"

CHAPTER 29

LONDON

The Gatwick Airport UK and EU immigration lines had crawled quickly, with six international flights processed together. Hundreds of tired overseas passengers formed lines as directed by airport staff. Border Force officer Steve Joel asked Abu, "What is the purpose of your stay in the UK."

"A short holiday, then back to work," replied Abu.

Steve Joel put Abu's passport on the digital reader. The green light came on, indicating it had been read and sent to the database. The computer chip in Abu's biometric e-passport revealed his name, place of birth, date of birth, passport number and expiry date. But it was the passport photo. Joel looked up, examined Abu's face, and asked, "Where will you be staying?"

The hair and eye colour were different. He was squinting in the passport photo. This guy is vain, wearing coloured contacts and trying to look younger. He chuckled to himself.

"The Grand Brighton, on the waterfront," said Abu Sarek. "I do hope it is a nice place."

Unknown to the UK Border Force and Abu, every passenger had their picture taken by a 12K video camera minutes before entering the immigration hall. It was illegal and violated human rights. This camera took thousands of images and videos of all incoming passengers from all flights. It's connected to a 128-core server tucked away in an electrical service cupboard and used by MI5 to gather intelligence on all individuals entering the UK. This server used a controversial facial recognition program called Bio-Metric Face Fit (BMFF) Beta Version 5.0. With 200,000Tb memory bandwidth and 3000 teraflops performance, thousands of faces and video images are processed in milliseconds and compared against a collection of databases using AI software. Two more identical systems were secretly working at Heathrow and London Airport. This unit was called Joyce.

Abu Sarek's image set off an alarm on Warren Driscoll's office PC at the MI5 counter-terrorism unit in the basement of Thames House, London. Driscoll wrote the code for the AI servers. He watched his BMFF software generate a confidence threshold of 63% with a 1983 Jakarta Police Photo-E Fit of known terrorist Hussain Humid. Driscoll didn't pick up his phone to report the match or notify his colleague.

"It does not seem to be the same person," said Driscoll. "This was the second time this week, Joyce!" He named the three computers Joyce, Debra and Victoria. All are named after his ex-girlfriends.

Driscoll was late for a department meeting. He noted the alert on the BMFF database and collected the historical and current pictures and videos into a marked digital file as an unconfirmed match of the wanted terrorist. He phoned his boss, apologised and said he would attend morning prayers in a minute.

"Damn you, Joyce," said Driscoll. He logged into the MI5 data program and entered the name Hussain Humid.

'No wonder Joyce is confused. Humid is a different guy,' thought Driscoll.

The original Photo-E Fit was a Police artist's drawing based on a witness's verbal description.

"No wonder. But why twice?" Driscoll wondered. He kept reading the MI5 report on Humid. He looked around, seeing if others had left for the meeting.

"The Police used an old Nokia brick phone to take a picture of the drawing. Then, they scanned the image into Police data files, photocopied it, and mailed it to other agencies, including Interpol. Were there cell phones in 1983?" wondered Driscoll. The new BMFF software wasn't just an upgrade. It went further, much further.

Driscoll's AI algorithms analyse the position, size, and shape of the eyes, noses, cheekbones, and jaw. The latest version focuses on the periocular region, the space surrounding the eyes, which is better than a fingerprint. He also coded a person's stride, leg length, weight, and hand preference into the software. He looked at Joyce's summary. "The hair was different, but the periocular region brought the match. Could Humid and Sarek be twins? No, it's an image problem," thought Driscoll.

The hand-drawn pictures in the MI5 and MI6 databases were all scanned, stored, and written descriptions, if any. Then, a 3D facial recognition system reconstructs the periocular region as a 3-D model of the face. If the person's weight and height are known, all the better. Driscoll fed everything into the AI algorithm. Once analysed, Joyce will observe that person. She records a person's walking manner, pace and how they stand. Driscoll combined all these features plus gave her access to CCTV street footage, stores and train surveillance to accomplish the profile and track the person.

"These old hand sketches are causing problems. There are few accurate markers to match," said Driscoll to himself.

When the first alert occurred, Driscoll saw the poor condition of the Photo-E Fit. Debra first alerted him that Hussain Humid was standing at the immigration counter at Heathrow International. He had alerted his supervisor and Heathrow Police. They questioned a UK African Pentecostal pastor with identical facial proportions. Driscol gave a personal apology, and he was released. Driscoll sensed someone behind him, "Why weren't you in morning prayers?" asked Noel Adams.

"Is it over already?" asked Driscoll.

"Yes. You are in the doghouse. Here comes the boss, buddy," replied Noel.

"I need to improve this source code," said Driscoll.

"Why, what's taken place?" asked Noel as he concentrated on Driscoll's PC.

"Joyce has created another discrepancy, but it's not her fault," Driscoll explained why he was absent from the meeting and explained the problem to his boss, Alan James.

Driscoll's supervisor, Alan James, responded, "Warren, some politicians may argue this unregulated technology can threaten civil liberties. We are lucky that the pastor didn't contact his local MP. We need a win, okay? Does it have a problematic algorithmic bias?"

"I will fix it," said Driscoll sheepishly.

"You better. We can't feed flawed data to the floor above," declared James.

"The software struggles with two elements: hand drawings by Police artists. Some are excellent, and others are awful," said Driscoll, justifying himself.

"And?" urged James.

"Very dark skin tones appear to be a problem. I will correct the code and retest it," said Driscoll.

"If that got out into the public, some human rights lawyer would accuse us of focusing on a black religious minority... Look, get it right," stated James.

"It's happened once, that's all, okay," Driscoll responded with a slight tone of anger. "We should expect bugs."

"It doesn't matter. Once is enough," replied James.

"Okay, okay!" said Driscoll as Alan James returned to his office. Warren Driscoll watched him take off. "Time to recode."

Driscoll called up the video of Hussain Humid walking through the airport hallway. The guy stood in line at the immigration counter. Driscoll watched him move his head.

"Hussain Humid appears to be scanning the crowd. Or maybe searching for a smaller isle," said Driscoll. He then reread the witness description of the 2004 Malaysian bombing of the Australian Embassy in Kuala Lumpur. The composite image worked up by the police artist was the source of the false alarms.

"But the eyes do not lie," said Driscoll.

Driscoll told Noel, "These old Police drawings are the obstacle."

"In what sense?" asked Noel.

"Well, accuracy. This police sketch is bad," replied Driscoll.

"You prefer to dispose of all sketches from the '80s?" suggested Noel.

"No. What do I do with sketches?" asked Driscoll.

Noel replied, "Tag all old drawings. Read each file and note the false alert. Keep all the false strike images in the same digital folder. Identify at least two particular features and rerun them with those qualities."

"Two features will not work, Noel. I'll adjust the coding and place an alert status on all Police Drawing pre-1990," said Driscoll.

"Police artists are used now. It is a legitimate form of recognition," answered Noel.

"Yeah, but it undermines my coding," said Driscoll.

"My opinion. Tag and code those sketches. Then, search for some more pictures of Hussain Humid. Okay," replied Noel.

"Other records on Humid, yeah, okay," said Driscoll.

"We need to show our face in the meeting now. Report updates on all three machines and keep it brief. You're ironing out bugs, okay? Be positive," said Noel with a scowl.

"Okay," said Driscoll as he followed Noel into the meeting, mumbling, "Joyce!"

Directly after the meeting, Driscoll followed Noel's advice. He pulled up every record with Hussain Humid from the MI5 database and searched the internet. He struck gold in a Kuala Lumpur report. It was an identical terrorism report with the same date and exact location, but the names differed. Instead of Hussain Humid, this report had Ducat Abuti. "Is Ducat Abuti the guy's middle name or a different person?" said Driscoll, surprised, speculating what it meant.

In 1989, Malaysian Police made a Photo E-fit from a witness. Driscoll noted in the record that this witness was 40 meters from the bomber. Investigators received confirmation from two other witnesses that the bomber parked a van full of C-4 behind another delivery truck waiting to enter the Australian embassy security perimeter. With a cap tugged low over his head, the driver, Ducat Abuti, left the van. He walked around the corner of the wire security fence, invisible to the security camera, crouched and detonated the C-4 by mobile phone.

"Three witnesses. Which witness described the bomber for the

Police drawing?" asked Driscoll. He looked at the bottom of the report. There were three names tagged as witnesses. Two witnesses were at the bus stop on the far side of the road and were injured and hospitalised. Detectives interviewed them both. The van exploded, killing one person and two Embassy guards. A total of twelve wounded were taken to hospital and later released.

"Who was the third witness?" wondered Driscoll.

Noel gave up working and pushed his chair to be beside Driscoll.

"What?" asked Driscoll.

"You talk when you think, mate," replied Noel.

"Sorry," said Driscoll.

"Who was the individual who described Abuti to the Police artist?" asked Noel.

"Not the office workers at the bus stop. They were brothers, Joshua and Jay Chen. I think it was the third witness," said Driscoll.

"I found it. Zikri Hakim, a photographer for the Kuala Lumpur Times, had taken twelve photos of the Australian Embassy," said Noel.

"Why target the Embassy?" asked Driscoll.

"Okay, let me read it. It says animal rights activists wanted to stop live cattle exports from Australia to Malaysia," said Noel.

"Were the protestors present when the bomb exploded?" asked Driscoll.

"Not sure, maybe," said Noel.

Noel Adams searched for the details online and found plenty of angry comments from both sides of the debate. Adams summarised as he read it.

"Okay. It's a big business. Australian Cattle owners hate the activists. Malaysia doesn't want to be lectured to by activists. Activists don't like the way Malaysians slaughter animals. Here we go. The activists protested the day before the bombing. Somebody put banners on the fence. The Police were present in riot gear," said Adams.

"They protested the day before the bombing. Is there a connection between the cattle and the bombing?" asked Driscoll.

"They are killing people to stop people from killing animals. Doesn't make sense to me," said Noel.

"Were the protestors present on the day of the bombing?" asked Driscoll.

"The same reporter was most likely there on both days. Where are his photos?" asked Noel.

After several minutes of reading, Warren said, "Here we go. Zikri Hakim, the paper photographer, was also injured, taken to hospital and interviewed by the same detectives as the other two witnesses. It was Hakim who described the bomber to the Police artist."

"Search for Hakim and the newspaper, 1989," replied Noel.

"Oh. Somebody murdered Zikri Hakim on the same day outside the hospital," said Driscoll.

"Murdered. How convenient!" said Noel. "Print me a copy of that report, will you?"

"Yes. Murdered for taking photographs," said Driscoll.

"Pictures of the bomber," replied Noel.

"We need those pictures. Where are they?" asked Driscoll.

Noel phoned Paul the Apostle, his MI5 equivalent in their Kuala Lumpur Embassy. After several minutes of talk, Noel ended the call.

"He'll get back to us with a contact and phone number," answered Noel.

"Why do you call him that?" asked Driscoll.

"When MI5 recruited him from the university with post-doctoral degrees in philosophy and theology, He thought morning prayers were, you know, morning prayers. The name stuck," answered Noel.

"Post-Doctoral studies in Philosophy. Why isn't a professor at some university?" asked Driscoll.

"He's a brilliant thinker," replied Noel.

Paul got the interviewing detective's name, now Superintendent Jayanbalan. The Superintendent's office emailed the full interview with Hakim, witness statements and photos. Noel printed the documents, and they sat closely, split up the papers and got to work. Driscoll said, "Hakim's editor sent him to get a photo of the Australian Embassy and a quote from their public relations person. Here we go; Hakim took photos of the van arriving, the bomber leaving the van and the explosion."

Noel said, "I have all the 12 photos. Okay, we have the face of the bomber, Hussain Humid."

"I'll let Joyce work on these twelve pictures and contrast them with this morning's photographs from Gatwick," said Driscoll.

"Okay, Jayanbalan says; Hakim survived and suffered a minor concussion. An ambulance took him to the Metro Hospital for observation. He worked with the Police artists describing the bomber. The doctors released him with medication at 10:46 pm," answered Noel.

"What transpired with the photos?" asked Driscoll.

"Jayanbalan requested the newspaper for a full set of Hakim's photos," said Noel. "For both days."

"Does request mean bully?" asked Driscoll.

"There might be different rules in Malaysia," noted Noel.

"They found Hakim dead on the footpath at 10:50 pm. The body was near the taxi rank outside the hospital, and there was no bag or camera," said Driscoll.

Noel said, "Jayanbalan states the murderer was Hussain Humid."

"Murdered because of the photographs," asked Driscoll.

"Yes, because of the photographs implicating him 100%," affirmed Noel.

"Autopsy?" asked Driscoll.

"Hey wait, a minute. Here it is. This is interesting. Not a dagger, something narrower, between the ribs puncturing the heart," replied Noel.

"A silent assassin," mumbled Driscoll.

"Yes, a thing of crime stories or a personal signature," replied Noel.

Driscoll stopped reading. He ordered up his Malaysian database and entered 'Zikri Hakim.' Some of these stories needed translating. He scanned all the newspaper articles for the last one, dated 1989. It was a funeral notice. Noel, it reads here that Hakim died in the hospital, not on the street," Driscoll said.

"Jayanbalan again," replied Noel with his eyebrows raised in suspicion.

"Hakim identified Hussain Humid as the bomber," said Driscoll

"Says Jayanbalan?" replied Noel.

Driscoll kept reading the report out loud: "Malaysian and

Australian Federal Police interviewed Wira Harun, who worked in the Malaysian Road Transport Department. Harun was arrested at his home in Bukit Kepong and then transferred to Bukit Aman Police headquarters in Kuala Lumpur for interrogation."

"I bet that wasn't subtle," suggested Noel.

"Jayanbalan says the Special Branch of the Royal Malaysian Police took over the investigation," said Driscoll.

"Sounds like a takeover. You know a takeover happened, and Jayabalan got his nose out of joint?" suggested Noel.

"Yes. The Special Branch fired Detective Jayanbalan and interviewed Harun, who illegally printed three driver's licenses for 2,500 Ringgit," said Driscoll.

"All Malaysian car licenses?" asked Noel.

"No. He printed a Malaysian, UK and Australian ones. The name on each car license was the same, Ducat Abuti," said Driscoll.

"Wira Harun stated that Ducat Abuti contacted him originally. He paid him for the driver's license. Ducat Abuti was not the person who picked up the forged driver's licenses," replied Noel.

"Ducat Abuti used a courier?" replied Driscoll

Who knows? Jayanbalan implies the Special Branch developed tunnel vision. Once you latch onto one individual, you become oblivious to any alternatives," replied Noel as he continued reading.

"Okay, so Hakim, the photographer from the city newspaper, takes pictures of the bomber while photographing the Australian Embassy. At some point, Jayanbalan confiscates Hakim's twelve photos. A police sketch artist who can't draw goes to the hospital," said Driscoll.

Noel interrupts and says, "Hakim provides an inferior description of Ducat Abuti to the Police artist because Hakim has a front-page exclusive feature and explicit photos."

"Hakim leaves the hospital, and Ducat Abuti murders him on the street," said Driscoll.

"That makes sense. That lousy sketch of Ducat Abuti from the Special Branch has been on our database for years," replied Noel.

"Correct. I wonder why Jayanbalan kept the photos from the Special Branch?" asked Driscoll.

"Somebody only gave the Special Branch the drawing," wondered Noel.

"Jayanbalan, was that somebody," laughed Driscoll.

Driscoll turned and looked at Joyce's response to Gatwick and the twelve pictures. "It is a 94% match. Joyce says an older Ducat Abuti was at Gatwick this morning."

Noel kept reading out loud. "Australian Federal Police Forensic investigators worked with the Malaysian Special Branch detectives. They sifted through the bomb debris." He turned the page. "This is interesting. They found a part of the engine block and obtained a partial engine number. The van belonged to a Singapore-based truck rental company located in an industrial park in Selangor. The company handed over a copy of the van rental contract with a photo of the driver who hired it. They have a camera behind their counter. Wait a minute. Here's the picture," said Noel.

"What?" asked Driscoll.

"Where's the Jayanbalan report?" asked Noel.

"Here. Got it," said Driscoll.

"Does Jayanbalan comment on the van hire?" suggested Noel.

Driscoll said after reading the entire report. "No, there's nothing on the van. The Special Branch interviewed, charged and jailed Wira Harun. But Jayanbalan followed up and interviewed Harun later in prison. I think Jayanbalan struck a deal."

Noel lifted his head from his reading and asked, "What type of deal?"

"Reduced sentence," said Driscoll with his eyebrows lifted.

"Harun said to Jayanbalan he had a video," replied Noel.

"Of what?" asked Driscoll.

"It doesn't say. We don't have it, but it got Harun a reduced sentence from killer to accomplice," answered Noel.

Noel just stared at Driscoll. He moved his armchair over to the phone and called Jayanbalan back.

The phone rang. Jayanbalan answered with his Indian accent, "Hello."

"Inspector Jayanbalan,? This is Noel Adams from MI5 again. Thank you for taking my call." Noel looked at Driscoll, who was listening in on the conversation.

"I've been waiting to see how good you were as an investigator," said Jayanbalan.

"What do you mean? Harun's video, his insurance?" asked Noel.

"I will email the video," said Jayanbalan. The phone call ended.

Noel held the phone and said to Driscoll, "We just got played. Jayanbalan has been waiting for someone to put the pieces together."

Noel opened his secure email account and found Jayabalan's three MP4 videos. Driscoll stood and leaned over Noel's shoulder to watch.

"This video shows the courier for Ducat Abuti entering Harun's shop. He pays for the driving license and then leaves. The courier is wearing a cap. Let's look at the second video. Harun has his hand stretching up above his head to the camera," said Noel

"What is he holding?" asked Driscoll.

"He is holding all three licenses to the camera. Harun does the same thing with the passport," said Noel.

"And the third video?" asked Driscoll.

"Interesting. The courier enters the shop, and Harun hands over a package. The courier turns and leaves," said Noel.

"Go back to the second video," asked Driscoll. "What is the name on the passport?"

Noel rewound the second video and expanded the dimensions of the image. Driscoll's desk PC made a tone alert. Driscoll said, "Joyce has just matched the twelve photos of the KL bomber with Ducat Abuti at Gatwick this morning. 94%."

Noel turned back to his screen and said, "Look. It is not Ducat Abuti."

"What do you mean?" asked Driscoll.

"Look at the second video. The bomber, Hakim's murderer, the van hirer, the courier, now I suspect the Gatwick guy are the same person. That passport in the video says his name is Abu Sarek. Can you see that face in the passport?" said Noel.

"Who is Abu Sarek?" asked Driscoll, now confused.

Driscoll entered the name 'Abu Sarek' into the MI5 database. "Here we go. I'll read it out. The US coalition killed Abu Sarek in Bagdad,

Iraq. Sarek, his family and a group of insurgents died in a CIA drone strike. He's dead," replied Driscoll.

"Does the CIA terrorist database have a photo of Abu Sarek?" asked Noel.

"Yes. The CIA has a picture. But this is not the guy at Gatwick or in that passport," said Driscoll.

"Well, who the hell is the person at Gatwick?" asked Noel.

Driscoll swapped over to his immigration database from Joyce and called up the passports' video recording. "The name on the passport this morning is Milton Kant. Kahnt looks like Abu Sarek. Harun's passport was not used at Gatwick," replied Driscoll.

Noel said, "Now I am confused. Joyce told us Abu Sarek was at Gatwick this morning. Joyce compared the passenger with the Police sketch. The passenger's name is Milton Kahnt. Based on the sketch, Kahnt has biometric data similar to Abu Sarek. That proves it, Warren. It is a coding issue. Joyce is giving a false positive on similar biodata, plus that Police sketch?"

"Who is Milton Kahnt?" asked Driscoll.

Noel reviewed Joyce's social media data for a few minutes and said, "Kahnt was born in the UK, as per his passport. There you go!"

Noel lifted his phone, spoke to their boss, Alan James, first, then phoned Paul the Apostle back in Malaysia. They needed more information on Abu Sarek.

CHAPTER 30

LONDON GATWICK AIRPORT

Abu Sarek noticed a slight shift in tension on Border Force officer Steve Joel's face. Abu leaned over the counter and pointed to his passport, asking, "Sir, is there a problem with my passport?"

Abu then lowered a narrow, transparent, carbon-based Flexi stiletto from his left sleeve, a deadly weapon invisible to airport screening.

Steve Joel looked up and replied, "No, it's fine. Your passport picture could be better. Enjoy your stay, Mr. Kahnt."

Sarek thanked him, and he made sure that nobody saw his stiletto retract. He then took the shuttle to the train station and waited for the next train to Brighton.

CHAPTER 31

MURMANSK RUSSIA

A navy worker nicknamed the Russian naval new ICBM missiles the 'Red Banners.' The missile's body is painted shimmering silver with fire engine red expandable wings.

A single Red Banner is eight meters in height and 7,000 kilograms in weight. It will carry either a 15,000-kiloton nuclear warhead or multiple smaller warheads and have a range of 16,000 km. The P-900 missiles entered employment with the Russian Northern Submarine Fleet as part of the Oscar class guided-missile armoury. The engineers designed the 'Red Banners' for a new stealth submarine.

Nerpichya Bay Naval Base is 60 km from Murmansk and is the graveyard of many Cold War Soviet submarines. It is in the Litsa Fjord of the Kola Peninsula, 45 km from the Norwegian border. Severe climate, strong winds, and a long polar night make this area unpleasant and uninviting. The Government abandoned these Cold War Soviet submarines, which now sit like beached whales, leaking radioactive waste—a disaster in the making.

The Russian Naval Base of Nerpichya was dead quiet. It was a restricted base for irradiated submarines, awaiting deconstruction. But today, it was busy. Six men and one retired nuclear engineer from

Moscow dismantled two Red Banners missiles from a crippled submarine.

They were all members of a Moscow mafia group.

Russia has 237 retired Cold War nuclear-powered submarines. One hundred eighty submarines have been decommissioned, leaving fifty-seven beached in distant harbours in Russia's extreme north. Scientists developed the Regional Centre for Radioactive Waste Conditioning and Disposal site opposite the abandoned Nerpichya Naval Base in Saida Bay.

The scientists asked that their project be located somewhere other than the infamous Andreeva Bay. They filled 48 steel containers, each weighing 600 tons of nuclear waste.

An international charity had devoted over 100 million euros in assistance to ballistic missile submarine dismantlement. Previously, the Soviet Union dumped liquid radioactive waste into the ocean, avoiding the expensive draining, storing and filtering process of this deadly legacy from the Cold War.

The Spanish and London Dumping Convention now forces Russia from sinking submarines. Submarine dismantlement is a slow, dangerous, and costly exercise. An international environmental group funded the security, protecting the stock of spent naval fuel. Rumours surfaced, and the money went elsewhere, resulting in abysmal security, especially during winter.

The used fuel rods are radioactive, requiring careful handling. Spent fuel requires reprocessing to separate the plutonium for use in weapons. Russia is aware of a possible threat posed by a rogue state or terrorist groups attempting to seize the fissile material from decommissioned nuclear submarines. The Russian Federal Inspectorate for Nuclear and Radiation Safety questioned why fuel inventories differed from actual fuel stored at individual sites. It was a mess.

Isaakovich Apresyan was a bully.

He trusted nobody. The guy looked like a heavyweight boxer who had gone in the ring too many rounds. Apart from the fatty flattened nose, massive hands, no hair and heavy eyebrows, he was also significantly overweight. He was walking from a heart attack.

Apresyan's father was part of the Moscow criminal syndicate or the mafia and bled young Isaak into the cartel.

Apresyan offered 5,000 euros to a secretary from the Inspectorate to obtain a copy of a classified report of a recently damaged Khabarovsk Class submarine and its current location and status. These new stealth attack class submarines were built in Workshop 35 Construction Hall 3 at the Sevmash yard in Severodvinsk. The design included lithium-ion batteries as a secondary power source when hunting. First and foremost, they were nuclear-powered, nuclear-armed and expensive at one billion USD each.

Something happened on the first test run.

The submarine was moving at maximum speed and collided with an unknown object. Ten thousand tons of nuclear-powered steel rammed into something, causing significant catastrophic damage.

It was an expensive epic mistake, or was it?

The NavyNavy had removed eight undamaged Red Banner missiles, leaving two mangled missiles in their loading bays. The heavy eight-foot-diameter missile hatches were twisted and jammed closed. Usually, to open a missile hatch, the locking pins retract, and then a piston under pressurized fluid punches the 9,000-kilogram hatch open. Other designs use explosives.

Further damage was caused to the superstructure and pressure hull around both missile tubes. The report estimated the cost of repair at 700 million USD. The Navy delayed removing the remaining missiles because radioactive waste was leaking from the two reactors. The report stated that it was uncertain how this had occurred. Apresyan had paid the Reactor Control Chief 90,000 Euros. Reactor Control Chief Vlad Drovopsky was to cause a reactor scram during the sea exercise. However, the unexpected collision allowed Drovopsky to destroy the vessel.

Drovopsky triggered the plant's protection circuitry, and in less than two seconds, the (CRDM) control rod drive mechanism drove the control rods to the core's bottom. The core was no longer generating heat. Without heat, there was no steam for the turbine generators and main engines. He opened the primary coolant circuit bypass valve for fifty seconds, releasing massive amounts of contaminated moisture through an internal valve. Alarms sounded, and Drovopsky announced a radioactive leak. He detonated a small charge, causing the air purification unit to catch fire. Drovopsky broke the billion-dollar submarine.

It surfaced, and the crew evacuated.

The unexpected collision worked in Apresyan's favour, although the damage made his work more difficult. Murmansk Oblast Federal Security Service and the Russian naval crews from the PM class service ships had selected an empty wharf at the Nerpichya Naval Base to dock for the submarine. Radioactive waste was to be removed from the sub and transported to Saida Bay Center for processing.

A date had yet to be set.

Isaakovich said, "You will each receive 200,000 Euros to separate the two warheads. We will secure them to transport frames and encase them into two lead-lined shipping containers. It has possible health risks, so take precautions at all times," said Apresyan.

He knew the men would take the risk because of the money.

Their exit strategy was straightforward. Upon delivery of the two missile nuclear devices, each man would receive cash payments. The plan was that each worker would return home separately. Apresyan said each worker would receive new passports and open-air tickets with 200,000 Euros. The nuclear engineer had to secure and arm the 'Red Banners.'

The plan was to approach the Bay without raising suspicion. Apresyan purchased a retired 'roll-on/roll-off car ferry to transport three Ural-4320-555 off-road 6x6 trucks with shipping containers loaded with machinery and supplies. There was also a Scania R500 V8 tractor-trailer with lead-lined shipping containers and a Liebherr LTZ 22300 mobile crane.

The darkened ferry remained in an isolated inlet, waiting until early morning. Apresyan's helmsman wore Enhanced Night Vision Goggle-Binoculars. He steered the ferry out into the channel, moving slowly. The ferry arrived at the Nerpichya Naval Base wharf at 2:16 am and docked beside the damaged submarine.

It was winter and a polar night.

"There should be two guards. Divide into two groups. Secure the wharf. Secure the guards in that building," said Apresyan. Armed with silenced weapons, night goggles, and black clothes, the first team found the guard's accommodation empty.

The radio clicked, "Apresyan, both guards are sitting on chairs on the pier facing the ferry, unarmed and dead drunk. We've taken them to the guard building and restrained them with their handcuffs," said Maxim. "We have their roster. It is a ten-day on and four days off; we're on day three, leaving us seven days before anybody comes looking."

The Liebherr LTZ 22300 mobile crane was the last truck to come off the ferry. The high tide helped the balancing act as the crane crept onto the concrete pier without sinking the ferry. It had a telescopic boom with 1200 metric tons lifting capacity to lift each missile. They had three days to dismantle the 'Red Banner.'

CHAPTER 32

BRIGHTON UK

The train from Gatwick Airport to Brighton Rail Station took 45 minutes. Abu blended in, but nobody paid him any attention. The accommodation was an 8-minute walk downhill on Queens Road, then left into the second North Street, to the Premier Inn. He chose this inn because of the automatic person-less reception.

The machine asked for his passport, booking number, and credit card. It returned the credit card with a magnetized receipt for digital entry into his room.

Abu unpacked, dressed in casual clothes he had purchased in a Barcelona beachside store, and went for a walk to the beach. 'Barcelona's promenade has white sand, and Brighton Beach has rocks. How different? People are sitting on beach towels on large rocks. That can't be pleasant,' thought Sarek. Hundreds of families were wandering along the beach footpath and pier. Abu admired the relaxed atmosphere. It was hot and sunny, and a slight breeze ran off the ocean. Children were playing, and people were laughing and talking. Abu purchased a takeaway coffee and searched for a place to eat.

Returning from the Brighton Pier, he crossed the road and walked up Black Lion Street. The Meeting House Lane was on his right. Abu noted the title, 'Friends Meeting House.' It was a place of worship but looked more like an ancient Roman temple.

Across the lane were graffiti-laden trendy cafes, a cannabis oil store and an artisan bakery.

He watched three elderly ladies leave the ancient building. Their clothing was the opposite of those sitting in the open-air café. The contrast for Abu was confusing.

Sarek weaved through an alley with stores and attractive cafes selling delicious food. On Union Street, he ran across a pub called -The Font. UK pubs were fascinating with their odd names and outdoor flower arrangements.

He read the marble plaque affixed to the Font's brick wall near the entrance. A steel picket fence provided a space for patrons to leave their dogs to drink water. Abu raised an eyebrow as he studied the old foundation plaque.

It read, 'Henry Varley came here in the 1700s and opened the London Free Tabernacle. He moved to Brighton to this Gospel Hall.'

Abu looked up at the structure, "This building was a church? Today, it is a pub."

Abu knew that in Istanbul, the Church of Hagia Sophia or Holy Wisdom was a place of worship built in 537 as a Christian cathedral. In its day, it was the largest Catholic church of the Eastern Roman Empire. It was the first to use a pendentive dome. It represented the peak, the ultimate of Byzantine-built structures. It was said to have changed the concept of architecture. The Islamic Government recently ordered it to be converted into a Grand Mosque. The Pope and many Christian Church leaders expressed their objections. But few Catholics today live in Istanbul.

'I can't image the Islamic Government turning the Holy Wisdom into a pub,' he thought. 'Perhaps an area for tourists to admire but not a pub.'

He examined the Font's age, 'At least the building wasn't abandoned. These patrons worship a different god.' Abu chided himself, "Stop being judgemental." He read about Union Chapel's history. It was also called Union Street Chapel for non-Anglican Christians.

'Non-Anglicans, what does that mean?' thought Abu. 'After 300 years of use by various churches, it passed into secular hands in 1988 when the current owners converted it into a tavern called -The Font.'

'Now, I'm intrigued.' Abu entered, ordering a medium-cooked steak, chips with salad, and a lemon-lime juice drink. The waiter walked him upstairs and placed the food on a small round table with one chair beside the old wooden balcony.

"Thank you. Where is the restroom?" Abu asked. The attendant pointed to a door to his right, smiled, and disappeared.

He was hungry, and the aroma of steak was delightful. It was different from lamb or veal. The breakdown in protein and fat caused by the cooking, the fresh olive oil, and the appealing creaminess and juiciness created delicious scents rushing towards his nose.

It was a delicious meal, and Sarek, now relaxed, drank his lemon and lime drink. He peered over the balcony. The bar was below, following the semi-circular frame of the raised church platform. The bar staff had stacked bottles of alcohol on and across the front of the stage. Overhead but within easy reach for the barman were different brands and odd-shaped bottles of spirits, stacked three bottles deep into an overhead system. He looked at the balcony and saw how professional stage lighting focused on the bar and alcohol.

He then glanced at the wooden platform. Towards the front was a discoloured square pattern. The preacher stood behind his podium. 'They changed their God with a different spirit,' thought Abu.

'Alcohol was prohibited, indeed considered sinful by most Muslims. Yet a minority of Muslims could probably outdrink western drunks.' He thought of the stone plaque and the thousands of people over 300 years coming here to worship their God, Jesus.

'Why didn't they sell the building to Muslims for a mosque?' wondered Abu.

He left the Font and was weaving through laneways, heading to his room. 'Why am I feeling agitated?' wondered Abu. Was he going through an inner restlessness, or was it confusion, something he couldn't understand? 'I have no problem with the People of the Book. I don't see them as infidels that commit polytheism with their God the Father, God the Son and God the Holy Spirit,' thought Abu. He kept wandering in the general direction towards his hotel, squeezing past people and thinking.

'So, what is it? Has the UK abandoned their Christianity? Was it disrespect, did they see their faith as brainwashing, or were people cynical and indifferent to anything spiritual?' wondered Abu.

He bought ice cream. 'I've heard Western people say they are spiritual.' He smiled at people as they moved through the narrow lanes. 'Being spiritual meant they did or didn't have a god? Their Christian faith had faded. But didn't Christianity shape their history, culture and welfare?' thought Abu. 'They disregard a church as a sacred place but not Stonehenge? Are people subjected to enforced secularism? If their Christianity is irrelevant, then so must be my Islam?' thought Abu. He stopped walking.

When he reached his room, he opened the door, entered, and then locked the door. He turned and walked over to the window, opened the curtains and the window.

"Such a pleasant warm breeze," said Abu.

He looked at the night view, the coloured lights, the pier, the Brighton wheel spinning in circles. He watched people walking the streets. There were families with children eating ice cream and couples holding hands, talking and laughing. They seemed content and happy.

'Happiness is their ultimate goal? Then what I believe belongs in a museum,' thought Abu. He cut short his stay in Brighton and focused on his work ahead. He had to establish his company as he only had four years to embed himself and prepare for Ahmed's plan.

He wondered about the US Marshall relocation program. 'Do people stay in their new, unfamiliar location, can I?' thought Abu.

CHAPTER 33

RUSSIA
Malyshev's morning alarm chimed. "I'm very tired of all of this," said Vyacheslav Malyshev. He was 55 years of age, born in Australia to Russian immigrants. He had thick silvery hair and a handlebar moustache. Since his Moscow wife's death, he had lost weight and focus. His one great passion was the environment. Vyacheslav was the Australian consultant with the Nuclear Materials Security Task Force Program. It was an international project with Russia to remove radioactive waste from submarines.

Malyshev crawled out of bed, made himself a cup of coffee and looked out his kitchen window. 'Polar nights!' he murmured. After a hot shower and shave, he was ready for data recording. The funding for the program ceased a year ago, but he continued his work. 'I have nothing else left to do.' He lived in Murmansk and had the authority to visit each bay in the Kola Peninsula to obtain readings. He made his way to his car with his flask of hot coffee. He lit a cigarette while sitting in his 30-year-old car, waiting for the engine to warm. Once the car heater produced warmth, he inspected four bays. No sunrise, just darkness.

"What does it take to wake people up to the environmental nuclear destruction of the Kola Peninsula?" said Malyshev. He knew the answer. They were so isolated and out of sight of the population. He constantly complained about the radioactive waste pollution from used fuel cores from sunk submarines in the Barents and Kara Sea. Nobody cared. He had written letters to Government departments enclosing photos showing how each sub was falling, slipping deeper into the water and showing further signs of rust and decay, exposing the environment to radiation contamination. He kept precise records with a confident hope that they would someday assist a new generation of bureaucrats who cared more about the environment than keeping their jobs.

Saida Bay Center worked while it had money. However, mutual mistrust, Russian denial of access to individual facilities, and the lack of liability agreements caused divisions. Then, disputes over the location of the spent naval fuel storage facilities stopped the program.

"Some preferred argument rather than environmental solutions," said Malyshev.

He took his pictures and made notes, and then he would leave. It was the final bay. He got out of his car, put on his protective clothing, hoisted his equipment bag over his shoulder, and shuffled two hundred feet through the snow to the overlook of the abandoned Naval Base of Nerpichya. He set up his tripod and attached a long-distance lens to his Canon 750D digital camera. It was switched to a night setting, and each submarine was shot in the distance.

"We never got around to fixing so many of these rust buckets," complained Malyshev. Every high ground had a yellow-painted steel peg forced into the ground. He placed the tripod over the steel peg at each location. Retired submarines had a spot of yellow iridescent paint at the level of the nuclear reactor. When that spot of yellow touched the water, he knew that, in time, nuclear contaminants would ultimately enter the sea.

As he approached the last bay, he was surprised to see the pier illuminated. "Someone started work on that sub," said Malyshev.

Malyshev had attached Wi-Fi to his camera, which was capable of recording video like a cell phone. The camera sent images and video to his home server.

The recently damaged Khabramvsk Class submarine was his last set of photographs for the morning. "What a squandering of a billion dollars," said Malyshev.

'Something odd is happening on the pier,' he thought. He swung his camera to the dockside warehouse that stored the wrecking equipment. The electric warehouse doors were open. Malyshev knew all the gear off by heart. They had used it all in the project. He counted all the equipment - oxyacetylene torches, plasma cutters, mobile cranes, conveyors, cable-cutting machines and giant guillotine shears.

"Why is the equipment scattered all over the pier? Why are the lights on inside the warehouse, but the lights in the GG warehouse next door were off?" asked Malyshev.

The GG warehouse was called the "Gravel Gerties" by the Americans. Its roof is covered with tons of sand and gravel. If a detonation occurs when dismantling and recycling bomb cores, the building collapses, burying the hazardous material and the employees.

Malyshev knew the fuel cores of decommissioned Russian warheads were diluted, sold, and delivered to the US to power 104 nuclear reactors. Salvaged bomb material now generates 10% of electricity in the United States. 'If the American public knew those details!' "The gravel warehouse was dark?" said Malyshev. He turned his camera back to the dock from the warehouses.

"Why on earth is a vehicle ferry alongside the submarine?" wondered Malyshev. A crane was lifting a shipping container onto a Ural truck. Thick black cables stretched from a silenced 500 kV power generator to five independent hydraulic arch-lighting towers.

'This doesn't look like a repair job. Between the stern and bow, the entire section had been ripped open,' thought Malyshev. By law, missile dismantling had to be done in the GG warehouse, not on the dock where the equipment lay scattered,' he thought.

"The outer light hull and the stronger inner pressure hull midsection were torn apart. The missile housing is visible and empty," said Malyshev. He watched the Liebert 36-wheeler crane tear apart a missile.

Malyshev's camera had taken dozens of photographs and video

"This is not right." He was aware the missiles were the final two from the billion-dollar wreck. But tearing the sub apart was dangerous. "They're wearing CBRN suits?" said an astonished Malyshev.

CBRN suits are charcoal-impregnated protective clothing. CBRN replaced the Cold War term NBC (nuclear, biological, and chemical) with 'R', which stood for a radiological or dirty bomb.

'Several CBRN suits lay scattered on the pier. Exposed naval workers normally wear CT-12 NBC Respirators,' thought Malyshev.

"Those respirators are for the British SAS or counter-terrorism group. Moscow is allowing UK SAS teams to work here?" asked Malyshev. He focused the camera on the containers and then recognized what was inside. The video kept recording everything.

"It just doesn't make any sense!" said Malyshev.

"By law, the navy must dismantle missiles inside the GG warehouse, not on the pier. Now they are loading the warheads inside a shipping container?" He saw an old RDS-7 inside a shipping container on a Ural off-road 6x6 truck.

"An RDS-7, that's impossible?" said Malyshev.

Malyshev's father was involved in the Soviet atomic program in 1959. He disappeared to Australia through China. Along with other physicists, they had successfully tested the RDS-7, a 'layer cake' thermonuclear device that used fusion in lithium deuteride to enhance a fission bomb's yield. The two-stage radiation compression design ultimately changed the design configuration of the RDS-7. But before its change, then abandonment, Malyshev's dad had introduced a rare Li-6 isotope to enrich the fuel. Still, a miscalculation in measuring the nuclear reaction rate involving the dominant Li-7 isotope yielded an unexpected twenty million TNT tons. When tested at Kazakhatov, the fireball measured nearly twelve miles high and threw radioactive debris over 50,000 square miles. The addition of the isotope even surprised Malyshev's father.

He grabbed his phone off the tripod hook, checked the USB cable to his camera, adjusted the settings, and then sent everything to his former project boss. "The British are stealing nuclear warheads? No, that doesn't make any sense." He thumbed through his contact list for George Phillips, his ex-boss from the Department of Energy in Melbourne, Australia.

George awoke from a deep sleep, looked at his bedside clock, 11:37 pm, cursed and answered his phone. "George, is that you? Malyshev here.

"Umm...how are you?" said Phillips, now half-awake.

"Sorry, George, I know it's late, but I don't know who to call. Something is going on that I don't understand," said Malyshev.

"What do you mean?" said Phillips.

"British SAS is loading an old RDS-7 nuclear bomb onto Russian 6X6 along with two P-1200 or Red Banner warheads. The 6X6 has two shipping containers on a tractor-trailer. The missiles are from the damaged Khabramvsk class submarine," said Malyshev.

"Yes, the one that hit the mountain. The RDS-7 don't exist," said Phillips.

"Some of these UK soldiers are wearing UK protective clothing. The car ferry is a domestic transport vehicle! I am perplexed. Why would the British be doing this?" said Malyshev.

Phillips asked where Malyshev was, but Malyshev kept talking. "Look, I will send you pictures and video right now. Something is not right. Russian Naval Command was about to remove the crushed missiles. I am sending you everything. Okay? I didn't know who to."

Philipps heard a grunt and then a slight thump. Malyshev had stopped talking. Isaakovich Apresyan lowered his bolt action M40A3 Sniper Rifle, lifted his binoculars and scanned the area. He spoke into his hand radio, "Zatk'nis, we leave now! Load the ferries now," Apresyan ordered. "Secure the cargo containers, get those trucks on board, and leave everything else on the pier. We go now!" He raised the rifle and looked through his 4th generation NVXS-7 scope to ensure the person was dead. He grunted and bent down to pick up his 338 Lapua shell casing.

The cell phone lay on the ground, still sending images. Australia's HQJOC computers captured the contents of the conversation. Karen Richards and ASIS director Paul Adam automatically received the photos.

CHAPTER 34

SYDNEY, AUSTRALIA

Hunter Wyatt was riding his Ducati Diavel from Leichhardt to Darlinghurst ASIS offices. Karen Richards had called Hunter to an urgent meeting with Dr. John Moody. The counterterrorism operative checked his watch and knew he would be late for his 7:00 am meeting. He opened the throttle and started weaving through stalled traffic, receiving various honks and hand gestures.

"Yeah, yeah!" said Hunter with a smile.

Hunter had a sharp intellect and the build of a soldier. He was raised and attended private schools on the Gold Coast. After graduating from the Royal Australian Military College, he joined SASR or Tier 1 Commandos. Hunter's first mission became legendary for the wrong reasons.

An Australia's SASR team were undercover in Belarus to stop a military weapon supply transfer. South Korean ASIS agent Kwon reported that the Russian military would transport weapons from Moscow to Minsk onto Vladivostok for North Korea. The cargo would be transferred from the Antonov 124 to a fake badged Finnair C5 Galaxy at Minsk. Karen passed that intelligence onto SASR.

For the SASR, it was a waiting game. Team leader Black Rhino's strategy was to board the loaded C5 and fly it to Yokota US Air Base in Japan. The team bunked down in an abandoned shed. After ten days, the Antonov 124 was a no-show. Black Rhino then booked rooms at a city hotel 26 miles east of the airport.

"Hunter, you're staying. New team members get boring jobs. If the Antonov lands, call me," said Black Rhino.

"Yes, BR," replied Hunter. He thought Black Rhino's name was probably Bruce or Billy. He wondered if his surname was Rabbit, Rudolph or Rogers. 'That would be so embarrassing if his leader's name were Billy Rabbit,' thought Hunter.

Hunter figured the exchange would be at the end of the runway after midnight, where both aircraft would park and do their business out of sight. The airport closed at 10 pm. Satisfied he was invisible, Hunter crossed the runway and headed to a mound covered with scrub. He did the black makeup and covered his hair and clothing with mud.

The C5 Galaxy arrived three days later at 2 a.m. The runway lights came on at 1:55 a.m. and were turned off again at 1:59 a.m. The sound of the Galaxy awoke Hunter. It was not a Finnair plane. The Galaxy taxied to a warehouse and stopped; the pilot lowered the rear cargo door. The lights came on in the cargo doors. Hunter counted rows of large wooden crates strapped to flatbed dollies.

'I can't read Russian,' thought Hunter. He concentrated on using his digital binoculars and wiped his eyes several times. Okay, wooden crates, two meters square. There were lots of different boxes he couldn't see. The number' 50' is spray-painted on the box with an image of a landmine.

"Fifty landmines?" said Hunter. He lowered his binoculars and looked up at the sky. "I can't see the C5."

Armed Spetsnaz soldiers were walking down the rear cargo doors, chatting and ready to smoke. The aircraft re-fueler standing behind his truck shouted abuse at them. Hunter laughed. He rechecked the sky.

Hunter could almost read the bloke's lips, 'You don't smoke here, you idiots, you morons. Are you as blind as bats? I have millions of litres of fuel. Get over there!'

"No Finnair badge on that plane and no Antonov," odd thought Hunter. The soldiers were smoking near the warehouse. He moved his binoculars back to the rear of the Galaxy, "The flight crew are not leaving the plane," said Hunter.

He radioed Billy Rabbit, "Boss, an unbranded Galaxy C5, has landed. The plane is full of Russian military equipment. The Antonov isn't here, and the flight crew has not left the aircraft. There is no transfer happening, only refuelling. The Spetsnaz are extinguishing their cigarettes," said Hunter.

"We'll be there in 10 minutes," replied Black Rhino.

"The soldiers are being waved back on board," said Hunter. His voice pitched higher.

"Shoot the tyres, Hunter. That plane can't leave," replied Black Rhino.

"Seriously! It has about 26 tyres! Black Rhino, hello?" said Hunter. Billy Rabbit had disconnected. Hunter repeated the order as he got his rifle ready.

"Shoot the tyres? It's not a car Billy Rabbit face."

The C5 Galaxy started to taxi, then stopped at the end of the runway. It was spooling up, ready to accelerate and lift at 3700 meters. Hunter was halfway up the runway by now. He adjusted his Barrett M107A1 sniper rifle and shot one tyre, and nothing happened. He tried again.

'Billy Rabbit said it can't leave.'

Hunter fired five 50 BMG calibre bullets into each of the two engines on his side of the runway just seconds before rotation. Once an aircraft reaches takeoff speed, the pilot will say 'rotate.' The plane flew past Hunter, and he poured bullets into the rear of the two engines and wings.

Hunter didn't know there were three million rounds of ammunition, 700 antipersonnel mines, and 300 shoulder-held ground-to-air missiles on board. As the jet fuel lines and engines exploded, everything inside added to the fireball. Hunter was running full speed in the opposite direction.

Hunter's radio chirped, "Hey, junior, we're one minute out. We can see a fireball. What happened?"

"I shot the plane!" shouted Hunter

"You shot the tyres, you mean," said RB.

"I tried!" shouted Hunter.

CHAPTER 35

Hunter wondered if that event triggered an invitation to join ASIS after being kicked out of SASR for not following Billy Rabbit's outrageous orders, 'Shoot the tyres.' The Ducati Diavel was Hunter's joy. Hunter's old man and medical practitioner called them 'donor bikes.'

But Hunter enjoyed the feeling, sound, power, and muscular grunt of the bike as he cruised the road to ASIS headquarters, which was filled with office workers. He needed to fully understand why there were so many ASIS office workers and hardly any field workers. 'Not my circus, not my monkeys,' thought Hunter. He entered Karen Richard's office and parked beside his team member, Dr John Moody.

Karen Richards was 40 years of age, married with children, and lived nearby with their husband, Ben, a theology professor at Alphacrucis University. Karen finished her doctoral studies in International Affairs from Bond University. She was brilliant, with average stature, with dark brown hair. She had a friendly personality, but intelligence was her strength. Hunter checked her empty room and looked perplexed. "What's happening? Did I miss the convention? Is the coffee fresh? Where is everybody?" asked Hunter.

John Moody grunted, "Nothing, no and yes and who knows," and went on studying the morning news on his tablet.

"John, I heard you travelled to Canada or New Zealand to qualify with some hot shots. What is your latest distance?" Hunter asked.

"2000," replied John.

"Splendid!" answered Hunter. He poured coffee into a mug and sat beside John. Assistant ASIS director of Operation Karen Richards arrived with a sullen expression.

"How bad is it?" asked Hunter.

Karen Richards glanced at Hunter and replied, "Very!"

"What's taken place?" John asked, closing his digital tablet.

Looking down at her notes, she replied, "Gideon Downer, secretary of the Department of Defence, received a midnight phone call from George Phillips." Karen read from her digital notes, "At 11:37 pm Sydney time, Philips took a phone call at his home from an old Australian co-worker living in Murmansk Oblast, Russia. Philips was the lead engineer from the Department of Energy in Melbourne. He was involved in an internationally funded program to extract and store spent nuclear fuel and radioactive waste from contaminated Russian cold war submarines. It included experts from lots of countries, including Australia. The recycling program lasted for about 18 months. It ran out of money."

She looked at Hunter, then John, expecting questions. She continued.

"George Phillips reported to Gideon that one of his Australian friends, Vyacheslav Malyshev, had observed men dressed in UK SAS CBRN clothing, loading two, maybe three Russian missile warheads onto a vehicle ferry."

Hunter asked, "What sort of missile warheads?"

Karen looked back at her meeting notes and said, "Malyshev said that there were two or three Russian nuclear submarines, Granit P-900 or P-1200, but he wasn't sure. But he was certain he saw an old Cold War RDS-7. I have some photos and video." Karen opened her tablet, and the images went to the LED screen on the office wall.

"Does Malyshev know the difference between a missile and bits and pieces from the submarine?" asked John. Karen didn't answer.

"Hang on," said Karen. She examined the enlarged colour photo of two men standing in front of what looked like an untrained eye as a large 1980s rotary car engine. In the background was an industrial building.

"The Russian military employed Malyshev's father to help design and develop the first RDS-7," replied Karen. "According to George Phillips, Malyshev's parents came to Australia in the 1960s. They read the writing on the wall, so to speak."

"So the guy knows all about nuclear bombs and submarines," replied John. "Where did these photos come from?"

Karen's cell phone buzzed. She held up a finger, listened, hung up and said, "Okay, I have IT coming in with a copy and transcript of Malyshev's call to Phillips. The photos are from Malyshev's camera. All the images and videos came through his camera Wi-Fi to his server, onto Phillips, then our servers," answered Karen. She transferred the image to a screen.

"What a mess!" declared John.

"That submarine looks like an open can of beans. Has it been identified?" asked Hunter.

"Yes. It is the new Khabramvsk Class sub. One of five," replied Karen.

"Abandoned gas tanks and hoses, tools," said Hunter. "Look here. Is that a body? More bodies are lying on the pier. Radiation poisoning? Dead guards?"

"Yes," said Karen.

"They've removed a portion of the damaged structure, exposed the empty missile silos and their empty cradles," said John. "Those two silos still have the base of the missiles. They have cut off the heads of the two missiles. Talk about risky! No naval engineer worth his salt operates like these amateurs. See that weird warehouse? That's a GG. Missiles are worked on inside in a GG building, never outside. If something goes wrong, tons of gravel collapses on top of you. It's a 'Hail Mary.'"

"Those blokes are wearing UK SAS CBRN suits," said Hunter.

"What are you saying, Hunter? UK SAS troops are stealing nuclear devices from Russia?" asked John. "That doesn't make sense."

Karen's look said it all. "Okay," said Hunter, with his hands up, "too early to speculate."

The following photos showed three new Russian Ural-4320-5556, 6X6 all-wheel drive terrain trucks carrying a shipping container. "These guys have left open the doors of one shipping container. Can we identify what's inside?" asked John.

Hunter studied the picture and replied, "It's a suspended cradle for a nuclear device to be transported on the vehicle ferry. The container walls look thick. John, look at the right of the picture, bottom right-hand corner," asked Hunter. "The bloke in a CBRN suit with binoculars. He's pointing a rifle at the camera." Hunter turned to Karen, "Is Malyshev dead?"

"He is dead," replied Karen. "The phone call stopped, but the camera kept running."

The door opened, and Peter Jonas from IT walked in. Peter was young, eager, sharp, and turned out with a bowtie. He was a professional coder and software engineer. "I have the video recording and transcript of the phone call from Malyshev to Philips," replied Jonas. He handed each person a copy and played the digital video recording on the LED TV on the wall. When it ended, Jonas added, "The camera's battery only stopped three hours ago, 3:30 am our time. We obtained an exact location because of the phone's GPS. It is east of Olenya Bay, Kola Peninsula, Russia. The conversation ends suddenly after the gunshot."

Everybody nodded as they continued reading. Hunter asked, "Is he injured or dead?"

John asked, "Hunter, he hasn't moved. He didn't phone the local Police, just his friend."

Jonas returned to the video. They could hear Malyshev talking and hear the rifle shot. They watched the ferry being loaded and leaving. Jonas opened his laptop and pointed to the LED TV on the wall. "Okay, this is the satellite image of Olenya Bay. Malyshev took these photos around four hours ago. Malyshev's phone is hooked to his tripod, giving us a GPS position."

With the LED pointer, Lucas stated, "This is the navy pier and sub.

The abandoned equipment is here and here. These are mobile flood-lights here. The car ferry has fled."

Lucas turned off his pointer and sat down.

"I want you in Stockholm, John," said Karen. "You will work with our embassy ASIS officer, Jess Vanderbilt and her assistant, Karin Smirnov."

She checked her watch. "Paul Adams and I will Livestream with Canberra in an hour. The PM wants an update. At this point, this is not Australia's problem. Who knows what Russia will do? But we must retrieve his body," said Karen.

"Fair enough, I assume other agencies will also try and track the theft," asked John. Karen gave an affirming nod as she read her cell-phone text.

Hunter turned to Jonas, asking, "Can you get some intel on the car ferry? Its direction and identity?"

Jonas opened another map showing a shipping route on the Baltic and pointed to Norway, 200 miles elsewhere. He replied, "Let's assume they want to reach a port, disembark, then disappear. Kirkenes would be first, then Vadso and maybe Vardo. Both are in Norway, each with single roads leading both ways out from each town. It is hazardous if road-blocked. I doubt those choices."

"How do you disappear with those trucks?" asked John.

Lucas jumped in, saying, "Another possible destination could be Atomflot in Murmansk. They could sail the White Sea down to Archangel or anywhere in between if brave. A ferry is not an icebreaker, so no, I wouldn't go that way."

Hunter said, "The Commander of the Russian Northern fleet could launch a dozen ships from their base at Severomorsk. Norway could do the same. A car ferry would stand out unless they always use ferries in that area."

Karen replied, "They have, about an hour ago."

"They have what an hour ago launched boats?" asked Hunter.

"It might all be over," replied John.

Jonas answered, "Let me break this down. The Khabramvsk Class sub cost USD 1 billion. It hit something, but they isolated it near the machinery sheds George Phillips's international dismantling team used. Those sheds had machinery capable of removing warheads and nuclear fuel."

Moody spoke with a grin, "And?"

"Second, the Russian Naval command isolated the sub for a reason. It may have had a radioactive leak. Third, the Navy munitions depot is in Okolnaya Bay, just outside the main fleet's base of Severomorsk. This sub only does one thing. It carries 'The Red Banners' or SLBM Bulava Missiles, not the P-900 or P-1200 missiles. Malyshev was mistaken. This sub was undergoing sea tests, and they do not carry missiles on the first seagoing tests."

Hunter asked, "Would Malyshev know the difference between an SLBM Bulava Missiles and a P-1200 warhead?"

Jonas replied, "Maybe, maybe not. He is the expert."

"But you're sure we're dealing with the 'Red Banners' because the cradle design doesn't match the P-900 or P-1200 missiles?" asked Hunter.

"The Red Banner's missiles carry a much bigger payload, 15,000KT," said Lucas. "The Navy should have towed this damaged sub to the Zvezdochka repair facility. But they didn't, and that says something."

"So, a new billion-dollar embarrassment is floating in an isolated bay and is radioactive," replied John. "It leaked radiation, exploded, killed sailors and is now abandoned?"

Hunter said, "You're speculating."

Lucas lost his patience, "The crew and sub-captain may be dead from accidental radioactive poisoning. I would suggest it has been placed there, out of the sight of the navy and public!"

"Or they are wine-testing their way across France because they loaded the 'Red Banners' and sold them to these idiots,' replied Hunter, pointing at the pictures.

"What? Nobody walks out of the warehouse with a missile in a shopping trolley. Were you not listening to me? May I continue?" asked Lucas.

"Yes, of course, go on," replied John, scowling at Hunter.

"That ferry does not need a wharf," said Lucas. "You drive the ferry into the ground, and bye-bye 6x6 trucks."

"But not the tractor-trailer," replied Hunter.

"Correct. Everything else is abandoned or dumped overboard," answered Lucas.

"Where? Russian 6x6 trucks are obvious to spot!" replied Hunter.

"They may have a plane nearby," replied John.

Jonas glanced at his tablet and replied, "Vadso has a small airport, and Murmansk has an industrial and commercial airport."

"These guys might be sick or dead," replied John.

Karen Richards turned to Hunter. "I want you on our plane heading to either Vadso or Murmansk. You retrieve the body. If invited, Hunter, you work with these other agencies. Your ID will be the Australian Department of Energy. Jonas, I want you to ID the ferry's owner and try to track its direction. John, go to Stockholm and fly the commercial. If those trucks offload the 'Red Banners', they could go anywhere in Europe or Asia. Who knows where? Jessica will help you with transport. Hunter, you go on the Gulfstream 800. John on the 700. Upon arrival, wait at the airport for more intelligence. If that ferry heads west, hire a car and join up with John."

"We will tread on sovereign toes, Karen. We might get thrown out of Russia," replied Hunter. He knew the US, UK, EU, and Russian agencies would mobilize. Nobody wants those Red Banners in their part of the woods, and neither would Australia. He wondered why they were involved, but these were orders.

CHAPTER 36

SYDNEY AIRPORT

The nine-mile helicopter ride from the ASIS heliport to Sydney International was fast. They landed in a distant part of the airport, away from the public view. Hunter boarded the ASIS's Gulfstream, put his go-bag on his seat, then speed-dialled Jonas.

The Rolls-Royce BR910 turbofan engines on the Gulfstream 800 Turbo spooled up, and the plane moved gracefully across the apron to the runway. Jonas was on the phone, "Your departure from Sydney to Murmansk will take twenty-four hours, a distance of 14,600 km, and you'll arrive at 9 am local time. It's a polar night, with no sunrise or sunlight, okay?"

"Got it," replied Hunter.

"Your credentials will be that of an investigator through the Department of Energy. Your Gulfstream can travel at 904 km/h with two pilots and one refuelling stop. From Murmansk, you can take off to Norway or remain in Murmansk. I will have satellite information arriving in 10 minutes. I will call on the Gulfstream satellite and deliver any images to your tablet through the Gulfstream Broad Band Multi-link (BBML). Keep it powered," answered Lucas.

"Jonas, Malyshev photographed the ferry and then phoned

Philipps," said Hunter. Assuming it took the car ferry crew an additional hour to load the trucks and then leave, what is the ferry's top speed and direction? Get me a list of possible harbours, ferry terminals, or towns where these trucks would not look out of place."

Lucas replied, "Seven to ten miles every hour, depending on weather and the sea conditions. Hunter, when you reach Murmansk, the ferry will have a 28-hour advantage."

He was scrolling through his tablet, loaded by Jonas, which had images, maps, and a chart of airports. "Jonas, there are twenty-five airports within a range of 400 miles from Murmansk. Ten within 200 miles, with most in either Finland or Norway. That car ferry could go to any small town or double back to Murmansk. Or, as you suggested, they could lower the ferry ramp onto an isolated rocky outcrop near a major road. Then offload the 6X6 trucks, travel fast to an airport, and disappear."

Jonas said, "I can scan all ten airports within 200 to 400 miles. However, infrared satellite images at night will show all types of trucks around planes. I'll scan the Ural 6X6 and see if that shape truck appears at any of those airports."

"Jonas, I require some sense of the proportions and weight of the warheads. That will determine the type of plane they need. They would require a forklift to transfer the 'Red Banners' from the shipping container to a box suitable for an aircraft. I suppose a small airport might have that equipment and wooden flight crates. Maybe not." said Hunter.

"I will look into that," replied Lucas.

"Does any airport operate 24/7? If they do, check the images for open cargo containers, sheds, and forklifts. Is there any information on the ferry?" asked Hunter.

"No. All airports have sheds and equipment, Hunter. They could land a plane on a grass runway, load the boxes, and fly off. Hold on, I will call you back on the app," replied Jonas.

"Okay, check for any disused airports. Bye," replied Hunter.

CHAPTER 37

MURMANSK RUSSIA

The weather-battered, black-hulled ferry slithered into the cramped mix of bulk container ships, tugboats, tankers, naval ships, and other sleeping vessels. Isaakovich Apresyan stood at the bow of the car ferry. He instructed Darko Gusev to reduce the speed and stop the ferry with his handheld radio.

"Turn all the lights off. Stay 100 meters from the pier," said Apresyan. He scanned the buildings on the hillside of Leninskiy Okrug for any human activity from the naval accommodation blocks facing the inlet.'With so many ships in the harbour, few would immediately notice a car ferry. This small, isolated harbour area was quiet. It was dark," thought Apresyan. "Okay. No movement on the pier. There are no lights on the hill." He radioed Darko Gusev, "Stay dark, move forward slowly." The tide was high. "Darko, I want you to lower the ferry loading ramp slowly," said Apresyan.

The ferry moved slowly forward and then came to a halt. "Don't grind the ramp on the concrete. That's it, nice and slow, brilliant," said Apresyan. Darko killed the ferry engines, exited the ferry cabin, descended the stairs, jumped into the Scania tractor-trailer's cab and started the engine. Apresyan went on the radio, "No truck lights.

Night vision goggles on. No music. No smoking. Drive-in convoy. Drive fast, and don't stop."

The Scania tractor-trailer came off the ferry first, followed by the 6X6 trucks. They drove in convoy through the outskirts of Murmansk, then got onto the E105. It was pitch black as they moved through Kona. Apresyan knew the 20-minute drive from the ferry to the Murmashi rail yards was risky.

"All it took was just one person, some insomniac, to show interest," said Apresyan.

They approached the warehouse where the exchange would occur and waited. Apresyan parked one street away, within WiFi coverage. He opened his text app and typed, "Vlad, are you finished?" This app encrypts all messages and texts.

"Yes. The welding is complete, and the timer is running. I will be with you in 45 minutes," replied Vlad. Once the app transmits a text or phone call, it deletes it permanently. Vlad Vasin had walked off the ferry and through the township. He found an old car, around 1980s vintage, with no car alarm. He broke in, hot-wired it and was now driving towards Murmashi, the outer suburb of Murmansk.

Apresyan used his phone to log onto his WAN system. He waited. His survival within the Russian mafia depended on his never trusting anyone. 'Could he trust the buyer?' he wondered. He installed a 1080P 6-megapixel security WiFi camera. Long-life batteries powered it. The built-in IR LED enabled Apresyan to watch the factory at night.

He watched live WiFi images taking place inside the warehouse. One person was pacing. He switched to infra-red to see if any other people were waiting. A vehicle was cooling off, and maybe a kettle was boiling. Satisfied, Apresyan switched off his WiFi connection and phoned his contact in the warehouse. "We're here. Open the door."

The warehouse was rundown, old, and cold. There was nothing to draw the eye, no signage, and dirty windows. The electrical roller door opened, and the trucks entered, parked, and the door closed. Waiting for them was Ahmed.

CHAPTER 38

NORWAY

Hunter asked the pilots, "Can we land at Kirkenes, Vadso, Kilberg, Skallelv, or Vardo?"

The co-pilot replied, "Give me a few minutes."

Hunter's tablet beeped. A video screen appeared with Jonas talking to someone else. He turned his head to Hunter and said, "Hunter, can you hear me?"

"Yes," replied Hunter.

"Our satellite passed over the Murmansk region ten hours ago, showing an unidentified boat. It is heading west outside of the inlet to maybe Norway. The image should be on your screen now," added Jonas.

"The image is not very good, Jonas," stated Hunter.

"It's cloudy; remember the polar night. Infrared has picked up two vessels. The first vessel is hugging the coast. Its destination could be Kirkenes, Vardo or Kiberg. The second vessel is further out to sea," said Lucas.

Hunter said, "How would they choose?"

Lucas responded, "Hunter, the longer this ferry stays at sea, somebody will find it. This region has low shorelines and not the steep-sided fjords typical of parts of the Norwegian west coast."

Hunter searched for information on Kirkenes, "Talk to me regarding the town of Kirkenes."

"It's a small township under a thousand people. The town is in the extreme northeastern part of Norway on the peninsula along the Bokfjorden. It has a vast bay connected to the Barents Sea near the Russian-Norwegian border. Kirkenes is home to a military base which supplies troops to the six Russian border stations," said Lucas.

Hunter was reading from his tablet, "The military base and border stations are to defend against illegal immigrants and other illegal activities. No. I wouldn't choose Kirkenes. A military base has too many trained eyes. Jonas, Vadso or Vardo?" asked Hunter.

Lucas replied, "Vadso trades with Russia. They had a fortress to keep the Russians out. The Germans destroyed the place, and the Cold War gave them a naval base and airport. Today, they fish the Barents Sea."

Hunter asked, "Where is it?"

Lucas stated, "Vadso is on the European route E75 highway. The airport is at Kiby, just east of the township. The Murtigrabben ferry services the township."

Hunter said, "I would mimic a Murtigrabben ferry route."

"That's a real possibility," replied Lucas. Vardo is on an island. Access to the mainland is via an undersea tunnel. The township hosts a radar installation called Globus II. Russia installed it to track space junk, but many argue it tracks the now-defunct anti-missile systems. Norway's Murtigrabben express ferry service docks at Vardo."

Hunter looked up from his tablet. "Vadso or Vardo? A car ferry at Kilberg, Vadso or Vardo will not draw any attention if it's a Murtigrabben ferry."

"A different ferry might not attract any attention," said Lucas. "One ferry undergoes a lengthy service, and they hire a substitute."

Hunter kept thinking, "Vadso or Vardo?"

"Those Russian 6x6 trucks may not attract any attention either with Vardo's Globus II radar installation," said Lucas. "You have staff, security, repair vehicles, a Russian communication platform. It would be a busy place with trucks coming and going."

"They will have the same trucks," said Lucas. "Those trucks could merge onto the trans-Scandinavian highway which connects any of these seaports to Europe. It would be a military convoy with credentials. It happens at different times. I would change vehicles." Jonas repeated his theory, "The 6x6 trucks have the nukes. They drive the ferry on a riverbank, and then the trucks vanish."

"A beached ferry out in the open is obvious. A beached ferry in a shipyard speaks of repairs," said Hunter. "Nobody would take a second look."

Karen Richard's face appeared on Jonas's app; "The Norwegian Radiation Protection Authority and Norwegian Police Directorate have issued a nuclear theft or threat coming via the car ferry into several possible fishing ports," said Karen. Norway's VTS are on alert. We are waiting for their report. Data from VTS may be our best bet. Our PM said, 'tread lightly.'"

'Tread lightly?' he thought. "VTS?" Hunter asked.

"Vessel Tracking Service. If a boat is not registered, they will stand out," replied Karen.

"The 'Red Banners' could go anywhere in Europe by now, truck or plane. We may know more once I land," said Hunter.

Jonas spoke again, "The VTS, Norway's Vessel Traffic Service, monitors the ships sailing the Barents Sea and along the coast of Northern Norway. I will record and translate their conversations and forward any relevant information."

"Thanks, Lucas," said Hunter.

"Can I assume that if the NRPA has issued an alert, the local Police from Norway and Russia have roadblocks working? Is that your understanding, Lucas?"

Lucas said, "Yes, correct. That is my understanding from their Police Directorate. I can confirm that Norway has activated the Beredskapstroppen. Russia may have airlifted their Alpha or Spetsgruppa group, but I can't confirm that."

"We must find the ferry," replied Hunter.

Jonas leaned into the image again and said, "Hunter the Beredskapstroppen is within a military compound outside Elverum. Unless they have units across the country, they must fly commercially or by plane to Tromso, then take a smaller plane to any Norwegian ports."

Hunter asked, "What is the estimated timeframe for the Russian Alpha or Spetsgruppa group?"

Lucas calculated, "I have no idea. They may have people living in Murmansk."

"Okay, thanks. Jonas, look at the colours on the ferry diesel exhaust funnels and compare them with the Murtigrabben Express Ferry Service," Hunter asked.

The co-pilot Ross. M. Lee came through the cabin and sat in front of Hunter.

"Okay, Hunter. The Gulfstream is not fully laden. We need nine hundred meters to land and one thousand five hundred meters to leave. We can land at Vadso, but the runway is too short to take off. We can land and leave at Vardo, Kilberg and Murmansk with our tanks empty or full."

"Okay, let's plan for Vardo first, Murmansk second," said Hunter.

"Okay, Vardo first, then Murmansk." Lee stood and returned to the cockpit.

Jonas overheard the conversation and continued, "Hunter, the Murtigrabben group, has a fleet of high-speed express passenger and cargo ships. According to their website, they own eleven vessels. A newspaper report two months ago says that the Murtigrabben Group sold off the 'MS Midpolar.' an older passenger and cargo vehicle ferry, to a shipping broker in Jamaica called Universal Freight Customs Brokers. The UFCB website has an image of the MS Midpolar, which is still available for lease."

"That's our ferry," replied Hunter.

Lucas examined the night images. "The stripe pattern on the funnel is the Murtigrabben Group."

"The second ferry?" asked Hunter.

"I asked," replied Lucas. "They didn't sell or lease a second ferry. There are no reports of theft."

Hunter said, "How would they know?"

"I didn't think of that. I'll ask the VTS," replied Lucas.

"Norway's VTS, do they track everything?" asked Hunter.

Jonas responded, "I will ask how they track?"

"Thank you, Lucas," replied Hunter.

The MS Midpolar sat at the Vardo wharf. Its vehicle ramp was down. The vessel lights were off, and the diesel engines were silent. Two Police constables and the Chief of Police Alvald stood on the pier staring at the now quiet and abandoned MS Midpolar.

"What's so dangerous, chief?" asked one constable.

"Look, VTS and the NRPA have ordered us to secure the ferry. That is all I know. Just wait, okay? Stand over there," said Chief Alvald.

"We've been waiting here for twelve hours, chief!" complained the constable. Everybody from Vardo, including Chief Alvald, had travelled on the old Midpolar. It didn't look dangerous; it was just older—more rusty. Chief Alvald could see that the truck cargo bay was empty except for one Russian Ural-5557.

"Why is that truck there?" asked the other constable.

"I don't know," replied Chief Alvald. "I am still waiting for an update. We may need some portable lighting. Go to the hiring company and bring back a lighting tower. Use this credit card."

Chief Alvald knew help was coming. The NRPA said it might be a radiation event requiring an evacuation. The Chief mumbled, "What does 'radiation event' have to do with a ferry?"

The lighting tower arrived and was close to the lowered ferry lamp in the middle of the road. "It has fuel to last 30 hours," the constable told Chief Alvald.

"Turn it on," replied Chief Alvard. Now, they stared at an abandoned truck. Alvard's phone chirped. He listened, then hung up. "Okay, we need to evacuate the town. It's a radiation event. We text everybody on the island to go to the mainland. You do a headcount."

"This will take hours," replied one constable. Chief Alvard stared at him, "Okay, I'm on it."

A car tunnel passes under the Bussesundet Strait and connects the Vardoya island to the Svartnes village. The tunnel reaches a depth of 28 meters with a length of 1,000 meters.

There were 2,535 citizens of Vardo standing by their cars, vehicles, bikes, and school buses near the Airport at Svartnes, on the tunnel's mainland entrance. People were chatting, drinking coffee from flasks and catching up with friends, creating a party atmosphere.

Annual evacuation drills were necessary because of the Globus II Radar installation. They were annoying and inconvenient, but they were a normal part of Vardo's life. Chief Alvald was waiting for further instructions from the Norwegian Radiation Protection Authority, VTS, or the Russian Beredskapstroppen. He was more than happy to hand over full responsibility.

"I saw two Norwegian Coast Guard vessels on my final house round. Both are 500 meters behind the MS Midpolar," said the constable.

"Really? Do you have an accurate headcount?" asked the Chief.

"Three families are away on holidays, and we have five tourists. The town is empty," replied the constable. 'I think.'

Hunter's phone chirped. "I've just heard from the VTS," said Jonas. "A ferry is sitting at the Vardo wharf. The Police report a Ural 6X6 is on board. There is no crew, and it looks abandoned. The Police evacuated the town under the guise of the annual Globis evacuation drill. NRPA will arrive in 17 minutes."

Hunter buzzed the pilots and confirmed Vardo was the destination. "We are 14 minutes away. I can cut that to eleven minutes. Buckle up, now," said the co-pilot. The Gulfstream Captain informed Vardo Airport of their approach.

"This is Bombardier Dash 8 from Tromso calling Vardo Tower. We are carrying the Radiation Protection Authority agents and will land after the Gulfstream," the captain informed.

Ten meters beyond the end of the runway at Vardo Airport was the road designated as European route E75. It curves and hugs the fenced airport boundary and then enters the Vardo tunnel. It was 9:35 p.m., and 2,535 people turned to see the Gulfstream G700 approach towards them. Only propeller aircraft land at Vardo. The Gulfstream' Forward-Looking Infra-Red' (FLIR) sensor displayed the runway lights and heat signatures at the end of the runway, coming from vehicles, torches, and LED lights.

The HUD and Kollsman Enhanced Vision System enabled the Gulf-stream G700 to land safely, but the runway was short. Captain Kone flared the plane, almost stalling it to decrease its descent and airspeed rates. It landed, pitched down, and stopped at the edge of the runway. The landing lights lit up the faces of the people staring, many with their mouths wide open.

Hunter moved forward to the cockpit. "Ah, good landing, guys. Can we go to the tower and unload?"

The Gulfstream powered up to 30 knots and moved onto the taxiway leading to the tower. The Bombardier Dash 8 landed and followed the Gulfstream G700 to the same building. Twenty minutes later, a Lockheed C-130 Hercules with Norwegian FSK insignia circled above, dropping white flares. It was unable to land.

Jonas was wrong. The FSK or Beredskapstroppen was equivalent to the U.S. Delta Force. A stream of parachutes emerged from the rear of the plane. The first parachute had a red flare, and everybody lined up behind him. They were challenging to see, wearing black clothing, helmets, and goggles. Each soldier's helmet had a blue LED light attached to the back to stop stacking and gauge distance in the dark. It was an impressive sight, a choreographed precision swirling dance. The crowd clapped.

Hunter attached his credentials, took his backpack and gear, and introduced himself to the three NRPA agents from Bombardier. The FSK soldiers quickly gathered with the NRPA agents, the local Police, and Hunter. They formed an easy circle. FSK team leader Vegard took charge, ordering everybody into CBRN radiation suits. He explained that the FSK would secure the ferry. Later, the three RPA agents would examine the ferry and the truck. Chief Alvald called in two minibuses to take them to the pier.

When Vegard shook Hunter's hand, he paused. There was a slight hint of recognition, but he moved on. Hunter had worked under ASIS cover as an advisor to NORSOF during their final days in Bagdad. He had seen Norway's "secret warriors" in action. Hunter's mission confidence increased. Vegard checked, and everybody was now in radiation suits, oxygen tanks, and face masks. FSK agents reattached their SIG Sauer P226 gun utility belts. One police vehicle led the minibuses through the crowd into the tunnel entrance, then to the ferry.

The dock was quiet, except for the humming sound of a 20,000-watt water-cooled diesel engine generator. It powered a 20-foot telescoping tower full of LED floodlights. The white piercing light shone into the opened bowel of the roll-on/roll-off car ferry.

Chief Alvald and his two constables watched as armed FSK soldiers dressed in black CBRN suits with respirators moved up the ramp onto the ferry. The constables had their mouths open in amazement. They only dealt with drunk tourists and bar fights. Hunter approached the police chief before putting on his respirator and mask, asking, "Did any vehicles or people leave the ferry?"

"Australian?" asked Alvald. "We've been here now 10 hours. No vehicles left the ferry."

Alvald glanced at Hunter's 'Commission of Energy' ID badge.

"Any surveillance cameras around here?" asked Hunter.

"That café there, on that corner to the right, has one," replied Alvard. "Vardo Sparebank ATM beside the shop has a camera. There is an exterior camera at the Vardo Hotel on Kaigata 12-14, and another ATM with an external security camera pointing onto Kaigata 18 street."

"Thanks, Chief," said Hunter, grabbing his satellite phone from his backpack. "Jonas, I need you to hack Norway's Sparebank network, ATM at Vardo on Kaigata 18, and the Vardo Hotel on Kaigata 12-14. Check and ID any vehicles from the pier from 16 to 24 hours. Okay? Put Karen on," asked Hunter.

"Hunter?" said Karen.

"Karen, the ferry is the 'MS Midpolar.' There is one Ural 6X6 on the ferry. I am looking at it now," added Hunter.

"Are you sure?" replied Karen.

"The FSK is securing the ferry. We will board in a minute. The NRPA will check for radiation. Then, we will check the truck. It's odd. Something is not right," answered Hunter.

Jonas came back on the phone. "Hunter, I've got one camera feed. I'm fast-forwarding. Wait a moment. I've got it. The ferry arrives, and the ramp is coming down. No vehicles are coming off the ferry. One person is walking from the ferry towards the camera. I will try to get a face."

"No vehicles are exiting the ferry?" replied Hunter.

"No, the ferry arrived with the one Ural, and one person walked down the ramp. The trucks have gotten off someplace else," said Lucas.

"Why would they bring the ferry here and leave a truck?" wondered Hunter. "It's a diversion? They are buying time. Jonas, I need you to follow and ID the second ferry," asked Hunter.

"I'll get the latest WRESAT satellite to do the tracking," replied Lucas.

"Lucas put some fire under them. Get Karen to do it. Can you ID the walker? He wears height-weight clothing. See where he goes. Send me a copy," asked Hunter.

CHAPTER 39

MURMANSK RUSSIA

The warehouse roller door closed with a screech and grind. Darko then parked the Ural 6X6 trucks parallel to the Scania tractor-trailer inside the warehouse. Apresyan's men opened the shipping container on one of the Ural trucks. Darko moved the forklift and transferred both cradled nuclear devices from the Ural 6X6s onto the Scania-enclosed tractor-trailer. It took 35 minutes to secure the load.

Apresyan's phone beeped. He looked at the text. "Ahmed, Vlad is here. He's waiting outside." Ahmed opened the warehouse roller doors just enough for Vlad's vehicle to enter. The doors were closed, and Ahmed walked over to Apresyan.

"On this table are seven mobile suitcases. They will fit into the overhead of any plane. Each case has 200,000 Euros in 500 euro notes. Also, there are wallets with new forged passports and car licenses, two credit cards loaded with $2000 in local currency and pre-purchased open plane tickets to any European country, plus underwear and toiletries," said Ahmed.

"Where are the rest of your men?" asked Ahmed.

"Three are dead from radioactive poisoning," replied Apresyan.

"Where are the bodies?" asked Ahmed. He raised his eyebrows.

"They went overboard, gone. Don't worry," said Apresyan. he smiled to bat away Ahmed's concern. Ahmed considered if he was lying, and he had them killed. Apresyan saw a slight hesitation and said to Ahmed, "Look, Ahmed, don't worry."

"That briefcase with the blue handle is yours. The one million Euros as promised inside" said Ahmed. He motioned to the vehicles and said, "These three BMW X7s are for you and your team. They are ready to go wherever you want. Use them or leave them at any airport. I have them registered with a Dutch Amsterdam company."

"Thank you," said Apresyan, suspicious of Ahmed's generosity. He trusted nobody, including this man. But he said nothing.

Ahmed said, "That table has a range of new clothes, jackets, shoes, and shoes in a range of sizes. Everybody must dump their old clothes in those black plastic bags; otherwise, radioactive particles will trigger alarms at the airport."

Ahmed had to be careful how he spoke to this man. He sensed this man was always in charge and rarely took any advice.

"With your approval, might I suggest that everyone shower first? I have set up two portable radiation decontamination showers. The water is warm, and they must wash gently. They must not scrub their skin; it protects their body from any radiation material. Use shampoo. No hair conditioner as it will hold radiation particles. After the towels themselves, everything goes into the plastic bags," said Ahmed.

"You don't want any traces or evidence lines," replied Apresyan.

"Sorry, it came across as a lecture. Can you translate that for me?" asked Ahmed.

The third table had folding chairs and two enormous baskets of fresh sweet buns with cream and strawberry jam—a box of Vodka and two large coffee urns. The aroma of the coffee and buns filled the stale warehouse. Ahmed served the coffee plus Vodka, expressing his thanks to each team member for their success. They toasted their success and the men who died.

While they ate, Ahmed, dressed in protective clothing, sealed the plastic bags. He dismantled the showers and placed the pieces into additional plastic bags. Ahmed would dump everything miles from the factory.

CHAPTER 40

VARDO NORWAY
At the Vardo wharf, Vegard told two FSK soldiers to verify nobody was on board. Vegard waved the NPRA team and Hunter onto the boat, "Nobody is on board."

Hunter pulled out his own P-90Z Dosimeter Counter, attached it to his clothing, and put it on vibrate. When he stepped onto the ferry, his dosimeter vibrated.

'That was quick,' thought Hunter. The group approached the Ural 6x6 truck with a cargo container on the back. Each member of the NPRA team had hand-held ionizing radiation survey instruments. These can detect alpha, beta, gamma and x-rays over four selectable ranges. All of them were beeping, showing radiation levels. "Switch them off. We have limited time," said Vegard over the radio coms.

NPRA team leader Greg Arnfinn opened a road case, assembled a large tripod, put an odd-looking lead-shield optical scintillator screen imaging machine onto the tripod, and powered it up. It reminded Hunter of a big ugly camera taken from a 1960s hospital ER ward.

Arnfinn said, "This machine took 1,000 thousands of images over days to determine the integrity of the pit." Everybody had ear radios inside their CBRN suits. "What is the pit?" asked one soldier.

"The pit is made of plutonium metal. It's the heart of a nuclear weapon. The machine collects photons and converts the photons into green light to create a digital image. I will do a fast 5-minute scan to set up a base reading."

Arnfinn turned to Vegard and held up a small whiteboard with his calculations. He wrote, "Plutonium core inside condition unknown. It is a nuclear bomb."

Everybody tensed.

Hunter pointed to Vegard to look at the truck's rear door. "It's locked and welded shut, suspicious." He walked to the truck's front, climbed onto the truck cab step, peered through the window, wiped the layer of sea moisture with his gloved hand, then put his NBC respirator mask up against the foggy glass window and looked in again.

"Vegard, I can see a box of wires on the passenger seat, feeding through a hole in the truck cabin," said Hunter on the radio.

Hunter grabbed the door handle and swung sideways to look into the space behind the truck cabin. "The wires from the truck cabin feed into the shipping container."

"What type of wires?" asked Arnfinn.

Hunter turned back to the box in the truck cabin. He wiped the window again to get a better view. This time, he saw a digital electronic control system with a timer.

"Bad news. There is a digital timer counting down. Three bridge wire detonators sit on the cabin truck floor. On the seat, the tray that normally holds twelve bridge wire detonators is empty," said Hunter. Arnfinn climbed up and confirmed what Hunter had just described.

Hunter and Arnfinn climbed from the truck cabin and got Everybody's attention.

Hunter said, "Based on that wiring, bridge wire detonators, and an electronic timer, we have 35 minutes." He held up his two hands— three fingers on his left hand, five fingers on his right hand. Hunter repeated to ensure Everybody understood, "We have 35 minutes."

Vegard set the alarm on his watch for 30 minutes.

Hunter walked around the back of the Ural 6x6 and pointed to the weld on the cargo container doors. Vegard signalled one of his men to the welded doors. He understood, took off his backpack, withdrew a drill, made a hole in the door, and then used a mini camera to check for any booby trap. He gave a thumbs up, 'All clear,' then cut the door hinges with a portable CNC plasma cutter. The doors slammed onto the ferry's steel floor.

Vegard and Hunter both jumped onto the tailgate of the truck container. Vegard shone his LED torch into the dark cavity. "Three dead men and a bomb," said Vegard.

'It sounds like a song,' thought Hunter. The bomb was tucked in close to the container wall, within easy reach of the truck cabin. Unknown to both men, it was an RDS-7 old layer cake Li-6, an isotope-enhanced thermos-nuclear device. It looked like a 1960s washing machine. Wires were everywhere.

Hunter took pictures of the three men and the nuclear device. He blue-toothed the images to his phone and sent them to Jonas with the typed words: "ID bomb." He spoke over the radio, "This bomb has rewired detonators, two new lithium batteries, and an open laptop in Russian wired to another digital box."

Hunter emailed pictures of the complicated wiring. They had 32 minutes left. He turned to Vegard and said, "The wiring is too complicated for 30 minutes."

Vegard agreed and shook his head, "What do we do?"

Hunter texted his pilots. "Leave now. Go to Norway or Murmansk." He tapped Vegard's shoulder and pointed to the soldier with the plasma cutter, then pointed to the dead men and said, "We need their fingerprints!" Hunter turned to the soldier, pointed to his wrist and slid his finger across his wrist. The soldier looked to Vegard for approval.

Vegard agreed and then said, "Everybody to the pier, now. Move it." The last person off the ferry was the soldier carrying six hands. Hunter placed each severed hand on his tablet. Hunter took an image and then sent it to Jonas.

They gathered in a small circle to make a decision. Vegard said, "We have 20 minutes before this thing detonates."

Hunter confirmed with PoliceChief Alvard, "Everybody is in the vehicle tunnel?"

"We could sink the ferry," said Vegard

"There's not enough time," replied Hunter. He turned to Chief Alvald, "How deep is this harbour?"

"40 meters directly below the ferry," replied the Chief.

"Can we push the Ural into the water?" asked Hunter.

One FSK soldier said, "The ferry has a cable-operated stern vehicle ramp. We can blow the cables with C-4, the ramp will drop, and plasma cut the truck handbrake cables and gearbox linkage." He looked around and pointed, "That Police 4WD can push it into the water."

Hunter asked: "Time frame?"

The FSK soldier said, "Six minutes."

Hunter asked, "Risk of exploding?"

Vegard, "Unknown."

As time was running out, their sentences were becoming shorter.

"Do it," said Hunter. His phone chirped. Hunter read the text to the group: "It is a Layer Cake bomb, old and unstable. The yield is 400 kilotons. Nagasaki was 20 kilotons."

Every person stood inside the tunnel. Police encouraged people to move closer to the mainland exit. Fear arrived, and many were crying, while others were stoic. Uncertainty gripped conversations as they waited for their deaths.

Arnfinn had the group in a tight circle. They kept their voices low. Arnfinn half-whispered. "The Bikini Atoll nuclear explosion in 1946 was 61 meters deep."

"We're around 20 to 25 meters underground?" guessed Hunter.

Arnfinn nodded his agreement about the depth. "The bomb is on the other side of the island underwater. The water will absorb energy. The water will illuminate due to the fireball. That rapidly expanding gas bubble will create a shock wave around the island. This tunnel is circular but old, and we should be okay."

They all looked relieved, turning towards the entrance and then turning back as Arnfinn continued. Now, with hesitation, "If the rising gas bubble breaks the surface, it will create a shock wave in the air, and the town may be gone. What may come through the tunnel entrance is my concern."

"What will come through the tunnel?" asked Chief Alvald.

"Surface waves or waves may move out from the centre, probably 3 to 10 meters in height. The waves may come over and or around the island. Water will pout into this tunnel," replied Arnfinn.

"Best guess," asked Hunter.

Arnfinn said, "It all depends on the nature of the explosive charge of that bomb. The tunnel is the safest place. But we may drown," said Arnfinn.

"What would be the speed of the wave?" asked Hunter.

The Police Chief turned and summoned his officers to move the townspeople towards the tunnel's mainland exit.

"It may be fast. A wall of water may follow the wave," whispered Arnfinn. They all looked at Arnfinn and wondered how that would play out. He continued, now sweating, wringing his hands and glancing around, trying to maintain a steady, casual voice. It wasn't working.

"Nuclear explosions come in kilotons," replied Arnfinn.

Hunter interrupted, repeating, "The 'Layer Cake' is 400 kilotons."

Arnfinn stopped and recalculated the impact, speaking more to himself than the group, "One kiloton nuclear weapon is 1,000 tons of TNT. Four hundred would be 400,000 tons of TNT. That's a lot of energy."

"It could misfire. All those new external wires," suggested Hunter.

Arnfinn continued as if he didn't hear Hunter, "The plutonium will compress to five to six times its average density. The more compression, the greater the explosive yield."

The Police Chief looked at him, "Give me the idiot's version, Arnfinn!"

"It could misfire because it is old and rewired," replied Arnfinn.

"A misfire is good or bad?" asked Chief Alvard.

In this case, the new detonators went off 15.34 nanoseconds later. The compression became inefficient, and the core squirted out in the direction where the shock wave was weaker. That inefficiency reduced the 400-kiloton yield.

CHAPTER 41

LONDON

He searched online for any bankrupt building companies that had appointed an external administrator. Administrative receivership, where the bank would liquidate everything and secured creditors could recoup their money, was of no interest to Abu. The preference is to negotiate with an administrator before that happens.

'ELB' is the perfect fit. He paid out all the debts and sent all assets except the inner-city office to auction. ELB now owns a registered building company called Kloder Holdings Group Ltd. It had several building contracts, and Abu would complete those construction jobs with the same subcontractors. KHG will approach the Anglican Church through his lawyer, offering to renovate, free of charge, the listed St. Mary-Le-Strand Church in London.

St Mary-le-Strand is a Church of England building at the east end of the Strand in the City of Westminster, London. To the north of the church is Somerset House, to the right is King's College London's Strand campus, and to the south is Bush House. The church now sits in the middle of a traffic island. Traffic noise and exhaust fumes are the sources of complaints by parishioners.

The next day, Abu was dressed in his suit, with a business tie and leather shoes. He caught the 14-minute tube ride from Euston Station to Charing Cross Embankment, followed by a brisk eight-minute walk to Kings College Chapel, opposite St. Mary-le-Strand. He crossed the road, avoided the heavy traffic, and stood before the church. He took pictures of the stone columns entrance with the magnolias shaping the ten half-circle steps leading to the porch. He looked up to the spire with the clock tower. Abu thought only women were allowed into the church as the gate entrance plaque said, 'The church of the Women's Royal Naval Service.' He had seen historical pictures of women and men inside. He put that thought away and walked around the church. He read that it cost £16,000 to build in 1714, with the steeple completed in September 1717.

The Roman Baroque influence was evident outside with extravagant ornamentation and decorative urns. In the past, a sandstone urn fell and killed somebody walking past. Abu looked up to ensure another one didn't do the same thing. He said to himself, "Imagine the newspaper headline - Church stone urn falls on terrorist head. Christian God's revenge."

He put his hand on the wall. It was flaky and soot-infected. The stone was blackened, displaying water damage at the base. The church had no money to upkeep the property. The semicircular porch and the tower, in his opinion, had dropped.

Business leaders proposed to the council to convert the street into a plaza. King's College London wanted to re-configure part of its campus, including the demolition of 154-158 Strand, leaving the Grade II-listed facade of 152-153.

Either way, the timing was perfect for an exterior renovation of St Mary-le-Strand. Satisfied, Abu took the nearest tube station to Temple to return to his accommodation. Tomorrow, he will hire staff and organize the former offices of KHG Ltd.

Abu's lawyer signed a contract with the Anglican church. They received permission to 'Urgent Works Notice' for the church from three government departments: the Ministry of Housing, the Department of Digital and Culture, Media and Sports, and the Department of Environment, Food and Rural Affairs. An architect with listed A1 building renovation experience submitted renovation work plans.

These included the replacement of the external roof and internal upgrades for the kitchen, restrooms and plumbing. Outside the walls, windows would be cleaned and sealed. The rising dampness would be addressed by lifting the building and replacing the foundations. The spire or bell tower had a list, and the front entrance had sunk over 200 cm.

Abu set an ambitious deadline for completion. Bishop Ian Stewart was pleased to move his parishioners from St. Mary-Le-Strand to another facility during the 2-year renovation. St. Mary-Le-Strand was on the main processional route between Westminster and St Paul's Cathedral. The Royal carriage had passed Somerset House and St Mary-Le-Strand on Queen Victoria's and Elizabeth II's Diamond Jubilee celebrations.

"The Strand is famous, ideal for my purposes," said Abu Sarek.

CHAPTER 42

MURMANSK RUSSIA

All the men showered, changed their clothing, and enjoyed the food and drink. They had worked hard for five days, and the area stank from stale perspiration. Ahmed served sweet buns, coffee, and alcohol.

The factory was now silent, and nobody was moving except Ahmed. Each sweet bun contained a white, odourless crystalline powder. The sweat cream and jam hid the bitterness of the barbiturate, and the alcohol masked the sedation. Apresyan and his team kept drinking, eating and laughing. At seven minutes, their speech began to blur. Ahmed knew this moment was critical. They might get suspicious and turn on him. To his amazement, they laughed at each other's attempts to talk. It was a festive atmosphere until the effects took hold, and it was anaesthesia. They were all conscious but unable to do anything. They could only move their eyes, watching Ahmed's every move. Ahmed filled eight small syringes with etorphine, an analgesic potency 3,000 times that of morphine, used to immobilize elephants. He was dealing with dangerous, violent men, so sedation had to occur first. Ahmed inserted the syringe between the toes and under the armpits.

"Dead within three minutes," said Ahmed.

From the BMW boot, he put on plastic gloves. He purchased a selection of guns from a dealer in France. Ahmed used Apresyan's hand to hold and fire one weapon. The gun residue would cover Apresyan and his clothing—one shot per person. But not with Vlad; it would be just one. Ahmed then placed a different gun in Vlad's hand and shot Apresyan. He fired two bullets into the table, then one into Apresyan.

"With this weather, each body will be frozen solid by the time the Police come looking," said Ahmed. He knew a dead human body releases chemical compounds, producing odours, including cadaverine and putrescine, which smell like rotting flesh. Skatole compound has a strong faeces odour. 'The freezing weather should diminish that process,' he thought.

Ahmed was banking on the Police interpreting the scene as an internal mafia takedown. He placed each empty bottle of vodka either in or near the hands of two men, then smashed several on the ground. The money went back into the BMW trunk. Ahmed then opened a small briefcase. One plastic bag had a half-empty bottle of vodka with Abu's fingerprints.

'I'll lay this vodka bottle on its side,' reflected Ahmed. "Too obvious." He removed the lid and swung the bottle around like a drunk, then placed it on the table and sprinkled Abu's blood on the neck of the bottle. Then, a few drops were placed inside a leather driving glove and under the forklift seat. The plastic bags went in with the dismantled shower bag.

"It's time to swap out the 'Red Banners'," said Ahmed.

The forklift eased the Red Banners from their shipping containers onto the factory concrete floor. The 'Red Banners' were suspended inside a steel frame, then enclosed in a marine-ply board box. Ahmed drove the Urals with the empty shipping containers to a different warehouse. After he walked back, he moved the Scania tractor-trailer to the second factory and returned with a car transport trailer loaded with his personal M235i BMW.

He forklifted and chained both bomb boxes onto the top of the double-car haulage trailer. Next, he wrapped both boxes like

Christmas gifts with an advertising vinyl canopy. The vinyl was black with large white printing: 'Next-generation car e-engine.'

Ahmed double-checked that he had collected everything: food, shower, briefcases, leftover clothing, and rubbish. He looked around on the ground: "Shell casing, fingerprints, smashed bottle." He loaded the BMWs onto the transport trailer, locked them, and secured them with chains. He placed large circular magnetic stickers on each vehicle door, reading 'Luxury London Motor Show Courtesy Vehicle.'

CHAPTER 43

DISAPPEAR
Ahmed registered a haulage company in the Netherlands, received a VAT number, and opened Bank Accounts online. He then purchased a small transport company to launder the money. He signed lease contracts on warehouses in Murmansk. The plan was to abandon the trucks and equipment. Repossession agents, followed by letters from lawyers, would discover an empty Amsterdam trucking company leased by Sarek Haulage in the name of Abu Sarek.

Wearing BMW-branded clothing and the radio tuned to the Police Channel, Ahmed checked his GPS and said, "Time to go!" He purchased twenty London Luxury Car Exhibition tickets, each worth 40 British pounds. If the vinyl-covered engines received any attention from law enforcement or migration officers, he'd offer a ticket to the exhibition.

"What is your destination?" inquired the Police officer working the Murmansk roadblock

"Munich, Germany," replied Ahmed.

"What are you carrying?" asked the officer, taking notes.

Ahem smiled, then pointed backwards, "BMW show cars. It is a

2148-mile trip, 38 hours of driving. I'm returning these leased vehicles to the BMW headquarters in Munich."

"Driver papers and registration, please," asked the Police officer. Ahmed slid a London ticket and registration underneath his papers. "I do hope you can come. I have a VIP Hospitality ticket for you."

A Police commander approached, shaking his head. The Commander spoke with the Police officer and then continued walking down the line of halted vehicles.

"Thank you for your cooperation and the ticket," said the Police officer. Ahmed glanced in his rear view mirror. The Police were removing the roadblock.

CHAPTER 44

MOSCOW

In the 1950s, Metro-20 was the name given to a secret underground metro network. It ran parallel with and 20 meters deeper than the main domestic metro lines. Metro-20 ran under the Kremlin, Federal Security Service Headquarters, now SVR and the Defense Force building, then onto the Vnukovo International Airport, 17 miles southwest of Moscow. The purpose was to transport leaders, politicians, and their families in case of nuclear war.

Near the Moscow State University, an old stone building is hidden among trees in the now-modern Ramenki district. It had steel bars across the opaque glass windows, a red-tiled roof and old grey-brown red brick walls. If you had seen this building, you'd have guessed it was a water pumping station because of the sizeable green-painted metal pipes protruding from its left side, bending 90 degrees and descending into the ground.

Attached to the rear of the building were two five-meter brick ventilation stacks to pump air in and out. The building looked abandoned.

An old, broken concrete road led to the building's only entrance. It had a wide steel door with a faded letter 'R' welded to the side. This steel door was the entrance to the 4-mile gradual zig-zag road tunnel that led to the infamous Metro-20. A warning sign stated, 'Danger Asbestos Contamination.'

Like a spider's web, these tunnels held military hardware, three rail platform heads, a depot for vehicle maintenance and emergency rooms. Not to be outdone, the engineers created a gigantic cave to hold the thousands of citizens and military as they waited for their train ride to safety.

Ahmed unlocked the doors and drove the Scania tractor-trailer inside the building. He attached a second sign warning; 'Danger Asbestos Storage dump–prohibited entry.'

He closed the gates, then welded them shut from the inside. With the truck's high beam and extra fog lights switched on, the truck descended in low gear mile by mile, reaching the railway maintenance depot.

Ahmed felt like he was in a time tunnel going backwards in history. The military blocked the rail tunnels in the 1970s, but the 500-meter platform remained, decorated with striking Soviet-era posters and white tiled walls.

With no other footprints visible or car tyre tracks, Ahmed drove the truck into the rail maintenance depot's vehicle entrance, past the skeletons of abandoned 1950s lorries to the far corner of the depot where he had a 30-ton refrigerator truck and forklift. He got out of the truck and stretched. It had been a long journey, and the rain had helped. Ahmed stood with his arms folded momentarily to take in the surroundings.

'I might move the 'Red Banners' into the refrigerator truck. But not now. Those hire cars can wait a day or two before I return them,' thought Ahmed.

"I'm exhausted." He patted the Scania truck, "We made it."

The rail maintenance area included a rail yard and workshop. At the end of the platform, the train entrance had a single spur line, leaving the main metro line and entering a large industrial warehouse-sized room. The single line then splits into ten separate lines.

To the left was the maintenance area where Ahmed had parked his trucks, and to his right were 10 Seven-car V2 type former Berlin Class C-2 metro trains. Abandoned and dead, like ghosts, can no longer carry 3460 frightened people to safety. He took his sleeping bag, climbed into a carriage, and fell asleep.

The following day, refreshed, Ahmed walked over to an unmarked steel door. The door led to a small stairwell to the current metro line. If needed, this would be his second emergency exit. He changed the locks at both ends.

"My friend, darkness and silence," said Ahmed. He stood there thinking of death, his death., knowing what he was going to do. The attraction of silence and darkness would swallow his pain and emptiness. He now understood the power of hate and what it does to a person.

He climbed the second emergency exit. It is a steel spiral staircase to the surface. He replaced the lock on the steel plate and buried the entrance with branches.

The drive from Murmansk to Moscow gave him time to adjust to the mission. He had also shaved his beard and hair. At a tanning salon, all that pale skin was now dark.

It was early morning, cool and damp, as he rode a city bus downtown to his one-bedroom unit. Moscow is the second most populated city in Europe, right after Istanbul. He would stay here for some time.

"A city in which I can hide."

CHAPTER 45

VARDO NORWAY

Satellites recorded the explosion. The NSA and Russia's FAPSI analysts speculated it was nuclear with a yield of 400 kilotons. The island suffered one massive surface wave, ploughing through the town. Its energy expired, and the water retreated to the ocean, dragging everything.

There was no fireball, and no fire entered the tunnel. The first wave came around the island and entered the tunnel. The blast wave carried people out of the tunnel onto the snowy mainland. Nobody drowned, but now they were wet and freezing. Young men enjoyed the water ride. You could hear the laughter. Chief Alvald unlocked a steel box and started the tunnel's emergency independent water pumps. The diesel engines growled into action. "That will take hours to pump out the seawater."

Hunter turned to NPRA leader Greg Arnfinn and asked: "Will there be another wave?"

"No. It was an underwater burst. The fireball instantly boiled that water. I will test the contaminated," replied Arnfinn. People were now pointing and shouting. Arnfinn and Hunter turned to see a rising cloud of steam and mud, plus whatever else it picked up, gracefully rising in the air.

Arnfinn said, "Good, the cloud is moving away from us."

"And my town?" inquired Chief Alvard.

"Chief, people must avoid that cloud, as it could change direction. Second, the town may need to be tested for radioactive contamination," replied Arnfinn.

"Are you saying you don't know?" asked Chief Alvard.

"Correct. An underwater nuclear explosion doesn't behave like a tsunami," explained Arnfinn. "It may have pushed contaminated water into the township, but then it also left, taking everything with it. We need to wait and test."

"So the town isn't safe?" asked Chief Alvard.

"You saw the tunnel water wasn't black. It might be the same in town," said Arnfinn. "Let me check to see if the water is hot," said Arnfinn.

Alvald looked at Hunter, "Does he mean hot as in a cup of hot tea?"

"If the water is muddy," said Hunter. "Arnfinn believes it's radioactive."

Alvard needed clarification.

"An underwater nuclear fireball creates a high-pressure gas bubble. The bubble rises to the surface and forms that cloud. But the boiling water grabs radioactively affected dirt from the bottom of the bay, creating a pressure wave," said Hunter.

"If that contaminated dirt got pushed into the tunnel, do we need to wash the dirt off people," replied Chief Alvard. "But you're saying the same thing happened to the town."

"Arnfinn's team will send a team to test that possibility," said Hunter.

Arnfinn walked back, "I can't get a good reading. Vehicles can't go through the tunnel until I get accurate readings." He crouched to retrieve equipment from his case. "Chief, if you can wait a moment until I test the water.,

He said."What type of test?" asked Chief Alvald.

"Saltwater absorbs neutrons, and it turns into sodium-23 and chlorine-35 atoms, which change to radioactive isotopes," said Arnfinn.

Hunter heard Chief Alvald repeatedly ask, "So it is radioactive or poisoned with sodium or what?"

"Okay. Let me check," said Arnfinn.

Several minutes passed, and he returned and gathered the group into a small circle. "The sea salt water is hot. It has Sodium-24 with a 15-hour half-life, but there is also chlorine-36 with a half-life of a few hundred thousand years," said Arnfinn.

"Yes or No—is it dangerous?" Chief Alvald asked. Hunter looked at Arnfinn and saw a look of concern.

"It is dangerous. Further investigations are required. The pier area will be irradiated if not dissolved. The floodwater in the tunnel is harmless except for Chlorine-36. But that steam cloud is the problem, Chief," said Arnfinn. "Look, the tides may take care of all these problems."

Chief Alvald, "I got it. No one goes into the tunnel or town. Nobody touches the dirty, hot water; we all run if the cloud comes our way. Do people need to hose the water off them?"

"Yes," replied Arnfinn.

Police Chief Alvald repeated his interpretation of the scene to all the township families. "We need to take off to Kilberg. It would help if you avoided the wind and any particles landing on us. The scientists will investigate our town and inform us if and when it is safe to return. You must also hose particles off your clothing and body with water. We will work this out."

Crowds of freezing people started talking as they walked south to Kiberg.

Hunter received several texts on his tablet. The fingerprint IDs were positive. The three deceased men were representatives of a Russian organized crime network called GPG. The subsequent text confirmed that the Russian Military Police had located another abandoned ferry in Murmansk.

Hunter called Vegard over. "There is another ferry. We need to go to Murmansk."

"Can we use the Bombardier Dash 8?" asked Hunter.

"We can't take the FSK guys with us," said Vegard. "Russia SVR will turn us around."

"Maybe," replied Hunter. "We should leave now. Vegard, that's the pilots over there? Get them to review the aircraft. We'll negotiate with the Russians when we arrive. I have the identities of the dead guys. That's our ticket to the second ferry," replied Hunter.

"It may not work, Hunter. Those Russians are territorial," said Vegard.

"We'll inform the Russian Police or whoever we have intelligence on the deceased. I have the fingerprint scans. We let them learn their identification."

"They might shoot us out of the air," laughed Vegard.

The Gulfstream G700 co-pilot Lee preferred to touch down at Vadso Airport in Finnmark county, Norway. The obstacle was the airstrip was only 997 meters in duration. They could touch down, but they needed 1300 meters to lift off. Instead, they travelled to Kirkenes Airport in Hoybuktmoen and waited for Hunter's call.

"Lee, the damaged Bombardier blocks the Vardo runway," added Hunter.

"Hunter, there's a helicopter here. They will bring you to us at Kirkenes," suggested Lee. Vegard and Hunter were now on the CIA Gulfstream V Turbo flying to Murmansk. Arnfinn's Bombardier Dash 8 was on its side and unrepairable, just like the township. Vegard contacted Rena Military, outlining the need for troops, medical people, potassium iodide tablets, food, water, mobile showers, clothing and soap.

"Chief Alvard?" asked the Government spokesperson. Oslo's Department of Emergency Services will coordinate from Oslo. Our investigation team from PST, Norway's security agency, and Police emergency liaison officers will land in Vardo in sixty minutes."

"Thank you, but we need help with radioactive medical supplies. You can investigate later!" shouted Chief Alvard. He and NPRA Arnfinn both received text copies to stand down. Some idiot politician cancelled the emergency Rema military request.

Chief Alvald thanked the lady and then phoned Oslo's Government Department of Emergency Services. He demanded resources, not more Police. Frustrated, he disconnected his phone and motioned his constables over. "Oslo is sending a planeload of detectives. I have informed them our runway is still not operational, but we will offer any assistance," said Alvald. "Damn politics!"

Asbjorn, Alvald's youngest constable, said, "A tractor road scraper is down the road. We could drag the Bombardier off the runway." Constable Asbjorn looked in horror at Alvald's face, "Chief, are you okay? You're sweating."

Alvald felt radiating pain in the jaw and neck. It was a heart attack. Before Alvald could ask for help, he collapsed on the ground. The local doctor started performing CPR. The doctor threw his keys to Asbjorn, "Get the defibrillator and medical bag from my car!"

"Will he survive?" asked a worried Asbjorn. The doctor didn't answer. He knew 90% of people survive myocardial infarction if helped in the next few hours. The defibrillator worked. A Vardo hospital nurse opened the doctor's bag. "Nurse, give him two aspirin tablets and water. I will need 5 mg of Metoprolol IV ready to inject."

Alvard opened his eyes. The doctor then administered some anticoagulants and calcium channel blockers. "You need to rest, Alvard," the doctor said, taking his blood pressure. That was very close."

Chief Alvald's phone chirped. Arnfinn picked it out of Alvard's pocket and answered. It was Hunter phoning from the Gulfstream. "Chief Alvard, are the people okay?"

Arnfinn said, "Chief Alvald just had a heart attack. The doctor says he should be okay."

"What?" replied Hunter, shocked.

"Hunter, Oslo is sending detectives, not the army. The Chief was screaming at them and had a heart attack. A doctor performed CPR, but we nearly lost him," replied Arnfinn.

"I'm sorry. I don't know what to say. The people need to be safe," said Hunter

Arnfinn said, "They're calling for a report. Shall I give them your name and this number?"

"Arnfinn, yes," replied Hunter. "They must think another Red Banner is in town? Arnfinn used Alvard's cellphone and the last Oslo number. Don't take no for an answer. If that doesn't work, get a mother to Livestream the crisis. Please forward a copy to an Oslo TV news station, get her to scream incompetence. Sorry, I've got to go."

Jonas was taking on Hunter's tablet. "The two gentlemen are Mr Bratva Xasin and Mr Sergi Moghailov. Both have criminal records. I have nothing on the third man. Sergi and Xasin are involved in trafficking in narcotics, money laundering, and prostitution. They have Russian mafia connections. Xasin was a nuclear engineer," said Jonas.

Hunter suggested, "Get more information on Xasin's and his skill sets."

Karen came online, "John is coordinating from Stockholm with Jessica Von Berg from our Embassy. She has her contact standing outside the Police barrier of the second ferry. Murmansk Military Police have secured the ferry. There are no dead bodies or trucks on the ferry."

Lucas said, "The state weather monitoring agency, Roshydromet, released a report stating a large spike in radiation at Vardo."

"I'm not surprised," replied Hunter.

"The layer cake didn't reach its maximum kilotons," said Lucas.

"Look, Xasin might be unqualified or made a mistake," replied Hunter.

"Xasin may mess up the Red Banners?" asked Lucas.

"Yes. The Red Banners are more sophisticated," replied Hunter. "Whoever has those two devices may wonder if Xasin is incompetent. He may reach out to another engineer. We may need to gather a list of alternative nuclear engineers, jobless or retired," replied Hunter.

"Good idea, but the layer cake was ancient, Hunter, regardless of who worked on it. Xasin could be the best in his field but knew he was dealing with something unstable."

"True. Please research the bloke and try to verify his skill, Lucas," Hunter said.

"Karen, you mentioned the trucks had gone? Did Emma mention if anybody saw them leave the ferry?"

"I sent you Emma Smirnov's cell phone number," replied Karen.

Emma Smirnov was born in Moscow, trained in Canada, and completed doctoral studies in languages, critical thinking, and communication at Queensland University, Australia. She joined ASIS and excelled in investigative and observation skills. Kyokushin karate was her great love. Smirnov's first posting was at the Australian Embassy in Oslo.

"Karen, we're heading to Murmansk now," said Hunter.

"Hunter, I assume the Military Police don't have the names of Xasin and Sergi?" asked Karen.

"Those hands are floating out to sea, but their ID might get us an open door. Am I still an employee of the Department of Energy Melbourne?" asked Hunter.

Karen replied, "Yes, nuclear liaison research and development investigator. Jonas has already printed your credentials." He walked to the Gulfstream compact office, opened the printer hatch and removed his new credentials.

CHAPTER 46

MURMASHI RUSSIA

Hunter called Emma Smirnov, introduced himself and asked, "I understand you are watching the ferry. Can you locate any CCTV near the ferry? I need to know what came off the ferry and when."

"Got it," responded Emma.

"Pay attention to anything odd," replied Hunter.

"Like what?" asked Emma.

"Someone with a trigger who wants to sink the ferry with the Police detectives on board," replied Hunter. "Lucas is also searching for CCTV. I need to know what came off that ferry. See you shortly." Hunter disconnected the call.

Jonas phoned, "Hunter, there were experiments with the layer cake using an isotope to increase yield. It worked. I'm uncertain what that means for us. I have a list of nuclear engineers. Some are dead, and most live in Moscow, but our guy seems to be the expert."

Hunter replied, "Thanks, Lucas. Can you check for CCTV near the ferry? I need to know what came off and when. Does any satellite help?"

Lucas replied, "No. It's over the horizon, out of the orbit reference frame."

Vegard showered, then Hunter. They gently washed their hair to remove any radioactive particles. "I didn't know a Gulfstream had a shower, Hunter," said Vegard.

Hunter smiled, "Put your clothes in this plastic bag." He offered Vegard his second grab bag.

The Gulfstream turned to prepare for landing. Hunter asked the pilots, "Have we got approval to land?"

"Yes, and we have a welcoming party," replied Lee. The Gulfstream landed at Murmansk International Airport, located near the township of Murmashi in Murmansk's southern outskirts. Hunter glanced at his tablet and asked Vegard, "We're 25 miles from Murmansk city centre and 21 miles from the second ferry. Where do we start?"

The tower directed the Gulfstream pilot to taxi to the end of the runway and proceeded to a separate hanger.

"I was considering hiring a car," said Vegard. "However, it looks like that will not be happening." He tilted his head to the Gulfstream window as it turned and slowed.

"The welcoming party," replied Hunter. "Nobody is wearing law enforcement uniforms. See the older gentleman with silver hair, suit, shirt, striped tie and coat?"

"Yes," said Vegard.

"He's in charge," replied Hunter. As the engines spooled down, Hunter and Vegard glanced again out the window to ascertain the type of reception they were about to receive. "I expect they're the Politsiya, Federal Law enforcement. One armoured truck, a BMP-2 with four armed men, and two unmarked Nissan Skyline R34. That's an impressive option for a pursuit car."

Vegard peered at the four armed individuals. Hunter suggested, "Vegard, they're showing no hostility. Their arms are relaxed, and their hands are by their side. They're experts. They have their heads in the game. We'll be okay."

"I get it, Hunter; you're a liaison specialist with Australia's Department of Energy with other amazing perceptive skills," said Vegard with a grin.

As the pilots opened the cabin door, Hunter told Vegard, "Having said all that, this can go several ways. We get thrown in that BMP, questioned, jailed, or told to turn around and get lost."

"I thought you mentioned they looked okay," replied Vegard.

"That was for your benefit," replied Hunter with a smile.

Ivan Bely finished his call and stepped forward to greet the two men. Ivan introduced himself, and instead of moving towards the waiting vehicles, Ivan gestured to his own Gulfstream. "Let's talk, gentlemen."

His armed detail followed and established a loose perimeter around Bely's Gulfstream. Inside, they sat in the leather seats. Bely said, "The second ferry is secured. Low levels of radiation are visible, but there are no individuals or dead bodies on the ferry. There are no vehicles and no bombs on the ferry. Local Police are door-knocking all the houses from the ferry to the road intersection."

Hunter thought perfect English, a slightly British accent, perfectly dressed, tailored suit, and expensive shoes. This guy is not from the Politsiya, FSB Federal Security Service, national security, counterintelligence, organized crime, or drug smuggling. Perhaps his ASIS equivalent, SVR Foreign Intelligence Service.

Hunter's phone was recording the discussion. Bely looked at Vegard, "You cut the hands off the deceased men from the Vardo ferry? Do you have them?" asked Bely. Vegard looked awkward and gestured to Hunter, who replied, "Yes and No."

Bely looked at both men, waiting for a further response. Hunter thought, definitely SVR.

"The two guys are Mr Bratva Xasin and Mr Sergi Moghailov," replied Hunter. He stopped talking and waited.

Bely asked, "The third person?"

"The third person, we have no identity. Xasin and Moghailov both have a history of trafficking in narcotics, money laundering, and prostitution. Both have Russian mafia connections. Xasin was a nuclear engineer."

Bely said nothing at first. "Mr Hunter, you're a nuclear liaison expert with the Australian Department of Energy?"

Hunter replied, "Yes, that is correct."

Vegard asked, "Have your roadblocks reported any sightings of the army trucks?"

Bely stared at them both and did not believe who they said they were. "No."

"The roadblocks," asked Hunter. "Are they on both highways, and how far out are they?"

Bely pulled out a map and pointed out, "There are Double road-blocks on both highways. Based on the timelines of both ferries, we estimated the Ural truck's maximum speed fully loaded and in convoy. The first roadblock is 40 miles south of the airport, and the second is 150 miles. No army trucks have passed any roadblocks," replied Bely.

"No convoys." Hunter asked, "Will you check passenger vehicles?"

"No, just convoys and trucks. Nothing so far," replied Bely.

"Do the roadblock crews have radiation detectors?" asked Hunter.

"Not sure, most likely," replied Bely.

"Can we go to the roadblocks nearest this airport?" asked Hunter.

Bely nodded an affirmation, then raised one eyebrow. "Why?"

"The Ural truck convoy may have already passed the first road-block and are waiting at the 150-mile roadblock," said Hunter. "I suspect they have swapped vehicles. A convoy of Ural's is too obvious. The Urals are in a warehouse close to this airport. Some have left by plane, others by car. Or they have gone to ground, which I doubt."

Bely nodded.

"Do you have people at the airport?" Hunter asked.

"We closed the airport. Your plane was the last plane to land. A commercial flight to Oslo has returned, and the Police are interviewing the 181 passengers. As of now, there are no fake passports. There is nothing suspicious."

Hunter inquired, "No fraudulent passports and nothing unusual presented at the four roadblocks?"

"No," replied Bely.

"Okay, they are hiding, gone or dead," said Hunter.

"Why deceased?" Without revealing it, Bely liked Hunter's instinct.

"I would have one large truck carrying the devices, leaving no witnesses behind," said Hunter.

"Based on what took place on the Vardo ferry?" responded Bely.

"Correct. I would have open plane tickets. They went to the airport, and when they saw it was closed, they hired a car and fled," replied Hunter. "Plus, they are sick."

"Like at Vardo," answered Vegard.

"An open ticket is bought in advance, allowing passengers to schedule their travels as they wish." Hunter asked, "We need to check to see if anybody has booked later flights today using an open ticket, even if the airport remains closed."

Hunter turned to Bely. " On the Oslo flight with the 131 passengers, were there any 'No Shows'?"

Bely pulled out his phone, spoke for a minute, disconnected, and then put it away. "They are checking."

CHAPTER 47

FERRY MURMANSK RUSSIA
ASIS agent Emma Smirnov was standing five meters from the second ferry. The Naval Police had set up a simple barrier to keep nosy locals at bay. She spoke to them. But they knew nothing and were waiting for police detectives to arrive.

'The ferry is deserted. There are no trucks and no dead bodies,' thought Emma. She looked down and noticed truck tyre imprints in the sludge between the bitumen road and the ferry vehicle ramp. Emma took a picture of the tyre tracks with her phone. Looking up, she wondered if the ferry crew had switched off their onboard CCTV.

An unmarked Police vehicle arrived on the scene. They were arguing. The male detective wore jeans and a crumpled business shirt with a wool-lined jacket, got out of the car and slammed the door. The female was embarrassed.

The Police vehicle's motor was cooling off and ticking away. Saying nothing, the male detective moved to the car boot and pulled out two radiation suits. Emma considered the woman an investigative technician, as she was carrying a camera, a dosimeter, and an equipment bag. The female technician walked down Emma's side of the police vehicle and stopped to examine the ferry.

Emma tapped her arm. She pointed at the truck tyre imprints in the mud. The technician acknowledged the evidence with a nod, bent down, captured the tyre imprint on film, and followed the grumpy male.

The male detective returned, "I want fingerprints from the bridge?"

Emma overheard them talking. "There are no Ural trucks, no ferry crew and no CCTV, but there are traces of radiation."

Smirnov wondered if anybody up the street had a CCTV camera. 'This is the only way the truck could have left the ferry,' she thought, as the opposite direction goes to the military housing block. 'Perhaps they have garages on the housing estate? No,' thought Emma.

Walking up the hill, she stopped and looked back at the ferry, "I saw something odd. What was it?" She rewound her cellphone video.

'A journalist spoke to the male Military Police officer. He then spoke to the lady technician. No. Two navy workers were talking with unlit cigars. No. One teenager was out too late. No. The guy beside the journalist. Him. He took out his phone and spoke for less than four seconds. He scanned the crowd. He wasn't speaking in Russian or English. He was checking in with someone,' thought Emma.

Jessica Von Berg received a picture from Emma's video. "Can this man be identified?" asked Emma.

"Zhang Jing owns the 'Golden Door' Chinese Restaurant downtown," replied Jessica.

Emma asked, "So, why would he be here?"

"Jing lives in town," replied Jessica. "He also owns the Meg Nightclub. He lives in a unit at the back of the club. Is he still at the ferry?"

"No, he called somebody. The call lasted four to five seconds, then he left," replied Emma.

"It seems like he reports to his handler or his wife. What are you working on now?" Jessica asked.

"I'm checking the route the URAL trucks took for any CCTV. The alternative direction goes to the military housing estate. Okay, wait a moment. I have a pawnbroker's store with CCTV pointing out. That makes sense; he has mesh on the windows. The store street number is 34a; Dmitri Yevdokimov is the proprietor," replied Emma.

"Got it. I'll hand that to Lucas. Thanks, Emma," answered Jessica. Emma clicked off her encrypted phone as she walked to her car.

The MP-443 Grach is the Russian Army's standard gun. Even with a quality suppressor, the Grach is unreliable. But it didn't suffer any reliability issues in the car park. Zhang Jing, the proprietor of the Golden Door, followed Emma to her car. He would shoot her, wipe his fingerprints off, and then drop the gun on the ground. 'The type of gun will implicate a military police assassination,' reasoned Jing. 'A glorious payback for raiding my club.' He smiled. Jing raised the weapon to shoot through the driver's window, but the silencer knocked on the driver's window. Emma's reaction was instant. Her door flew open, slamming the gun aside. From a hunched position, she launched herself at Jing with a single punch to the throat. He fell backwards, his head hitting the concrete road.

Emma checked his pulse and breathing. 'He is dead,' thought Emma. She glanced around, watching to see if anybody saw what had happened. She pocketed his phone. The pawnbroker's CCTV cameras were not facing the car park. She heaved, then folded the man into her trunk along with his gun. As she drove, she updated her boss. "I'm returning to Oslo. I have disposable luggage in my boot."

CHAPTER 48

CANBERRA AUSTRALIA HQJOC

"Hey John, you got a minute, mate?" asked Wayne.

"What, you need some coffee, Wayne?" replied John.

"No mate, you remember our $75 million thieves from China, our hacker friend, Mr Wang Li Jun?" said Wayne.

John Lewis walked over to Wayne's desk, which looked like a capsule with numerous computers and screens.

"Yeah, what has this bloke Li Jun done now?" suggested John.

"Do you realize I've been tapping his phone, tablet, and work computer? I also bugged their server," Wayne replied.

"Get to the point," replied John with a weary smile. He stretched his arms and yawned.

"Well, I hacked into their local traffic video the last few weeks and followed the bloke. Every week, he goes to the same coffee shop. They have excellent CCTV—probably lousy coffee. Anyway, my AI server has identified another chap called Mr Liu Wei.

"Is that Wang Li Jun's contact?" asked John.

"Yep," replied Wayne.

"Who employs Liv Wei?" asked John

"He works for the Joint Staff Department Intelligence Bureau," replied Wayne.

"That's unusual," said John. "Two different government bodies."

"I tell you, John, these two are up to no good. Especially Wei. Do you know why? He claims he invented a cryptocurrency, Big Coin," added Wayne.

"Big Coin?" responded Lewis.

"Yeah. This bloke stole USD 100 million from ordinary Chinese people who invested in his pyramid scheme. What do you want me to do?" asked Wayne.

"Big Coin? Keep tabs on them both for the moment," replied Lewis.

"Before you run off, John, is anything happening in Murmansk, Russia?" Wayne asked.

"What?" asked John.

"Well, Wang Li Jun, you know USD 705 million-dollar man just got a phone call from a Mr Zhang Jing in Murmansk, Russia. I translated the message, 'Ames has both.' That's the message."

John remained there momentarily, considering, "Murmansk, Russia. Okay, examine if any news is coming out of that area. I'll give my ASIS friend a buzz," replied John, returning to his desk to make some phone calls.

"Hey, John!" shouted Wayne.

John didn't get easily annoyed. But with Wayne, sometimes he did. "Yes, Wayne!" replied Lewis.

"All hell is tearing loose, mate! It's a dog's breakfast. Stone the crows!" added Wayne.

"What is it, Wayne?" asked John.

"It's a big bloody bomb!" replied Wayne.

"What do you mean? Where?" demanded John.

"Norway," replied Wayne.

"Norway?" answered a surprised John.

"The location is Vardo, Norway," replied Wayne. He worked on his server and opened a few programs. "Our satellite imagery is not good. It is a polar night. It's a dirty cloud puff!" added Wayne. "I can see people on the other side of an island. A plane is on its side. A lot of people are walking away. It does not look good. Oh! I got a phone call happening."

"What phone call?" demanded John, frustrated now.

"Murmansk, Russia, is a minute's drive along the road. Mr Zhang Jing is in Murmansk and just phoned those dodgy guys, Liu Wei and Mr Hacker Wang Li Jung. Do you think there is a connection?" asked Wayne.

CHAPTER 49

MURMANSK AIRPORT RUSSIA

Bely pointed to his convoy of vehicles, "Warehouse district or roadblocks?"

Hunter nodded and said, "Can we go to the two roadblocks from the Airport?"

"Why?" Bely, Hunter, and Vegard got into the lead vehicle. The turbocharged diesel engine thundered into operation. Gears crunched loudly, and wheels spun on the bitumen.

Hunter kept thinking about how he would escape. "If this were me, I would have a tractor-trailer or truck that you would ignore at a road-block. Perhaps a morgue or sewer vacuum truck, you would not look twice or even want to open," added Hunter.

Bely's phone rang through the vehicle console. "Yes." He listened. "How many, and the destinations? Text me everything to this number. Thank you, yes."

Bely turned to Hunter and Vegard, "Nine no-shows at the airport. Details are coming soon" Bely's. Three vehicles travelled through the outer suburbs at top speed, ploughing through snow. Hunter was fiddling with his phone, launching another app Jonas had loaded.

When Bely said, 'Nine no-shows,' Hunter pushed those details through to Jonas.

Hunter said to Bely, "They would not travel as a group. Maybe one or two. Can we obtain all the names of the no-shows for elimination?"

Bely nodded his agreement. His phone rang. Bely listened for several minutes. "There are 179 different vehicles in total at the four roadblocks. All different makes and types. The Police have photographed and checked the IDs of every motorist."

The truck swerved hard around a corner, tyres squealing. Bely waited, then continued. "Each vehicle was checked for traces of radioactivity but not opened, emptied or inspected. It was snowing. The breeze had just picked up, cutting down visibility."

They arrived at the outer roadblock and slowly drove past all the parked vehicles. "No Ural's," said Bely.

"They have dumped the Ural's Bely," said Hunter, now frustrated.

Bely questioned the officer in charge. "Did any Ural trucks pass through before the roadblock was operational?" asked Bely. The answer was no.

"We will return to the Command Centre at the first roadblock," said Bely. Hunter remained silent.

Detective Leonid Prokhor was in charge of the mobile Police Command unit. The three vehicles parked as close as possible to the entrance of the mobile trailer. "Detective Prokhor, are you in charge?" asked Bely, displaying his credentials. "Did your officers see any Ural army trucks approach the roadblock, line up, then leave?" asked Bely.

"No Ural trucks have passed through our blockades," replied Prokhor.

"Any tractor-trailers giving off radiation?" asked Bely.

"There are plenty of tractor-trailers at each roadblock. We've checked all the vehicle registrations and driver identity tickets. Nothing is standing out," replied Detective Prokhor. "We had a few cars with expired vehicle registrations. One naval cadet was drunk and was driving a stolen car. We have a total of 179 vehicles. That number is increasing. My officers are reporting nothing unusual."

Hunter caught a slight hesitancy in Prokhor's report. His vocal tone and eyes said something different. He asked Detective Prokhor, "Did any heavy trucks go through as you set up the roadblocks?"

Prokhor said, "Yes."

Bely said to Prokhor, "I need all vehicles, especially tractor-trailers, to be opened and inspected. Make sure each officer is armed."

Hunter felt Prokhor's response needed to be longer. He was hiding something. "Do the Police cars have video cameras?" asked Hunter. Detective Prokhor's eyes moved from Hunter back to Bely. He needed to figure out the chain of authority here. Bely nodded approval.

"Yes, one Police vehicle per roadblock was capturing on video every vehicle that got through before each roadblock," said Prokhor.

"Where are the videos?" asked Bely.

"Everything is uploaded via satellite to headquarters in Moscow. You wish to look?" asked Prokhor.

"We need to search for a Scania tractor-trailer from all Police vehicle videos before the roadblocks," asked Hunter.

Prokhor lifted his shoulder radio and said to the second Command centre, "Check for any Scania Tractor-trailers before the roadblocks? Call me if you find anything."

Hunter noticed his finger didn't entirely depress the side button on the radio.

"It can be a Scania truck with a sewer vacuum trailer, even a rubbish truck," replied Hunter, now watching any micro-expressions from Prokhor.

"There will be less snow on the truck's roof," Bely told Prokhor. If you get a hit, phone me and forward the video. Here is my cellphone number."

Hunter text: 'Do you see where I am?'

Lucas's text: 'Yes. I picked up the conversation. I'll get the videos.'

Hunter's text: 'Hold off for a moment. Check CCTV footage from any intersection off the major road heading into the industrial estate near the airport.'

Lucas's text: 'Watch for Ural 6x6 trucks turning into an industrial precinct. Got it.'

Hunter disconnected and looked up. Bely asked, "Anything?"

"My associate is searching for heavy trucks moving from the ferry along the main road, then turning into an industrial precinct," replied Hunter.

"Your associate?" asked Bely.

Bely, Vegard, and Hunter left the Command centre and watched armed Police officers opening and inspecting trucks inside the roadblock.

"How long will this take?" asked Vegard.

"I'd estimate two hours," said Bely. "But more trucks are arriving."

"The Ural's are in a warehouse adjacent to or near the Airport," said Hunter. It's an unremarkable old warehouse with no domestic housing nearby. We need to move."

"How do we find an unremarkable warehouse?" asked Vegard.

"You'll know it when you see it," replied Hunter.

Bely watched the snow falling as police officers continued to inspect each truck. Hunter's idea was a logical next step. Bely's phone buzzed. He turned and walked away from them, listened, hung up and turned back.

"Okay, let's move towards the industrial areas. I estimate we have fifty-five minutes. RET Russian agents are landing in fifty minutes and will replace me and throw you both back on your plane. Let's move," said Bely.

Hunter replied, "Good friends, are they?"

Bely called his team over. "We have one hour to hunt. We must cover three large industrial precincts and locate two URAL 6X6 trucks and maybe a Scania Tractor-trailer."

Hunter and Vegard got into the BMP as Bely drove. Hunter's phone rang. "Hunter, the time frame seems okay. I have a gas station CCTV at a junction. A convoy of three trucks, one of which was a tractor-trailer. They drove with no lights on. The drivers were wearing ENVG-B night-vision goggles. The camera is at a fuel station on Kolsky Road in Kola," answered Lucas.

Hunter pulled out his earplugs and said, "CCTV at a fuel station on Kolsky Road in Kola captured three trucks, two Urals and the Scania. They were driving without lights. Drivers wore night-vision goggles."

"Got them!" said Vegard.

Bely drove the BMP to the fuel terminal and watched the CCTV footage. "It's them." He spoke with the after-hours attendant regarding details of the closest industrial precinct. The BMP turned into Pribrezh-naya Road. Bely drove at a slow pace as they passed warehouse after warehouse. Their initial excitement abated, as there were so many old warehouses.

"What are we searching for again?" asked Bely.

"Something strange, an inconsistency," replied Hunter.

Vegard said, "That definition is not helpful, Hunter."

New industrial warehouses lined the road on the left side, and the older warehouses were on the right side. Hunter said, "Go away from the main road."

The BMP turned and slowed to a crawl. "Nothing is standing out," said Bely. They reversed and went further down the road. They turned into the next side road, which had less visible, older, and cheaper warehouses.

"Stop. Look. See the tyre ridges. They are just visible."

Bely turned to Hunter, "There are more side road warehouses further down."

"It's impossible, Hunter," said Vegard. "Any truck could have produced those lines."

Hunter wasn't listening. He was watching a disused shop wedged between two old run-down warehouses. It had a faded sign and a wooden chair leaning against the outside wall. Hunter thought of an older man or woman living alone. More likely, the wife had died, and so did the store.

"Stop—the closed shop. Look at the second window from the left. See the gap in the window? Someone is standing in the shadows, smoking." The BMP stopped. Hunter saw the edge of the yellowed newspaper move as they walked over. Hunter knocked on the door with Bely standing beside him, holding his gun beside his leg. The door opened, and a thin, older man stood there. He glanced at the BMP, Bely, and then Hunter.

Hunter asked Bely, "Translate."

Hunter said, "Many trucks."

The older man heard Hunter's odd Australian accent and smiled. He pointed his bony yellow-stained fingers to the third warehouse.

Bely checked his watch and swore as he walked over to the BMP. He recalled the two vehicles.

Hunter felt the older man's hand clutch his arm. He lifted two fingers in the shape of a gun and mouthed, "Puff, puff, puff." Then pointed at the warehouse. The two turbo supercharged Nissan Skyline R34 arrived from the other warehouse districts in record time. You could hear the sharp-pitched turbo whistle as they changed gears. They could hear the roar of the engine even from a block away. It was distinct. These guys were flying. 'They must be ex-racing car drivers,' thought Hunter as the cars slid sideways to a perfect handbrake stop. Bely pointed to the warehouse across the road, tapped his chest, made his hand into a gun, and put his finger to his lips, showing silence.

Hunter laughed, 'Silence after the car announced their arrival.'

The bulletproof vests were new and light. They formed a single line and approached the warehouse. The warehouse was old based on the dryness of the wooden clapboards and the faded signs. It had two entrances: a steel mesh-covered wooden office door and a large industrial roller door. One of Bely's men used a crowbar to open the door. He stood to the right as Bely and his guy ran inside, then followed. They were shouting in Russian, guns ready to fire.

The factory was silent and cold. Their LED torches displayed a scene of devastation. Dead bodies lay on the warehouse floor. Tables and chairs were upturned. Two deceased men were holding guns. There were no trucks, just one Forklift, empty shipping containers and no 'Red Banners.'

Bely shouted, "Switch on the lights!" He scanned the warehouse and asked Hunter, "Are they the ferry guys?"

"Yes," said Hunter. He pointed to one of the dead men, "Vyacheslav Malyshev photographed this gentleman in Saida Bay. This dead guy shot Malyshev with a rifle from the submarine pier."

Hunter crouched down to examine each individual, moving from one body to the next. Something was off. As he kept checking each body, Hunter said to Bely, "Prokhor was lying." Bely was confused by Hunter's random comment.

"The bullet trajectory is odd," said Hunter. "The bullet entered this man's shoulder. It went through his heart and out his lower back. He turned him to confirm. It is the same with this guy. Who has a pen?" Hunter pushed the pen into the chest wound. Hunter stood back, moved around and pointed his finger at both bodies. He removed the pen and put it in the bullet entrance on the second body. Stepping back, he calculated where the shooter stood and fired the gun.

Hunter then started looking at the Vodka bottles. "The smashed bottles of vodka indicate a struggle or an argument." He looked at Bely and Vegard. "But glance at this bottle of Vodka on its side. Look at the top of the bottle." He pointed with the bloody pen.

"See the two slight blemishes. That's leftover gum paste, like removing a bottle's label. That bottle will have planted prints. The killer has kept a person's prints on a sticky plaster or tape. The gum has aged," replied Hunter. He thought of something and asked Vegard to look at the victim's hands.

"They are all a little greasy, especially under their fingernail. It is black grease," said Vegard. "These guys worked on the sub."

"What is in their pockets?" asked Hunter.

Vegard frisked every person, "There are no cell phones, no money clips, no coins, no credit cards, no keys, no hair comb, nothing?"

"That is interesting," mumbled Hunter. He stood with his arms folded, thinking.

"No ID?" asked Bely. "Maybe this was just a turf war. Somebody stole everything, plus the Red Banners."

"Correct," said Hunter. "But it was not a turf war. That's what the driver wants you to think. Their hands are dirty, but their clothes are clean, if not new. Look at the soles of the shoes; they are new. The clothes don't fit him and him. There are no cigarettes and no cell phones. They've got dressed, got drunk, then murdered."

"Why would the driver bother to get them to wear new clothes?" asked Bely.

"The driver didn't want their clothes setting off alarms at the airport. It was part of his ploy. 'I'm on your side; here are some new clothes, food and money. Give me those irradiated clothing you are wearing.' Hunter looked up and walked around the factory. "Here is

the drain and a puddle of water. They washed off the radioactive particles." He walked back to one body to confirm they showered. He felt
the deceased hair. "Clean, no grease and no hair conditioner."

"Why no hair conditioner?" asked Vegard.

"When exposed, you don't scrub. You wash gently, no conditioner," replied Hunter.

"I need to call this in," said Bely. "We have about ten minutes
remaining before RET removes us. Hunter, do what you need to do.
Okay? I expect our medical examiner to work on this scene. I'll get that
report to you. You give me what you have."

Hunter took his tablet out and took pictures of hands with faces.
He turned to Bely. "Can you get your men at the ferry to email me the
ship registration and logs?"

Bely pointed at the dead men, "I expect one of them is the owner."

"No. I think the driver set this all up," said Hunter. "We discovered
this warehouse ahead of time."

"Meaning?" asked Bely.

"The driver expected these bodies to freeze. There would be no
putrid smell until spring. Do you have a Spring?" asked Hunter.
"Somebody will complain about the smell. A detective will not connect
it to the Red Banners. The detective will write it off as an internal mob
fight," said Hunter, looking at Bely.

"Where are their cars?" asked Hunter. "This is murder."

Bely said, "Explain?"

"You can't fool hardened streetwise Russian mobsters," argued
Hunter. "You do it another way."

"You show them lots of cash," replied Vegard.

"The mob would never wander into a trap," said
Hunter. "They're not stupid, just exhausted."

"The boss, this guy," said Bely, pointing to the man holding the gun.
"The driver pays for the ferries, trucks, tractor-trailers, and this ware-
house. A mobster feeds them, pays them, then shoots them," argued
Bely.

"You are correct, except that person is the driver and not a
mobster," said Hunter. "Okay, so we have two scenarios. I believe the
driver brought cash to pay for all these men. He brought clothing,

drinks, cash and a shower. The driver kills them all, then sets the scene."

Bely was not happy to be contradicted and looked at Hunter. "For example, look at this glove on the Forklift. Compare that with the boss, his hands. See the dilemma?"

Bely said, "The glove is too small."

"There will be blood or skin inside," said Hunter. That blood or skin will not be the driver's, and it will be either identical to the print on the vodka bottle or not. But it will point an investigation to another unknown person, or perhaps, as you say, another mobster," said Hunter.

Bely said, "Or a mafia boss."

"It will point to another person, not here," replied Hunter. "The driver was here before these blokes arrived. The driver purchased everything and hired these guys to do the job. He then got rid of all the witnesses."

Vegard said, "What about the guns?"

"The driver only used that gun in his hand," replied Hunter. "I doubt the boss has any gun residue on his hands."

Vegard sniffed each gun barrel. He used a clean cloth to sniff each gun barrel. "Only these two guns have been fired. The driver fired this gun once." He walked and crouched down beside the boss. "The driver fired this other gun many times and then placed it in the hand of the boss."

Bely asked, "What does that mean?"

"Okay. The driver or another mobster stood over them and shot them all with that one weapon. He'll be buried in GSR after ten to twelve shots. The driver places the gun in the hands of the boss to portray a falling out. Or if the Police realize these guys stole the nukes, then it portrays the boss wanted all the money but got killed by that one shot," replied Hunter.

Vegard said, "Based on cordite residue, you're on target, Hunter."

"Here is the kicker," said Hunter. "They were dead before the driver shot them with that weapon."

Bely was about to contradict Hunter.

Hunter bent down and sniffed the lips of several men. "There is a sweet aroma," said Hunter. He wiped the bloody pen on his clothes and then opened their mouths. "Look at this. Can you see the fragments of sweet bread in several of their mouths? You can smell the Vodka plus another strong sweetness."

"So, what happened?" asked Vegard.

"The driver used a drug to immobilize them. It's not in the Vodka. It's in the jam or bread," replied Hunter.

Bely said, "Okay, your scenario is this. They all drank Vodka, ate the bread, and became comatose. The driver rose above them and shot at a forty-five-degree angle. Then, they placed the weapons in their hands to appear like an internal conflict."

Hunter said, "Correct."

Vegard said, "The boss knew the driver?"

"Yes," replied Hunter. "The driver arranged a meeting with the mafia boss."

"The boss uses his contacts to set everything up," said Vegard.

"We won't know who purchased or leased the equipment. It would be better if it were the driver," said Hunter.

"Because there would be paperwork or digital evidence of purchases or hire contracts for all the equipment?" Bely asked.

"Well, if I was him," said Hunter, pointing to the dead boss. "I would keep some ransom evidence for a rainy day, wouldn't you? Revenge and all that!"

Hunter spotted a camera in the corner of the warehouse. Then his tablet pinged. "Here are their identities. Bely, turn your phone's Bluetooth on; they're yours." Vegard also wanted the images and identities. Hunter went to the western wall of the warehouse. He looked up and saw two scuff marks on his shoes. Disturbed dust. "Shoe prints and hands prints here, Bely. If the driver installed it, we need the prints," said Hunter. Bely got one of his guys to climb the wall. Hunter handed him his tablet. "Close shots of those prints," requested Hunter.

"The camera is battery operated. No hard wiring," said Bely's guy. "It looks brand new."

"Use your shirt to hold the camera. Fingerprints. Okay. We might be lucky," said Vegard.

"Someone was watching?" said Bely.

"Ambush insurance," said Vegard. Bely nodded in agreement as he looked at his watch, wondering how much time he had left.

Hunter's tablet beeped; it found the camera's Wi-Fi connection. Hunter sent the details.

Jonas' response was immediate: "It is only a camera. There is no hard drive. There are no images. Someone had a laptop or cell phone a maximum of twenty meters away. It has only two transmission dates."

"Only two? Not continuous?" asked Hunter.

"No. Someone logged in and looked for a few minutes a day ago," said Lucas. "The older transmission was three weeks ago."

"Someone switched the camera on yesterday and three weeks ago," repeated Hunter, looking at Bely.

Hunter's tablet beeped again. "The password was Volgograd."

"Volgograd is a Russian city," said Bely

"These dead guys checked the warehouse before entering. They were looking for an ambush. They drive the 'Red Banners' into the factory. The guys are paid. They ate the food and were immobilized. They die, and then they are all shot dead. The 'Red Banners' were removed from the Urals and put into another truck. Then the driver left."

Bely, "Who transferred the 'Red Banners' from the Urals to another truck?"

Hunter pointed to small circles of tyre tracks in the dust. Hunter said, "Forklift. There, and then there. The driver did the transfer either before or after the murders. An autopsy will determine death and method. The transfer of the 'Red Banners' happened here, and the army vehicles left this building. Considering the time frame, they are stored nearby."

Vegard asked, "Why not leave them here?"

Hunter said, "The driver wanted time to get away. He severed the connection between the Red Banners, the mafia, and the URAL trucks. He wanted three investigations and some misdirection to give him hours or days to disappear."

Hunter started walking away and nodded with his head for Bely to follow him. They headed back to the older man in the shop. Bely translated the questions: "What was the last truck that left today or yesterday?"

Bely needed clarification. "Last?"

"Final truck to leave?" said Hunter.

The old man grunted in a bit of Russian and broken English and said, "Trucks, they come, then they go."

Hunter asked, "How long between come and go?"

"Long. It's been 30 minutes. The truck is terrible. The driver is not good. He's a stupid driver; he crunches gears," said the old man.

Hunter smiled, then repeated his original question. "The last vehicle?"

"Yes, it was odd, enormous," said the old man.

"How was it odd?" asked Hunter.

"It was new and very big. It carried many beautiful cars—all very beautiful. The ladies like those cars," said the old man.

Bely had his radio out instantly, transmitting the news to the roadblock command centre. Hunter tapped Bely's shoulder. He had a few more questions.

"What colour was the truck?" asked Hunter.

"Colour was white," said the old man.

"How many vehicles are on the trailer?" asked Hunter.

The old man kept talking, "Lots of beautiful cars. Very expensive."

"What brand were the cars?" asked Hunter.

"My favourite, lovely, best car," said the old man. "I tell you a secret. My wife married me because of my beautiful car. I bought the 1950's BMW 507 roadster. Beautiful, I say. All the ladies loved my car. That is how I got married. No, ladies love me now," said the old man.

"The cars were BMW?" asked Bely.

"Yes, beautiful luxury cars," replied the old man.

"Old or new?" asked Hunter.

"They are new. You're not listening! They were brand new X7 SUVs. Very expensive. Very luxury," said the old man.

CHAPTER 50

ASIA AUSTRALIA
        Lucas had heard the entire conversation live. He downloaded a picture of a Scania truck with a vehicle haulage trailer. He inserted BMW X7 cars with a drawing program and then loaded the new image into a facial recognition program. The program found the truck on the Police vehicle video from each roadblock and allowed it to pass through each blockade.

He calculated the time the loaded tractor-trailer passed through the last roadblock. The average speed would be 80-90km per hour. The double fuel tanks would enable him to drive up to 50 hours, as far as Germany, then onto France, perhaps further within forty-eight hours.

'Which direction did you go?' wondered Lucas.

He searched for CCTV on highways and roadside video cameras on the E105 or P21, Paris or Sweden. Lucas found nothing.

Hunter and Bely walked back to the factory. "The Scania was captured on the Police vehicle camera and was allowed through two roadblocks," said Hunter. He read Lucas's comments and pulled up a map. He repeated what Lucas said to Bely and Vegard.

"4,000 km distance in 48 hours to Paris," said Hunter. "Bely, E105 /

P21 to Saint Petersburg or Sweden? Would you take the Crimea Highway?"

Bely said, "I'd choose Paris or Germany, not Sweden."

Hunter's phone chirped. "Hunter, Karen here. Could you take me off speakerphone? Something interesting just happened. John Moody just informed us that Emma Smirnov left the second ferry looking for CCTV, and Zhang Jing attacked her."

"Is she okay?" asked Hunter.

"Jing's dead. Emma is okay," said Karen.

"Who is he?" asked Hunter.

"Jing owns a restaurant called the Golden Door and a nightclub in Murmansk. Emma saw him make a quick cellphone call. Jing noticed and waited for her in the car park. He pulled a silenced gun on her while she was in her car. It didn't go well for him. Jing is in her boot, and she is heading to Oslo," said Karen.

Bely whispered, "Hunter, we must go now!"

Hunter nodded his acknowledgement to Bely and said to Karen, "Okay, thanks."

"Wait," said Karen. "Jessica Von Berg received a call from John Lewis, our guys at HQJOC in Canberra, inquiring about Vardo and Murmansk."

"Why is HQJOC involved?" asked Hunter.

"One of their IT guys has been listening in on phone calls and following Liv Wei from the Joint Staff Dept Intelligence Bureau and another person, Wang Li Jun from JSD Intelligence Bureau. So tonight, Zhang Jing phoned Wang Li Jun and said, 'He has both,'" said Karen.

"He has both," repeated Hunter. "Both meaning the 'Red Banners.'"

"I would say yes. Lewis from HQJOC said his IT genius assistant has been watching Wang Li Jun for weeks. Jung digitally stole $75 million from a US Bank, and Lewis's IT guy followed it to Bagdad."

"Really?" said Hunter. "$75 million, and it went to Bagdad? So, China is sponsoring the theft of two nuclear devices using a bloke from Bagdad. Then, the Bagdad bloke uses a Russian gang to commit theft. So what is the end goal here?" asked Hunter.

"That's the question, isn't it?" said Karen.

"Karen, I've got to go," said Hunter. "The Russian SVR above Bely are about to throw us out." Hunter turned to Bely and Vegard to explain this new development, but Vegard interrupted and said, "We overheard you. China. So, what does that mean?"

Bely said, "Let's talk in the vehicle; we need to go." Before leaving the factory, Bely turned to his team and said, "Forensics will be here soon. Keep the place secured. You will probably be relieved when they stand me down. Tell them everything. Stay as long as possible. Good job, well done."

Bely turned to Vegard and Hunter. "Okay, Airport." They all turned away from the murder scene, loaded into the BMP and headed to the Airport, thinking about China.

Hunter's phone chirped. "Hunter, the fingerprints on the camera and wall have come back. Excellent prints. The prints were not on a criminal database but a Police database. A Commander Leonid Prokhor owns them."

"Thanks, Lucas," said Hunter.

Bely was driving the BMP. Hunter said, "The fingerprints on the camera and wall belong to Commander Leonid Prokhor."

There was silence. Bely swore under his breath.

"Leonid Prokhor let the truck through the roadblocks," said Vegard. "Prokhor was paid off. I guarantee the sub people were also on the payroll."

"I don't understand China's role here," said Hunter more to himself. At the Airport, Hunter asked Bely, "SVR want you off the case. Will you play ball?"

Bely smiled but didn't answer. He gave Hunter a half-wave salute, and Vegard turned and walked back to his BMP. He dialled his FSB/SVR boss.

"I've been waiting. Update me, please," said the FSB/SVR boss.

"The Red Banners are gone," replied Bely.

"What happened?" asked Bely's boss.

"A team of men stole the Red Banners. The guy who planned the theft drives the Red Banners to France or Sweden. We don't know his target. We know he is from Bagdad, and two Chinese agents are funding the plan -USD 75 million," said Bely.

"Where did the murders happen?" asked Bely's boss.

"A 30-minute drive from the second ferry in a deserted warehouse near the Airport. I shut the Airport down and ordered one plane to return. We were holding and questioning the passengers and checking for no-shows. Nothing came from that," said Bely. "Since then, we discovered the men who stole the 'Red Banners' were anaesthetized, drugged, and then shot. We have their fingerprints and identity," said Bely.

"Who were they?" asked Bely's boss.

"OPG," said Bely.

"Organized Crime. Moscow mafia?" asked Bely's boss.

"Yes. I'll forward the names to you now. The factory was the location for the exchange of money for nuclear devices. Somebody moved the two Ural 6X6 trucks to another factory. I have a team searching. The tractor-trailer driver is behind the entire plan," said Bely.

"How are the Red Banners being transported?" asked Bely's boss.

"On a vehicle haulage tractor-trailer carrying the Red Banners and BMW cars. I arrested a local Police commander who let the truck carrying the 'Red Banners' through the inner and outer roadblocks. His child was abducted and told the boy would be released if he let the tractor-trailer through," said Bely.

"Destination?" asked Bely's boss.

"No idea, anywhere in Europe. I am about to board my plane. I will be back in the Yasenevo district in three hours. Do you want me to lead those raids?" asked Bely.

"No. The names have come through. We will raid immediately," said Bely's boss.

"Naval Military Police need to interview all serving on the submarine on the day of the accident. Full background checks, debts, bank account, everything and arrest warrants for anybody who has recently resigned and or has disappeared," said Bely.

"You have suspicions?" asked Bely's boss.

"It was a setup," said Bely.

Bely disconnected, then took three deep breaths, punched in a seldom-used number, entered his code, plus an access code. Bely gave the same report to Igor Medkov, the interim member of the Security Council of Russia and the Defense Council. Bely knew the council was in session and demanded precise intelligence. Any decisions would pass to the SVR Director, who would notify President Denya Driminov later. Driminov would anticipate the international reaction and lock it down hard. Bely wondered if ZL would take over from him. Zukenal, or ZL, is a highly classified elite undercover unit of one hundred operatives who execute black covert operations overseas. Russia denies its existence, and Bely knew the President would order ZL to hunt for the 'Red Banners.' It would be barbarous and a bloodbath. He had no desire to get in their way or even brief them.

Hunter stopped watching Bely and leaned into the Gulfstream cockpit. "Submit a flight plan to Arlanda Airport, Stockholm, Sweden. Be ready to change direction."

"Vegard, is that okay with you? Perhaps we can coordinate our next steps with the Swedish Security Service. Do you have contacts?" asked Hunter.

Vegard nodded. He had reported to the director of Norway's FSK and was scrolling his contacts for a name.

John Moody phoned Hunter. "The Swedes have roads blocked. Where are you?"

"We are leaving now," replied Hunter. Vegard showed him his contact.

"We're heading to Solina, Sweden's Security Service at Bolstomtavagen 2. John, let's meet up there. Vegard will be with us. Something might click," said Hunter.

"Emma and I will travel by embassy car. I will check some truck fuel and food stops," said John.

"The bloke may not need to stop," replied Hunter. "Is Emma okay?"

"Yes, it was a bit of a shock," replied John. "Her fast response saved her."

Hunter then phoned Karen, providing her with an update. Karen asked several questions but swung back to Bely. "What's your take on, Bely?"

"He reported in when we were leaving," said Hunter. "To whom I don't know. He is SVR, but I don't know his status or rank."

Karen said, "Our Russian contact has informed us that a ZL team has been authorized to retrieve the 'Red Banners.' They are dangerous people. Hunter, who bought off the submarine crew, the driver or the Russian mafia?"

"I believe the Russian mob leader used his contacts in Murmansk," said Hunter. "His pockets were empty. We have no names or details. Why do you ask?"

"Our Navy wants information on the sub," said Karen. "We need to grab one of those paid naval people from the submarine."

"You mean we will kidnap you before they imprison you," replied Hunter.

"Yes, that is the plan," replied Karen.

"There would at least be a few naval people within critical jobs," said Hunter. "Get your contact information on that investigation team fast because everything may disappear, including the submarine and the crew people you want."

"True," said Karen. Hunter said, "We don't know the driver's destination. There are only two highways out of Murmansk, one to Moscow and the other to Europe. When we land, I will meet up with John and Emma. I need sleep. It's seven hours to Stockholm, and my body clock is confused," said Hunter.

"I'll get the Stockholm station to pick you up," replied Karen.

CHAPTER 51

STOCKHOLM

Frank Warren is the head of the ASIS station in Stockholm. He was waiting at Arlanda International Airport for a 2 am pickup of Agent Hunter Wyatt. Warren would drop Hunter off at the arranged accommodation. Frank was grumpy because of a terrible migraine, and the coffee machine gobbled up his coins twice before offering the worst coffee he had ever tasted. It didn't help his mood. Frank had a successful career as an investigator in the Canberra ASIS office, and Stockholm was his final posting before retirement.

The FSK ordered Vegard to be dropped off at the Gardermoen Airport to debrief their security services. Hunter was sound asleep when the ASIS Gulfstream left Gardermoen, Norway, heading to Arlanda International, Stockholm. Arlanda Tower directed the Gulfstream to taxi to the Graber Jet Centre. Hunter disembarked as the Gulfstream spooled up and returned in the air within minutes, heading to London for another pickup. He exited the Graber Jet Centre lounge and entered the car lot. There was only one person outside. "Are you, Hunter?"

Hunter nodded. "My car is over here, please. I've booked you a hotel room near the Embassy?"

"That's good. Thanks," replied Hunter. They left the Highway 273 airport road loop and came onto the E4.

"It's twenty-five minutes to the city," said the driver.

"Do you have a security car following us?" asked Hunter.

"What, no!" said the driver.

"Well, you have one now," said Hunter. "I saw two men waiting in the adjacent car park on the other side of the Graber Jet Centre."

"It's a busy airport; several flights came in at once from overseas, sometimes freight airlines, mostly at this time of the morning," replied the driver. "It can get rather busy at night."

Hunter turned his head to watch the approaching car. It was a Subaru WRX STI, the latest model, 2.5L turbocharged. Warren's car had not increased in speed. "Is this vehicle bulletproof, the windows?" asked Hunter.

"What? No. Don't worry. This is Sweden," replied the driver. The Subaru came along alongside the car. The passenger window was coming down, and a gun appeared.

Hunter shouted, "Gun!"

The driver turned to Hunter, confused. "What?"

Hunter pulled the handbrake for a split second, then spun the steering, releasing the handbrake to reduce speed. He hit the rear corner of the Subaru, causing it to turn in a circle. It didn't flip because the vehicle had low suspension. The bullet flew over the hood of the car. Hunter released Warren's seatbelt, flicked the back of the seat down, threw him in the rear seat, then jumped into the driver's seat and brought the seat back up while watching the Subaru. Both vehicles were now stationary and facing each other 30 meters apart.

Hunter threw the car into reverse, pumped the gas, and the engine howled in reverse; he spun the car around and then took off. "Keep your head down." The Subaru also gave chase. The car was slower than the Subaru, and Hunter only had a second to take these guys off the board. They were both heading up the E4 the wrong way. The Subaru caught up and was directly behind Hunter. The shooter was now going for maximum damage. The gun was on full auto. Shattered glass sprayed inside the car, and the internal rearview mirror exploded, with the dashboard ripping apart and then the front windscreen smashed. The shooter reloaded his gun, so Hunter moved sideways and checked his exterior mirror. He saw one headlight. Time to act. He shouted, "Hold on." Hunter hit the brakes; he snagged the front corner of the Subaru, causing it to lurch sideways and then spin. Hunter's vehicle was skidding to a stop.

Approaching both cars was a tractor-trailer already travelling at 120 km/hr with its brakes on full lock. The truck's ABS kicked in, and the rig shook uncontrollably. The truck and trailer started to hop, bumping and burning rubber, horn blaring, bouncing and sliding sideways, and then the truck's ABS failed. The driver resorted to pumping the brakes to prevent the wheels from locking, but it was too late. The car hit the Subaru at speed, crushing it and then pushing it along, with steel grinding into the bitumen, slowing the truck's forward movement, but not the trailer. Hunter saw the trailer swinging around like a fly swat, and he would be the fly.

He threw the car into reverse but stalled the engine. He covered his head and threw himself down on the seat. The trailer, acting like a weighted pendulum, swung around to imprison both cars in a crushing death embrace. Hunter pushed the passenger door open. Then he saw it. He looked up. The trailer was precariously leaning, ready to topple over. Then he heard a loud bang. Something had come loose inside the trailer. Then it happened again. The trailer's balance would topple and crush Hunter's car. The sound of twisting metal ceased, and a cloud of burnt tyre rubber caught up to the truck. Time was running out. The Subaru erupted into flames.

"Warren, my leg is stuck, Warren!" Hunter twisted his body to see into the back seat. Warren was dead, with multiple bullet wounds. By rotating to look at Warren, Hunter felt his leg shift slightly, giving him hope. He lifted his free leg and pushed hard, crawled over Warren, through the car's rear window onto the trunk, falling hard onto the road. A broken arm and leg didn't deter him from crawling away from the imminent danger of fire. The trailer dropped and crushed Hunter's car.

Dr John Moody was leaning over Hunter, looking at his injuries. Emma Smirnov was on her phone, updating Karen Richards and Jessica Reid. They were in the Capio Saint Goran's Hospital recovery ward. Hunter's left arm and leg were both in fibreglass casts. The doctors had wrapped his right arm in a thin film of non-stick gauze dressing impregnated with paraffin for second-degree burns. But more concerning was his head injury. A large piece of metal from the exploding Subaru had lodged into Hunter's skull. Hunter was not fully awake but was listening to Moody describe his injuries. The usual drips and monitors were attached and working silently in the background.

"You have a fractured arm and leg, which will take four to five weeks to recover. You have second-degree burns on your other arm. You also managed to have some of the Subaru lodged in your head," said Moody. Emma was standing beside Moody as he spoke. With her phone on video, Karen and Jessica were watching and listening.

"Your head CT scan didn't clearly show the relationship between the foreign body and the surrounding structure," said Moody.

Emma whispered to Moody, "Speak English."

Moody corrected himself. "We are unsure of any brain penetration by the Subaru metal. The surgeons performed a procedure called craniectomy 24 hours ago. They removed the metal object then the bone flap was not replaced but secured in place with screws. Full recovery will range from 4 to 6 weeks. The surgeons are confident there was no penetration, but infection and management of the vascular injuries are critical at this point," said Moody.

Emma looked over his body, various cuts and bruises, stitches, and used her phone to give Karen and Jessica the best overall perspective possible. Hunter fell asleep.

Karen asked Emma, "Would you kindly hand the phone to John?" John took the phone from Emma while looking closely at the surgeons' work. He was very pleased with their work.

"John, what happened?" asked Karen.

John moved away from Hunter and walked to the large windows overlooking the Hospital car park; he saw a church steeple and watched the rain falling steadily, causing the snow to turn to mush. "He almost died. All we have is one witness, a tractor-trailer driver. He says two cars were speeding towards him on the wrong side of the airport's E4 highway. The truck driver said he lost control of his tractor-trailer, and all three collided. Everything went up in flames. The truck driver is in the hospital with minor burns."

"The wrong side of the road means a high-speed car pursuit," said Karen.

"Yes," replied John.

"How many dead?" asked Karen.

"Three. Two dead men in a high-performance muscle car loaded with guns. The third was in the other car, Hunter's car," replied John.

"Hunter's car. Was it a rental?" asked Karen.

"I'm not sure if Hunter's car was a rental. Somebody shot the person in his car several times," replied John.

"Who shot who?" asked Karen.

"The Police found one gun in Hunter's vehicle. Crash investigators finished with the scene two hours ago. Karen, the dead guy in Hunter's rear seat, had an issued SIG Sauer P226. The two in the Subaru had two QCW05 5.8mm silenced submachine guns," said John.

"Hunter's dead guy was a Swedish Police Officer?" gasped Karen.

"We don't know. A Swedish Police Detective came to interview Hunter, but he was out cold. Emma and I showed our credentials. That just raised more questions. The detective asked the nursing staff to contact her when Hunter was ready to talk. Based on the detectives' verbal responses, I doubt they will share any DNA evidence on the other two dead men. I don't blame them. We're outsiders, and they don't have the full story," said John with a hint of frustration.

"Neither do we have the full story," replied Karen.

"It can't be a random attack. Can you get access to the autopsy and investigation?" asked Karen.

"Yes, I will contact RPS," replied John.

"Are they up to speed on Murmansk?" asked Karen.

"The counter-terrorism National Task Force and RPS know of the theft of the Red Banners, but not the Swedish Police Authority," replied John.

CHAPTER 52

MOSCOW RUSSIA

Ahmed unpacked, showered, shaved, and dressed in a suit inside his one-bedroom modern flat. He placed all his clothing in an enormous plastic bag and went out to find an evening meal. Ahmed found a bin to dispose of his coats, underwear, shoes, and jackets.

Around the corner was a local bar called 'AF', which served food and alcohol. The bar was in a renovated factory complex in a fashionable suburb of Moscow. AF attracted crowds of people with loud music and trendy décor. Ahmed figured He could fit in without being noticed. LED TVs lined the entire length of the bar. The 20 X 85inch LED TV was extraordinary. There are sports, news, and fashion, serving as crowd ambience. The music was pumping, so all the TVs had no sound. He sat at the seat below the TV running 24/7 News. The waiter approached, and because of the music, Ahmed lifted the menu, pointed at the steak and vegetables and kvas combo, smiled and handed over two 50 Euro notes.

Annika Federova always greets and talks to everybody who comes into her bar. She would chat, even sweat talk, every male with lots of loving touches, asking about business. She used humour, laughing with the ladies, commenting on fashion, and making sure empty glasses were constantly full of alcohol. She was good at it, in fact, too good. Ahmed watched Annika using subtle hand signals. Without a word, someone would produce more alcohol. He noticed the sign several times. If a person didn't like the food, she would apologize and order a replacement meal by pointing her finger in the air. When the replacement meal reached the patron, they received a 50 Euro voucher for a later visit.

'Smart,' thought Ahmed.

Annika was a blonde, five foot ten inches in stature, slim, charismatic, charming, and functioned as an informant for the SVR. She worked the room quickly, one person at a time. The bartenders would watch for any signal to supply drinks or bring side plates. Ahmed followed her reflection in the mirror behind all the bottles of spirits. He understood why the place was so attractive. He had finished his meal when Annika approached and presented herself. She said in Russian, "You are new; welcome to AF." She recognized the look and, smilingly, "You speak English, French, German?"

Ahmed smiled and answered, "English."

"My name is Annika. Yours?"

Ahmed didn't wish to give his name. He hesitated and said, "Robert."

Annika recognized the hesitation. She perceived he was about to lie but smiled and said, "Welcome, Robert. I hope you enjoyed your meal. Thank you for being our guest tonight. Would you like another drink?" She did a different hand signal. Ahmed knew what it meant.

"Thank you, but no. I must run," replied Ahmed.

Annika lifted her hand and pointed with two fingers, and the barman brought over a 50 Euro meal voucher. "Please come again very soon. Your next meal will be on me," said Annika.

Ahmed stood, looked at Annika and said, "Thank you, you are most generous."

Ahmed worked his way out of the bar to return to his unit. Annika briefly held up three fingers to the barman, then moved to the next person and introduced herself.

As Ahmed opened the glass door, he saw the reflection of the bartender lifting Ahmed's drinking glass by placing his fingers inside the glass and putting it up on a shelf.

CHAPTER 53

STOCKHOLM HOSPITAL

Emma stays with Hunter in the emergency room while John follows a Swedish Security Intelligence agent, David Hallgren. John introduced himself, and Hallgren replied, "There might be a problem."

"What sort of problem?" asked Moody.

"We have 24 forensic medical specialists in Sweden. Doctors assist them. Other doctors work full-time at universities. The universities sometimes discharge them when required to carry out autopsies. As of today, half of the 24 are either on sick leave or holidays, hence delays," said Hallgren.

"How long are the delays?" asked Moody.

"Presently, you mean?" said Hallgren.

"Yes," asked Moody.

Hallgren's cell phone was chirping, "Ten days, but I have requested a favour."

He disconnected the call and responded, "We're up. This will cost me something," said Hallgren. They both showed their identities. The receptionist then escorted Hallgren and John from the Coroner's Office floor to the elevators, down to the autopsy rooms. They had to wait, as the forensic medical specialist rostered today was on the phone and would be with them in a minute. The receptionist left them to return to her desk.

"I hate the smell of this place," whispered Hallgren. "Disinfectants get up my nose, let alone burnt human tissue."

A door opened, and both men swung around to watch two assistants bring the bodies out on stainless steel lifting trolleys. One nodded at Hallgren and Moody, and the other repeated what the receptionist said. The second assistant returned to the refrigeration room and brought out the third body.

"The Government has spent $40 million on a bigger refrigerated space the size of the parking lot outside. This place is full right now. Backed right up," said Hallgren. "The new place is nearly finished. I think they went over budget." John understood some people talk to calm their nerves. Moody watched the coroner's young assistant transfer the three bodies from the hydraulic trolleys to the examination tables. The assistant placed trays filled with instruments, evidence bags, and tags on each table. She stopped working and waited with her hands clasped before her stiff rubber apron.

"Sorry, I'm late. I hope you didn't have to wait too long?" said Carol Gorstren.

John declared, "American?"

"Yes, my husband is Swedish. I am Dr Carol Gorstren. You must be Dr. John Moody. It's nice to meet you. GP?"

"Reserve Australian Army doctor; surgical trauma is my field," replied Moody.

"David, nice to see you again," said Gorstren. Moody looked at all three bodies; the smell of burnt flesh was not attractive, and they could see David's reaction. John gave him sixty seconds before he bailed.

"Shall we start?" asked Gorstren. She was draped in scrubs and had a spatter shield on. She tapped her foot on a steel button to start the audio and video recorder on the initial body. She began to remove all the organs and intestines.

David Hallgren turned to John. "She loves her job. I could think of much better things to do."

Gorstren could hear Hallgren. She smiled at David; she loved her job. She looked at him and went back to work.

"To me, this is the ultimate," he was about to say atrocity when he saw Gorstren lift her eyes at him. "Um, challenge. You get burnt up, and now you get picked apart, your brain weighed, and if a bullet gets stuck in your spinal column, it breaks your back. I mean, you're already dead. It's brutal, you know."

Then John saw the slight convulsion starting – the pre-vomit.

Gorstren kept working and said, "Hey David, perhaps I can have a cup of coffee for you in my office; this may take some time."

"Oh, okay, thanks," said Hallgren. He didn't need any encouragement. David left the room, relieved.

Gorstren turned the two damaged bullets over in her gloved hand. "I will give you a picture of these if you wish?" Her foot touched the recorder button to stop the recording. She placed each bullet in evidence bags.

"Okay, we can talk," motioned Gorstren. With her finger, she pointed to the first body. "Fire burns patterns start on the soft tissue, the fat and muscle, and later the fire continues to the skeleton. Those patterns tell me how each body burned in the vehicle. Dr Moody, are you familiar with burn patterns, blisters and skin split? You know this, yes?" asked Gorstren.

"Yes," replied Moody. He was examining the body as she spoke.

"The muscle protects the skeleton, but as the fire continues, the muscles shrink, exposing the bone. The inner bones on the head and the extremities, when exposed to fire, change colour," said Gorstren.

Looking at the other two corpses, Gorstren asked, "What do you see?" asked Gorstren.

"I have seen these identical patterns on the battlefield. Both have skeletal injury patterns from gunshot wounds. This body has more than the other. Plus, this third body has suffered some blunt force trauma in the past. With that level of physical trauma, I would suggest he was a self-medicated drug user," said Moody.

"At this stage, I would agree," said Gorstren.

"Those two corpses have been around violence and guns. But not this fellow," said Gorstren. She was pointing to the first corpse.

"DNA?" asked Moody.

"I need his DNA for identification. Unfortunately, their bones are bluey, grey and white." Moody followed Gorstren as she explained the problem with the other two bodies. "The fire intensity determines the damage." She looked at Moody, who said nothing. She continued. "In summary, burnt bodies come in three states. First, semi-burnt and preserved. The second stage is black. These two are in the final stage of highly degraded 'blue-grey' burn."

"I suspect you will not find any genetic markers or patterns," replied John.

"Correct. But we have teeth," said Gorstren.

Gorstren pointed to their feet. "Those toe bones are semi-burnt, which may interest you, John. They both wore heavy leather steel-capped boots and non-flammable socks," said Gorstren. "Military attire."

Moody responded, "That is intriguing that they both have identical shoes. Perhaps like a uniform? When will you have some results?"

"24 hours is the best I can do," said Gorstren.

"24 hours. Thank you, Dr Gorstren," replied Moody.

Gorstren came through with the DNA. The guy from Hunter's car, with three bullets, was Danish Police Officer Erik Hakansson. The fellow with blunt force trauma was Jansson Madsen, an identified offender. The third guy was unknown. The Danish Police raided a farmhouse on the edge of Stockholm. Erik Hakansson and two other men lived in one farmhouse. With the evidence gathered, Hallgren was optimistic that they could determine the third man's identity. There was a fourth bedroom with personal items.

Behind the farmhouse stood a shed where Danish detectives found explosives, C-4, detonators, Illegal guns from China and 235,000 Euros. When the bomb demolition expert confirmed the site was safe, forensics moved in and took fingerprints, photographed and collected evidence.

A forensic officer called Hallgren over. "This computer has no password. The browser history shows they are always looking at Jihadist sites. Somebody installed the Tor browser one day before the freeway car incident. Read the conversation."

Hallgren read it.

"I will need a hard copy of that conversation," replied Hallgren.

Hallgren repeated the Tor discussion to Moody in English, "An unnamed party offered cash to these men to murder Hunter. They even had the Gulfstream arrival details."

'Hunter plane must have got tagged by someone in Murmansk,' thought John. "This means we have another agent in the field." John immediately thought of the men Hunter worked with within Murmansk.

"Hunter's death was to be verified by a photo. Then the cash would come by courier," said Hallgren. "That is a short timeframe to organize a hit. Sloppy to send these idiots up against a professional. Smells desperate to me."

"It was a last-minute arrangement from someone in Murmansk," replied John

Hallgren shook his head. "Erik Hakansson, a law enforcement officer, was associated with these thugs. Who would have thought?" He shook his head in surprise.

"David, were they aware of the stolen 'Red Banners?'" asked John.

"No. These guys are all about blood lust and domination. I doubt they knew Hunter was ASIS. These people advocate a belief in racial superiority. They enlist the underemployed, project a sick vision and murder for publicity. They are dangerous people with a foolish cause."

"Hunter would have been a trophy," replied John. "When Hunter is awake, we will get the full story."

Hallgren phoned the hospital. He waited a minute for Hunter's doctor to give an update.

John only followed a few Swedish words. He thought of a TV puppet program with the Swedish chef and laughed.

"Hunter should be in reasonable condition to visit tomorrow at 10 am," replied Hallgren. "Get some rest. We will sort out this connection."

"10 am," replied John.

"By the way, the doctor said he may move Hunter from intensive care to a private hospital room depending on how he improves. I will organize some floor security," said Hallgren.

"He's a fierce old goat," said John. "When this surgery is complete, he may look like the rear end of a goat, ugly as hell." Hallgren didn't understand the Australian doctor's jab. They seemed to hate each other. John picked up Emma from the hospital's front and went to the Embassy-appointed hotel to rest. They would return at 10 am the following day.

Hunter's surgeon was satisfied with the improvement of his burns and his skull trauma. The heavy surgical medication had now worn off. It was just after 10 pm, and Hunter's doctor was on his final rounds for the night. The doctor advised Hunter that the nurse would administer any desired pain relief medication every two or three hours upon request.

"Do you have a migraine or headache?" asked the doctor.

"No. I can feel the head injury. It's not painful. It's like someone has super-glued a patch on my skin," replied Moody.

"That's a perfect description," replied the doctor. "Your bone and skin are in good condition. No infection, just a slight swelling, but it is going down."

"My thinking is sharper, and I'm ravenous. This fibreglass cast will not stop me from forking some food into my mouth," laughed Hunter.

"Okay, what would you like?" urged the doctor.

"Some steak and legumes. I can't stand any more yoghurt and gelatin," replied Hunter.

The doctor laughed. "I will ask the kitchen for a meal. I will see you tomorrow at 9 am. Your colleagues will visit you at 10 am. At 9 am, if your condition improves, I will transfer you to a private room. Apart from the meal, can I do anything for you tonight?" inquired the doctor.

"Thank you for your help. See you tomorrow," replied Hunter.

"Tomorrow," repeated the doctor. The doctor left, and Hunter counted the ceiling tiles.

The badge affixed to his blue uniform shirt read, 'Lucas. Food Services Aide'. "I could smell the steak before you entered the room," said Hunter. The Police officer watched the aide. Lucas, the Food Services Aide, smiled as he pointed to the food on the trolley. "This is the meal you requested."

Lucas helped Hunter to sit up and placed a pillow behind his back. The aide swung a small table towards the Hunter and put the dinner plate on the table. "Will I cut the steak into pieces for you?" asked the aide.

"Thanks," replied Hunter.

As he cut the steak, he paused and spoke to the Police Officer. "The kitchen told me to bring a meal for you—the same meal as Hunter. Is that okay?" replied Lucas.

Hunter watched Lucas cut the steak into small pieces.

'Lucas called me by name. He said Hunter, not patient or sir.' thought Hunter.

Hunter knew the doctors had withdrawn his name from the board behind his bed and chart, but he wasn't sure what name was on the nurse's registrar. Without moving his head, Hunter looked at the floor and saw thick leather steel-capped boots. Lucas wore dirty jeans under his Hospital blue uniform top that went below his waist. As Lucas cut the steak, his body moved, and Hunter saw a familiar shape under the uniform, stuffed down his jeans. A form he has seen thousands of times.

Hunter looked at his food and asked the Police Officer, "How is your steak?"

He glanced at him briefly. His gun was in his belt holster, under the tray, and the Police officer had wedged himself into the small armchair. Buying a few seconds, Hunter pointed to two pieces of steak and asked, "Would you kindly cut those two pieces in half."

Rookies always make mistakes with silencers. Hunter expected the gun to be a SIG Sauer P226. An attached silencer to any firearm in an outside or inside the waistband holster, chest, pocket, or shoulder holster, or shoved in the front or back of your jeans means you have to lift your shooting arm much higher so the silencer is free from any entanglement. By doing so, you lose valuable seconds.

Those seconds determine whether you will live or die.

Hunter picked up his fork with his bandaged, burnt left hand and asked for the steak knife so he could try to eat. "Could you pour a drink for me?" He spun the steak knife in his hand and knew his shoulder was able to give him leverage.

The aide picked up the jug of fruit juice and poured it into a cup as Hunter struck the steak knife into Lucas's stomach above the gun.

Hunter then struck two times near his thigh, below the groin where his abdomen ends and his leg begins. The first strike sliced the femoral leg artery close to the surface of the skin. The final strikes were fast, with deep penetration above the top of the gun. Lucas fell back in shock, hitting the wall. He was then trying to lift his smock and grab his weapon, now soaked in blood.

Hunter shouted, "Gun, gun!"

"What?" asked the Police Officer. His mouth was open and full of food. He looked at the TV and then back at Hunter.

Hunter tried to lunge for Lucas but fell off the bed, bringing saline tubes, hospital machines, and blankets with him. Hunter was shouting to the Police Officer again, "Gun, shoot."

The Police officer stood, with his food falling to the ground. He had his gun in his hand and raised his arm to shoot when Lucas fired and missed the Police Officer. The Officer's hand was shaking, and instead of firing back, he hit the floor to hide. Lucas's gun was so slippery he fired and shot the wall over the door. Lucas rubbed one hand on his smock, lowered his weapon, and fired through the mattress, killing the police officer.

Hunter, though entanglement, stuck multiple times with the steak knife, splicing Lucas's femoral artery on his other leg. Hunter tore the burnt skin on his arm, and blood was now pouring over him. Lucas was groaning, his face turning pale, staggering heavy against the wall, breathing, trying not to lose consciousness, still attempting to point the gun at Hunter. With only seconds left in his life, he turned the gun towards Hunter. Hunter grabbed what strength he had left and held the burning silencer, attempting to push it away when it fired and hit him in the shoulder. Lucas died, slipped in his blood, and then fell hard on the floor. The Police Officer was dead, and Hunter knew he was in trouble, then he lost consciousness. It was over in seconds.

The nursing staff check their patients every two hours, from 10 pm to 6 am. The nurse enters the room to observe the patient's condition and checks the medication and electronic equipment without waking the patient. Hunter's nurse was alone at her station, ready to do her midnight patient rounds. The ward was silent and dark. Her patient, Mr No Name, underwent surgery, was seen by the surgeon at 10 pm, and then had a meal. "Do I let him sleep and check him at 2 am?"

The nurse finished her cup of coffee. She commenced her rounds with her mini LED torch and patient clipboards stacked on her medication cart. First up was Mr No Name. She read the patient details, then the special notations.

'A Police Officer will guard Mr No Name 24/7. Entry is restricted to hospital staff only. The guard will check ID.'

She shone her torch on an empty chair. "And where is this courageous law enforcement officer? Probably, he is outside smoking?" She grunted in frustration and stomped to the exit door.

"The door is not pegged open. The cop locked himself out." She opened the door to check. Sure enough, nobody was there. She lifted her radio. "Security, has a cop come down the external fire stairs? Did he come back inside? Can you have a look, please? Thanks." She then checked the toilets while waiting for the night security officer to respond. "The toilets were empty."

She turned her radio down, then checked on Mr' No Name.'

Hallgren, John and Emma burst through the hospital ward doors. As they entered an armed 'Sarskilda Operationsgruppen,' or SOG, the Swedish Police's tactical division raised his weapon. This guy was in full tactical gear, pointing his Glock 17M handgun at them. John saw two stun grenades, flash-bang grenades, a taser, and an MP5/10 submachine over his shoulder. John glanced beyond the armed Officer and saw several more SOGs at the exit door.

For a moment, nobody moved.

The SOG officer verified their credentials. Only then did he lower his gun. Hallgren, John, and Emma ran to Hunter's room. "Turn off that alarm!" shouted the doctor. The head nurse switched off the emergency alarm. Silence returned to the ward, but not calm. Doctors worked on Hunter while nurses moved other patients to other hospital floors.

A resident and three nurses had lifted Hunter back onto his blood-soaked ICU bed. The crash cart had revived him, and now they were trying to stabilize his vitals. The surgeon arrived and, with one quick look, shouted, "Theatre 8 now! You and you get prepped. I'll get the anesthesiologist. Let's go now. Make way! Move everybody!"

Everybody stepped back and watched the nurses scramble. One nurse slipped on the blood and then fell hard on the floor. Two SOG officers took over and hauled Hunter's blood-soaked ICU bed out of the room to the operating theatre, followed by the remaining tactical officers.

John helped the nurse to her feet. Emma looked aghast, watching footprints of the blood being created by the nurses and SOGs pushing Hunter's bed, "John, there's too much blood," said Emma. "There's too much blood!"

John looked at Hallgren, who turned white. "David, sit down. Emma, come and sit here for a moment."

John helped him sit on the floor in the hospital corridor. "Thanks," said Hallgren.

He took several deep breaths, dialled numbers, and lifted his phone. "This is Chief Inspector David Hallgren, RPS. I'm at Capio Saint Goran's Hospital recovery ward and need a forensic team. Thanks."

Before, there was shouting. Now, there was silence.

John stepped carefully into Hunter's room. The medical team had switched on the room lights. He was trying to understand what he was seeing. To his right, Moody saw a dead uniformed Police officer, weapon holstered. The elderly Police Officer was lying on his side, with a food tray beside his leg, food scattered, and bullet exit wounds on his neck. He looked to be on retirement, probably on prescribed blood thinners. He bled out fast, tragic.

Hunter's ICU bed gone, John saw another dead man in a hospital uniform slumped on the floor. There was a copious amount of blood on his clothing near his stomach and thigh. A silenced SIG was swimming in a large pool of blood. There was a knife embedded in his inner thigh. John retreated to check on David and Emma.

"I'm sorry, John," Hallgren said, embarrassed.

"If you are both up to it, I want to show you something." John motioned Hallgren and Emma over to the doorway.

"Buckets of blood," said Emma through tears.

"I think all this blood is from him, not Hunter. His femoral artery was severed. See the knife in his leg. David, look at his boots," said John. "We've seen those boots before!"

"Damn. Steel-capped, thick leather. The farmhouse, fourth bed," replied David.

Hunter was in good spirits after surgery. His bullet wound was now one of many, creating an ugly landscape and deforming his first teenage tattoo, a small fish now looking like a whale. He was starving and asked again for a steak and vegetable meal. John explained what they had pieced together as he ate his dinner from the two attacks.

"I can't see the Jihadist and Red Banner connection," replied Emma.

Emma, Hallgren, and Stockholm's ASIS head of the Embassy, Frank Warren, were crowded together in Hunter's room. The armed SOG team of three was outside the room. Frank apologized to Hunter, saying, "I am sorry. I was in Terminal 5, waiting for your transfer. I contacted the pilots and checked the car rental desks when you didn't show. My mistake, Hunter."

Hunter held up his hands. "It's okay, Frank. I got fooled." Frank was relieved.

John jumped into the awkward silence to change the subject, saying, "Can I bring everybody up to date? The tractor-trailer with the BMW cars and 'Red Banners' has vanished. The roadblocks gave us nothing. CCTV on different routes and different time frames gave us nothing. The only conclusion is the driver did not use the highway through this country."

All their faces showed frustration. Hunter caught the words, 'this country.'

Karen came online. "John, hold the tablet so I can see Hunter."

"How are you, Hunter?" asked Karen.

"I am okay, alive," replied Hunter. "The best sleep I have had in a while. My arm may take a while to heal."

Karen said, "John, pivot me around so I can see everybody. "Okay, Bely came through on the ferry details, auction dates, auction company and current owners. The successful bidder of the boat was AMVGT Corporation. They had deposited the payment online to the auction house from their bank in Luxembourg. Those banks will never talk, ever. Lucas said he would look into it."

"What's our next step?" asked John.

"We need to find the vet," said Emma. "The vet who supplied the medication to sedate the Russians might have CCTV."

"Why a vet?" asked John.

"First, the drug has to be more powerful than morphine, so that leaves us with a vet and large animals," replied Emma. "No, forget it. The driver could have ordered the stuff from the UK. It's a dead end."

"Maybe, maybe not," replied John.

"It's frustrating, isn't it?" said Hunter to Emma. "One step forward, two steps back."

Emma smiled, but she was frustrated. 'We are being outwitted daily.' She opened and closed her fists. She was more than frustrated—it was anger.

John asked, "I was wondering about the connections between the Bagdad driver, the Chinese agents and the Jihadists who attacked you?"

Karen spoke first. "Based on these local Jihadists' accommodation and skill set that David described, I doubt the driver would sell or give the 'Red Banners' to them. They are violent amateurs. Their job was simple. To stall the hunt by killing Hunter. The question is, who contacted them?" 'It can only be ZL,' she thought. She'd wait for that to be confirmed. Karen knew ZL were dangerous people.

"The Chinese guys have a plan," replied Hunter. "Either it is personal or state-based. The driver knows what he is doing and has done missions before. He's organized and confident. The Chinese are the moneymen. The Jihadists are local amateurs paid by the driver or ZL. They failed. It's a distraction. We're now aware of them, but we must remain focused."

"The Chinese agents could short the share market. They would have a specific date," said John.

"Why do that? You can short the market in other ways without using a nuclear weapon. It would be very suspicious. Brokers would identify who was shorting the market," said Emma. "With the amount of money they have, they could invest and double it. But they are not doing that. Therefore, they are under orders."

John wondered about 'under orders from whom.' "But they stole the money?"

"It makes no difference, John," replied Emma. "They stole the money because they were under orders from their superiors, hence our Bagdad cutout."

Hunter's phone chirped. He put it on speakerphone, "Hey Bely, it's me. Thanks for the information on the ferry."

"I hope it goes somewhere," said Bely. "Look, the Military Police still have an ongoing enquiry, but at least they found one person with too much money, and he is talking," said Bely.

"Who paid them?" asked Hunter.

"Asperyan. Cash in hand. Euros. Also, the autopsies are back," said Bely.

"Drugged?" asked Hunter

"Yes. The buns contained a barbiturate. They ate, drank and were sedated, total anaesthesia," said Bely.

"Neutralized the threat," replied Hunter.

"Correct. Forensics discovered the usual syringe marks under the arms and between their toes. The drug was Etorphine, used to immobilize horses and elephants. It's more potent than morphine. A vet told me you are required to order this drug. Normally, they don't keep it in stock. Look, Hunter, I am no longer on the case," said Bely.

Emma smiled.

"You said that would happen," said Hunter.

"Are your phones encrypted?" asked Bely.

"Yes," said Hunter.

"President Driminov has handed the hunt for the 'Red Banners' over to ZL," replied Bely. "Everything will disappear: the ferry, the sub, and your team. Moscow will deny even the existence of the 'Red Banners'. It was a military exercise. Already, on social media, the Vardo bomb wasn't a bomb. It was the ferry fuel tanks. Hunter, watch your back and good luck," said Bely.

'I thought so,' thought Karen.

CHAPTER 54

MOSCOW RUSSIA

Ahmed realized he had made a fatal error at the bar. He thought through each step that happened in the bar. 'She asked my name. I hesitated. There were no tells, rapid eye blinking, facial tics, nervousness, sweating or blushing. I didn't look right. I didn't touch my face and gave no fake smile,' thought Ahmed.

'I saw her reaction when I didn't give my name. It was a microsecond hesitation,' thought Ahmed. 'She has a particular skill set? Who is her employer?' wondered Ahmed, reflecting on those few minutes. He rolled it over in his mind as he walked back to his unit.

'She collects names and matches them to a face using the bar's CCTV. Does she work for the mafia? Is it extortion? Perhaps an informant?' thought Ahmed.

He stopped walking, turned and returned to the restaurant. He waited in the shadow of a shop door opposite the car until the final customer left, then went inside the restaurant. "I left my wallet here," said Ahmed. "Have you seen it? It's leather black, the usual."

The barman checked the lost property box under the bar. "There is no wallet here. I will go and check the office," replied the barman.

"Thanks," said Ahmed.

The room was silent except for the rattling of the air conditioning and refrigerators. Ahmed was confident the place would have CCTV. Then, he noticed miniature cameras underneath the LED TVs.

'She records every day, plus my glass with my fingerprints is still on the shelf,' thought Ahmed.

When Ahmed first left the bar, he saw the waiter's reflection opening the all-glass door. The waiter placed his fingers inside the drinking glass on the shelf. He walked behind the bar and swapped the glasses using the barman's cleaning cloth.

The barman returned, "Sorry, there is no wallet," Ahmed thanked him and left.

'Faces and fingerprints, what the hell,' thought Ahmed. He waited in the dark until 3 am, then walked around the back. There were no lights and no movement. With nitrile gloves under his black leather gloves and two paperclips, he opened the padlock on the waterproof outdoor power board and switched everything off.

The climb up the rain pipe to the second floor gave him access to an ajar window. It was a storage room with a chair beside the window with a bottle full of cigarette butts. Ahmed found the office, disconnected the backup battery inside the alarm and unplugged the telephone connection.

"I should burn this restaurant down," said Ahmed. It's too obvious. The CCTV computer is a basic model with no internet connection.' He inserted a USB with a battery backup into the surveillance computer. He waited 30 seconds for everything to be scrambled, then pocketed the USB.

'What if he missed something?' thought Ahmed. He found the upstairs staff kitchen. Beside the rubbish bin was empty cardboard boxes. He tore off two pieces of thick cardboard and jammed them into the plastic toaster. He pushed the plunger down and turned it on its side.

Once back on the street, He performed an SDR to expose hostile surveillance. If it was some network, he needed to be cautious. He heard a sound. A polyurethane shoe sole will sometimes squeak on a polished surface. Ahmed memorized his surveillance route to lure a person into following him if it was a tail. The sound was faint but recognizable, and it was a fatal error.

Ahmed stopped walking. It was a tactical decision presenting Ahmed with a detection opportunity. The footsteps also stopped. Anybody following him now has to figure out how to keep track without displaying any signs of surprise. Ahmed stepped around a corner and waited. After a minute of indecision, he heard the footsteps start again. This time, they were slower, more cautious.

'It was the barman. He probably lived upstairs,' thought Ahmed.

Ahmed had a small sealed syringe filled with a Botulinum nerve toxin, which causes respiratory failure.

Botulism is associated with poor food handling, so any investigation will go no further than the bar. Ahmed started stomping and turned one more corner. He was now in the dark. The footsteps speeded up, and the waiter came around the corner, directly into the syringe.

The bar burned to the ground.

CHAPTER 55

STOCKHOLM

"We have no face, no name," said John. "If Lucas examined Bagdad battle reports, would a name keep showing up?"

"The driver is a skilled jihadist leader?" replied Hunter.

"You said he had fighting experience," said Emma.

"Leave that with me," said Lucas. "I will do some coding to collect names that keep appearing on social media platforms."

"That elephant drug," said Emma. "It's a possibility that a Murmansk chemist sold it to the driver. Polar bears live along the coast from Murmansk in the west to Chukotka in the east. I might do a browser search for vets in Murmansk."

"Back to Bagdad," said John. "How would you move so much money? Wayne from HQJOC said seventy-five million in cash?"

"75 million USD," replied Hunter, thinking how he would move pallets of cash.

"There are only ten vets in Murmansk," said Emma. "I will email pretending to be a Naval officer investigating sailors ordering the drug to smuggle the bears."

"Good," said John to Emma, but he was lost in thought. "You need a truck with air cargo transport boxes. How do you wash so much cash above $10,000 without banks being suspicious?"

Without looking up, Emma said, "Most banks have that $10,000 limit cash deposit. They also have legislation for 'Anti-Money Laundering and Counter-Terrorism Financing Acts.' If you try to deposit more than $10,000 cash into a bank account, that bank has to report the deposit to the government. The driver hires an idiot to work in his office to perform menial tasks. After a while, the driver asks him to deposit money in twenty banks. So he walks around carrying bags of cash, depositing 9,990 dollars at different banks. Or I would set up many fake companies and wash the money through cash businesses."

"The driver did that somewhere in Europe but not in Bagdad," said Hunter. "The Chinese guys probably delivered the money to Bagdad by private plane."

"Do you mean directly or through a bank?" asked Emma.

"The driver takes cash to Murmansk to pay the mafia guys. He leases ferries, cranes, Ural's equipment, and BMWs. He uses a Luxenberg bank," said John. That means he deposited the money somewhere else and transferred it to Luxenberg."

"Laundering that amount of money and then transferring it in big chunks to Luxenberg takes time. Maybe a year?" replied Emma. "Either way, John, those purchases or leases do not equal seventy-five million, maybe five million maximum. There is another game at play here."

"I would pack the money in several crates," replied Hunter. "They would be labelled machinery and flown out from Bagdad. One crate would have gone to Murmansk and the others to the end locations or the two Red Banner targets," said Hunter.

"No. Thirty-five million USD to Murmansk? I don't think so. Maybe five USD. It is too much money for what he needed to do, Hunter," said Emma. I would send the crates to different storage companies in other countries. You know those storage sheds where people send their junk they no longer use but want to keep their junk?"

"If the driver's mission goes belly up, he goes to Argentina, where he sent a few crates of cash," said John.

"The driver could be in France organizing all the Murmansk leases using laundered money through French cash businesses that he has purchased. That would take time. He can only do that in one country at a time. He can't fly with a crate of money from France to Murmansk, so he uses storage companies in several countries to spread the risk. So, as Emma suggested, the Murmansk storage would have only five or seven million USD."

"He can do it in two countries," said Emma. The driver isn't the only person who can."

John looked at Emma, then to Hunter, who said, "Another person with a 'Red Banner' is in the target country laundering the money. Why not set the timer on the nuke and leave? No, he doesn't have the 'Red Banner' yet. He is setting everything up."

Hunter stopped talking to think. "How would I do it? I would purchase a few cash businesses to launder the money. That will take time. I want to avoid scrutiny, so I need to be legitimate. The second person establishes a business near the target and waits for a Red Banner to arrive."

"The money laundering timeline makes sense," replied Emma. "The amount of cash speaks about buying something expensive, like a twenty-storey building in Berlin with a Red Banner on the roof. It could be any capital city."

"I was thinking about transporting the Red Banners by air freight and radiation," said John.

Hunter called Karen, "Sorry for the late call, Karen. We're thinking out loud. Most major European airports have radiation detection systems that intercept and classify radiological and nuclear materials for security. If so, can we get a list of which airports don't have them installed? The driver may use one to move the 'Red Banners' to his final location."

"Yes. I get Lucas and Wayne onto that," said Karen. "Since Japan's Fukushima power plant disaster, airports have awakened to the risk. You're thinking a cargo plane or amateur airport?"

Lucas came online, "Helsinki-Vantaa Airport has a radiation monitoring system. It avoids false-positive alarms. And I am reading, hold on, US planes from Tokyo set off radiation detection alarms in Dallas and Chicago. I have found the company that did the installation in

Helsinki, and they worked with Finnish Radiation and Nuclear Authority...."

"Lucas, Lucas!" said Hunter.

"Yes?" replied Lucas.

"Let's assume the driver has done detailed research on airports," said Hunter.

"An airport may not disclose whether it has them or not," replied Emma. "Or it may advertise its super security as a passenger advantage."

John groaned.

"Taking the 'Red Banners' to an airport is a big risk," replied Karen.

"Okay, he's driving, not flying, so the final destination is Europe," said Hunter.

"Not just Europe, Hunter," said John. "A container boat to the US mainland, a truck from France to the UK through the tunnel, even a courier van down to Italy, then onto a ferry—the list is endless. We need more intel."

"The money went to Bagdad. The driver comes from Bagdad," said Emma. "He hated the US-led coalition war, so the West is his target."

"Okay," replied Hunter. "If he is a fair dinkum Jihadist, he wants an Islamic country void of Westerners, which, I believe, is impossible. Anyways, the Red Banners are his bargaining chip. So which country does he bargain with?"

"It doesn't work, Hunter," said Emma. "He bargains with the US and says clear this whole desert area, or else I blow up Rome. So the US sends one hundred soldiers over, packs everybody into trucks and moves them out to God knows where, then they say, "Hey, Mr Terrible Terrorist, here is your land. They wait and see who arrives. It doesn't work unless the driver has 100,000 people on board, ready to pack up and move to the desert. An independent Islamic country is not his plan. If it is his plan, he's an idiot. So far, we have not seen idiot behaviour; we see calculated planning."

"If the driver makes any demands, it entails traceable communication," John replied.

Hunter read, "We need more intel on his motive, plan and target."

"A vet just answered my email," said Emma. "I am translating the drug names. Yes, only the elephant drug was stolen. The vet didn't know it was gone until I emailed."

CHAPTER 56

LONDON
Information Technology Director Alan James told Driscoll to close off any unfinished files on illegal or suspicious immigrants and hand them over to Noel to sign them off into storage. Then, start working on a new batch of files.

"Here you go, Driscoll; five are near completion and the remaining seventy need work. I have put them in order of priority. They date from six years ago to two months ago," said Alan James.

As Alan James left the room, Driscoll turned to Noel and said, "But I want to keep working on the Milton Kahnt file. There's something about it that doesn't add up, something that could be a breakthrough in our investigations."

"Okay, I'll sign these off and file them. But there are seventy waiting for you, buddy. Why that file?" asked Noel.

"I need to be sure. The Apostle Paul, Jayabalan and Joyce," said Driscoll. "We're on to something!"

"Didn't you fix Joyce?" asked Noel, raising his eyebrows.

"Yes, don't you trust me? I made the adjustments and did some offline testing. It is working," replied Driscoll, now angry.

"Okay, cool, your jets! So, what is the interest?" Noel gathered his files and looked back at Driscoll, waiting for a reasonable, logical response.

"I took a second run at Milton Kahnt and Abu Sarek. Joyce repeated her initial conclusion. Kahnt is Sarek, even though Sarek is dead," said Driscoll. "There are too many similarities, too many coincidences. Joyce is saying they are the same person. It's a mystery. I need to fix it, but only if Joyce is wrong, which I doubt."

"Does Joyce understand the concept of death?" inquired Noel, referring to the fact that Joyce, being an AI, might not fully comprehend the finality of death.

"No, she doesn't. She matches faces perfectly!" replied Driscoll.

"You need to put the concept of death into your coding. So what are you going to do?" asked Noel.

"I'm planning to pay him a visit," Driscoll declared. Noel, who had started to walk towards the storage room, halted and turned back, leaning in close. "You can't do that. You're an analyst, for heaven's sake. We're not spies or field agents. We don't carry guns and we have no field training."

Driscoll said, "I know that! Look, I thought I would swing by a company called Elite Renovation Builders.' Listen to this. The ERB website says they are renovating the A1-listed St. Mary Le Strand Church in London. It's located on the eastern end of the Strand in the City of Westminster. You know, the one where the road splits and goes around both sides."

Noel said, "Well, good for them. That church is a dump. So, you're going to walk in and say, 'Hello, I'm an MI5 IT analyst and a software genius, and my Atari server, called Joyce, says you're a bloody terrorist?'"

"No, I'm not stupid," shouted Driscoll. He sat down and looked around, waving and smiling at the people who were now gazing at him.

Noel replied with a tight grin, "You'll get thrown out on your ear, mate."

Driscoll responded defeatedly, "I just want to see Milton Kahnt, not talk to him. That's all."

"Warren, you've already seen him," Noel reminded. "You have

photographic evidence! Kahnt is not Sarek. They may look alike, and Joyce's analysis suggests they are the same person but two different individuals. One is deceased, and the other bears a striking resemblance. With those odds, you might as well buy a lottery ticket!"

Driscoll said, "I think he is Sarek!"

"Really?" said Noel. "That's all you've got, 'I think it is him.'"

"And I checked his bank account," said Driscoll. "I think it looks suspicious."

Noel raised his eyebrows and replied, "How does it look suspicious?"

"He has millions, coming in and going out," said Driscoll.

"It's a building company, mate!" said Noel. There should be lots of sales and expenses. These guys start with tons of borrowed cash; delays happen, cost blowouts, contractors demand cash under the table sometimes, deals are made, more delays occur, no sales are made, and then they go bankrupt. Their bank accounts jump all over the place."

"Anyway, do you want to come along?" asked Driscoll. Lunch and beer are on me."

Noel smiled and said, "You should have started with that!"

"The church has scaffolding everywhere. Look at that! Attached to the scaffolding is a mesh graphic image of the original church design," said Driscoll.

"When I was on holiday in Berlin, I caught the train to the Potsdamer Platz. The war flattened the place. And then I think the Berlin Wall ran right through the middle of the road. Today, the Sony Center is on one side, and office buildings are undergoing renovation on the other. The builders wrap the buildings in the same printed mesh. You had to look twice and realize it was a massive painted mesh enclosing the scaffolding. Just like here," said Noel, admiring the mesh portrait. "It is rather impressive."

Driscoll said, "I can't see inside!"

"I think that's the idea," said Noel. "You have this pleasant image and do not emit trucks, dust, or machinery. The public is protected from gents with hard hats with their bums sticking out the back of their shorts."

"Lovely Noel. Concrete road barriers surround the church, so how do we get in?" asked Driscoll.

They strolled past the church, and Noel said, "Normally, those plastic water-filled barriers would be hit by buses. The Americans call these concrete barriers, Jersey barriers."

"Rather narrow for the buses to squeeze through on the left side," responded Driscoll.

"Look, there is the entrance at the back. The building company has removed the bike racks and the extended concrete island on both ends, with scaffolding right to the edge of the concrete barrier. Everything looks normal to me. What were you expecting to see?" asked Noel. "A guy with a machine gun up in the tower yelling 'Make my day punk!'"

Driscoll looked at Noel, smiled, and said, "I'm not sure."

"You're not sure? Do you want to get closer or try to get in and look around?" asked Noel.

"No. I just wanted to get a feel of the place," said Driscoll.

"Really? How does it feel?" said Noel.

Driscoll gave him a withering look.

"Well, I'm feeling hungry," said Noel.

"Let's get lunch," said Driscoll. "Tomorrow, we go to his office."

Noel said, "We? Not me, mate. And what are you going to say? 'Hi Mr Sarek, are you that dead terrorist wanted by the CIA and MI6? It would help if you had stayed dead. How come you're alive?"

A downcast Driscoll said, "Let's get lunch."

Noel replied, "Your shout!"

The next day, Warren Driscoll went to Elite Renovation Builders' registered office and introduced himself as a journalist. Laura Ruby, the office manager, spoke in rather glowing terms of the opportunity to renovate St. Mary-le-Strand. She pointed to the large portraits attached to the walls, ranging from historic church images to renovated drawings.

"We're replacing the external roof with care," Laura explained. The interior ceiling is both ornate and fragile. The kitchen, restrooms, and plumbing downstairs will all be upgraded to current standards."

"When will your company complete the project?" asked Driscoll.

"We're having discussions with the architects, the Government Department and a specialist in building removals," said Laura.

"Are you moving the church?" asked Driscoll.

"No," said Laura. "It is staying. We will restore it to the original design with some upgrades."

"So it has some history ?" asked Driscoll.

"People danced around a maypole. May Day festivals were annual events. The Puritans pulled it down," said Laura. She pointed to a painting and said, "James Gibbs, the architect, built this Baroque-style church in 1714 for 16,000 pounds. Charles Dickens's parents were married in St. Mary's. I believe there was an older version of some sort from 1222."

"It has lots of history. Rather sad, it's now a traffic island," replied Driscoll.

"True. The outside had suffered from soot, traffic fumes and wear. That has all been repaired and cleaned, repointed, and the windows fixed. It will look wonderful. We're now at the most delicate stage. The foundations at the front have sunk, so the spire has started to list," said Laura.

"So, the whole thing could fall over?" said Driscoll.

"No, no! We are talking with a company that transports stone buildings from one location to another. Their suggestion is to lift the entire building, build a new foundation, and then put it back down," replied Laura.

"Sounds rather risky and expensive," said Driscoll.

"You're correct. We're talking with a Swiss Engineering company that moved a large Railway stone building 200 meters to lay a new railway line. That building was much bigger than St. Mary-le-Strand. We examined their procedure in detail and are confident of a successful outcome," sparkled Laura.

"How do they lift it without causing damage," asked Driscoll.

"The Church is approximately 70 feet x 22 feet. Think of 70 steel girders, side by side, starting from the front of the church to the back, inserted directly underneath, and then two steel girders welded to the 70 running up both sides of the church. A synchronous lifting system is then used to lift and level the building. We will build a new basement upon a stronger foundation," said Laura.

"How long will it take?" asked Driscoll.

"We anticipate four months as most of the work will be done at night between 9 pm and midnight due to sound and traffic restrictions. One vehicle lane on either side will be closed each night, enabling trucks to come and go. We will redesign the front garden, fence and path," said Laura.

"The Magnolia trees are a feature of the site. Will they be destroyed," asked Driscoll.

"We will return those trees. Our company has imported a scooping truck from the USA. Think of four large dessert spoons, facing inwards, going down into ice cream. It picks up the tree and the root ball and gets replanted. We now have the truck franchise to build these units in the UK. There's lots of interest," said Laura with a smile.

"Sounds amazing," said Driscoll.

"Let me get my tablet. I have a video of the transfer of the Magnolias. See, it's a long truck. That excavator's arm has six large spoons, sorry spades. It digs down to cut a massive root ball. It then lifts the entire tree and its root ball and takes it to another location to be replanted. Instant park!" said Laura with a big smile. "Just amazing!"

Driscoll said, "How will the local businesses respond to road closures with the church?"

You could ask them, but I have heard there is a push to close off all traffic and make it a plaza for people. This renovation may push that idea along. We now have five significant renovations similar to those in the city. But for the church, we have to go slowly now," said Laura.

Driscoll asked if he could interview the boss, Mr Milton Kahnt. "I'm sure he would love for you to profile the work on the church for you. I think it has become a passion for him. He's decided to pay for it himself."

"Really?" said Driscoll, caught off guard. "The entire renovation? Everything? That is rather expensive and generous."

Driscoll saw large framed photos of the church on the office walls, plus pictures of the other projects. "The church project won't bankrupt him?" asked Driscoll.

"I doubt it. Mr Kahnt is a smart businessman and very generous. I think St. Mary's renovation will bring more business. The Strand is ready for suitable renovation, and nobody wants a repeat of the brutal Barbican monster near St Giles, Cripplegate, do you? St. Mary-Le-Strand will shine again. The new plaza has no traffic, soot, trees, or coffee places. I can see it all," said Laura.

"That sounds great. Maybe I can interview Mr Kahnt when he's available," Driscoll said.

"He would love to chat about saving old buildings," said Laura. "Thank you for your interest. Here is our business card. Please call, and I will arrange a time for you to meet with Mr Kahnt." Laura handed him an ELB card.

Driscoll left the building and phoned Noel. "I think I'm wrong. I've just come from the ELB office. I met the office manager. There are lots of visions and projects on the go. The guy is spending money on renovating St. Mary's," said Driscoll.

"Milton Kahnt and Abu Sarek are different people who look the same. But you didn't see Mr Kahnt?" asked Noel.

"No, I didn't. I'm coming back to the office," said Driscoll.

Warren Driscoll still had a doubt. 'Is it doubt, or am I offended? Did I fail to anticipate something in the coding? I didn't code a pathway or a process when Joyce captures images of two identical or very similar-looking individuals but not twins.'

CHAPTER 57

MOSCOW RUSSIA

Ahmed hired luxury BMW cars from different rental firms in Moscow. He returned the vehicles to each rental company using the contactless key drop. However, someone had already booked the BMW X6. The detailer completed the post-hire report, which showed no damages. But when he recorded the kilometres, he was surprised to see that the car had only been driven a few kilometres during the four-month lease. He thought the digital odometer must be faulty, so he reset the GPS. However, the GPS showed that the car had been in Murmansk, meaning the odometer must have been broken.

The detailer brought the completed post-rental form to the office and told the manager there was a problem with the digital odometer reading for the BMW X6 that had been leased long-term. The manager, who seemed distracted, asked what was wrong with it. The detailer explained that the digital odometer only showed a few kilometres, but the GPS showed that the car had been in Murmansk. The manager replied that wealthy people love flashy vehicles to drive to restaurants. The detailer pointed out that the car had been in Murmansk, so the odometer must have been broken. He asked if he should order a replacement unit, but the manager didn't respond and just kept typing. The detailer put the paperwork on the returns tray and returned to his cleaning station, shrugging his shoulders.

CHAPTER 58

L ONDON

Abu sent a text message to Ahmed using the W.A.S. platform, saying, "I have a lot of work. When do you need my help?" Ahmed replied, "Keep working. I will let you know." However, Abu was unaware of the increased workload at E.R.B. due to their successful acquisition of Kloder Holding Group. They had also picked up several unfulfilled contracts and five more profitable deals. Laura, his office manager, informed him that a newspaper article on the renovation of St. Mary's was coming out soon, meaning he could expect more renovation contracts. Abu had changed his name to Milton Kahnt, which he liked. Milton had bought laundromats and a large restaurant to launder his money through these businesses, which took him two years. He renovated the laundromats, upgraded them to use EFTPOS and WiFi credit cards, and sold them. He kept the restaurant and even bought two more.

Milton's bank account doubled after he completed two projects without using laundered money. He hired a manager and a small team for each building contract to manage his workload, paying them above the award rate. However, the team enjoyed their work, the money, and the conditions, so Milton's office manager suggested that he retain all the teams, which he agreed to.

External companies were hired to handle finance, compliance, and staffing regulations, which turned out to be costly. However, Milton only cared if E.L.B. ran out of money, as it needed to run down slowly until Ahmed's mission was complete. However, the opposite occurred. He was winning more contracts because of his team's quality work. As a result, this popularity required Milton to visit multiple sites, filling his working hours. He realized that his business was growing and needed to adapt to the changing circumstances.

Despite his lack of knowledge about construction, Milton's day was brightened by supporting and motivating his teams and managers. He had a talent for listening, encouraging, smiling, and shaking hands. He made it a point to remember people's names, including details about their children and birthdays. Laura Ruby organized celebratory restaurant visits after each successful project, and Milton generously rewarded his team, workers, and sub-contractors with large bonuses. Over time, friendships developed, but so did a sense of guilt. Milton had never anticipated feeling this way about his success and friendships.

Milton lived at St. Giles Hotel on Bedford Avenue, just off Tottenham Court Road, while his office was located in the Centre Point complex on Charing Cross Road and New Oxford Street, a 15-minute walk away. At the end of his workday, he enjoyed walking along Bainbridge Street onto Bloomsbury Street to the Bedford Square Garden or Russell Square, where he would buy a takeaway meal. He was also fond of attending public lectures at nearby universities and visiting exhibitions at the British Museum.

Despite all of this, he was troubled. Milton never attended the local mosque and sensed that he was changing, even though Ahmed's mission remained unchanged. His contact with Ahmed became minimal after six years of working in London. Milton never confided in Ahmed about the internal struggle he was experiencing. He had doubts about the mission finding purpose in his work, even though it brought him satisfaction and joy. His thoughts often returned to Brighton, remembering the agitation about the indifference to faith at the converted church. Yet he loved working with his team and the people on the building sites, including gracious managers and some agnostic, Christian or from different religions. They were people he loved and considered his friends.

"I never thought this would be my life," Milton reflected on how this would happen,' wondered Milton.

Because of these incremental changes in his life, no more judging or looking down his nose at people of other faiths or no faith, he was horrified when he watched the news. U.K. Muslim brothers used knives and guns to murder strangers and pedestrians enjoying a meal or drink at night. He could not see how it benefitted Islam.

He recalled a newspaper opinion piece saying, "They want publicity, desire political change or revenge but lack the political power to enforce their desires, so they cause terror to inflict mass casualties. They seek to gain public attention." He stopped reading. The opinion piece described his old life. It was a life he didn't want anymore. He no longer wanted violence or blood lust.

Milton read of an ex-Muslim, now atheist, who was hacked to death in Bangladesh by some street Muslims. "I feel shame, how hate had filled every part of my life."

It was a painful process of questioning.

He knew if Ahmed discovered the change, he would be ostracized and rejected. Yet again, He reflected on the brutal punishments in Sharia law. The penalty for apostasy is capital punishment. 'I don't want to be part of this mad collective, Ahmed. Why do I feel guilt?"

Milton rarely worked on a Sunday but had a good afternoon finishing paperwork and was ready for a relaxing walk home. It was now dark, and he was entering Bainbridge Street, heading home. His thoughts went back to his growing indifference to any form of Islam, his increasing distance from Ahmed, and now guilt.

'What do I do with my guilt?' He was lost in thought when a shadow passed behind him. Somebody dragged him into the dark alley behind the Dominion Theatre. He attempted to break free, but the grip increased. The hand tightened over his mouth; he couldn't breathe; he slumped and lost consciousness. When he came to, he felt dazed and confused. It felt like a giant octopus had wrapped his eight arms around him and was squeezing, or a wrestler who had pinned him down and refused to let go.

"Help! Help, can anyone hear me? Help!" screamed Milton. His voice felt like gravel. The music playing in the theatre was drowning out his pathetic screams. When he stopped shouting, Milton asked, "What do you want? Who are you?"

No answer.

"I have money. Do you need money? What do you want? Are you going to kill me?" Milton was in full panic. It felt like an hour passed, minute by minute, with no response from his captor. Milton's fear was growing. 'This guy is high on some drug. Some adrenaline-heightened drug-induced strength was the only explanation. There was no other explanation. But he didn't demand money. No, this guy loves to torture.'

"I don't understand what you want. Who are you?" asked Milton again. He was confused by the silence of his captor. The music or movie was still playing. No street lights were shining into where he lay trapped. The alley was black, dark, and confusing; the only comfort was the music. It rained, then poured. Once the rain stopped, Milton lifted his eyes. There were no stars, just dark clouds. 'Death is waiting for me?' He knew it and could feel it. The scales of justice were not in his favour. A tear formed as he thought about his life, and then Milton stopped struggling. He gave up, ready for his fate. He thought of his parents and his new friends.

"What is your name?"

"What? My name?" asked Milton, now startled—the first words from this psychopath.

"My name is Milton Kahnt." He managed to slow his panic and breathing.

"Liar. What is your name?" He was now confused, weighing his options, and finally making a decision.

"My name is Milton Kahnt."

"Liar. That is not your name. There is darkness over you. Death."

"Darkness?" whispered Milton.

Milton felt his leg twist, and he felt a crack, vomited, and then fainted.

Milton awoke thirty-six hours later, post-surgery. He was confused and unable to comprehend where he was. 'There are tubes in his hand covered by tape. Why are my legs wrapped in bandages?' When he woke an hour later, food was on a table, and a doctor took details on the digital board attached to his bed.

"You are awake?" said a man in a white coat. Milton was confused and unable to speak a single word.

"You are at Portland Hospital London. Can you tell me your name?" the doctor asked.

Milton looked at him. 'My name? What is my name, liar!' He jolted.

"Okay," said the doctor. "You are safe."

Milton stared, confused and unable to understand what was happening. "They found you unconscious in an alley," said the doctor. "An ambulance brought you here this morning."

"An alley?" asked Milton.

The doctor smiled. "We operated on your thigh and broken bones. The 'Rectus Femoris' muscles, tendon or fibrous tissues, and hamstring muscles come away from your hip joint. We reattached everything. You will recover in time, and you'll have a limp, but physio will help you. I will see you again tomorrow morning. If you are in pain, see that button there; press it, and the nurses will bring medication," said the doctor.

Milton could only stare. He struggled to recall anything and then went back to sleep.

CHAPTER 59

MOSCOW RUSSIA

The text below has been reviewed and corrected for spelling, grammar, and punctuation errors and has been rewritten to improve clarity:

The medical surgeon Izak Vandabelt parked his BMW in the short-term airport parking lot. He exited the car, stretched, and dragged his suitcase and carry-on bag out of the trunk. After locking the car, he caught the courtesy bus to the Pushkin Departure terminal. He was meeting his wife in Paris for a four-day layover with their new baby daughter, and from Paris, they would return to South Africa.

Upon arriving at the airport, Izak joined the long line of passengers ready to go through the new body scanners. He placed his shoes, belt, laptop, watch, and wallet on the conveyor to be scanned. Izak was hungry and looking forward to a full breakfast with endless coffee inside the terminal precinct.

He couldn't recall the last time he had eaten; his schedule had been chaotic. After gathering his shoulder bag and personal items from the conveyor, he found a seat and dressed.

"Time for food!" the attendant at the chemical screening service ushered him over. 'Random testing is not random,' he murmured more to himself.

The officer heard his comment and swabbed his jacket, jeans, and shoulder bag. "This will not take long, sir," the officer promised.

The cotton-tipped swab was inserted into the machine and came up negative. There were no traces of explosive elements or chemicals. Then, a screeching alarm sounded. The airport screener stared at a small yellow box with a flashing red light.

"What is that?" asked Izak.

"I don't know what it is?" replied the officer. "It was not here on my last shift." The airport officer looked around, searching for his supervisor. The alarm got louder. Everybody in the screening room stopped working and stared at the two men. The security supervisor rushed from his office. He picked up the solid-state radiation detector and switched off the alarm.

"I am sorry, sir, but these new machines are now part of our screening procedure. Your clothes and your carry-on luggage appear to be giving off a particular type of ionization," said the security supervisor.

"I'm a medical surgeon, but I don't work in radiology," replied Izak.

The supervisor looked up from the machine. "Sir, the machine is showing 250 Rads. The reading is low, but it is still a concern. Have you come in contact with something radioactive?"

"Not as far as I know," replied Izak.

"Unfortunately, this may delay your trip," said the supervisor. "When is your flight, may I ask?"

Dr Vandabelt replied, "Paris in 2 hours. I was planning on having breakfast before boarding."

"Not a problem, sir. We have an on-site specialist. Please follow me," asked the security supervisor. The specialist radiation machine was a more precise instrument than the little Mickey Mouse yellow box. The supervisor is organizing the return of your checked-in luggage. I apologize for the delay," said the specialist. Ten minutes later, the luggage arrived.

"This will be over quickly," replied the specialist. "Your luggage is showing a radiation peak of only 250 Rads. Your clothes are okay, but not your shoulder bag." She had a clipboard and was taking notes. "You have come in contact with something radiating. Is that plausible?"

"I'm surprised. I use this bag constantly and have never had any problems," said Izak.

"This would be recent," said the specialist. "Something radioactive at your work?"

"No, it is not possible. Our team finished ten hours of surgery. I came here directly," said Dr Vandabelt.

"Where was your luggage during those ten hours?" she asked.

"Locked in my office," replied Izak.

"Did you come by taxi?" she asked.

"No, I used a rental car," said Izak.

"May I see the hire car contract?" she asked. The specialist recorded the details.

"Unfortunately, I must keep your luggage and clothes for our investigation," she said.

"That is not a problem," said Izak. "I can buy replacement clothes either here or in Paris."

"You can keep your passport, phone, and wallet," replied the specialist.

"I have my business cards and contact details here," said Izak, handing the card to the woman. "You can phone the hospital, or I can. But I guarantee my luggage has not come into contact with radioactive medicine. It is a separate department. It is not even in our building."

"Your return ticket is in eight weeks?" asked the specialist.

"Yes, I have surgery booked. I apologize again for causing any problems. I am confused about how this happened," said Izak.

Airport security informed the car rental company that they had confiscated the BMW for national security purposes. Izak caught his scheduled flight to Paris.

CHAPTER 60

STOCKHOLM.

They had rolled by six long weeks without any development or fresh leads. Hunter's team was disheartened and getting on each other's nerves. Hunter rebuilt his strength daily after being released from the hospital. He was pleased to be back working at the Embassy. The surgeons had performed an outstanding job, and he was satisfied with his rehabilitation. They gathered on a Monday morning after breakfast. It was week seven. They all knew they needed a fresh lead. Hunter knew other European countries were investigating. But they had nothing. Lucas also reported no new information.

"Let's review what we know," said Hunter.

Hunter glanced first at Emma. She looked at her tablet. "Wayne Scott from HQJOC Canberra says that Liv Wei from the Joint Staff Department Intelligence Bureau and Wang Li Jun from JSD Intelligence Bureau has not been absent for eight days."

"What does that mean?" asked John.

"Holidays. Jail. Dead. Wayne says he is monitoring their passports. That's it."

Hunter turned to John. "Bely, as we know, was dismissed from the investigation. He warned us about ZL. Bely said we need to watch our backs. They may shadow us and others. ZL will eliminate whoever gets to the Red Banners first. Then ZL and the Red Banners will disappear."

Emma replied, "What lazy buggers! We do the hard work, and they get all the glory, then kill us!"

Moody laughed at Emma's comment. Hunter's tablet lit up; it was Lucas.

"Good morning, Lucas," replied Hunter.

"Good morning. I just found something interesting. Weeks back, we spoke about radiation detectors in Helsinki. Do you remember? I've been reading reports. There have been twelve incidents. Some are false alarms, but I checked each incident. Anyways, one caught my eye. It happened a month ago, at Pushkin International Airport, Moscow."

"Curious," replied Emma.

"Yes. Get this. A medical Doctor triggered a dosimeter at the airport. Doctor Izak Vandabelt is a South African surgeon and a specialist who is not in radiology. He goes backwards and forwards from South Africa and Moscow," said Lucas.

"Is he dead, radiation poisoning?" asked John.

"No. The doctor's luggage was irradiated. According to the report, the radiation was minor, and only his luggage showed contamination from the boot of his hire car, a BMW X6," said Lucas.

There was silence.

"A surgeon is our driver?" asked Emma, not believing a word of it.

Lucas excitedly said, "We've got a break here, people."

"Well done, Lucas," replied Hunter. "The old guy who lived near the warehouse in Murmansk said the haulage truck had BMW vehicles."

Emma asked Hunter, "More than one?"

"More than one," replied Hunter.

Lucas said, "Dr Vandabelt said his luggage was locked in his office, and the radiology department is in another building. The Airport guys suggested the contamination may have happened at the hospital. But Dr Vandabelt dismissed that suggestion."

John said, "The removal of radioactive medicine in hospitals follows strict protocols."

Emma asked, "And the car?"

Lucas said, "Airport security and a radiation specialist spoke with the car rental company, informing them they were keeping the car for National Security reasons."

"Hunter, I'll email you the car rental phone number," said Lucas. "I don't speak Russian."

"I do! Give it to me," said Emma.

Hunter turned his tablet around so Emma could read the number. Emma pretended to be a Police detective with follow-up questions on BMW radiation contamination. She spoke for several minutes, listened, and then disconnected.

"The rental manager used some interesting swear words. He knew very little and demanded I return the car. He handed the phone to his detailer. The detailer checks the rentals for damage, cleans them and resets the GPS. He remembers the BMW very well. His words were, 'It was odd.'"

"Odd in what way?" replied Hunter.

"The rental was a four-month long-term rental. The odometer only showed the car went ten kilometres. But here's the kicker: The detailer normally deletes GPS entries from the earlier hire, ready for a fresh hire. He was curious that a four-month hire only went ten kilometres. He checked the GPS. The car was in Murmansk," said Emma. "The detailer believes either the GPS or the odometer is faulty."

"Those inbuilt GPS units, don't they send location details back to the manufacturer?" asked John. "For theft purposes."

Emma replied, "Yes, for locating a stolen vehicle. They will even start your car if you have lost your fob. If you do steal a car, they can turn it off."

She continued, "Munich affirmed the detailer story. The car had been in Murmansk, Russia. So he asked his boss to swap out the odometer. The boss said, drive around the block and see what happens. The odometer worked as did the GPS."

Hunter said, "So, the driver hires all the cars in Moscow, or at least this one. He then drives each car from the rental company to his truck. Then, he transports all of them to Murmansk and uses them to fool the mafia blokes. The driver then returns the BMWs to each Moscow rental company with only a few kilometres recorded."

"The driver unloaded the Red Banners in a warehouse in Moscow and then returned the BMWs," said Emma.

"Moscow is his target?" asked John.

"Hunter, you said the mafia blokes changed their clothes," inquired Emma. "Didn't you say they were also wearing new shoes? So, the driver collects the dead guys' contaminated clothing, puts everything into plastic bags, and then into the BMW X6 trunk. Those bags then disappear into some industrial bin. Their greed killed them."

"In what way," asked John.

Emma said, "Hey, here are new clothes, fellas. Give me those contaminated clothes. Have a shower, drink vodka, and eat these lovely poisoned buns. Here is a million dollars each and a free BMW car! They are all yours. Aren't I generous? Greed killed them. Their eye was on the money and expensive car, not the driver."

"Emma, very poetic!" said John.

"The car rental place only has CCTV behind their reception desk," said Lucas. "This company, like many, uses contactless key drop-off. We don't have a picture of his face."

"Lucas found one car, now what?" asked John.

"Hang on for a moment. Why return the vehicles? Why does the driver even bother?" Emma asked. He had money, and it's not like he cared about his credit card rating or the deposit hold."

"They don't release that hold until 24 hours after you return the car," said John. "But you're right, why bother?"

"ZL may already have caught and killed him," replied Hunter. "They also may have the Red Banners, and we would never know. Bely may not even know. We know he drove that Scania tractor-trailer haulage vehicle from Murmansk to Moscow because he returned the BMWs."

"He did it on one fuel tank, with no stops and no CCTV at a fuelling station," said John.

"24-hour straight drive," replied Lucas. "A seasoned truck driver could achieve that."

"Lucas, what name did he use for hiring the BMW?" asked Hunter.

"An Amsterdam-registered company with a sole director, Abu Sarek," replied Lucas.

"A simple search and bingo, we find him," said Emma with a tone of scepticism

"Sarek and his family died four years ago in a CIA drone attack in Bagdad," replied Lucas.

"Dead or alive, his name keeps popping up," said Hunter.

"The driver will not use his real name," replied Emma. "They must look alike if the driver uses his Sarek's ID."

"Who did the CIA drone kill?" asked John.

"Abu Sarek," said Hunter.

"Don't they verify their target before they push the missile button?" asked Emma.

"Of course they do with a 70-90% confirmation," said Hunter.

"Deception takes forethought and organization, just like our driver," said Lucas. Everyone was silent for a moment.

"So the driver has planned his mission," replied Hunter. He registered that company online with no face-to-face contact, and everything is in the dead guy's name. Lucas, can you research that Amsterdam company?"

John asked, "I will look at Abu Sarek. Background, history, contacts, friends, family and the bombing."

"John, our CIA mates, will swear black and blue that Sarek is dead," said Hunter. "There's no point. They look alike, but the driver, still unknown, will have multiple passports to bolt at any time."

"Why multiple passports?" asked John.

"He is already using Abu Sarek. Therefore, he would have other backups," replied Hunter.

After a few minutes of silence, Emma said, "Nobody answered my question. Why does the driver return the cars?"

"Because he hired them," John said with a smile.

She tilted her head and stared at John. "It makes little sense," said Emma. "Rentals involve insurance, right? Rental companies want to make more money, so they try to upsell you 'no excess' insurance. If you pay more cash, that excess drops from $4000 to $50."

John grumbled, "I'm not following."

Emma gave him a dirty look but continued, "You purchase this extra insurance to lower your excess. Such a luxury car like these BMW vehicles might have an excess of $7,000. You pay $7000 if you wreck the vehicle or if the vehicle gets stolen."

"Okay, I'm still not following," teased John.

"Keep going, Emma." Hunter gave John a look, which said stop.

"Why does he return the BMW rental? Why not dump them in a lake?" asked Emma.

"It's suspicious, the same as torching them. It attracts attention," replied Hunter.

"Okay. When I return a rental, I want that 'credit hold' removed from my credit card," declared Emma. The rental guy checks for dings in the panels. I don't want to pay any excess for any small damages. The Chinese spies gave the driver a ton of money. He could have dumped the cars, never returned them, closed the credit card, and couldn't care less. The driver returns a contaminated rental and potentially exposes his face. Why?"

"And used other rental companies for the rest," replied Lucas.

"So, the driver knows we're watching for any radiation alerts, airports, whatever," argued Emma. "So he returns a contaminated vehicle on purpose."

"It is a diversion," said Hunter.

"He wants us and ZL or anybody who is chasing him to go to Moscow and waste time searching every factory for the Red Banners," said John.

"So where is Mr Tricky Smarty Pants driver?" asked Emma.

CHAPTER 61

LONDON
Detective Carol Ian from the Albany Street Police knocked on the door frame of the hospital suite. "Hello, Milton Kahnt? I'm Detective Ian, and this is Constable Glenn Bree. Can we chat?"

"Yes, please come in," said Milton.

"Mr Kahnt, thank you for seeing us," said Detective Ian.

"Yes, of course," replied Milton. "Please, have a seat."

"We are following up on an ambulance officers report. She said, 'You appear to have been attacked or involved in a violent incident in the alley at the back of the Dominion Theatre'. Can you tell us what happened?"

"Um, I," said Milton, unable to recall a thing.

Detective Ian said, "A cleaner found you and phoned the ambulance. Our officers came to the scene. But no witnesses have come forward."

"Is that where it happened?" asked Milton.

"You don't know what happened?" asked Detective Ian.

"I'm sorry. I awoke here," replied Milton.

"Where do you work?" asked Detective Ian

"I work at Elite......" He stopped speaking and tried to finish his sentence but then felt confused. He looked embarrassed, knowing he couldn't remember.

"It's okay," Detective Ian replied. I can return when you are feeling better."

"The doctor said my memory would return, and my leg would recover. He wants me to get up and walk small steps. I'm sorry, but now I can't stop talking," said Milton, embarrassed again.

"Okay. I will leave my card. If you remember any details, please get in touch with me. Nobody wants to see another incident like this again. Get better," replied Detective Ian.

He held her business card and stared at it.

'Darkness.'

Detective Carol Ian dropped the Constable off at Albany Street Station. Then, using her phone's browser, she typed 'Elite + Dominion Theatre.'

"Okay, we have Elite Renovation Builders," said Carol. She drove to the building and caught the elevator to the 12th floor.

The ERB office was spacious, with decent views. The office manager came over to greet the visitor.

"My name is Detective Carol Ian. Do you have a worker who hasn't turned up for work?" asked the Detective.

Laura looked at the Detective, uncertain how to respond. "We have dozens of construction workers and managers on different sites across London. I would need to phone each manager to answer your question."

Carol described the man in the hospital and the incident that had happened. Laura's facial expression said it all. "You know this person?"

"Yes, he is my boss, Mr Milton Kahnt. He hasn't been here for three days. I was getting worried as he constantly texted instructions. I thought he was having a break. Is he okay? Which hospital?" asked Laura. She was almost in a panic and started to hyperventilate.

"It's okay. Take your time." Detective Ian said, "Mr Kahnt has suffered memory loss. The doctor informed me his memory would return. He will have a permanent limp. Can you fill me in on his movements from three days ago?"

Laura said, "A permanent limp." This time, she went white. "Is he okay?"

Detective Ian replied, "Yes. I asked him where he worked, and he said, 'Elite.'

Laura wasn't listening. Ian said, "It's okay. The doctors are confident of a full recovery."

"Would you excuse me for a moment," said Laura. Ian could hear her vomiting in the restroom. She returned, shaken.

"Take your time. Are these Elite's projects on the wall?" asked Detective Ian, trying to change her focus.

"Yes, St Mary-Le-Strand plus other buildings," Laura said with sadness.

"Is Mr Kahnt married? Does he have children?" asked Detective Ian.

"No. Mr Kahnt is a single man," replied Laura. The Detective walked over to the building windows and looked out, then down. "It happened there."

Laura came over and stood beside her. "Where?"

"He was found in that alley towards the back. An office cleaner found Mr Kahnt laying on the ground in the dark three days ago around five o'clock in the morning. No wallet, watch, money or phone."

"No. Mr Kahnt's wallet, watch, money, and phone are in his office. Mr Kahnt often walks home with nothing. I have always assumed he had duplicates at home," said Laura.

"Where does he live?" asked Detective Ian.

"St. Giles Hotel. Mr Kahnt has a small unit. On the way home, he regularly goes to the Museum or the university to read or enjoy guest lecturers," said Laura. "That's how he relaxes after work. He likes to walk the parks before he reaches his unit," said Laura.

"Has anyone made threats?" asked Detective Ian.

"Threats? No," replied Laura.

"These renovations you are doing, have there been any union problems, sackings or bribery, or walk-offs?" asked Detective Ian.

"Not as far as I know. We meet each week, and all issues are discussed," replied Laura.

"If there were threats, would you know? Would Mr Kahnt know?" asked Detective Ian.

"I would assume they would speak with Mr Kahnt. I am the office manager. I bring all issues to him. He raises all issues at the team meeting. I can ask the site managers if there have been some threats they have not reported," replied Laura.

"No, that's okay if I could have their contacts. Best if I do that," said Detective Ian.

"Do you have an email?" asked Laura.

"My card. Forward the contacts to that email," asked Detective Ian. "If you recall any suspicious contacts or characters, please let me know."

"Okay. I might lock the office and go to the hospital. Detective, do you think the attack was intentional or random?" asked Laura.

"Good question. At this point, I don't know. Perhaps when Mr Kahnt's memory returns, we will have a better idea. Will you be okay?" asked Detective Ian.

"Yes. I will lock up here now and go to the hospital," said Laura.

"Do you need a lift?" asked Detective Ian.

"That would be very kind. Thanks," replied Laura.

Laura Ruby arrived at the hospital and inquired at reception about Milton Kahnt. She stopped and turned back to the receptionist and asked, "Will the nurse's station give me an update on his condition? He is my boss. There are no other family members," said Laura.

"Ask them. You'll be fine," said the receptionist.

"Thanks," said Laura.

She approached the nurse's station, introduced herself, and got the same story Detective Ian had given her. She knocked on the open door and peeked to see if he was okay. He smiled and waved her in.

"Mr Kahnt, I only found out what happened! Are you okay?" said Laura.

"I'm okay, I think. Are you a doctor?" asked Milton.

It was a little awkward as Laura scanned the room, which was void of flowers and other personal things. "Mr Kahnt, I am your office manager, Laura Ruby."

"Right, very good," replied Milton. "Sorry, my memory. They said it would come back in time."

"Detective Ian came to the office and showed me where the attack happened," said Laura. "She said they had no leads. Do you remember what happened?"

"I have the Detective's card," replied Milton. The Detective asked me to contact her if I remember anything," said Milton. "I've tried to remember, but I can't."

"What about clothes?" asked Laura. "I can buy you a fresh set."

"Thank you," said Milton.

"So sorry to hear what happened to you. I'll be back within the hour," said Laura.

Milton smiled as she left. He did remember something, a single word: darkness.

CHAPTER 62

France 1 Year Later.

The Chunnel is a 31-mile railway tunnel that connects Folkestone, Kent, in the UK, with Coquelles in France. It runs beneath the English Channel at the Strait of Dover.

Ahmed was exhausted and approached the congestion of trucks for the Channel crossing, but was met with a hundreds of stationary tractor-trailers. He climbed out of his rig, pulled his cap on low, and strolled over to a group of drivers. One driver acknowledged Ahmed with a slight nod and said, "This place is in crisis, mate."

"A couple of hundred migrants have tried to enter the tunnel on foot! Some have died inside the tunnel. It's tragic madness, mate. The place is crawling with French authorities and Eurotunnel personnel," said the British driver.

Ahmed asked, "Police?"

"Yeah. Reckon, there are two hundred Police on the demolished boundary fence," replied the British driver.

Another driver said, "They're setting up lights. They're looking for migrants holding on for dear life under the rigs."

The Pas de Calais had ordered the floodlights so immigration agents could alert the Police if migrants were trying to jump onto their trucks. A French police officer walked down and handed a slip of paper to each driver in the group. In broken English, the officer said, "If you see a migrant running to your truck, sound your horn. Ring this number. We'll come."

Finally, at 3 am, after 12 hours of waiting, the 59 Eurotunnel shuttle wagons filled with tractor-trailers restarted their Folkestone journey. Ahmed joined a group of drivers in the lorry drivers' club car for a meal. At Calais, Ahmed looked out the window, smiled, and turned to order his meal. He had a map in front of him while he waited for his dinner.

'I'll start from Folkestone, take the M20 through Maidstone, and maybe get off to avoid as many traffic cameras as possible. Then, the A2, then the A282 to Romford. Maybe stop for coffee and check surveillance. Head back to Alfred's Way, then to Newham Way, followed by India Dock Road, which joins Commercial Road to A11 to a large storage facility in Dagenham. That seems like an okay route,' thought Ahmed. His meal arrived.

CHAPTER 63

STOCKHOLM
Jessica Von Berg summoned the team to the Australian Embassy for a chat. The Embassy staff set up light refreshments.

John leaned over to Hunter. "I've been in these chat meetings before. They are friendly at first, and then they sack you."

"A politician butts into the mission," replied Hunter. "But don't worry."

John stood and poured himself a cup of percolated coffee. "Why are we here?" asked John, looking at Jessica.

"Give me a minute. We're waiting for Karen and Lucas to come online," replied Jessica. John looked at Hunter with a look that said, 'I told you.'

There were two 85-inch LED UHD TVs attached to the wall. One came alive with Karen and Lucas. Karen's face said everything. Hunter knew what was going to happen. He picked up his empty cup of coffee, walked over to the coffee urn, and refilled his mug. Hunter stirred in sugar and cream, stepped three feet to his left, and leaned against the wall. John watched and was ready.

The second 85-inch LED UHD TV showed the 'Director of the ASIS emblem.' The live streaming came up with Gideon Downer's face. There was a twenty-second lag time. Right then, the Embassy fire alarms came on, followed by the electronic whoop, whoop. Speakers in the ceiling announced: "Evacuate, Evacuate, this is not a drill."

It kept repeating the phrase, followed by the ear-shattering whoop-whoop alarm. The air conditioning and electricity were switched off. The battery-operated emergency exit signs and small emergency LED ceiling lights came on.

John was on his feet, shouting, "Move it! Let's go, people, move, move!"

People were pouring out of the building.

The Australian Army management division serves in Australian embassies around the world. Within seconds, they appeared, weapons live. They carried their protectee, Jessica Von Berg, out of the building. Hunter left the room last and lifted the alarm lever back to the off position.

The Embassy fire warden stood ten meters outside the exit doors. He used a bullhorn to perform a headcount and asked everybody to step back and allow the Swedish Fire Services to enter the building.

Hunter turned to the group and said, "I suggest we leave for the hotel now."

Nobody noticed them leaving except Jessica Von Berg, who smiled and returned to the building to wait for the all-clear.

Emma said as they walked, "There was no smoke."

John replied, "The fire probably is in the basement, or maybe it was an electrical fault."

Back at the Hotel, Hunter opened his tablet and brought Karen and Lucas back online. "Okay, let's update each other, John. You go first," said Hunter.

"Abu Sarek had a reputation as a jihadist warrior. He speaks five languages. Lots of talk regarding his missions, him being present but never seen. He blew things up in churches, government buildings, and a police station. They were all empty every time. He didn't kill any local people. They had a plan to destabilize the government and form their own Islamic State," said John. 'That is the rumour."

Hunter said, "Was this the start of ISIL?"

John replied, "That is possible. One mission goes pear-shaped. Sarek's team suffered injuries, as did the US Coalition forces. The coalition captured his team. Sarek got away. Later, he steals C-4 from the CIA arms bunker, blows up Abu Ghraib, gets his team back plus others, and the US coalition places one million USD reward online for his capture."

Emma muttered, "Five languages? A well-educated bloke."

"It's only a rumour," replied John. "A tip comes in with his photo and prior unknown mission details. The reward goes to an overseas account. One drone verifies Sarek's identity outside the family home based on the picture supplied for the bounty. The other drone wipes him out."

Hunter asked, "Where is that picture?"

John stretched and said, "Good question. Nobody knows. But one more thing. We might have his fingerprints, just partials, though, and in poor condition."

Emma asked, "But he's dead. Why do we need his fingerprints? Oh. Right then! He's not dead. It was a setup. Goodbye, one million dollars. Jihadists now have overseas banking accounts in the Bahamas?"

Karen asked, "John Moody, is the Au Sarek dead or alive?" John thought his mother was in the room, hands on her hips, accusing him of something, using his full name with that tone.

John lifted his eyebrows. "The army said it was 100% Sarek, and he is 100% dead. What else would they say? But I also have something else. I have an old ASIS buddy who is almost retired in Bagdad. He looks and acts like a local and hangs around cafes and places to pick up gossip and whatever from his paid informants. He observed an exchange of money in one café. He said the exchange was odd, different. It drew his attention. At the time, there was no connection to Abu Sarek," said John.

Emma says, "No connection at all?"

John continued, "He follows the guy who returns the money to his place. It turns out it is a factory with attached accommodation and a kitchen. He installs a camera across the street to try to capture a face. No luck; he breaks into the factory to work out who the guy is. The factory has the machinery to make stuff. But he sees two separate used beds. He thinks nobody is home, but he is wrong. There were two empty glasses on the kitchen sink. He grabs them, looks up and sees CCTV."

"He blew it?" asked Emma.

"He immediately leaves through the back door. He couldn't email a report. Halfway up the alley, he's knocked to the ground. The factory was pre-wired to blow up with the same stolen C-4. He is now totally deaf from the explosion and has suffered extensive burns in his body," said John.

"Where is he now?" asked Emma.

"Before being shipped to Germany for skin grafts, he gave a report. It was the same C-4 with the same signature as the bombing at the prison. The army investigation team found an escape tunnel leading from the factory to another property. The secondary explosion was deafening. The factory had surface-to-air missiles, weapons, mines, and the army found shredded Kevlar vests and other stolen bits and pieces."

Hunter asked, "Kevlar vests? That is interesting."

"Yes, bits of them torn apart by the explosives," replied John. "Potts says he had partials of Abu Sarek, but the drinking glasses got lost somehow in the explosion. Anyway, Potts says there are two people, not one. There were also books with the guts hollowed out."

"Money in gutted books," said Emma. "Smart bloke."

"When you pre-wire your factory with C4, that says, 'I was expecting you, but you will die and never catch me,'" said Hunter. He is organized. It makes sense. The driver steals the 'Red Banners' to the final destination. Mr Dead Sarek is at that location and ready to receive the 'Red Banners'. Two people."

Emma smiled.

"Hunter, I agree with you, but their relationship has gone sour," said Lucas. "Sarek is the sole director of the Amsterdam company. The driver is Sarek, plus there is another person. Right?"

"The driver is using Sarek's name," said Emma. "He has portrayed Sarek as dead. The driver is someone else who slept in the bed."

"Roughly, 10 million Euros appears to have been washed into the

Amsterdam company bank account over 36 months from six different banks," said Lucas. "That is a feat in itself. The deposit descriptions on the company's bank account show six opaque cash business operations with regular deposits of different amounts at each of the six banks, several times a week."

Hunter calculated, "One bank three deposits a week would total $15,000."

Lucas continued. "Varying amounts. But another $10 million was deposited directly into the company account from a Lithuanian Bank. That bank no longer exists because a Russian investment bank set up a financial network to help their clients move money out of the country, and it just got busted."

"Lucky, the driver, got his money out," said Emma.

"Lucas, you said the deposits were always in varying amounts? How many Casinos are in Amsterdam?" asked John.

"Nine. I thought of that. Camera footage is available, but we don't have a face. But to answer your question directly, numerous checks from casinos show up in the deposits," replied Lucas.

"How does he do that?" asked Emma.

"The driver buys his chips, plays for a short time, and then cashes in his chips. He gets a check and receipts to claim gambling winnings. It's standard," said Lucas.

"Any CCTV? I assume the driver only used bank deposit machines?" asked Emma.

"He only used ATMs. I checked the cameras at all the deposit sites. I can't be sure, but his head is always down in heavy disguise, and deposits are made at night after hours. No face. Mind you, there may be other people making deposits and not being the driver," said Lucas.

"You said three times a week at each bank," asked Hunter.

"Yes, and I observed him rotating clothes weekly," said Lucas. "He is a man of disguises. No, luck there. I have an approximate height of only six feet. The Amsterdam company account is now empty, and based on the bank statements and the size of the purchases, I believe the ferries, trucks, and cars were hired or purchased through this account. He spent fifteen million USD, leaving fifty million for the next stage. This is all the driver's work, and I expect Sarek doesn't know his name appears over every transaction," said Lucas.

"Sorry, can we clarify a few things, please? Sarek is not dead. The driver is not Abu Sarek but is using Sarek's name. Therefore, the driver is someone else, and the name is unknown," asked Emma.

Hunter replied, "Correct, as far as we know. Either way, we are dealing with two people, and one is setting up the other to be the fall guy."

"I have a question," asked John. "The money didn't go directly to Murmansk but to Amsterdam. Why does the driver need so much money?"

Lucas interrupted and said, "Sorry, John—one more thing. I hacked into the Russian Motor registry before and after the timeframe when the driver returned the BMWs. I wondered if the driver registered or transferred a vehicle registration to another truck under the Amsterdam company name. Nothing showed. He may have bought a truck with cash, not registered it yet, or stole it."

"John, the driver, will pocket 80% of the 70 million," replied Emma. "He has two 'Red Banners.' That says to me, two locations. You are correct. It is too much money to position two nukes unless he buys two expensive tall buildings to increase the blast potential."

"Two locations. This gets worse by the hour," replied John.

"They would need to be strategic buildings," said Hunter. "The driver either just wants to kill people or kill certain people. Therefore, the buildings are in a particular location and are expensive."

Another question pushed its way through the crowd and stood in front of Hunter. Hunter closed his eyes for a moment. "Lucas, I have a question about email and browser searching," Hunter said.

"Fire away," replied Lucas.

"Let's say I type 'Abu Sarek' into my browser. That entry will stay in my computer search history. Is that right?" asked Hunter.

"Yes," replied Lucas. "It can stay, or you can clear your entire search history."

"Good. Does my browser data centre keep my search data?" asked Hunter.

"Yes, by default," replied Lucas. "But you can set a limit of either three or 18 months. What you watch, read or search works together to help you get things done more efficiently. Oh! I'm with you. Great idea! I should have thought of that!"

Hunter said, "So, is it possible?"

Lucas smiled and said, "Yes. It is called 'Dorking.' Locating a specific text string with 'Abu Sarek.' Dorking is a challenge. I'll need Wayne's help."

Hunter smiled and said, "Right, 'Dorking.' I'll leave that with you, then."

CHAPTER 64

ONDON

Milton's physiotherapy restored his mobility and well-being. The pain and swelling had reduced, and he was finally glad to leave the hospital. He hoped the walking stick was temporary. He thanked the nursing staff for their care. Laura Ruby had purchased an entire set of clothing for him to wear to return to work. She placed the clothes on his bed.

"Hopefully, I got the right sizes. In this bag are a shaver, cologne, hairbrush and underwear," said Laura.

"This is very stylish. You have a good eye for fashion. Thank you for doing this for me. You are most kind," said Milton.

"I will go and get two coffees. You can shower, shave, and get dressed. Say, thirty minutes?" Laura asked.

"Thirty minutes. Thanks again," replied Milton.

She returned the coffee to the room and waited for Milton to finish. "Before your accident, you said you wanted to go to each construction site. I have arranged times with each site manager. But before that, I have also made an appointment for you at the hairdresser," said Laura.

Milton smiled at her thoughtfulness, touched his hair, realizing it had grown, and then wiped a tear away. He felt disorientated and confused by her kindness. "Thanks. I never thought I would recover. Laura, you have been such an encouragement to me. Shall we go?"

"Coffee first?" asked Laura.

As they strolled out of the hospital room to the lift, Laura said, "I hope you don't mind, but I asked your hotel manager to replace the expired food in your refrigerator, and tonight, some frozen meals are ready. I apologize; I should have asked your permission to enter your unit. I hope you don't mind."

"Laura, you have treated me so well," replied Milton. All his memories had returned, but some dark spots nibbled away in his mind. Milton was not concerned about his passports, cash, credit cards and 'WAS' phone, as they were in his locked safe. Then he wondered if Ahmed had sent a text. Immediately, Ahmed's plan washed over him, bringing darkness and death. Then he smiled at Laura and waved goodbye to some hospital staff who had cared for him.

He was conflicted.

The site managers were glad to see Milton and embarrassed about the attack, but Milton waved that off. "It is what it is," said Milton with a genuine smile. They saw the walking stick and the limp, knowing Milton was trying to hide his disability. All the building projects and renovations were progressing exceptionally well. Again, Milton thanked all the site managers for doing a magnificent job and then shook hands with some of the workers he now knew by name. He was pleased that he could recall their names. That surprised him and delighted him.

"How is your family? How are the kids?" asked Milton, always genuinely interested in them. 'I even remember their names.' For every worker who had children, he gave them fifty pounds and said, "This is for your children, not you," then laughed after patting them on the back. Internally, Milton felt like a piece of clothing caught in a washing machine. Doubts and beliefs are being tossed around in his mind. He thought he was facing a new start, but the past had a firm grip on his heart.

'I had a strong faith, or was I just a violent, unknowledgeable arrogant man?' thought Milton. "I was violent." He looked up at the construction site with scaffolding holding things together.

'My faith now feels like a skeleton. It lacks love and meaning, a future, and joy. It pulls down. All I saw was hate, and I was full of hate. Hate invited me to its house, and I became an angry, ignorant man.

'Why do I feel so conflicted? Ahmed, my brother, and my darkness,' thought Milton.

His thoughts scrambled as he looked up at the sun's warmth and savoured the light on his face. Closing his eyes, Milton began to topple and fell over.

Laura raced over. "Are you okay? You were talking to yourself." She and a manager helped him to stand. He opened his eyes. "Laura, you have been so kind. Do you have time to drop me off at my unit? I probably need to rest," said Milton.

When he returned to the unit, he locked the door and made himself a cup of tea. He moved the small table and chair to the large glass windows, then sat and drank his tea. He sat for hours gazing at the safe, then back at the view.

He felt the warmth of the setting sun on his face, 'I am blessed.' He looked at the view but felt a demon in the safe, waiting for him.

CHAPTER 65

STOCKHOLM

Hunter turned to John, "I need to stretch my interest?"

They left the hotel through the front entrance and began a medium-paced walk down the street.

"I am hoping Lucas will generate a lead with his 'Dorking.' We need a fresh lead soon," said Hunter.

"Hey, we know more today than we did a few weeks back," said John.

"True. We know how the 'Red Banners' were stolen. We know how they laundered the money to pay for everything. We know about the BMW's. We now know there are two people," replied Hunter. "But we don't know the target or the time frame."

"What's bugging you, Hunter?" asked John.

"I can't put my finger on it. It's not the leftover $50 million that's bugging me. If I steal a bomb, I want it to blow something sky-high. But these blokes are waiting. They have an extended time frame. What that says to me is they have a date and a location in the future," said Hunter.

"Like the Olympics or the G7," replied John. "You're thinking of a specific event with a date and time?"

"Yes. The driver has hidden the 'Red Banners.' He may have already bought a building. That requires starting a business, dealing with a bank, and dealing with real estate agents," replied Hunter. I mean, he could own a building in Paris or Washington DC for $50 million, put a 'Red Banner' on top, and wait for Bastille Day or Memorial Day."

"That is a lot of money to blow up," replied John.

They kept walking until they found a café where they could order food and decent coffee. "Did you notice somebody followed us?" whispered Hunter as he drank his coffee.

CHAPTER 66

ONDON

Milton opened his digital safe and retrieved the 'WAS' phone, and started texting. He typed, "I've been in the hospital. It took weeks to recover." He looked up and placed the phone on the table, then heated up a frozen meal Laura had organized. He thought about what he wanted to say to Ahmed. He knew that Ahmed might want to talk face-to-face, but that was risky, and they had discussed that scenario several times. He glanced at the phone again, which connected him to his old life, a life he did not want, a life he now hated.

Milton had experienced the American interrogation techniques in Abu Ghraib. The idea was to keep everything separate and never to know what the other person was doing or where they lived. Ahmed said texting on the 'WAS' phone would be their only communication. He picked up the 'WAS' phone again, found some alloy foil, wrapped it around the cell phone several times, returned it to the safe and locked it.

"Getting paranoid? Definitely," mumbled Milton. "Next, I'll be wearing an aluminum hat!" He laughed at his silly joke.

The balcony was small but offered a decent view. While in the hospital, Milton had read a newspaper report about the Metropolitan Police Service raiding numerous criminal organizations and seizing over fourteen million pounds in cash. The Police had worked with a European Crime Agency. The ECA had informed UK Police that crime syndicates used encrypted communication phone software called Endochat. Like 'WAS,' Endochat was an impenetrable secure communication network used by over 1,900 London-based criminals until the ECA dismantled it.

Detectives had monitored hundreds of the handsets and analyzed thousands of encrypted messages to build dozens of cases for arrest and court. Previously unknown crime figures who thought they were untouchable and beyond the Police's reach were arrested and jailed.

Milton thought momentarily, 'Can the 'WAS' system be dismantled?

The answer was simple. "Yes."

CHAPTER 67

STOCKHOLM

Sweden time is 9:00 hours behind Sydney. Karen organized an 8 am morning briefing. "Good morning, everyone. I have some news. First, Hunter, how is your recovery?"

"Good, better day by day," replied Hunter.

"Okay. Updates?" asked Karen.

"There are two people, the driver and Abu Sarek," said Hunter. We don't believe Sarek died in the drone attack. The driver is using Abu Sarek's name and did the Amsterdam money and the Murmansk job. Sarek may not know that the driver is using his name everywhere. We are thinking now, that Sarek is in place to receive the 'Red Banners', but we don't know where. The driver has a long time frame, so he is looking at a date or an event. Finally, yesterday, somebody was following John and me. We lost them before we returned to our hotel."

"ZL?" asked Karen.

"Yes," said Hunter. "I expect so."

John said, "The driver took a long time to wash the money in Amsterdam, and the way they did it says to me that they are not in a rush. They have settled in, blended in, and are preparing for their next move. Nothing sudden. It was all thought through, step by step, well planned."

Hunter continued, "They are waiting for a significant event."

"Like a grand football final," Karen asked.

Lucas interrupted the conversation. "Excuse me, Karen; Hunter asked me to do some 'Dorking.'" Lucas waited without saying anything further.

Emma rolled her eyes, and John saw it and smiled. "Okay, I'll bite. What is 'Dorking' again, Lucas?" asked Emma.

Lucas said, "Okay, your laptop browser keeps your browsing history. Right? So, let's say you search for the name 'Abu Sarek.' Those two words, 'Abu Sarek,' will stay in your browser PC history and also remain on a server in a data centre. Dorking is hacking into the data centre, typically to find security holes. You can also do a search string that uses an advanced search query to find information."

"Lucas, to the point, please," Emma pleaded.

"Before I got kicked off the server," said Lucas. "As I said, I did a string search for 'Abu Sarek.' Bingo. Everybody! Hello!"

Emma scowled and shouted, "Lucas!"

Lucas, now deflated, said, "Probably a home PC or cell phone: unprotected IP, no VPN scrambler. Mr. Alan James searched for the name Abu Sarek. Alan James lives in London and works for MI5."

"Why would he do that search privately?" asked Hunter.

"Beats me!" replied Lucas.

"Lucas, when did he do this search?" asked John.

"Three years ago," replied Lucas.

"What?" replied John.

"That is a possible scenario," said Emma. The driver sent Sarek to the UK three or four years ago to settle in and get a job. Sarek comes in on a new passport and a new, different name, like Bob Jones. The driver steals the 'Red Banners' and is waiting for the day."

"What he posts them to London?" replied John. "Just because an MI5 agent in the UK does a digital search on Sarek doesn't necessarily mean Sarek is in the UK," replied John. "We would need to know why he did the search."

"Okay. Why is MI5 interested in Sarek? Sorry, why is James searching for his name privately?" asked Emma. "Privately, John."

"Okay, correct. It feels odd to search unprotected from home," replied John. "He doesn't trust his MI5 mates or something."

Lucas said, "I tagged Alan James' phone just to be on the safe side. He received a text a few days ago saying, 'Green-tree to orange box.' I followed the text back to Igor Medkov."

There was silence.

"Really," replied Emma.

"Now that is interesting," replied Hunter. "Igor Medkov, the handler, an action code of some sort and an MI5 traitor, who searches for our boy Sarek."

Karen came back on. "I suggest you guys pack and fly out today. 'Five Eyes' will get you in."

"We finally have a new lead," said John. "Well done, Lucas!"

Emma turned to John and asked, "Five Eyes?"

"It is an intelligence alliance of Canada, New Zealand, the USA, the UK, and us. It is a multilateral agreement of cooperation in signal intelligence. It's essentially an espionage alliance. We share intelligence," said John.

"Does everybody shares?" asked Emma.

"I guess we will find out!" replied John.

CHAPTER 68

ONDON

Igor Medkov received a text from Aleksandr Izvestia from Stockholm. "Red Banners most likely are in London. ASIS team is leaving for London today."

Aleksandr was a Russian undercover agent working for Sarskilda Skyddsgruppen or SSG. He had agents watching Hunter, Moody and Smirnov. Izvestia's phone pinged, 'Enjoy your holiday in London.'

Medkov sent a text. One text went to Assistant Commissioner Mitch Burleigh at the UK National Counter Terrorism Security Office. The second text went to an MI5 agent.

The message read, "Pick up the orange box for the orange house."

Burleigh had thick black hair, olive-toned skin, and blue eyes. He was fit and handsome. His international travels included attending counterterrorism seminars run by ex-FBI specialists. The workshops were certified and attached to an American University, where accrued seminar units contributed to a Master's degree. Burleigh graduated that evening with colleagues. Later that night, he met his handler. Burleigh was born in Russia, educated in Pakistan, and worked in the UK police force.

Mitch Burleigh deleted the message and signed off for the day. He took the stairwell down to the car park, badged his car out through security, and drove to York Road Station, one of the 49 abandoned London Tube Stations. York Road Station is north of King's Cross St Pancras. It was closed in 1932. Local politicians tried to reopen it but failed due to the cost, and it would add journey time to the Piccadilly Line.

Burleigh was in his black uniform when he approached the disused underground tube station entrance. 'Somebody changed the locks,' he said.

He picked up the lock and entered the station entrance. Burleigh saw construction equipment, scaffolding, bags of concrete, and stacked boxes of tiles.

'The place has been sold.'

Burleigh heard no sounds or movement. He switched on the master fuse in the electrical switchboard panel. The lights for the stairway down the platform all came on. His storage room was at the end of the station platform. Burleigh stared at the steel door. The lock was gone, and the space was empty. He retraced his steps and exited the Station. He saw that the second red door had an attached sign, 'Elite Renovation Builders. Three unique modern underground apartments for sale. Enquire now at ERB.com.'

He sat in his car. "ERB found my weapons." He wondered if ERB called the Police or kept them. Burleigh opened his glove box, found his torch, and went back. He examined the door. Burleigh opened the door and peered into the darkness, shining the torchlight on a contact sensor. "Got you." The wires triggered an infrared camera. The camera was hard-wired into an electric switch, and Burleigh was back-lit by the platform lighting.

'Who is watching?' thought Burleigh. "That camera only records a person entering the room," said Burleigh. "I would place a second camera outside." He turned and saw the second larger camera. Burleigh thought, 'I'm wearing a Counterterrorism uniform. Somebody has seen my face twice.

He walked up to the camera, pulled out his Counterterrorism credentials, and placed them in front of it. He was now convinced ERB had called the local Police. The National Crime Agency (NCA) installed the cameras, removed the weapons, and deactivated the guns. Then, the National Ballistics Intelligence Service (NABIS) generated a record of the guns.

Burleigh's counterterrorism officers would have witnessed the disposal and recycling of metal parts at a local incinerator while wooden gun parts burnt. "Damn!"

He held up his cell phone to the camera, showing his number. Burleigh's phone rang. A senior officer from the NCA called, and Burleigh identified himself and explained, in no uncertain terms, that the NCA had ruined a 12-month undercover counterterrorism operation.

Burleigh had a backup plan to get new weapons to the safe house.

CHAPTER 69

MI5 THAMES HOUSE

Alan James received a text message from MI5's IT division at Thames House, London. "Green Tree to Orange Box to the Orange House." Alan James left Thames House by car and drove the 20 miles to Rodling Valley, off High Road, Chigwell, Essex.

The UK Government sold the disused WMO Nuclear bunker decades ago. James had renovated it into a home financed by an intermediary and an unknown ex-Russian billionaire. He retrieved a cache of weapons, loaded them into the boot of his car, drove to a safe house called 'Orange Box,' and then returned to his office.

Hunter, John and Emma arrived at Heathrow in the ASIS Gulfstream. The Australian Embassy driver dropped them off at a safe house near Euston Station. A five-member ZL kill team flew together on a budget airline from Lisbon to Gatwick. Joyce watched and filmed every flight and every passenger, sorting, recording, and analyzing.

Two men from the Lisbon flight triggered an alarm at Warren Driscoll's desk.

AI Joyce based the warning on comparing the picture taken at the airport and an online newspaper report. Driscoll adjusted the coding to record a periocular recognition of the eyes and eyebrows whenever Joyce triggered an alert.

Driscoll opened the app and read, then watched what Joyce had collated. Joyce identified the two men as Russian intelligence officers from photos taken in Montenegro. Joyce pulled up newspaper articles and intelligence reports, stating both were from Moscow's 171st Special Purpose Intelligence Centre.

Warren called Noel Adams and his boss, Alan James, over to his desk. "We have two Russian agents, either former GRU or from Unit 29556. They arrived from Lisbon at Gatwick. Joyce has matched them and their history."

"Put those images up on the screen," asked Alan.

Noel turned to Alan and asked, "Is something happening?"

Driscoll replied without waiting for Alan to answer, "This could be a ZL kill team."

"ZL doesn't exist. Only two? Any other names?" asked Alan.

"Joyce only found two. Do you think there are others?" wondered Driscoll.

"Push those details to my tablet. I'll go upstairs," motioned James.

Alan James went upstairs to the operations room, went to the operations manager, and then returned downstairs. "Upstairs needs names and their final destination," replied James.

"Let's see where they go," said Driscoll. He gave Joyce access to Government CCTV cameras, switched off her airport filming and processing, coded in the two men's periocular recognition and told Joyce to follow. "They hired a car, and three more joined them. See how they walk. No question, they are soldiers."

"Can Joyce record the three other faces?" asked Alan James

"Yes, of course. Their names will come up in a minute. Joyce is also accessing CCTV anticipating their route," said Driscoll. "Here are the names. We have passports but no history."

The five ZL agents drove to an Orange Bravo safe house. Orange Bravo was a Russian safe house. The Russian sleeper agents had delivered weapons as instructed by Medkov.

Noel and Driscoll were looking at the LED TV screen. "We have five names. Two Unit 29556 guys and three unknown recruits. At Gatwick, they hired a car, and Joyce followed them to a Russian safe house, the third house on the left," said Driscoll.

"Can you get any closer," asked Noel. "Get the address."

"Got it! The street address is on the screen," said Driscoll, turning to look at Alan.

"Counterterrorism needs to scoop these guys up, now," replied Noel, looking to Alan.

"This is an upstairs area of responsibility," replied Alan. Driscoll noticed he left without his tablet. Alan went upstairs again, and as he walked up to the operations floor, he sent a one-word text, "Zoo 2."

"Look at that, Noel," said Driscoll. "All five agents just abandoned the house. They have their gear and are leaving at speed. Joyce followed the vehicle street by street until they arrived at an underground car park attached to a shopping centre.

"Did we lose them?" asked Noel.

"They're dumping the hire rental, for sure," replied Driscoll. "The shopping centre has too many exits. They won't steal a late-model vehicle. They are impossible to hot-wire."

"Have you tried?" asked Noel

"What, no! I read about it. Only one exit has CCTV. They're gone," replied Driscoll. I'll keep Joyce on the car lot and surrounding streets. Counterterrorism needs this new address."

"That shopping centre, they will not be happy with Counterterrorism running around!" said Noel. "They arrived at that safe house and then shot through. What happened?" asked Noel.

"Good question. There's only one answer," said Driscoll. "They got spooked. Something was not right." Driscoll asked Noel, "Can you do a property search on the house? The owner, company or who is leasing it? Okay. I'll be back in a minute."

Warren Driscoll looked over to Alan's empty office. "Noel, I'm going upstairs to update the boss."

Driscoll climbed the stairs to the next floor, saw Ric the Drummer, and walked to his desk.

"Hey Ric, have you seen Alan?" asked Driscoll.

"Alan hasn't been here," replied Ric.

"Thanks," said Driscoll. He returned to his desk. An hour later, Alan

James returned to his office. Warren walked over, tapped the door frame and said, "They left the house, and we lost them at a shopping centre underground car lot. Noel researched the house. It has links to a Russian billionaire. We can help you toss the place, boss."

"Okay, thanks. There is no need; Warren upstairs will take care of it." Alan stood again to go upstairs.

"Alan, it's the Two Rivers Shopping Mall, Staines-upon-Thames. The rental was a red Mercedes E-class vehicle."

Alan said, "Yeah, thanks."

Driscoll thought, 'He didn't ask which shopping centre. He is in a panic.'

Alan returned later and told Noel and Driscoll, "Upstairs has the case. I want you both to go back to your other work." He returned to his office.

"Noel, do you want a coffee?" asked Driscoll.

"Sure, thanks," said Noel. Driscoll went upstairs, and Ric repeated his no-show answer. He caught the lift to the ground floor cafe and returned with the coffee.

Driscoll sat with Noel, "Here is your coffee." They both sat and drank. "Alan didn't go upstairs twice. He didn't pass the intelligence on. I told Alan about the Russian safe house. The next minute, that ZL 'kill team' left fast. Guess who alerted them?" Driscoll nodded his head towards Alan's office.

Noel whispered, "Come on, Warren. Is the boss a Russian spy? You're mad!"

Driscoll whispered, "Ric the Drummer told me that Alan did not come up to see the boss. Ric hasn't seen Alan at all today. We need to go to the Director-General."

"And rat on our boss?" replied Noel, looking around, now worried.

"No. Alan is the rat," replied Driscoll. "They are a Russian kill team, and our boss phoned them and told them to run. Alan is a sleeper agent. Let's go. We go to the boss first, then the shopping centre parking lot."

"After we speak to the boss, how food? Get some takeaway," asked Noel. Driscoll rolled his eyes. They ate as Driscoll drove.

"You're making a complete mess of my car." Arriving at the shopping centre park, Driscoll asked, "Can you see any Police vehicles? Interesting, I gave Alan the address and look, no Police."

"We should phone them," replied Noel, now close to panic.

"We need proof that Alan didn't instruct upstairs to send a team," said Driscoll. "Proof that he phoned that ZL team."

They entered the shopping centre car lot, looking for the abandoned red Mercedes. "What a stupid car to hire. It stands out like a pimple on your nose," said Noel. "Go down to the bottom level. That's what they do in the movies. Somewhere in a darker area. Can we make this fast and then leave?"

"Okay, down to the dungeon," said Driscoll.

"I don't want to meet any ZL people," murmured Noel. They arrived in the parking lot's basement. I can't see any cars. If our boss isn't a Russian mole, you and I are in deep yoghurt. Look, over there in the corner. It's a red Mercedes. Stop the car, Warren."

They were at least twenty meters from the only car in the basement. "There is no police barricade tape and no Russian spies. Noel, phone the Police, identify yourself, and ask for a forensic team," said Driscoll. You'll need to go up the lift to get a signal."

It took two hours before a Metropolitan Police forensic scientist arrived. She got out of her car. "Who are you guys?" they asked, holding up their IDs. "I'm Rachel from Victoria Embankment Police Station."

Warren smiled, "I'm Warren; this is Noel. We're from the MI5 IT section, Thames House."

She looked at them. "Why are two computer guys here?"

Noel piped in, "Everybody is busy. We're following up on a piece of evidence."

"Okay, what sort of evidence," replied Rachel with a level of scepticism.

"This is a Heathrow Airport rental," said Warren. "We followed Russian agents to their safe house, online, not physically. They got spooked and came here. They dumped the car." He lowered his voice and whispered, "We think our MI5 IT boss alerted them."

"He's a Russian sleeper," added Noel.

"We have photographs of all five Russian agents, but we are missing three identities," said Warren.

"So, you need fingerprints to identify the remaining three, correct?" Rachel asked, "Have you touched anything?"

Noel replied, "No."

Warren said, "No, sir. I mean, Mam."

Rachel grunted, "Good." She set up her equipment and then went to work. Her portable LED lights brought daylight to the scene. She lifted the Mercedes trunk lid. "Was it unlocked when you arrived?"

Driscoll said, "We didn't touch anything."

Rachel motioned them over, "Okay, let's look inside. It's a good thing you got here. It's unlocked with the keys in the ignition. Some thirteen-year-old would love this car." She took forty minutes and had plenty of prints, finished up, and gave them her card.

"I'll have something by tomorrow or the day after," replied Rachel. "By the way, you didn't touch the door handles by chance?"

"No," both replied in unison.

"All four door handles were smeared with a deadly nerve agent, Novichok. If you do, you'll have breathing problems and vomiting. Your muscles will contract involuntarily, including your heart. So, you didn't touch the door handles?" asked Rachel

"No," both replied in unison. Warren said, "Thanks, Rachel. Will your database have these sorts of overseas prints?"

Rachel dropped her case and fell to the ground. Both Noel and Warren stared.

"Is she okay?" asked Noel.

The silenced MP5SFA3 semi-automatic carbine didn't make that much sound, more like a person coughing. They heard footsteps approaching. Both men turned and saw the gun, then the shooter. Driscoll recognized the face.

"Where are the Red Banners?" demanded the shooter.

Warren said, "We don't know. We are here to steal this lovely car." It was the wrong answer. The shooter took Rachel's case with the prints, her ID, and all the phones, wallets, and MI5 swipe cards from Noel and Warren.

He looked at the badges, "MI5 IT, specialist, Thames House. What are IT guys doing here?"

The shooter placed their bodies inside the Mercedes' trunk and locked it, then drove Noel's car to the MI5 underground car park, used the passcodes to enter the building through the underground car lot and went to the now-empty IT division.

He looked through folders on their desks. I read as many as possible and found one that spoke of 'Abu Sarek.' He stuffed that into his clothing. The cleaner's closet had four plastic containers holding twenty litres of flammable cleaning fluid. The Russians emptied the containers and then turned off the fire sensors.

He lit the fire and left.

CHAPTER 70

USTRALIAN EMBASSY

Hunter and his team arrived at the Australian Embassy early in the afternoon to brief Brian Clinton, London's ASIS leader and head of the station. After several additions and questions, Brian summarized the situation. "Abu Sarek came up a few years back, possibly at immigration. James privately inquired about him. Sarek is working with the driver to receive the 'Red Banners.' The Russians want the 'Red Banners' back, and Alan James, an MI5 IT supervisor, receives a coded message from Igor Medkov. So the cat out of the bag for James."

"James may be coordinating the ZL kill team to recover the Red Banners for the Russians," said Hunter. Or he may be the door opener. ZL are dangerous to us all," added Hunter.

Brian made a last-minute appointment with MI5 Director-General Allen at Thames House. Security performed ID checks, verified the meeting, and escorted them to Director Allen's office.

"Nice to see you, Brian. Are you well?" asked Sir Robert Allen.

"Sir Robert, I have never been better, my friend. First, may I apologize for this intrusion and the lateness of the hour? I am sure you are busy. May I introduce Mr Hunter Wyatt, Dr John Moody and Ms

Emma Smirnov? These three ASIS agents have been chasing the Red Banners since the beginning."

"Nice to meet you all. Please be seated. Drinks?" asked Sir Robert Allen.

Allen's secretary entered, served the drinks, left, and closed the door.

"Sir Robert. You are aware of the Red Banners?" asked Brian Clinton.

"Yes, we have been on alert. There have been many anti-terrorism meetings with little outcomes," replied Sir Robert Allen.

"Best if Hunter summarizes for you," said Brian.

"Two Chinese agents stole money from a US bank to underwrite the theft of the 'Red Banners.' They used a Bagdad man we call the 'Driver.' He organized a group of Russian mafia gangsters to steal the Red Banner, murdered them, then fled with the Red Banners," said Hunter. "The driver was last seen in Moscow."

Sir Robert Allen asked, "You don't know the identity of this driver?"

"No," replied Hunter. "We call him 'The Driver' because we think he has driven the 'Red Banners' to Moscow, went into hiding, and is now brought them here to London. He is the brains of the mission and goes by Abu Sarek or is using that name. Sarek, we thought, was killed by a US drone strike years ago. He is in London and will take the 'Red Banners' to the two target sites. We don't know the target, but we know this is an extended plan and points towards a significant event or events."

"A significant event? How did you come to that conclusion?" asked Sir Allen.

"The intentional delays. The dead Sarek arrived first. Money was laundered, which took time. Sarek has settled in for years now. The 'Red Banners' went into hiding in Moscow," said Hunter. "They are waiting for an event. They have time on their side."

"Why London?" asked Sir Allen.

"Our IT guy hunted server farms for the name 'Abu Sarek.' Alan James, your IT supervisor, searched Sarek's name privately on an unprotected phone. I believe he was given the name as a part of an organized plan. But he was curious about what the plan entailed. So he looks up Abu Sarek privately on his home computer. We know Igor Medkov sent Alan James a message. So, based on that connection from Moscow three years ago, either Medkov heard of a plan to steal their nuclear devices or initiated that plan. James searched for Sarek's name three years ago. That timeframe matches Sarek's arrival in the UK.

"You and your team come to the UK based on an internet search?" replied Sir Allen with one eyebrow raised. "Amazing deduction, dear fellow and Medkov's text was confirmation."

"But that does not confirm that the Red Banners are here yet; only Sarek," said Brian. It also doesn't confirm the target but is one step closer."

Sir Robert thought, "A dead, non-existent Sarek is a great cover for this driver. Does he exist, or is he a cutout?"

"Good question," replied Hunter, raising his hands.

Sir Robert looked at Brian and then back toward Hunter. "Alan is a Russian mole inside our MI5 IT office but is now in custody. He has been with us for over 20 years, and his own IT team was suspicious when he didn't take an arrest warrant for a Russian ZL kill team that arrived this morning. They flew in as you arrived."

Brian repeated, "Twenty years."

Sir Robert turned to Brian, "Sleeper agents. I suspect we all have them. Damn, nuisance they are, old boy. Two of James' team met with me today. They identified and followed a ZL kill team of five that arrived from Lisbon this morning. Alan then warned them. They fled their safehouse by car to an undercover shopping mall car park and then disappeared. Alan James said he informed operations, but he didn't. One of the two IT guys checked."

John turned to Hunter, then turned back to Sir Robert, "How do they know it was a ZL kill team?"

Sir Robert Allen said, "Joyce, our AI supercomputer, identified several of them from an attack in Europe through facial recognition, based on online news reports."

Hunter said, "Moscow wants the RBs back, at any cost."

Sir Robert finished the sentence. "Watch your backs. We have eyes on the streets, Brian. If those 'Red Banners' are in London, we face a dark future. Good hunting, and do your best, my friends. If I can assist, do not hesitate."

Sir Robert Allen stood, and his secretary entered to usher them out. Brian walked over to Sir Robert and shook hands. "I will keep you updated. Thanks for your time, Sir Robert." He acknowledged Brian's assurance with a slight nod and returned to his desk. The secretary ushered them to the elevator. When the doors closed, Emma asked, "Do you think that..."

Brian held a finger to his lips and coughed.

Then, a fire alarm shrieked. It was pitching and wavering throughout the building. Air conditioners stopped and were replaced by glowing exit signs. Ceiling lights flickered as the battery backups took control. As the elevator descended, it jerked to a bouncing halt, and then the backup battery system took control, lowering the elevator car to the ground floor.

The elevator doors opened. The room was thick with a choking fog of smoke. Hunter took a quick look. First, he saw a silenced MP5SFA3 semi-automatic carbine, then a leg, then a man emerging from the downstairs emergency stairwell onto the ground floor. 'He is coming up from downstairs and alone,' thought Hunter.

"Don't move," Hunter whispered to those behind him. The gunman looked at the entrance door, then checked his six. Hunter recognized the behaviour, and there was no shouting, 'Evacuate!' This guy was not an MI5 agent. The automatic sprinklers were hissing water mist and reducing visibility. 'His body language was wrong. This guy is hunting or protecting his exit.'

Hunter fired one shot from the elevator corner, then slid across the floor. The ZL agent fired his silenced MP5SFA3 carbine on full auto, where Hunter was a second before. The high-powered gun minced the plaster wall, sending sharp spikes of granite tiles flying and bouncing into the dead elevator car.

Emma and John stayed in the darkened elevator while Brian prepared to return fire but hesitated. Hunter was sliding across the polished, wet marble floor, firing his Glock 22 into the ankles of the shooter, causing him to topple over. At the same time, John took Brian's Glock and shot the ZL arsonist twice in the chest. The fire alarm's volume now matched the shouting of people running down the stairwell heading towards the entrance. Nobody heard or witnessed the gunfight.

"Brian, Emma, it's safe. Let's go now. Brian, are you okay? Let's get out of here," shouted Hunter.

Hunter grabbed the ZL's MP5SFA3 gun and threw it over his shoulder. John shoved Brian's Glock 22 into his belt.

Hunter dragged the ZL killer outside by his collar. "John, gun up! There may be more," shouted Hunter.

Fire appliances and Police were arriving on mass. Brian was looking up, fire pouring out of windows, large yellow and explosive red flames. John leaned over. "What about Sir Robert?" Brian kept dialling Sir Robert's cell phone, but there was no answer. "Sir Robert has his private lift," said Brian, but his facial expression said something else.

Brian phoned London's counter-terrorism police commander, identified himself using a code word, and then spoke, "A Russian kill team has attacked Thames house and set it alight. Sir Robert is still in the building. There may be more armed terrorists in the crowd."

The crowd consisted of MI5 night staff, cleaners, and pedestrians. As Brian talked, he could hear more Police sirens, fire appliances and ambulances approaching.

"The counter-terrorism team is five minutes out. Hold tight, Brian," said the Commander.

Brian thanked the officer, disconnected, and went to find Hunter and the team. The smoke, fire and confusion ramped up the panic in the crowd. Shrieks and gasps of fear came after each explosion. The glass was exploding, showering people, then bouncing after hitting the payment. One MI5 senior night supervisor was attempting a head-count. He was shouting in vain.

The explosions forced everybody to step further back, directly into the path of another silenced MP5SFA3 gun on full auto. Hunter was crouched down over the dead ZL killer, knowing there would be no identification. He found the folder of papers. "Emma, can you take these," said Hunter as he took a photo of the face of the dead assailant.

Hunter heard the shooting first, then saw people falling and others running. The ZL shooter emptied his clip and was ready to reload. Hunter raised his own Glock 22, prepared to return fire, when he saw two men firing at the ZL killer, hitting an arm.

Hunter pursued the ZL assailant, scattering the now panicked crowd. The guy dropped his weapon and was running full pace towards Vauxhall Bridge. The other two gunmen took up the chase, with Hunter coming in behind. The ZL guy did an Olympic dive off the Bridge. The two men emptied their weapons into the Thames River.

"Did you hit him?" Hunter asked, taking deep breaths. He spat out some of the fire's burnt particles.

"Not sure. There is no blood." They spoke in a French accent.

"DGSE?" asked Hunter with a surprised look.

"Yes. You're ASIS, no? We are hunting some Syrians on diplomatic immunity who have received the 'Red Banners,'" said one French agent.

"Syrians?" asked Hunter, now astonished that DGSE knew him.

"Yes, our intel was that radical Islamists were employed as baggage handlers at Charles de Gaulle Airport to load one of the 'Red Banners' onto a freight aircraft to land at Heathrow Airport. The Syrians then transported it here to somewhere in London. We lost them in transit. The other 'Red Banner' has stayed in France. Our team has been here in London for three months now, chasing, as you say, our tails," said the French agent.

"Syrians?" Hunter shook his head. "We confirmed today that a Russian ZL kill team is in London to retrieve the 'Red Banners.'"

"You said 'Red Banners,' plural. Are both nukes here? Are you sure?" asked one DGSE agent.

"We have no intelligence that one is in France or if both are here at all," replied Hunter.

"Syrians and Russians are working together. Very possible," said the French agent. Hunter wasn't so sure. Police vehicles raced past, and the DGSE agents swapped phone numbers with Hunter and left.

CHAPTER 71

AUSTRALIA HQJOC

It was 9 a.m. Canberra time and the end of the shift was approaching. It was a slow night in the IT ASIS department, and John Lewis was asleep at his desk.

Wayne Scott yelled, "Hey, John! Are you awake?"

"What?" he awoke with a jerking motion. "Wayne, you don't need to yell!" He stretched his arms and legs, only half awake, yawning and asked, "Mate, is it time to go home? What time is it?"

Wayne said, "Mate, the UK terrorism threat level is severe. It's through the roof, mate!"

John stood, stretched, and wandered over to the office coffee machine. He switched it on and waited for it to boil as he watched the LED TV on the wall. "What does that mean again, the threat level status?" asked John.

"Their threat level is different from ours. Guys run around London with guns, and it pops to the top." The coffee engine rumbled to life; he put his cup underneath and filled it with a fresh brew. "Ah!"

Wayne shouted, "Um, they are saying a militant attack is highly likely. Oh no! MI5 headquarters, Thames House, is on fire. Now, there's gunfire. Look! All hell is breaking loose."

Wayne was entering keyboard data, launching several pre-coded programs, and typing away quickly.

John asked, "Is this live?"

Wayne kept typing, "They are in trouble, man! There is a lot of shooting on full auto. You can hear it."

John said, "Oh! What's on fire?" He ran over to watch the overhead LED TVs.

Wayne said, "John, do you think I should help?"

"How?" asked John, entirely focused on the live TV reports.

Wayne said, "You don't want to know, do you?"

John ignored Wayne and returned to his desk to watch the news broadcast.

Wayne had hacked into the MI5 servers through an abandoned PC. He checked their server battery backup system. It had twelve minutes of juice. "I can work with that, maybe."

Wayne's coded programs closed the server firewalls, antivirus and other unnecessary programs. He opened up the multi-fibre bandwidth and shut down all other broadband usages in the burning building. Wayne's coded backup software started. He used multi-threading to speed everything up to the cloud. 'Ten minutes and counting,' thought Wayne. He found another broadband backbone that led to another government department. He repeated the same process.

There was nothing more he could do. He was unsure if the IT room was protected, onsite or off-site, and whether it would burn or not.

'I can't worry about that now,' thought Wayne.

An alert came up on his screen. Wayne watched the screen as the translation software translated the conversation.

"Hey, John?" yelled Wayne.

John was watching the aftermath of the fire. There were bodies everywhere. 'Unbelievable! Who did the shooting?' wondered John.

News vans were everywhere. It looked like absolute chaos.

"Hey, John?" shouted Wayne for the second time.

"Yeah, Wayne." He didn't turn his head or look back to Wayne. He kept watching the news.

"You know those two Chinese spy blokes who stole the USD 75 million?" shouted Wayne.

"Yes, Liv Wei and Wang Li Jun. What about them?" replied John.

"Yes, them. It's rather exciting, mate," said Wayne. John looked at him when he said the word exciting. "Get to the point, Wayne. I'm watching the fire." The door opened, and John watched as the day team entered. They were also watching the MI5 news live on their phones. John turned back to Wayne.

"Those two Chinese blokes are together, and one is talking on a cell phone to some young bloke in London who studies at Kings College," said Wayne.

John finally wandered over, this time with his coffee mug, smiling as he passed some of the dayshift crew. In a few minutes, he would give a summary to the day supervisor.

'That could wait,' thought John. "Okay," said John. "What have you got?"

"I have a recording and a translation. Do you want to hear it?" asked Wayne. "Both blokes have booked tickets to fly to London."

"Really. Get the flight numbers and arrival times. Send that to me," replied John.

CHAPTER 72

ASIS, SYDNEY.

"Karen Richards? John Lewis ASIS HQJOC," said John.

"Hi, John," replied Karen.

"You got a minute to talk?" asked John.

"Yes, are you phoning about the fire? I've been up all night. That fire will cause problems for us and the UK," replied Karen. "How can I help?"

"It is not about the fire, Karen. We translated a cell phone call with Liv Wei from the Joint Staff Department Intelligence Bureau with Wang Li Jun from JSD Intelligence. You recall those two?" asked John.

Karen said, "Yes, the million-dollar money men behind the stolen 'Red Banners.'"

"Correct. Both agents talked to a Chinese International student studying at Kings College London on the Strand. Liv Wei told the students to watch the spire or tower of a church opposite the college, St Mary's-Le-Strand. Let me send you the exact translated words," John replied.

He waited a few minutes and could hear the translation playing in the background.

"This could be a breakthrough, John," said Karen. "Now, have I got it right? Wei phones the Kings College student. The student reports to Wei when he sees the church bell replaced with a Red Banner. Is that your take?"

"That's how I read it," Karen said. "Perhaps something has gone wrong."

She turned to a colleague and gave instructions. "Why do you say that?"

"Wei and Jun have booked a flight to Heathrow on China Airlines, leaving in 2 hours," said John. The total flight time is 10 hours."

CHAPTER 73

HIGH COMMISSION OF AUSTRALIA, THE STRAND LONDON.

It was 2 am. Hunter was exhausted and sound asleep on a sofa. They all stunk of smoke and had been watching the live TV reports.

Emma said, "They have lost control of the fire. I do hope Sir Robert Allen got out."

Brian switched off the feed. "Sleep is in order? Clean up, go to bed, get some sleep. The Police will request a report along with counterterrorism," said Brian.

Hunter's phone chirped. He opened his eyes. "Hunter, Karen. How is everybody?"

"We survived, but Sir Robert Allen is missing, presumed dead. ZL started the fire. We nailed the firebug, but there was another ZL zealot outside, killing people. That guy ran and jumped into the Thames. DSGE was pumping bullets into the river."

Karen said, "DSGE?"

Hunter replied, "DSGE's intel was that Syrians received the 'Red Banners' and flew one to London and the other to Paris."

Karen said, "That's new? Okay, we'll talk again in the morning, in London. I have some intelligence from HQJOC." Hunter said nothing. He was already asleep.

CHAPTER 74

S T. GILES HOTEL LONDON

Milton was watching the morning TV news. Twenty-six deaths, one police officer injured, and the head of MI5 was missing, presumed dead in the now burnt-out shell of a building. The TV news crossed over to the Prime Minister, with the London mayor by his side.

"Tragedy struck London last night. Our heartfelt prayers go to the families and loved ones who died in this cowardly act of terrorism. As of 6 am today, MI6 and our Counter-Terrorism Taskforce will take over the duties of MI5. We are working with our international partners and the National Crime Agency to hunt for these killers. Metropolitan Police will be out in force on the streets of London today. I ask for your patience with the expected delay today. Thank you."

Milton switched off the TV. He could see translucent plumes of black smoke floating in the distance. Milton gazed at the streets below his apartment—police vehicles parked on the footpath, less regular vehicle traffic, and fewer pedestrians.

An armed Police officer is holding a Heckler and Koch MP5, standing on one street corner.

Last night's sleep was fleeting because Milton searched online late into the night for A1-listed London properties. Most church buildings were A2-listed and abandoned. At midnight, Milton texted Laura to make offers for the United Reform Church in South Norwood, St. Lawrence's Church, Brentford, and Southwark All-Hallows Church.

His first preference is to renovate and then sell the buildings back to a Christian community, as these worship facilities were majestic in various styles, now lost to time. Last night, as he searched for abandoned buildings, an online advertisement caught his eye.

The advertisement promoted a foundation against nuclear weapons. Milton clicked the link and read several stories about dangerous nuclear mishaps over the decades.

The website had an estimation tool. The reader could choose between bombs, from the 15 KT 'Little Boy' to the 50,000 KT Tsar Bomba. Then, you could select whether the blast occurs at the surface or air level. Milton chose the Tsar Bomba, knowing the 'Red Banners' were similar. The website showed if somebody dropped the Tsar Bomba on London, the fireball would stretch for 45 miles and the radiation for 32 miles, with 4.6 million dead and 3 million injured. Also, it would send a shock wave of 350 square miles, with 3,200 square miles of the area hit by intense heat.

Milton sat at the computer and stared. His hands started to shake.

Something happened inside of him.

It was at first unexplainable. Milton felt dread, then dark black waves of guilt. His entire body then started to shake. He felt darkness consuming him. He couldn't stop it or control it. He staggered to the toilet and vomited.

Darkness came, then went.

CHAPTER 75

S T. MARY'S-LE-STRAND LONDON
John and Hunter walked from the Australian Embassy to St. Mary's-Le-Strand. To their surprise, you could throw a stone from the Embassy and hit the church. It was that close. Hunter purchased some second-hand construction clothing and boots from a second-hand store. A junior at the Embassy had purchased replacement clothing for Hunter's team early in the morning. She dumped their stinking, fire-saturated clothing in the bin.

"May I never wear a suit again," complained John.

"Wow, you are touchy this morning," replied Hunter. But you look good, mate! I don't remember ever seeing you wear a tie."

John smiled, that said, shut up.

They researched the church after Karen's early morning debrief. They walked for three minutes from the Embassy and gazed at the church under renovation as they bought some takeaway coffee. John caught the tube at Temple Station and went to Vauxhall Underground station, performed a counter-surveillance run, and returned to Temple. Hunter walked along the riverside. He lost the ZL tail after a quick run.

Emma followed Hunter at a distance and checked for other followers, swapping in and out. Satisfied they had lost all their tails, Hunter asked John to talk with the building site manager at St. Mary's on the Strand. Emma sat in a coffee shop to watch.

"Good morning. My name is John Moody, and this is James Hunter, my assistant. We're from Bloomfield Chapel Bell Foundry. We want to offer a more competitive quote for the bell," said John.

"Australian?" asked the manager. The onsite manager's mobile office had a wide window on both sides, enabling Hunter to check for anyone watching. "I just arrived a few months back and got this sales job," replied John, smiling.

"Okay, I assume you are not climbing?" said the on-site manager. John pointed to Hunter. "My assistant will climb." Hunter walked with the on-site manager into the church. He pointed to the door to the spiral staircase and then returned to his on-site office.

John asked, "The restoration looks excellent. When is your completion date?"

"I'd say another two months. Here is my card. Send the quote to me as soon as you can. Just a reminder, a new bell can only be installed from 11 pm to 3 am. It's tight. Road closure and a crane, you know the deal," replied the manager. The phone rang. "I look forward to your quote. Sorry, I've got to go."

"Thanks," said John. "We appreciate the opportunity."

Hunter returned within ten minutes, and they both left. "We have three following us. A woman is standing outside Emma's coffee shop. Two men are standing twenty meters from that shop close to the road," added Hunter.

"You saw them from up the tower?" asked John.

"Yes. I texted Emma to find a store. Stay there for ten minutes. After ten minutes, she will enter Temple Station. We will try to draw them all into the Tube Station," said Hunter.

"And the Bell?" asked John.

"It's still there, old as hell and massive. You'll need a crane to remove it," replied Hunter.

"I suppose there is no 'Red Banner' up there then?" replied John.

"There is not enough space for a bomb and a bell," said Hunter.

Even then, I don't think there is enough space for a bomb. Even if you remove the clapper, there is still not enough space."

"Any swap would need to happen using a crane at night," said John. "Rather an obvious move, don't you think?"

How tall was the bell?" asked Hunter

"Four feet high and probably four or five across," replied John. "The driver could weld a Red Banner inside the bell," said John. "Most bells are 80% copper and 20% tin."

"How do you know that?" inquired Hunter with a smile.

"The manager is a bell fan or expert. You can't trick him. So the bell swap would need to be camouflaged," replied John.

"Let's start walking towards Temple station," said Hunter. "If these guys are ZL, we must take them off the playing board." Hunter looked at John to make sure he agreed.

"Are they ZL or MI6?" asked John.

Hunter just raised his shoulders. "Beats me! We'll find out."

"It can only be ZL," replied John.

"Let me go into the Temple Café," said Hunter. I'll wait in the Café and come in behind you. Get onto Westbound Platform 1, the Men's restroom, and enter a cubicle. I've been here before. I know the layout. The platform is curved, so there should be blind spots. Use the Men's restroom if there are too many people."

"You've checked it out?" asked John. Hunter nodded.

The ZL team consisted of three people: two men and one woman. The woman made the first error by staying behind to watch Hunter in the Temple café. Hunter observed her backpack and a long-sleeved jacket, so no gun was within easy reach. Then he saw in her left hand a black blade. The remaining two ZL killers followed John down the staircase and the platform to the restroom. Hunter left the café, paid his fare, and then walked to the semi-circular stairs leading to the underground platform.

He anticipated the attack would happen on the curve of the stairs out of sight of any CCTV. He increased his pace, sensing her closing in, ready to strike. When he heard her take in a breath to lunge, he stopped and bent down low, and her momentum carried her over Hunter before rolling down the stairs. She knocked herself out and stabbed herself. Hunter removed the backpack and kept walking. Hunter found John sitting on a bench at the end of the platform, with the ZL guys sitting on either side of him.

"What happened?" Hunter asked.

"They're dead," said John. "Rather sad if you ask me."

"Really?" asked Hunter. "Both are dead?"

John asked, "Where's the girl?"

"She's not dead. She fell down the stairs and stabbed herself," said Hunter. "Broken arm and leg, self-inflicted."

CHAPTER 76

NORTH YORKSHIRE UK

Ahmed got a job as an HGV distribution HR driver for a large retailer with a large workforce of 12,000 people. He would be unnoticed. Ahmed's truck was one of 16,000 trucks that deliver goods to stores across the UK. It was a weekly delivery schedule that excluded Sundays.

Ahmed's daily deliveries included five large shopping centres, including the Princes Gate retail complex. The complex promoted itself as the town centre at Catterick Garrison, a military community south of Richmond with 14,000 people. The garrison occupies 2,400 acres and has a long military history. The North Yorkshire Police and the Royal Military Police oversee protection for the entire community.

The town Ahmed delivers to is a picturesque gem, brimming with life and charm. Its streets are lined with quaint shops and bustling cafes, and its residents, a mix of locals and military personnel, give it a unique character.

CHAPTER 77

HEATHROW AIRPORT UK.
Liv Wei and Wang Li Jun travelled together. They were picked up from Heathrow by a Chinese member of the Strategic Support Force who operated political interference in the UK and siphoned off military and commercial secrets.

The United Work Department was a division of the Chinese Communist Party and a core subversion group within Chinese embassies and consulates abroad. Its job was to use the Chinese diaspora to do Beijing's bidding by creating friendships with local politicians and funding their pet projects.

Their purpose is to shape a nation's political landscape by working with lazy politicians who will not object to anything China, like the South China Sea, Hong Kong and Taiwan. They wanted no political objections to purchasing strategic industrial companies, taking stakes in car manufacturers and promoting China's superior and cheaper 5G network. They wanted deals with companies that made high-tech stuff.

Secretary Me Yu told both men, "You have afternoon tea with a London City Council Politician today at 2 pm."

Jun asked, "Does he have any useful intel on the 'Red Banner' terrorists."

"Yes. We offered a fully funded business trip to China to the fat politician and his obese wife to attend the 22nd China Institute for International Strategic Studies Conference."

"Other appointments?" demanded Jun.

Me Yu said, "Yes. You will meet our operative, who is an IT specialist in Counterterrorism. Here is the cell phone number."

"Good," said Jug.

Liv Wei's department has sent many people to the UK as undercover operatives in companies, universities and other organizations. One organization was the UK Counterterrorism Unit.

The 2 pm appointment with the London City Council politician went badly. Jun was both demanding and demeaning. The politician confidently said the 'Red Banners' were brought to London by Algerians with diplomatic immunity. The intel came from a baggage handler who loaded them onto a domestic flight. The French secret service DGSE had followed the Algerians from Charles de Gaulle Airport to London, but neither group has resurfaced, and nobody knows where the 'Red Banners' have gone.

Wei and Jun knew the next meeting might yield more fruit. Their Chinese undercover operative, Zack Moon, was born in the UK to a Chinese mother and a British father. They met in a Chinese Restaurant near their embassy.

"A Russian ZL team had torched the MI5 headquarters," said Moon. "He had stolen some intel but died when confronted by French secret service agents operating in London. What he stole from MI5 has gone missing, contents unknown. Another ZL team member killed twenty-six MI5 staff workers, two MI5 IT specialists and a forensic scientist in a different location."

"So the Russians denied the 'Red Banners' theft, saying it is a hoax?" said Wei, looking at Jun. "They send a kill team to return the Red Banners and kill anybody in their way."

"Two of the ZL team are dead. One escaped capture by diving into the Thames, presumed dead," replied Moon. "I have intel on the deaths of two remaining ZL team. I believe another Garde A ZL team is already here, but I can't confirm that intel."

"They're exposed seeking the 'Red Banners,'" said Jun.

"They are dangerous and reckless idiots," replied Moon.

"Do you have any intel about the present location of the 'Red Banners'?" asked Jun.

"Only rumours from the DGSE. One is here. And the other is in Paris. I can't confirm those details," replied Moon.

"DGSE. This is getting messy," replied Wei.

"Two MI5 agents lured the leftovers of the first ZL team down the Strand," said Moon. "They killed both ZL guys in Temple Tube station. The third ZL team member broke her arms and legs and has disappeared. As I said, I believe there is another unknown 'A Grade ZL' kill team in London. I repeat myself. After all, you are both in danger because you travelled under your names."

"So what! Your job is to find the 'Red Banners,'" spat Wei.

"And Abu Sarek?" asked Jun, looking curiously at Moon. Zack knew this was a test.

"Abu Sarek disappeared three years ago in Bagdad. I traced him from Gatwick to Brighton, but it wasn't Abu Sarek. It was a guy who looked like him. Abu Sarek died in a US coalition drone attack on the outskirts of Bagdad years ago. But somebody has been using his identity, which is a common name. I found his name in several countries. All his pictures are different. I found a bankrupt transport company registered in his name in Amsterdam. Abu Sarek is a dead end," replied Moon.

"That is interesting but very odd," replied Jun.

"I will keep looking, but I believe the Americans killed the guy," replied Moon. He put his hand inside his jacket and withdrew a picture. "Is this him?"

"That's him," replied Jun.

"He's dead," said Moon.

"Here is a burner phone," said Wei. "It has my burner phone number. If you get any intel, phone me." Wei looked at Moon to ensure he got the message as Jun wandered off to get a taxi.

Counterterrorism agent and Chinese spy Zack Moon knew something had gone wrong. Wei and Jun supplied the $75 million. Zack's contact within Jun's office didn't know how they got the money or if this was a state-sanctioned mission, third-party arrangement, or personal.

Moon went over the conversation. 'Did Wei think I was withholding information? I answered their questions without hesitation. Why had they come to London? They could have researched Abu Sarek from their office in Beijing. There is only one answer. They have lost the 'Red Banners' and communication with their contact. It's the only thing that makes any sense.'

Zack Moon phoned his duty officer and only got her answering service. "Janine, I broke my ankle, and I am undergoing total ankle arthroplasty. The doctors say recovery is six weeks. I'll email you a doctor's certificate. Perhaps two weeks' holiday and four unpaid. Is that okay? I'll be in contact after the operation. Sorry if this messes up the rosters."

Moon grabbed his 'go bag' from his gym locker and headed to Euston Station, catching the first train to Edinburgh, Scotland. From there, he would go to Thurso.

'Those idiots have lost control of two nuclear weapons.'

CHAPTER 78

ST. MARY'S-LE-STRAND LONDON

Liv Wei pocketed his burner phone. "We'll meet the student from Kings College opposite St Mary's-Le-Strand in fifteen minutes."

Wei and Jun arrived early and stood outside the abandoned Strand Tube Station. Originally called Aldwych Station, it was later called the Strand because that was the name of the street. It was the terminus of the short Piccadilly line. The Strand Station entrance had two doors: a locked red metal door and a locked sliding mesh door. Above the now-closed main doors is a semi-circular, panelled glass window.

Hunter and John watched everybody from behind the panelled glass. Emma was looking down on the roof of a building on the opposite side. They had been there most of the day. Emma phoned Hunter, "Heads up, guys. I'm watching two Chinese men in suits. They have no cameras, and they're not tourists. They're standing directly below you. They are looking at St. Mary's."

Hunter looked down to street level, "All I can see is the top of two heads."

Emma kept talking. "They're waiting. They keep looking at King's College, then to the church."

"Are these our $75 million guys?" asked John. "They could be tourists admiring the sights."

"What a pathetic attempt at surveillance," Emma replied. Hang on. Someone is approaching." Moody and Hunter tried to get a better look, but they saw three heads now.

"It's a young Chinese guy. Look at that!" said Emma. "The young guy pointed to the top of the church spire and got his hand slapped down. They are now talking. No, they are not talking. It seems like the young guy is undergoing a verbal interrogation."

Hunter turned to John, "Let's grab them, pull them back into here, and ask a few questions."

Hunter opened the red door to the entrance, and John followed close behind. "Son, are you okay? Are these men bullying you?" asked Hunter.

All three turned around simultaneously and looked at Hunter and John. Hunter grabbed Wei, and John dragged Jun backwards into the station entrance. The Chinese student ran. Both Wei and Jun were screaming and kicking until the Glock 19s with silencers appeared. Hunter knocked both Chinese agents unconscious.

"Why didn't you knock them out after we descended this dark spiralling staircase?" complained John.

"They were making too much racket, mate," replied Hunter.

They looked around the darkened railway platform. "John, find a light and get Emma here," asked Hunter. The platform lights came on, displaying World War 2 posters. Hunter tied their hands behind their back with wire and then dragged them to a platform seat one by one. He then wired their feet to either end of the seat legs. Hunter sat in the middle and waited. The 1974 rail carriages sat there like a dead ghost in its tracks. Hunter looked around, thinking he had seen this platform before. It's a movie or something. He could hear footsteps echoing through the now silent tube station. John and Emma looked left, then right. "Over here!" said Hunter.

They hurried to the end of the platform where Hunter was sitting. "I got a signal up top. Lucas forwarded their images from Wayne at HQJOC. These two guys stole the $75 million from that USA bank," Emma read her phone. "Their names are Liv Wei and Wang Li Jun. I don't know who is who?"

Emma opened her phone. "Lucas has a dozen pictures of both men at a café or coffee shop in China somewhere, based on the signage and décor."

Hunter held up their passports. "He's Jun, and on my right is Wei. Odd to use your real name."

"I followed the kid," said Emma. He stopped and looked back, ready to phone somebody. I took the phone and informed him I was from the UK Counter-terrorism unit. I gave him ten hours to leave the country or go to prison now."

John looked at her and smiled. Wei awoke first and understood his predicament. He glanced at Jun, still cold, then looked up at three people staring at him. "Who are you? We are tourists. We come for a wonderful holiday. Let me go!" demanded Wei.

Hunter waited until he finished. "Liv Wei. Joint Staff Department of Intelligence Bureau. Wang Li Jun, JSD Intelligence China Bureau. Both of you are in London. You stole $75 million from a USA bank and transferred it to Bagdad to organize the theft of the 'Red Banners,' said Hunter. He stopped talking and waited for a response.

Wei stared, pretending he didn't understand English, but thought about escaping the situation. Hunter watched. "Stop. You have no moves left. I only have two questions. One. What is the name of the person in Bagdad? Two. What was your plan for the 'Red Banners' here in London?"

Wang Li Jun awoke slowly. He opened his eyes, looked at the three people, and saw Wei.

"Two simple questions, Wei," asked Hunter. "It is not complicated. Your mission failed."

Wei said nothing.

"We are on holiday. See Big Ben, see a show!" said Jun. We are tourists from China. We are friends. Do you want money? Are you muggers?"

John breathed and held the gun up, saying, "Wang Li Jun, you work for JSD." John showed him his tablet with his picture and Wei's picture.

Hunter placed the silencer on Wei's knee and said, "Two questions, Wei. I am giving you a choice."

"What two questions?" asked Jun. Wei spat and shouted at Jung in Mandarin to shut his mouth.

Hunter repeated the questions, this time looking at Jun. "One. What is the name of your contact in Bagdad? Two. What was your plan for the 'Red Banners' here in London?"

"Abu Sarek. Blow up the Royal family. But no bomb inside the Church tower," replied Jun.

Wei was livid. He spit and shouted at Jun. Jun lowered his head in shame, embarrassed that he was so weak. Wei kept yelling abuse.

Hunter looked at Wei and said. "Abu Sarek is dead. Who is the second person from Bagdad?"

Hunter, Moody and Emma saw it—a micro-expression of surprise by Wei.

"You didn't know Sarek was dead?" replied Hunter.

Wei said nothing. 'It was now confirmed again. Sarek was dead. We failed. They also don't know who has the 'Red Banners.'"

Emma looked back at Jun and said, "Your plan has failed. Jun, Jun!" She leaned in close and held up his slumped head. "He had bitten into an ampoule."

"Where did he get that?" asked John.

Hunter grabbed Wei's hair to pull it up, but it was too late. Wei smiled, and then his eyes rolled back into his skull. John examined Jun's business shirt, suit jacket and tie. "They both have smaller necks and one extra-size business shirt. It's loose, see. Jun and Wei attached the ampoule to the back of their ties," said John.

Emma rolled the top of Jun's tie forward and saw a plastic clip. "The clip held a glass cyanide pill or another concentrated toxin," replied Emma.

"Is it evening up top?" asked Hunter.

"Yes. It is dark," replied Emma.

"We wait a few more hours and call the Embassy," said Hunter. "There may be other watchers above. John, you go that way, Emma, you go that way. Find a place where we can stash the bodies, short term."

Emma returned a few minutes later. "That end is concreted and blocked. There are lots of rooms unsuitable for hiding dead bodies."

John returned. "We can walk down the tunnel about 300 feet in. It joins another tunnel, but halfway, there is a disused room. It's a perfect spot," replied John.

Emma removed their phones, wallets, and keys from their pockets. She patted them down and found a knife stitched into the suit jacket and a mini camera on both lapels. "These guys came prepared." She put everything in her backpack, pulled out her phone, and turned on the torch. John gave her his phone and did the same. Hunter picked up Wei, and John carried Jun.

"Take it slow," said Hunter. "Easy to twist an ankle."

"Okay, Dad," replied Emma with a smile. "Wei didn't know Sarek was dead. So, who has the 'Red Banners?'"

"John, how much further?" asked Hunter.

"We're about halfway," replied John. They continued to walk further into the tunnel.

"Wei dealt directly with Sarek," said Hunter. You saw the look. From the beginning, the driver has been pretending to be Sarek or maybe his agent or middle man. But in reality, he was the boss."

John tripped and fell. Emma came over and said, "Let me help you." He got up, dusted himself, picked up Jun, and used the fireman's hold instead.

"You okay?" asked Emma.

"All good, thanks," John grunted. We have always said there were two people: the driver, whatever his name is, and someone else, Sarek dead or alive, but always two people."

Emma said, "Neither of the two may be Sarek?"

"If you want to misdirect, you don't use a dead man. You point to a living person and plant false evidence. Sarek is not dead. So where is he?" asked Emma.

Hunter stopped walking and turned to Emma, "Sarek is here in London working with the driver."

"Either way, Sarek should not be our focus, dead or alive," growled Emma.

"Correct. The driver is our focus," replied Hunter.

"Wei and Jung's plan, which I don't quite understand," said John. "You blow up London, killing millions, including the Royal Family, for what benefit? It can't be money. They were swimming in it. To short the stock markets? These two bank robbers gave most of it to the driver or Sarek. So who benefits?"

"Who benefits? I can't see how China benefits?" replied Emma.

"Perhaps these two blokes had their agenda," said John.

"Maybe not just their agenda," replied Hunter.

"What? Some Chinese General wants to start a war?" asked John.

"A nuclear war?" replied Emma. "The repercussions would be enormous, and it is a stupid move. I still don't see how anyone benefits by killing the Royal Family?"

"The driver ignored Wei's plan," replied Hunter.

"The driver may have improved Wei's plan because the bell tower area was too small," said John.

"It could be in St. Clement Danes Church tower, further down the road," replied John. "We are almost there."

"Why did the Russians send a ZL kill team?" asked Emma.

"If the 'Red Banners' go kaboom, they don't want the blame," replied John as he lowered the body onto the ground.

Hunter said, "Let's get these bodies stashed and leave. Perhaps it's time to leave the embassy and use a safe house. We need to be less visible."

"I still can't see Wei and Jun's motive," said Emma.

CHAPTER 79

L ONDON TOWER HOTEL
Three nights later, Commander John Bryant Jones from Metropolitan Police Counter Terrorism Command organized a joint strategic meeting to respond to the terrorist threat of the 'Red Banners.' Jones wanted a rapid response to the 'Red Banner' threat. The National Security Advisor and an MP whose portfolio included counterterrorism wanted to chair the meeting. Hunter watched several small groups form, trying to hammer out who should chair the meeting.

'I hate these meetings,' thought Hunter. Brian was sitting beside Hunter and pointing out all the players in the room by name.

"He's from the Foreign Office. That's the Chief of the Defense Force by the wall, and he's Doctor somebody from the Global Counterterrorism Institute of Strategic Dialogue and Graham Barnes, a famous Human Rights lawyer. That chap is the Police chief, and sitting beside him is the MI6 boss. No MI5 person has replaced Sir Robert," said Brian Clinton.

The Five Eyes agreement meant this meeting was also livestreamed. Brian and Hunter sat at the rear of the room. He leaned over to Brian and whispered, "The fact that they are fighting over who will chair this meeting says that the person who doesn't get to chair the meeting will leak to the media."

"You seem to be rather cynical," replied Brian.

"I don't trust politicians in general," replied Hunter. The chair of the meeting ended up being Commander Bryant Jones. 'All that time wasted,' thought Hunter. Jones introduced everybody and then summarized the situation. He proposed three possible actions.

Bryant Jones said, "Let's pay attention. We should search all London properties for the 'Red Banners.' We identify and jail any ZL teams and hunt for Abu Sarek."

The representative from the Home Office said, "Regarding the ZL chaps, we expelled twenty-three Russian diplomats, all embassy-based spies. Hopefully, that will disrupt their jolly spy network."

"Only the first option was actionable immediately," whispered Hunter to Brian.

The human rights lawyer Graham Barnes stood and waited until he had everyone's attention. "What are the parameters of entering private property and performing a search?"

"Counterterrorism legislation allows warrantless entry," responded the Police Commissioner.

Barnes responded, "Based on evidence. A court would need to approve Police wandering into every building in London, dear boy."

The Police Commissioner spoke to the group, "Even if the Court approved, we don't have enough Police or staff to search all buildings, even if the army assists us. The public would need to assist, and they may refuse."

Commander John Bryant Jones replied, "I suggest we limit the search to all tall office buildings, building roofs, church spires, the Shard, and Big Ben, as the bomber would want an above-ground blast."

Hunter twigged at the mention of a church spire. 'Was that a guess, or does he know something about the Chinese agents?'

One MP held up his hand. "Let's keep Commander Bryant's first suggestion for the moment. Do we need some more ideas? Can we break into groups?" Everybody starts talking. Hunter was not surprised by the outcome. 'Something was better than nothing,' he thought.

Hunter wandered over to a small group and waited for a discussion between Graham Barnes and John William, the MI6 boss, to finish. "John, my name is Hunter from ASIS. May I have a word?" asked Hunter.

John shook his hand. "Brian has already spoken to me about what you and your team have done. Thank you, and well done, old boy."

"If we could step out of earshot of Barnes for a moment, John." Hunter said, "The night the ZL team burnt down Thames House, we met with Sir Robert."

"Poor old sod. About twenty selected Russian diplomats were frog-marched onto a plane this morning; one spy network is gone," said John. "Sorry, Sir Robert, yes?"

"Before that meeting, Sir Robert was told by his IT guys that Alan James, their boss, was a Russian sleeper agent."

"Correct. You terminated one ZL team member. The second ended up in the Thames," said Williams. "We believe one ZL operative killed those two MI5 IT agents you mentioned and a Police forensic officer."

"Sir Robert mentioned that one of their IT guys had developed an AI program called 'Joyce?'" said Hunter.

"Yes. Those servers were in the basement," said Williams. "The fire consumed everything."

"IT geeks normally break protocols and have things backed up at home or in the cloud, or even keep home copies of programs so they can improve in their spare time," said Hunter.

"I assume if that were the case, they would be breaking some interesting laws," replied Williams.

"Of course, yes," acknowledged Hunter.

"What's on your mind?" asked Williams.

"If there is a copy of Joyce at his home, and if we can get it running." Hunter's eyes looked at Barnes, then back to Williams. "I would like to monitor all UK communications for the word, 'Abu Sarek,' or any combination of that name?" said Hunter.

Williams looked around as he considered the risks. Hunter spoke while John thought, "I have an IT guy who could do this, but I would need the addresses of those two IT MI5 guys," suggested Hunter.

"Your cellphone number?" John memorized it, too, took out his phone, and texted. "Good luck. Keep me in the loop," said Williams.

Hunter got out his phone and was about to make a call. He wondered if somebody was monitoring the room. He descended the stairs to the street and leaned against the entrance wall. It was the spot where everybody smoked. Hunter tapped his encryption app, then hit speed dial.

"Lucas, can you look for any digital communications connections between a Chinese Army General or Politician with Wei and Jun, if any? Then, is it the same with Commander Bryant Jones, Wei, and Jun? Jones commented on the church spire in a meeting tonight," said Hunter.

"Okay. The Chinese connections may take more time," replied Lucas.

"A ZL operative murdered two MI5 IT guys. I've asked for their home addresses," said Hunter. "I'm assuming these IT guys keep an AI backup at home?

"I would rather not answer that question, Hunter," replied Lucas.

"It's okay," said Hunter. "I have requested their home addresses. I want Joyce to monitor all UK communication for the word Abu Sarek."

"That would break a few privacy laws," replied Lucas.

"I think the MI6 boss palmed that to me," said Hunter.

The building behind Hunter exploded, throwing him onto the ground.

"Hunter! Are you there? You dropped out. Are you there?" asked Lucas.

The ground moved as bricks, walls, and timber tumbled like rain. Hunter shook his head, got up onto his knees, and fell back. Boiling air is passing over him. Dirt filled his eyes, and his ears rang. He tried again to stand but vomited.

Red and yellow flames were pouring out the Hotel's second floor, throwing spikes of shattered glass and body parts over the footpath and road. Glass and chunks of bricks showered down like a hailstorm.

Burning objects landed on Hunter.

Grit and ash filled his mouth, causing convulsive coughing. Blood was pouring into his eyes. He needed to move or get burnt to death. Trying to stand, he went into another coughing fit as he sucked in chemical-rich black smoke.

Cars and buses ploughed into each other and then caught fire. People were running. Pedestrians lay on the footpath, some dead, some injured, and some screaming in pain. Hunter helped a woman attempting to limp away from the expanding fires. Then he dragged a young guy with deep cuts and lacerations as far as he could. Unable to go any further with the heated air and melted hot plastic landing on him, he began to stagger.

Then, a second explosion, even more devastating, brought the building down, groaning as it collapsed. The blast threw Hunter sideways, landing hard on the bitumen road against a car door. The fire leapt over buildings. Bits of the building became deadly projectiles. Hunter tried again to get up on his knees but failed and fell. As he lay on the ground, he knew everybody in that meeting had perished.

There was nothing left except an inferno from hell.

The building beside the Hotel then collapsed onto the footpath and parked cars.

'I need to move. Stay, and you die, Hunter!' he thought. "Get on your feet,' said Hunter.

He stood, staggered, and then fell again between damaged vehicles. The smoke was suffocating, filled with burning particles. 'Move, Hunter,' he commanded himself. He watched as everybody was running away except for one person. The guy is looking at the burning Hotel with a look of satisfaction. He has no fear, not like those running past him. The man then looked at Hunter; something clicked. A generation 5 Glock 55 with a silencer came out of his underarm holster. Hunter fell to the ground as bullets skipped the road and thudded into the mangled car.

Hunter fired the Embassy Glock 9 from underneath the car, hitting the bomber's foot. The bomber limped down an alley and disappeared. Hunter stood swaying, determined to give chase. He lurched into the alley entrance, dropped his weapon and lost consciousness.

Emma shook John awake, "Lucas says there is a bombing at Hunter's meeting. Get dressed, let's go." The townhouses flew past, "Drive faster, John!" said Emma. "I can see the flames over there on our left."

John got as close as possible and double-parked the car. They ran to the fire as others ran away. Arriving at the fire, John felt he was back on the battlefield. He started assisting injured people. "I'll be with you soon, find Hunter," shouted John.

It was a devastating sight, with the fire consuming a block of buildings. Police, fire and ambulances packed the scene. The multiple flashing lights felt like a disco. The smoke was suffocating, adding to the distress of the many injured.

"I'm an ex-army trauma surgeon," said John to a paramedic.

"Okay, help me sort these injuries in order of priority," replied the paramedic. After sorting the most critical into ambulances, John asked a police officer to speak to the Emergency site commander.

"Is this important?" inquired the Police officer.

"Yes," replied John.

The site commander was giving orders to officers. "Sir, this chap is an ex-army trauma surgeon and asked to speak with you," said the Police officer. The officer turned and left.

"My name is John Moody. I am here looking for a friend," said John, but the Commander cut John off.

"I'm sorry, but we will get to victim identification in several hours," replied the Commander, ready to talk to another waiting person.

"Sir, you misunderstood," replied John. The Commander was understandably impatient.

"My friend Hunter is an ASIS agent. He was at a meeting at this Hotel. MI5, MI6, your head of Police, embassy officials, politicians and others were meeting there tonight," said John. "This is a possible terrorism act, not just a fire."

The Commander was caught off-guard. Emma ran over to John and dragged him to a small alley. A paramedic looked up and said, "You know this gent?"

"Yes," replied John.

"Okay, he has cuts and may have a concussion. He will have a nasty migraine, so I have given him a strong analgesic. If there is any decrease in cognitive function, lack of coordination, pupil dilation, or difficulty staying awake or sleepy, you take him to Emergency. He may have blurred vision and nausea. Any questions? Okay, if you help him up?" asked the paramedic.

"John, what about Brian?" asked Emma, now distressed as she gazed at the destruction.

"Let's get Hunter to the car," replied John.

"Emma, I can help out here. I'll get a taxi back later, okay?" said John. He put Hunter's gun into her jacket.

Dr John Moody, an army field trauma specialist, went to work.

Four mobile diesel-powered light towers quietly bathed the blood-soaked scene in pure white light. John felt it was identical to a war zone with destroyed vehicles and several double-decker London buses burnt out and now leaning over.

By 2 am, there were no more fires. Whispers of smoke lingered along with the repulsive aroma of burnt human flesh. Emergency services were now retrieving the dead.

The Police diverted traffic away from the site by closing surrounding streets. Police tractor-trailer drivers arrived and set up two mobile Police Command Centers near the site.

At 2:30 am, building contractors erected a vinyl-covered mobile fence stretching from one side of the road to the other at both ends. Emergency vehicles now clogged all the streets. Forensic tents, support vehicles and diesel generators filled the crowded space. Police instructed the contractors to extend the portable fence perimeter.

By morning, sixty-three tagged body bags lined the footpath side by side. It was a tragic scene, but emergency workers kept their heads down and kept working the scene. The forensic team were still gathering scattered body parts. If anything, it was precise and methodical. The investigation would take weeks. A few body bags were flat, and others less than half empty. A cafe nearby brought a van load of free food and tea urns for those working on-site.

At dawn, tired detectives and forensic officers could see the full extent of the destruction. The media were swarming the area, lined up outside the fence at both ends, holding video cameras above their heads over the temporary fencing, transmitting live images.

The UK Prime Minister arrived at 7:50 am and thanked all the emergency workers, detectives, forensic officers and Police. He shook hands, patted the backs of workers and had short conversations with everybody.

The detectives, forensic officers, emergency workers and Police stopped working.

They stood silent as the Prime Minister approached the body bags. It was a profoundly sobering sight. Surrounded by his armed security, the Prime Minister looked at each of the sixty-three body bags.

The TV cameras captured everything. The PM knew these folks; some were colleagues and friends. He bent down each time to read the name tags, of which there were only a few. The worst were the body parts in bags. Forensics would identify these later. Those bags had numbers and no names.

The Police Commander gave him a sheet of paper that contained the list of names of the dead as of 7 am. The list was short. Media photographers behind the barricade had their morning news shots. Other journalists were filming from the top of high rises nearby. The Prime Minister had lost friends and colleagues. Evidently, he was distraught, choosing not to make any media statement. The PM had called an emergency meeting at the Palace of Westminster, the House of Commons and the House of Lords. But now, he stood before his deceased friends, head bowed.

CHAPTER 80

BOMBSITE

"I stood beside the glass doors, against the wall. I was on my phone when the first explosion happened," said Hunter.

Two detectives from Scotland Yard had picked up Hunter from the Australian Embassy to take him to the scene. He had walked the detectives through what happened. "I saw the guy with his phone out over here," replied Hunter. He pointed from where he had fallen near the car. They walked from the car to the footpath leading to the alley. Hunter was limping.

"What made you suspicious?" asked the detective.

"Everybody was running—those who could run. Vehicles had stopped moving, and people were on fire. Many lay injured. People were abandoning their cars and running. But this guy stood with his phone out, taking pictures as people ran past him.

"Taking pictures, like a journalist?" asked the second detective.

"He may not have been taking photos, now that I think about it. It could have been a remote. He showed no fear. When he saw me looking at him, he pulled his gun," said Hunter.

"Did he recognize you?" asked the detective.

"No," said Hunter.

"Why did he withdraw his weapon?" asked the detective.

"He interpreted my staring at him as a threat or witness, I guess," replied Hunter.

"Do you remember what he looked like?" asked the detective.

"The flames behind me lit his face for a split second, but I was looking at the gun," said Hunter.

"Where were you?" asked the detective.

"I staggered about halfway across the road, stopped here. I was leaning on a car to get my breath. I had stopped and looked at him. When I saw the gun, I fell to the ground," said Hunter.

"He started shooting at you?" asked the detective.

"I couldn't hear a thing; my ears were ringing, but yes, he fired and hit the car that I was behind," replied Hunter.

"You returned fire from under a car, hitting his foot. And your weapon?" asked the detective.

"My team has it and is available for you," replied Hunter. They were now standing deep inside the alley across the road from the hotel. "I remember trying to follow the shooter's blood trail, but I was struggling. I collapsed on this path. My team retrieved me from here, and the paramedic "umm," mumbled Hunter, unable to finish his sentence.

"You don't look too good. Okay, let's take a break." Hunter sat on the ground at the entrance of a brick alcove from the alley. His head is between his legs, and his blood pressure is dropping. He took a few deep breaths, trying to fight it. "I feel light-headed."

"Take it easy," replied the detective. Hunter swallowed a tablet the paramedic gave him. His breathing slowed, and he knew he was about to pass out.

"I'll get you some water," said the detective.

The other detective asked Hunter a question and then stood back, watching the other detective.

CHAPTER 81

U K TV STUDIOS

Later that morning, a television journalist interviewed two experts: an explosives standards auditor and a professor from the International Studies Centre for Non-proliferation. The auditor described what had happened at the Hotel bombing site at 8:12 am, based on data from seismological sensors stationed across London. The television journalist asked, "What are your thoughts regarding these tragic events this morning?"

The auditor responded, "First, I offer my condolences and heartfelt prayers to the families who have lost their loved ones, and in particular to our emergency service workers. Second, based on both visual and seismological evidence, the damage assessment equals four tons of TNT, which is greater than the 1994 Oklahoma bombing. Today is a tragic day for London and its people."

CHAPTER 82

MILTON'S HOME

Like twenty-five million UK residents, Milton Kahnt sat in his room watching the live TV morning news. He turned the sound off and phoned Laura.

"Morning, Laura," said Milton. "Are you okay? Have you seen the news?"

"I can't believe it. It's tragic. The media is reporting that the PM is dead," replied Laura

"Yes, it is tragic," said Milton. "Laura, I think it best we don't open the office for three days. Everybody is on edge. Do you have family nearby?"

"Yes, I do. You're right, three days. Do you think we are safe?" asked Laura.

"I'm sure you are safe. Stay inside or go to your parents. It's best not to be by yourself. Okay? I will phone our site managers now and instruct a three-day paid break," said Milton.

He finished his phone calls except for one. The 'WAS' phone was on his lap. Milton sat back down, thinking what to say. 'Was that you, Ahmed? 'Ahmed would say,' Yes, wasn't it great?'

Milton knew his response. If he asked Ahmed why he did it, Milton also knew the answer. He put the phone on the balcony table, walked over to his small kitchen and made a cup of tea. He was agitated and deeply distanced from Ahmed's reckless actions.

The nuclear documentary with the enormous death rate was acting like cancer in Milton's mind. He finally admitted it to himself. 'I regret getting involved with Ahmed. I hate my old life. I hate what Ahmed did today,' thought Milton. 'I don't want my old violent life anymore.'

Waves of guilt washed over Milton. 'What do I do with my shame?' he thought. 'I know I have changed.' A fight raged inside of him, and the old Abu told him he could never change, that he was as guilty as Ahmed.

Abu whispered, 'Darkness surrounds me.'

He made breakfast but didn't touch the food. The diversion didn't work. He opened his tablet to play music but glimpsed at the latest news on his tablet. Joint Police and MI5 raids commenced in the early hours of the morning.

It was a response to the bombings. One of the men arrested had the word "Kafir" scratched on the barrels of his guns. The Arabic term means "unbeliever" and describes a person who disbelieves in god as defined by Islam. The Police also confiscated pipe bombs. MI5 raided a Birmingham home of a British-Egyptian national connected to a bombing in Tanzania. The Police found TNT and blasting caps in his basement. The evidence found on both the defendant's phones revealed their violent ideology, but not the perpetrator from last night.

'How to win people over to Islam by threatening them.' Milton had witnessed the same attitude and the same threats. He had thought the same way. 'I had thought the same way.'

One newspaper headline quoted an angry Police officer saying, "Islam is a bloody, ruthless and intolerant false religion, a menace to the world. Why is violence needed to defend their prophet? I question the morality and legitimacy of the Koran they hide behind. It is a warlike religion. Its power is of no value. It is not a loving religion but a brute force filled with fanaticism and violence. It has no grace and no forgiveness."

Milton agreed, 'That was me, warlike.'

It hit him hard, like solid punches to the gut. He hated himself, his old identity he had held with great pride.

'I killed in the name of a militant god, or was it me that had murder in my heart?' thought Milton. The internal battle aged. 'What kind of wretched, miserable man are you?'

'I don't want that old life, its memories, its darkness.'

Tears streamed down his face. "Is there forgiveness for me? Is it possible for me to have a new life?'

Milton looked at his shaking hands. He knew he had bleached them with the blood of the innocent.

CHAPTER 83

DOMINION THEATRE LONDON

Many shops were closed, except for one coffee shop where he ordered a coffee. There was silence in the coffee shop as everybody stared at the TV news anchors. He turned to the Barista, thanked her for the coffee, left the café and strolled away.

His mind was a million miles away as he ploughed into a portable street sign outside the Dominion Theatre entrance. It was an invitation asking people to pray for the victims.

He stood there momentarily, unsure what to do, then walked in and sat alone in a theatre seat. There were a few hundred people. Some were praying, some were crying, and others were silent. He listened to heartfelt prayers coming from the stage. Milton cried.

Milton wondered if St. Mary's-Le-Strand would have prayers; perhaps he should go there. But he felt glued to the seat, his guilt weighing him down, unable to stand. Prayer after prayer was given, but with no calls for revenge or hatred or fighting back. There was a profound sense of peace in the theatre, a stark contrast to the turmoil inside of him. He admitted to himself finally that he was trying to redeem himself by renovating St. Mary's for free.

'Can you buy redemption?' he wondered.

As he left, an usher handed him a bunch of flowers through the glass entrance doors. "If you pass the bomb site, please place them there or nearby."

He thanked the usher and glanced behind her. There were boxes and boxes of flowers. Milton said, "Thank you for what you are doing." He wiped away tears, "I'm an emotional wreck."

He didn't understand what was happening to him.

CHAPTER 84

ST. PANCRAS HOSPITAL

John found Hunter in surgery at St. Pancras Hospital, which was in chaos. "Emma, I found him. He is on the floor above you." He hung up his cell phone and waited for her.

"Bombs cause unique patterns of injury seldom seen outside of combat zones. Mr Hunter has survived. It was a high-order explosive producing a supersonic over-pressurized shock wave. Mr Hunter was sitting on the ground behind a concrete wall at the time of the explosion. It saved his life," said the doctor to John and Emma.

Emma was relieved. John replied, "He suffered a concussion from the first two blasts last night."

"That explains the other injuries," replied the surgeon. "There are no penetrating fragmentation or blunt injuries, and no amputation needed, just deep wounds. Those wounds are now clean. Each with twenty-odd stitches. Does he have asthma?"

"No," replied John.

"He has had breathing issues, most likely from the dust, smoke and toxic fumes. Mr Hunter is in good physical shape. He has significant past injuries, and I assume he is an ex-soldier based on his scars," said the doctor.

"Ex-soldier. You're correct," replied John.

"He needs rest. We will watch for any TBI. You can see him in thirty minutes. Okay, good luck," said the surgeon.

Emma said, "Thank you, doctor." They sat again to wait.

John said more to himself than Emma: "Good luck. Does luck rule everything? I'm sorry you ran out of luck. You're dead."

"You okay?" asked Emma.

"I don't like that saying," replied John.

Emma texted Karen with an update. She rested her elbows on her knees and held her face in her hands. "The UK is in crisis. I saw fear in the eyes of all the people downstairs."

John leaned back against the wall, "That is the definition of terrorism. It's the driver."

"Why did he kill those people?" asked Emma. "He killed the Police command, Counter-terrorism, MI5, MI6 and the PM?"

"Fear is his weapon," replied John. He saw a coffee vending machine and brought back two coffees. They sipped their coffee while thinking.

"The driver had the time and location of that meeting," said John. How did he get there, and how did he set up the explosives so fast?"

"Who chose that site?" Emma asked. That is where we start. Hunter said this morning that Counter-Terrorism Command called the meeting. The third explosion only happened when the PM arrived with a few politicians. The driver did it, or was this political?"

"The PM has already been replaced and will reassure the public the government is in control," said John. "A curfew will happen, and the army might be on the streets. It's about confidence and security. Don't they phone in and take the credit if it is political? No, it's the driver."

Emma's phone chirped. "Hi Lucas, you want an update? Okay. Unfortunately, Brian Clinton didn't make it. Hunter's surgery has finished. We will see him soon. Lucas, Counter-Terrorism Command, called the meeting. The driver knew about last night's meeting, the location and the time."

"You want me to find a connection," asked Lucas.

"There must be some procedure or protocol," replied Emma. "They

organize a strategy, a communication meeting with people on a prede-
termined list."

"I got this," replied Lucas.

Emma looked discouraged. She was crying, ready to walk away.

The Australian Ambassador to London, Dr Alice Wang, entered the
hospital hallway walking towards them, surrounded by security,
"Afternoon, any news on Hunter?"

"Ms Ambassador Hunter is in recovery," replied John. The surgeon
says he will be okay but need rest."

"Brian was one of the victims last night," said Wang. "I've spoken
with his family. The casket will go to Perth in about a week, but I
suspect it will be empty, considering ." She stopped for a moment. "I
believe you were about to move out of the Embassy. I've rescinded that
decision. We've increased our security. "I've asked Karen for more feet
on the ground to help you guys. She has chosen people you have
worked with before, plus a new head of the station. They will be here
in about nine hours, so let's regroup in twelve hours at the Embassy. If
Hunter is up to it, he can coordinate our next steps. If not, the new
head of station will."

Dr Wang and her armed protective detail left as they had come
fast.

"Just lovely," whispered Emma.

A surgery nurse informed them that Hunter was awake, had eaten
some food, and asked for you both.

"Talk about bruises, buddy. How are you?" asked John. "We will
have to call you Bluey!"

"Banged up, but okay," replied Hunter. "John, my phone is in the
cupboard. Hopefully, a text from the MI6 bloke's office with the
addresses of the two MI5 IT guys might be there. Sir Robert said one of
them had developed an AI surveillance server, and I think one of these
IT guys will have a duplicate at home."

"What do you want to do?" John asked. Emma was shocked to find
Hunter back in spy mode.

"Give Lucas and the Australian HQJOC IT guy access to monitor all
communications in the UK for the words, 'Abu Sarek,'" replied Hunter.

Emma found the phone. "It has two addresses." John summarized Ambassador Wang's decision. Hunter said nothing.

"So we're breaking into their home," asked Emma. She looked for confirmation.

"They can't object," said John.

"You are looking for a server or external hard drives and passwords. Have Lucas online; he will know it when he sees it," said Hunter.

"Yep," said Emma.

A Police inspector knocked on the open door, "Sorry to interrupt, Mr Hunter?"

"Yes?" replied Hunter. "Please come in."

"I am Inspector Brad Lynch from Scotland Yard." He held up his warrant card and said, "Do you mind? I have just a few questions. Is that okay?"

"Not a problem. These are my colleagues, John Moody and Emma Smirnov."

"Nice to meet you." Inspector Lynch said, "This is everyone's attendance list at last night's meeting. You and your supervisor, Brian Clinton, were on that list, and you are the only living witness."

"It was a tragic night. I can walk you through the meeting," replied Hunter.

"Great. Mind if I record this?" asked Lynch. He put his phone on Hunter's table.

"Brian and I were seated at the back of the room at the meeting," replied Hunter.

John asked Inspector Lynch, "Who gave you that list?"

Inspector Lynch replied, "Commander Jones from the National Counter Terrorism Security office organized the meeting. They have a protocol to follow, a set of names.

"Did Commander Jones add Brian and Hunter at the last minute?" asked Emma.

"Yes. Someone added Brian and Hunter's names," replied Lynch.

"Who chose the location?" asked John.

"Jones' secretary chooses a random location," replied Lynch. "An encrypted text is sent. You're asking because you think somebody compromised his system?"

"That was what we were wondering," replied Emma. The bomber got there first." Emma texted Lucas.

"We were discussing this before you arrived," said John to Lynch.

"The meeting came up with several unworkable suggestions, except one," said Hunter. "Then everybody started talking. I left early to make a call. I was on the street beside the hotel's front entrance when both explosions happened."

"The traffic had stopped due to the fires?" asked Lynch.

"People abandoned their cars and a couple of buses. Everyone was running away from the fire except for one person. I'm confident he had a remote and was watching the building," said Hunter. "Originally, I thought it was a phone; he was a journalist taking pictures."

John saw Emma's confusion and whispered, "You can trigger a bomb on your phone's Wi-Fi."

"He saw me and pulled a gun," said Hunter. "I returned fire, shooting under a car, and hit him in the foot. He bled and ran. I collapsed in the alley. Paramedics patched me up, and John and Emma took me to our Embassy."

Inspector Lynch asked, "You didn't come here first? You went back to the Embassy?"

"This morning around 8 am, a detective from your Scotland Yard picked me up, and we returned to the scene. I walked him through what happened and showed him the alley. A second detective asked more questions."

Inspector Lynch asked, "We only allocated one officer from the Yard to speak with you. Did the second detective identify himself?"

"Sorry. It's a blur," replied Hunter.

Inspector Lynch said, "Continue, please!"

"When the PM arrived, everybody stopped working. We were in the alley at the time. The interview stopped. I felt dizzy and sat on the ground," replied Hunter. "The first detective said he would get me some water. The other detective, I think, asked me questions. That's it. Then I woke up and saw these two knuckleheads."

Emma rolled her eyes. "Well, this knucklehead, Hunter, needs some coffee."

"Did you see the bomber again today?" asked Lynch.

"No," said Hunter. "He would have been outside the explosive radius with the line of sight, waiting for the PM to arrive."

"If I bring in a digital artist, can you describe the bomber's face from the first explosion," asked Lynch.

"Okay, but it may not be much," replied Hunter. "It was a glimpse only."

Inspector Lynch switched the recorder off. "We lost a lot of highly skilled people yesterday."

"Who replaces the PM, his deputy?" asked John.

Inspector Lynch said, "Yes, already done."

"How would you describe the new PM as ambitious?" replied John.

Inspector Lynch said, "My honest answer is, he is a mouse and won't last. He's not behind or involved in this if that is what you think."

"Is the army taking over security?" asked John.

"Yes. If you recall any other critical details, please contact me. Here is my card. I'll get an artist here within the hour," replied Inspector Lynch as he left. "Get better, and thank you for your time."

John took Karen's call, putting the phone on speaker. "Was Bomber the driver, not Sarek or ZL?" Karen asked.

"Correct," replied John. "Hunter saw his face briefly. We've asked Lucas to look for an assistant in Counter-terrorism. The driver got the location and time early enough to plant the bombs. The driver antici-pated the meeting."

"Emma and John are going to the home of the two deceased MI5 IT guys," said Hunter. "There should be a copy of their AI program. It will search all of the UK for any talk on Abu Sarek or a link to the driver."

Emma walked into the room with three coffees.

"Hunter, this morning, did the second detective have an accent?" asked Emma.

CHAPTER 85

AUSTRALIA HQJOC

"Hey, John?" yelled Wayne.

"Wayne, how often have I said you don't yell across the office?" said John.

"Hey John, I have some bloke from ASIS in Sydney on the phone wanting to talk to you, mate," said Wayne.

"Righto, put him through; what's his name?" asked John.

"Luke Skywalker. Hey, push the encryption button, mate," said Wayne.

John rolled his eyes. "John Lewis speaking."

"Hi John, my name is Lucas. I believe you have spoken with Karen," said Lucas.

John replied, "Yes. How can I help you?"

Lucas asked, "Are you up to speed with the events happening in the UK?"

"The Red Banners, bombing. Yeah, mate," replied John.

"I'm wondering if you guys can help with an MI5 AI server created by one of their now-deceased agents," asked Lucas

Wayne shouted from the other side of the room, saying, "Hey John, that would be Warren Driscoll, mate!" said Wayne.

John said, "Lucas, let me put you on hold for a moment."

"Are you listening to my conversation, mate?" said John.

Wayne said, "Hey John, I might have a copy of 'Joyce.'"

John smiled, then, switched back to Lucas' call.

"Lucas sorry. I'm going to pass you over to Wayne Scott. He has some intel on your request," said John.

"Hey, Luke, how are you, mate? Sorry about the confusion, mate. Look, when MI5 was burning down the other night, I got into their server and uploaded as much as possible before the backup batteries died. I think I got most of Joyce," said Wayne.

"Who is Joyce?" asked Lucas.

"That's what Warren Driscoll called his AI servers," said Wayne. "Driscoll has a bunch of servers at Gatwick and Heathrow plus London Airport. All named after old girlfriends."

"Heathrow, Gatwick and London were separate programs or the same," asked Lucas."

"Yeah, mate the same. Anyway, the coding is amazing, plus Warren had another server at his home. Everything at Thames house, including backups, got burnt to the ground."

"Have you got everything, including the entry codes?" asked Lucas.

"She was flirting with me until I worked out how to talk to her," said Wayne. "She thinks I'm Warren. She's ready to go. What do you want her to do, Luke?"

Lucas explained the plan and gave Wayne the name 'Abu Sarek' plus keywords, cell phone numbers, and any digital documents with the name.

"Okay, mate. I'll code it and get her at it. I'll call you back soon, buddy. Have a good one," said Wayne.

Lucas disconnected the call and turned to Karen.

"It's done. HQJOC Canberra will run the name."

He texted John to update him that Wayne from HQJOC had Joyce. There was no need to enter Driscoll's home. John and Emma retraced their steps, locked the Driscoll's back door, and left.

CHAPTER 86

BOMBSITE LONDON

Milton Kahnt had laid flowers near the bomb site's outer fence along with many other bouquets. People were standing around, some crying, and others standing silently. What he saw, he had seen many times before. He felt victorious before, and now he felt pain, sorrow, and regret.

'This isn't about me today, you fool. This is about others,' thought Milton.

He walked back to his unit, made some lunch, opened the balcony door, sat at the small table, and looked in the direction of the bomb site. He got up, went to the safe, opened it, removed the 'SAW' phone, walked back to the balcony chair, and switched the phone on. Ahmed had responded to Milton's questions about the bombing of emergency service people.

'What if it was me?' said the text.

'Indifferent and careless.' Milton noted the tone.

Milton typed: Are the RBs still only as a threat? Has something changed?

Ahmed responded: I had a wife and three sons. My family was murdered and run over.

Milton typed: I didn't know. I'm sorry.

'Ahmed had never spoken of them, ever. Is it even true?' thought Milton.

He thought about his next question. 'Ahmed has changed.'

He recalled conversations where Ahmed had made him the mysterious, victorious Jihadist while he was in prison. 'Maybe nothing changed at all. Ahmed planned to frame me for the Red Banners murders.

"An Islamic state was never the plan," said Milton.

Milton deleted: Islamic State or Revenge?

"Ahmed's plan was never to use the 'Red Banners' as a bargaining chip. They were to be instruments of revenge on millions of lives," said Milton. "Can I stop this?"

'I am not an innocent man in any of this mess. My past torments me daily. Even my new life runs on terrorism money. I feel shame when I reflect on the people I have hurt and killed. No, murdered,' thought Milton.

Milton changed into walking clothes and left his apartment to think.

'Ahmed had changed, and I have changed. But in opposite directions. My new name had given me the gift of life, a second chance, a career, a purpose, even pleasure and joy,' thought Milton.

As he walked, "What do I do with the guilt that washes over me daily?" whispered Milton. His walk brought him back again to the tragic bomb site. There were so many people there. Some held candles, others attached hand-drawn notes to the fence with the message of sympathy, and there were flowers everywhere. Milton read many of the heartbreaking letters. He wondered if there were family members here mourning. He looked around and saw one group of women embracing one distraught lady.

His shoulders dropped. Milton phoned Laura. "How are you?"

"I'm okay, Mr. Kahnt. I am at my parents' home. Have you called?" Laura asked.

"Laura, I'm at the bomb site. Can we do something for the loved ones left behind by this tragedy? I want to offer to pay for the funerals or burials personally and anonymously. I don't know how to do this. Can you organize that, Laura?"

"Do you mean everybody?" asked Laura.

"Yes, if they accept the offer," replied Milton.

CHAPTER 87

CHELSEA, WEST LONDON

Ahmed thought through all his steps over the last few nights: the secretary he had paid off, the man who had stared at him. 'Who was he? There was recognition there, even bravery.' Ahmed then reflected on Abu and the tone of his text questions. 'Would Abu betray me? Maybe he already has,' thought Ahmed.

Milton thought about Ahmed as he walked back to his unit. Milton recognized he was in mourning, feeling the loss of his brother, even with his betrayal and deception.

'Why didn't he tell me about his family? My brother's family died from a vehicle accident,' wondered Milton.

"Ahmed will have identified the regiment driver of a 'Stolly," said Milton to himself. "Those five-ton, bulky 6 x 6 high mobility units would crush anything in its path. The driver would know what he did."

He stopped walking. He heard the pedestrian lights changing to green. Distracted, Milton was walking across the road. When he looked up, he saw a green-painted British Army Stolly straddling the footpath facing him. Behind that was an Oshkosh wheeled tanker used for logistical support for fuel and water. He stood and stared. The soldiers were watching him. Milton saw M16 assault rifles, M4 carbines, Glock 17s, and one soldier had over his shoulder an L129A1 —no, it was an L115A3 sniper rifle.

There would be another way back to his unit. 'They are not hunting Ahmed. They act as security guards, like at a nightclub. A show of force.' thought Milton.

Out of the corner of his eye, he saw a payphone. He turned around, walked back, dialled 999, and waited for the call to go through. "Ahmed, the bomber will target the Army. It's revenge. The Army killed his family." He took a deep breath of relief, returned to his unit, made coffee and sat on the balcony. His body was shaking.

"I have betrayed my brother."

The streetlights shone below his balcony. The light rain was causing the lights to twinkle and blur. 'Where are the Red Banners? Ahmed's family, was it true? I didn't see any photos in the factory, none?'

Milton finished his coffee and tried to stop the tumble dryer of thoughts bouncing around, but he couldn't. "Would the police charge Ahmed with planning a terrorist act? Yes, but his arrest would save millions of lives," said Ahmed. "If I get arrested. So be it if it stops millions from dying."

After washing his coffee cup, he changed into casual wear, opened his safe, and removed the WAS phone. He locked his apartment and walked down the fire stairs to the underground car park.

Milton typed a message into the WAS phone. 'Ahmed will murder a Stolly driver and its crew as revenge for his family deaths.' He punched 999. He smashed the WAS phone with his foot and threw the remains in the industrial bin.

PREVIOUSLY AT THE BOMB SITE

Aleksandr Izvestia was standing behind the barriers, watching forensic officers process the bomb site. Igor Medkov had ordered him to go to London and to work independently of any ZL team. He was an undercover Russian agent working as a Police officer in Stockholm and hated ZL's work. They were animals and never helpful.

When he heard that Thames House was on fire, he arrived as fast as possible. He didn't watch the fire; he stood at the back and watched people. He watched the madness of ZL shooting carelessly into the crowd. He followed the chase to the bridge and watched, then walked across the bridge, trying to memorize the three faces of men talking and looking over the bridge railing into the Thames. When he heard of the bombing at the Hotel, he saw the same two men in the crowd being held back by police officers, and the third was inside the police cordon and was receiving assistance from paramedics. Then he saw two more people, the same three people from Stockholm. 'The Australian ASIS team, two men and one woman.'

Izvestia sent a text to Medkov, "The attack on the ASIS team in Stockholm failed, and they are here at the London bomb site, still investigating. Follow or kill?"

"Kill."

Aleksandr Izvestia knew police procedures when it came to bomb-ings. He watched who was present on the site. He saw what he needed and left the bomb site looking for a second-hand men's clothing store. He selected new underwear, a suit, shirt, tie, shoes, socks, and an old money wallet. He went to the dressing room, changed, paid the cashier, put his old clothes in the contribution bin, and left looking for a photocopy store.

He took out his phone, opened the browser, and then opened images, searching for a UK Warrant card. When he found one, he used software on his phone to insert his picture, fake name, and title, Detec-tive Alex Vesta.

He plugged his phone into the printer, adjusted the printed image, cut it to size, and inserted it inside the wallet's clear plastic holder. He paid and left. Next, he found a coffee shop, ordered six takeaway coffees, and then returned to the bomb site.

Emergency service contractors had erected a mobile fence structure on either end of the bombing site, and the company attached white vinyl for privacy. He walked confidently towards the constable on the fence, flashed his ID, knowing the guy was looking at the coffee and not the Warrant Card and asked, "How long have you been here, son? Doesn't matter here. Take one," said Aleksandr Izvestia. Izvestia went directly to the ambulances, offering coffee. "This is tragic. Anyone survive?" asked Aleksandr Izvestia.

"Not sure; we think only one," replied the paramedic.

"Just one. Will the woman survive?" asked Aleksandr Izvestia

"A man. Head trauma, lots of cuts. My name is Hunter. Only bodies are coming out now," replied the paramedic.

"At this point, he is the only witness. Was he concussed? Was he verbal? Do you think he's up for an interview?" Aleksandr Izvestia asked.

"Look, I'm not sure. I spoke briefly with the paramedic who took him to St. Pancras," the paramedic replied. You would need to go to St. Pancras. Sorry, I can't help anymore."

"You're busy. Thanks for your help," said Aleksandr Izvestia.

Aleksandr badged his way into emergency and surgery. He made his way to intensive care and found the nurse station. "Sorry to interrupt." He showed his Warrant Card. "I am Detective Vesta. The man from the bombing, Mr Hunter, when can I interview him?" asked Aleksandr Izvestia.

"He's got patched up on-site. He never came here," replied the nurse.

"Thanks. Would the patient be at another hospital?" asked Aleksandr Izvestia.

"Sorry, I have no idea," replied the nurse. "I have to go; we're full."

"Thank you for your time," said Aleksandr Izvestia.

It was now 6 am. The following day, Aleksandr Izvestia went to find breakfast and do the coffee routine again. Hunter arrived with another detective, and Aleksandr watched Hunter pointing to a place near the Hotel's wall. The PM had arrived, and everybody started to whisper. The workers stopped and waited. Vesta made his way over to Hunter without drawing attention.

"Hello, I'm Detective Alex Vesta. Are you Mr Hunter, the witness?" asked Aleksandr Izvestia.

Hunter answered with a nod.

Aleksandr Izvestia turned to the other detective. "Sorry to intrude, Detective. I missed him last night at St. Pancras. Mind if I tag along?"

All three entered the laneway. Hunter felt sick and sat down behind a concrete pillar. One detective went to get water for Hunter. Aleksandr had his opportunity. He leaned down to Hunter and asked, "Where are the 'Red Banners?'" Hunter was out cold. Aleksandr stood back up.

Then he died instantly.

CHAPTER 88

STATE FUNERAL LONDON
The new Commander of the Counterterrorism unit was Mitch Burleigh.

"We only have three team members alive in the city unit, and they were on leave. Contact all four counterterrorism units. I need a full team of twenty for a series of funerals. I want those calls made now. Then, organize accommodation and rosters," said Burleigh to his second in command.

"Leave is cancelled," said Burleigh.

They usually limit state funerals to monarchs but may include a distinguished person, such as the Prime Minister. Ceremonial burials were for the high-ranking officials who died in the bombing. An unknown sponsor had paid for the remaining funerals. The new PM allocated politicians to attend every public servant's funeral, law enforcement officer, and emergency workers who perished in the bombings. The first funeral was the Prime Minister's, followed by other funerals across Greater London over the next four days. There were no open coffins.

The new Prime Minister called for seven days of mourning. Few knew what that term meant. It was not a joyous occasion to celebrate a life well lived. It was the opposite. There was little joy. People gathered on the streets, watching and waiting for the PM's gun carriage to pass.

"I chose to defy this fear, and I refuse to cower to a bully with a bomb," said one man to the people on either side. Some mumbled agreements, and others remained silent.

Standing in front of these brave citizens were armed soldiers. Shoulder to shoulder, they lined the PM's funeral procession streets. The armed forces performed the same duty for the remaining funerals in the suburbs and towns. It was a clear statement. Their defiance was blatant.

Tomorrow's headline would read: 'The armed forces on the streets of the United Kingdom.' It was a show of strength. Military and Police vehicles lined the city intersections, and helicopters flew overhead, watching, searching, ready to respond—counterterrorism teams across the city and inside and outside St. Paul's Cathedral.

Five days after the bombing, the Royal Navy had the prime minister's coffin on a gun carriage draped by the UK flag. The gun carriage was moving at a slow walking pace from Westminster Hall to St. Paul's Cathedral. Armed sailors from the Royal Navy drew the gun carriage. Sailors always held their weapons in reverse as a sign of mourning.

But not today.

A military band marched in silence behind the gun carriage. After the military guard lowered the PM's coffin into the ground, they would play. You could hear the sound of the shoes of the Navy men and women moving along the bitumen road. There was no talking. The polished wooden wheels of the gun carriage were silent as it moved gracefully along the route. The four young children, the PM's wife and his successor walked behind the gun carriage.

The only sound the crowd and soldier heard were the cries of four children.

Television stations live-streamed the event. People were angry. Mitch Burleigh assigned three counterterrorism agents to Hunter and his expanded team to search buildings along the Strand. The gun carriage passed by St. Mary's-le-StrandMary s-le-Strand on its way to St. Paul's Cathedral without incident.

The search teams have yet to find anything.

Karen's boss, Gideon Downer, the director of Defense Intelligence and her Sydney team watched the Livestream. The Australian Prime Minister John Porter had expressed his condolences but was advised not to attend for security reasons. Other nations, including Russian President Denya Driminov, expressed sorrow at the tragic events.

CHAPTER 89

AUSTRALIA HQJOC

"Hey, John," said Wayne.

"Yeah, Wayne, what do you want? It's the start of the shift, and I'm busy," John replied.

"Hey, John. It's noon London time. Mate, they're live-streaming the UK PM's funeral," said Wayne.

"Wayne, I already have it on my screen. Don't you have any work to do?" asked John.

"Hey, John," called Wayne.

"Yes, Wayne," replied John.

"Do you think upstairs would mind if I use some satellite time?" asked Wayne.

"Mate, it's 9 p.m., mate. Only the night crew is upstairs," replied John. "They will need to make the decision, not me."

"Can I do it anyways, over the UK," asked Wayne.

"Why, Wayne?" asked John.

"Luke Skywalker asked me to use Joyce to find stuff on Sarek. The bloke took flying lessons a few years back, purchased a truck, and did some parachute jumping. Do you want me to email that to Luke Skywalker?" asked Wayne.

"Yeah, go ahead. I'm watching the funeral, mate," said John.

"So I can use a satellite?" asked Wayne.

"Whatever!" mumbled John, now engrossed in the sad procession.

Wayne had already logged into four satellites and waited. If nothing happened, he would do the same again with the next group of birds coming over the horizon. Wayne had a pre-determined text ready to go out to Dr John and Karen at ASIS in Sydney, Lucas, and Hunter. The cellphone text contained a GPS location, a message, and magnitude.

He had a hunch or more like a guess.

Wayne reached out to his IT geek friends to create a scene for a computer game. The winner would get one Bitcoin. The story had a nuclear bomb and a protagonist who could fly a plane and parachute. One competitor's story made Wayne think.

'Would Sarek do this?'

CHAPTER 90

DURHAM AIRPORT UK

Ahmed had travelled by hire car to Durham Teesside Airport from Otterburn. The previous day, he had driven his truck to the light plane section, unloaded it, and then gone to Otterburn, near the Northumberland National Park. Durham is an international airport that serves the North East of England. Light and heavy commercial planes use the runway, and it competes for traffic with Leeds Airport in Bradford. For many months, Ahmed had taken skydiving lessons and learned to fly a twin-engine plane.

The aircraft storage, repairs, and maintenance section is away from the main international airport. Ahmed's flying license was current for his Cessna 335. Now, with hundreds of hours of flying, he recognizes towns, roads, and many landmarks. The twin-powered Cessna had a capacity of 300 horsepower, a speed of 152 Km/h, and a range of 2604 km.

This Cessna had a maximum service ceiling of 29,800 feet. With the six passenger seats removed, it could now carry 1256 kgs. Ahmed had clearance to fly at 25,000 feet today, heading northwest. The maximum exit altitude for skydiving is 18,000 feet, where you don't need supplemental oxygen. Above that height, jumps are called 'MFF' or 'Military

Free Fall.' He had imported from the USA a HALO wingsuit with an oxygen mask. Today, he would jump at 25,000 feet. The jump included 75 seconds of freefall, and then he'd deploy his parachute and choose where to land.

He set the speed for 390km/hr and his rate of climb at 1400 feet per minute. It was 12:15 pm when he turned above the rural township of Otterburn. The Cessna was now on autopilot and would remain at 25,000 feet for another 18 to 21 minutes.

At 19 minutes, it would be above Catterick Garrison near Richmond, 21 miles from Teesside Airport. The Cessna was not a pressurized plane. He made a final check, opened the pilot's door, and slid off the wing without hitting the rear tail. Tumbling momentarily, he stabilized his freefall for 75 seconds, then opened his chute and aimed to land near Otterburn.

CHAPTER 91

CATTERICK GARRISON, RICHMOND UK

The 'Red Banner' exploded at 25,000 feet directly above Catterick Garrison, leaving a trail of absolute destruction up to two kilometres. The severe damage extended out to four kilometres, and the impact was felt as far as ten kilometres.

The horror of the thermal flash ignited fires that raged on relentlessly. The shockwave, travelling at the speed of sound, dispersed a lethal cloud of sickness. It took a full day for rescue teams to safely approach the site. The fallout, carried by the wind, moved eastward, towards the ocean, leaving a trail of devastation in its wake.

CHAPTER 92

AUSTRALIA HQJOC

"Hey, John, it happened," said Wayne. "John! John, come here!"

John raced over to Wayne's desk. He knew the difference between Wayne's annoying drone voice and the voice of panic. "What just happened, Wayne?"

"It is 12:19 pm London time. My coding identified the GPS location of the 'Red Banner'; its yield is 15,000 tons. Contamination cloud details, wind speed, and direction are all here on the screen," said Wayne.

They stared for several seconds in disbelief as Wayne scanned the readings. "It's a Red Banner. The GPS location is a military town, Catterick Garrison."

John swore under his breath and dropped his phone on the ground. He picked it up, contacted his boss, and was repeating Wayne's commentary.

"The blast wind travels 300 miles per second, but I hope the Ernst Mach will reduce its damage. No, no, my coding is giving a vaporization distance. It was an atmosphere-displacing shock wave. Somebody can calculate the gamma radiation and x-rays later," said Wayne.

"This is a disaster," whispered John.

"I just saw the double flash, John," said Wayne.

"I need to phone our guys in the UK," said John.

"They have already received a text with exact details."

His next coding step started automatically by sending satellite images after images and HD photos. They show wind direction and calculated contamination zones, adjusting as the wind changes speed or direction.

"What a disaster!"

CHAPTER 93

ST. PAUL'S CATHEDRAL, LONDON
The Anglican Rector from St. Marks, Darling Point Sydney, had married the Prime Minister and his wife in the early 1980s. He gave a gospel message on the promise of the resurrection. It was powerful, personal, and short.

The new Prime Minister was next. He knew he was not a public speaker. His secretary typed his speech in large fonts. He didn't need to hold the notes; just read them, line by line. But it didn't work. The shaking started with his hands, then his body. People turned away, embarrassed.

"We will never bow to those who wish to harm this great nation. Never again..." said the PM. At 12:23 pm, security teams raced to the podium and enacted their emergency extraction plan, carrying the PM out of the church. Cell phones were ringing, and more security entered the building, hastily escorting people to their vehicles. It was chaos. The rector looked at his phone text and saw the news. He best described it as an apocalypse. He didn't move, but bowing his head in prayer, he prayed for those who had now lost their lives in the town of Catterick Garrison.

The confusion outside the Cathedral was evident. Security now had their weapons out in plain sight. Some were escorting people to their vehicles others hunting for an invisible target. The crowds of people behind the barrier of soldiers turned and ran. Some were crying, and others were shouting as they fled. Soldiers experienced the same confusion until one soldier lowered his gun and ran towards the Cathedral, thinking an attack was happening inside. Then, all soldiers followed, pushing their way in to discover no one was shooting.

There was commotion everywhere. One soldier grabbed a security guard and demanded information. "I don't know. His security whipped away the PM. People were receiving texts and left quickly. Nothing has happened inside here."

The security guard freed himself from the grip of the soldier. The Cathedral had a large screen LED outside, showing a stunned and distraught PM carried to his vehicle by security. Havoc ruled as people attempted to escape, thinking the church would explode.

The church was empty, and silence returned.

The rector stood alongside the former PM's coffin. He invited the PM's wife and the four children to gather around the casket. The rector hugged each person in turn. He looked at the PM's wife, opened his Bible and re-read the wedding vows they had written and spoken to each other two decades back. The rector prayed with one hand on the coffin and as a personal friend. It was a heartfelt, moving prayer to God to bring comfort in the chaos. He named each child and asked for God's blessing upon each one. The two Parliamentary and Diplomatic Protection officers standing behind the former PM's wife wiped away tears.

CHAPTER 94

TEESSIDE AIRPORT UK

A dishevelled reporter replaced the PM's livestream. The word 'live' flashed across the bottom of the screen.

"I am at Teesside Airport, and we have just witnessed a massive explosion to the southwest. I saw a bright white flash, which was so intense that it blanked out the entire sky. Then, I saw a fireball, but there was no sound. It was completely silent. Thirty seconds later, I heard a sound like a loud, thundering growl. The ground shook, and I quickly retreated inside the airport building. As I entered, I felt a blast of hot, burning air wash over me. There is chaos inside the airport."

Milton was staring at the computer screen in disbelief. "Ahmed, what have you done? Oh no! You haven't murdered soldiers, you've murdered families, children and mothers. Why? Why did you do it? You lied. This is your revenge and you're mad," Milton cried. He held his face in his hands and wept for the innocent lives that had been lost.

As time passed, the news services were able to gather more information about what had happened. However, the reporters found themselves struggling to find the right words to describe the situation. It was evident from their tone that they were feeling a mix of shock and anger. Many people who were watching the live broadcast were left feeling numb, overwhelmed, and unable to articulate their thoughts and emotions.

One television news anchor brought in one representative from the Nuclear Energy industry and an environmental activist. It was a mistake. The activist charged in saying, "Our military has 215 nuclear weapons, of which 115 are operationally available, and our nuclear use policy is ambiguous, we have nuclear power plants, and today we saw what nuclear experts for years have denied, the great dangers of these devices in the wrongs hands," shouted the activist.

During a television news segment, the anchor made a mistake by bringing in a representative from the Nuclear Energy industry and an environmental activist. The activist argued that the country's military has 215 nuclear weapons, out of which 115 are operationally available, and that the nuclear use policy is ambiguous. They also highlighted the potential dangers associated with nuclear power plants and the recent demonstration of the risks of nuclear devices falling into the wrong hands.

The activist stood up and pointed her finger at the representative of Nuclear Energy. She then threw her lapel microphone on the floor and stormed out of the studio. While the activist may have made an error in judgement, her anger is a reflection of the mood of the nation in some way.

Milton was filled with regret. He turned off the TV, put on his coat, and left the apartment crying. He briefly considered getting drunk but changed his mind. His hands were shaking, and he was outraged. He stopped walking and vomited. After a few minutes, he said, "I should have said more. Didn't the police receive my call? I phoned twice." Milton continued, "Oh, Ahmed, you fool. Indiscriminate revenge will never bring back your loved ones."

He walked past several cafes, and everyone inside was watching the live broadcast as TV anchors scrambled for content. The pubs further down the street were the same. Milton could overhear conversations on the road. "Is it safe to be walking the streets?" He could read the shocked, sad, and angry expressions on people's faces, which mirrored his own emotions. He stopped walking and noticed the same prayer sign outside the Dominion Theatre.

"He needed help," thought Milton as he sat on a bench, feeling overwhelmed. Suddenly, a man approached him and asked, "How are you coping? Mind if I sit? The last few hours have been so sad and so hard." The man looked around, visibly upset.

Milton looked at the man in casual wear and asked, "You're the imam, I mean priest?"

"Pastor," corrected the man. His smile wasn't a smile but a look of sadness.

"How am I coping? I don't know what to do with my guilt and anger," said Milton, feeling the weight of his emotions.

The pastor gently repeated the words, "Anger and guilt." There was silence, and neither man spoke for several minutes.

Milton whispered in tears, "What do I do with my guilt? I could have done more."

"You feel guilty?" asked the pastor.

"My past haunts me daily, and it has returned today," replied Milton.

The pastor sensed that something authentic was happening in this man's life. Perhaps violence from his past was triggered by the bomb devastation. He may have been with the security services and had overlooked a clue to today's disaster.

The pastor fell silent, waiting for wisdom to come to him. He then spoke, saying that everyone deals with guilt at some point in their life, but sometimes it can become overwhelming. Milton whispered that his old life was now riddled with guilt and shame because of the current situation. The pastor then revealed that before he became a believer, he used to medicate his guilt daily just to function. Despite having a PhD, a job, and a family, he hated himself and brought destruction to those around him. He eventually realized that he couldn't change himself. However, he experienced unmerited grace and forgiveness from God through Christ, which he didn't fully understand at the time. When Milton looked at him, he felt a glimmer of hope.

"Did it work?" asked Milton.

"Yes, I found out the hard way," replied the pastor. "I trusted in a promise of forgiveness."

For the first time, Milton looked at the man and noticed his tattoos and deep scars. He then asked the pastor, "Would your God forgive my guilt? Is that how it works?"

"Yes," replied the pastor. "Your friends, spouse, society, and the government may not, but God does. If feelings of forgiveness come with it, that's a bonus, but I can't live a life based on feelings. I trusted in God's promise. Grace, my friend, is free."

Milton had his head down. He lifted his head, and his face was full of tears. He asked a genuine question, seeking a truthful answer. "Are you a changed man?"

"I was a wreck. I tried to drink my guilt away," whispered the pastor. "My conscience kept accusing me. I couldn't change myself. I couldn't wash away my past. Christ did."

After ten minutes of silence, they passed. Milton took a deep breath, looked at the pastor, offered his hand and said, "Thank you."

CHAPTER 95

ASIA AUSTRALIA

Lucas told Karen, "Wayne, our IT mate, sent me a copy of AI MI5 software. Hunter asked Wayne and me to look for everything about Sarek. Wayne found that Sarek had taken flying and parachuting lessons a few years back. Hence today's disaster."

"It is always easy to combine things after the event," replied Karen.

"I also found two things," replied Lucas. "Debra Hayes works for UK Counter-Terrorism. Her bank account averages four to seven hundred pounds, except for a recent deposit of five thousand pounds. Hayes used her cellphone to text the meeting time and location to a burner phone. I believe that the burner belongs to the driver. Hayes didn't delete her text messages. I found one long text of interest."

Karen asked, "From whom?"

"A Metropolitan Police Superintendent, Ms Gloria Smith March, who doesn't exist," replied Lucas. "March praised Hayes for her dedication and was paid for any extra hours or expenses incurred. March ordered Hayes to watch and report any meetings organized by John Jones. March gave the impression that Jones was on the take. He is now dead. Jones was the National Counter Terrorism Commander."

"When was that arrangement made?" asked Karen.

"Seven days before the Hotel bombings," said Lucas.

"Hunter will need that text for evidence," replied Karen.

"The phone is not responding. I've pinged it," said Lucas. "It is probably in a million pieces."

Karen was thinking aloud and said, "She may not even realize that Police Superintendent Gloria Smith March doesn't exist."

"Yeah, but to spy on your boss who dies in that meeting after giving away the details, come on, she'll be feeling guilty," said Lucas. "I have her home address."

"The driver fooled her," replied Karen.

"Also, her phone had a bug, and I don't think she knew," said Lucas. "This speaks to why I am raising this now. Her phone automatically sent a copy of all texts and voice conversations to another phone still in use. Inspector Mitch Burleigh uses that phone. He didn't attend the meeting and replaced the Commander. Burleigh also used the same phone to communicate with the ZL 'kill' team, attacking Thames House. I unravelled his cheap encryption."

"Burleigh knew and allowed the bombings to proceed?" Karen asked. Is he a sleeper agent for Russia?"

"I have the phone transcripts," replied Lucas. "Burleigh saw her texts, probably researched March and discovered she didn't exist, and put two and two together, stood back and let it happen, knowing he would benefit."

"Forward the transcripts to Hunter and include me," asked Karen.

Lucas jumped in before she hung up, "Burleigh's mistake was to send a short text, not encrypted, to Igor Medkov, Director of the Security Council and Defense Council SVR."

"He was rushed? What did it say?" asked Karen.

"Chase RB or stay?" said Lucas. "Medkov said stay, as in undercover."

"Should Hunter get this or the Metropolitan Police?" wondered Karen.

"Hunter," replied Lucas. "Medkov is hunting for the 'Red Banners' and doesn't want Burleigh involved, so he keeps him for another day.

Medkov is under pressure from President Driminov to get them back. The RBs are fatal for Driminov's presidency."

"Get the intel to Hunter immediately," said Karen

CHAPTER 96

AUSTRALIAN EMBASSY UK

Hunter sat with John and Emma. It was breakfast, and nobody was hungry. Their coffee was now lukewarm. They were second-guessing themselves, reviewing decisions, identifying missteps that cost how many lives? They all knew that they had failed badly.

Emma Smirnov asked, "How many people, John? How many did we fail?"

"Scientists and nuclear experts will be first in evaluating sampling. Someone will work out those who are missing. Then, as the radiation poisoning and death spread. You get the idea. The UK has a very long, tragic journey ahead," said John.

Emma was crying. "Why that army garrison? Is this personal? UK troops were a minor partner with the US coalition in Bagdad."

"The driver chose to wipe out an entire garrison," replied John. "I thought the 'Red Banners' were to destroy the entire Royal Family and Parliament. Either way, stock markets have responded."

"You said that several times now. I don't believe it is about the stock market," Emma replied. It's revenge, John, plain and simple!"

"The driver changed the target," replied Hunter. "It went from St

Mary's-Le-StrandMary' s-Le-Strand to an Army town. Something
happened in Bagdad, but what?"

"He murdered women, children, kids, and babies," shouted Emma.
"The soldiers weren't even there. He made a mistake! He's a mass
murderer, children, Hunter! Defenceless kids!" She started to cry and
threw her empty cup across the room. The glass smashed. She then sat
back down, her face in her hands.

Hunted walked over, picked up the pieces of glass, and put them
all in the bin. He then brought a flask of fresh coffee and tea back with
a plate of French pastries.

"He didn't make a mistake," said Hunter. He served food to Emma
and then to John.

Emma said it more firmly, "Yes, he did! He murdered women, children, babies and young people."

Hunter repeated it, slowly and softly: "He didn't make a mistake. It
was intentional."

Emma said, "Of course, it was intentional, Hunter!"

"I think UK troops killed his family," replied Hunter. "Think about
it. He murders politicians, police, and emergency workers and
weakens the government. They did what he anticipated."

Hunter waited a moment before he continued to talk.

"The Government called all the UK soldiers and armed forces out of
their barracks across the country to walk the streets and show strength,
confidence, power, and certainty. He knew they would do that, especially for the PM's funeral. He anticipated it."

"He went after their families because someone went after
his," replied John.

"Oh, God, help us! What a monster!" cried Emma. "It is totally out
of proportion, Hunter!"

"In the driver's mind, this is collective punishment," replied
Hunter.

"You mean retaliation?" asked John.

"The UK soldiers, their family, friends, their workmates, or an
entire ethnic group are all guilty by association," replied Hunter.

"Even though they did nothing and have no direct relationship
with others?" asked John.

"That is correct," said Hunter. "You can think about it in terms of war, where collective punishment results in atrocities. It is like a kid in class doing something wrong, and the whole class suffers. Back in military college, we studied the Qin Dynasty of China. The emperor maintained strict rules and enforced his judicial authority. If you did an act of treason, you were not the only one punished. They would kill your family, even your extended family. They were all put to death – collective punishment."

"I need some coffee, maybe something stronger. I don't like this discussion," John replied.

"It is ugly, sinful human nature, John. You know this from your scripture," said Hunter. "Korah in Numbers 16:32." John looked at Hunter and gave that half-smile of acknowledgement.

"Collective punishment is the execution of all relatives of the one individual. Guilt by association," explained Hunter. "Think about it; your parents, grandparents, children, grandchildren, those living with the culprit are all put to death. That's the driver's warped, out-of-proportion mindset."

There was silence again.

Emma stood, "I'll be back in a minute after I smash all the walls in the women's restroom." Emma returned an hour later, and nobody spoke.

Hunter's tablet chirped. He opened the encrypted app and read the message. "Lucas has some information we need to follow," said Hunter. "If you want to leave this, I don't blame you. However, there is a second 'Red Banner.' Yes, lives have perished. We could have read the scene better; we didn't. But I intend to stop this from happening again. I will not stop."

"That's your motivational speech?" asked Emma.

"That's the best you'll get," replied Hunter.

"So what does Lucas have for us?" inquired Emma.

CHAPTER 97

OTTERBURN UNITED KINGDOM
Mr Wang complained about a truck that had been parked near his farm entrance now for three weeks. The Otterburn Police chief sent Police Constable Ben Edwards to resolve the problem. The truck was in good condition; it was two years old, with current plates and a locked roller door.

"Ben, are you going to take this truck away soon?" asked Mr Wang. "Can't you confiscate it or something?"

"Yes, Mr Wang, good morning and hello to you," replied Edwards.

"Sorry, I didn't mean to be rude; I'm frustrated," replied Wang. "I know the disaster takes priority, and I feel a little ashamed raising this minor issue."

"It will go today. We have a tilt tray truck coming," said Ben. "You didn't happen to see the driver of this truck?"

"No. It just appeared," replied Mr Wang.

The vehicle was taken to the Otterburn Police Station, and the back was deposited with other car wrecks and burnt-out vehicles awaiting their insurance judgements.

CHAPTER 98

AUSTRALIA HQJOC
Wayne wandered over to John's desk, "Hey, John, you want a cup of coffee?"

John said, "Yeah, thanks, Wayne." He turned the machine on and waited. It was 3:30 am, a slow night with little to do. "Here's your coffee, mate."

"John, I think I made a mistake," said Wayne as he drank his coffee.

John looked up at him to continue, "What mistake?"

"Remember Liv Wei and Wang Li Jun?" asked Wayne. "UK immigration has no record of them leaving. Their visa's expired, and the cell phones are dead."

John said, "So? What was your mistake, Wayne?"

"What?" replied Wayne. "Oh yes, the USD 75 million. I don't think they stole the money from that USA bank."

"What do you mean?" asked John.

"I didn't find any police or insurance reports, nothing. It was like a normal transaction had taken place. So, I had a closer look, but then I got stuck," replied Wayne.

"Stuck meaning, what?" asked John

"The money bounced from a dummy company in Qatar," said

Wayne. "I saw the bounce; it was only there for a minute. It has come from somewhere else before Qatar. So, these two Chinese blokes aren't the guys in charge, even though I thought it looked that way."

"The Chinese guys are middlemen made to look like it was their gig. So where did the money come from?" asked John.

"That is the question," said Wayne.

CHAPTER 99

JOINT COUNTER-TERRORISM UK

Since the bombings, the Joint Counter Terrorism group met at 8.30 am every Tuesday. Their purpose was to coordinate everything related to terrorism. Today was an emergency meeting run by Cabinet Minister Carol Lapel, Secretary of State for the Home Department.

Lapel held the meeting in Scotland Yard.

"Okay, good morning, everybody. We have new people present today. I want to welcome our MI5 investigators, agent coordinators from MI6, the Metropolitan Police Special Branch, Counter-Terrorism, National Cyber Security officer and my boss from GCHQ signal Intelligence. You all have name tags, so get to know one another," said Lapel.

Carol Lapel only sometimes attends or chairs these meetings. However, today, she received instruction from the new PM.

"I want to acknowledge the tragedy of losing many of our dear colleagues in such brutal circumstances. We understand the public mood. When we finish today and leave this building, we will leave with a plan, work together, and succeed," said Carol Lapel, staring down any opposition.

"I also want to welcome and thank Estelle Grace, former head of

MI5 and Sir Brian Jackson, former head of MI6. Estelle and Brian have come out of retirement to help us in this critical hour. Thank you, Estelle, and thank you, Brian," said Lapel.

"Finally, I would also like to introduce Mr Hunter Wyatt. Hunter and his ASIS team have begun chasing the Red Banners. I have asked Mr Hunter to give us a background report," said Lapel.

Hunter knew by looking at a few faces that his presence as an Australian may not be welcomed, especially with what he was about to say first. Hunter stood. "Before I start, I have two transcripts that I need to bring to your attention," said Hunter.

He gave copies to Carol Lapel, then sat back down. Hunter turned to face the new Counter-Terrorism Commander, Mitch Burleigh. He waited until Lapel finished reading. When he saw her shocked face, Hunter said, "Mitch Burleigh is a Russian sleeper, a spy."

The room went silent. Everybody turned to Burleigh, who jumped to his feet, "How dare you make such an inflammatory accusation? I will see that you are arrested and charged with defamation!" spat Burleigh.

Brian Jackson said, "Sit down, old boy, your protesting is giving yourself away. Sit down."

"I can't believe the audacity that an Australian has the gall to accuse me of being a traitor," replied Burleigh.

Lapel looked up from the transcript and said, "I suggest you remain silent."

"Madam Lapel, I apologise, but I have prearranged with the Special Branch for armed officers to remove and arrest Burleigh," said Hunter. Burleigh considered running, but being in Scotland Yard, it would wait until later for a vehicle transfer.

Carol Lapel met Hunter's eyes and said uncertainly, "Mr Hunter, do you have any more surprises?"

"No. Shall I continue?" asked Hunter.

"Continue, old boy," said Sir Jackson. "This is the best meeting I've been to in a while. Sorry, Madam Chair." Jackson noted the tension eased in the room. He was happy.

"Burleigh reports directly to Igor Medkov, Russia's SVR leader. As you know, the PM appointed Burleigh to work with MI6. I have no idea what he has accessed or passed onto his superiors," said Hunter.

Estelle Davis' gaze went from Hunter back to Lapel. The look of astonishment. "Quieten down, everybody. Keep going," replied Carol.

"Medkov didn't want Burleigh chasing the 'Red Banners' but to maintain his position. Debra Hayes, an administrator at Counter-Terrorism, received a call from Superintendent Gloria Smith March to spy on her former boss commander, John Jones. March paid Hayes overtime for information. March doesn't exist, but we believe the person was the driver, the bomber."

Hunter waited for questions. There were none, so he continued. "The location and time of the Hotel meeting were given to the driver. These are copy cell text intercepts," said Hunter, handing them out.

"Burleigh bugged Hayes' phone and maybe others. He could have investigated March and stopped the first bombings but chose to do nothing. Why? To rise in the ranks, as per Medkov's wishes," said Hunter.

The Special Branch officer asked Hunter, "Who is this driver?"

"The driver, we believe, is the bomber. We believe he stole the 'Red Banner' in Murmansk, Russia. He then transported them here and detonated one 'Red Banner' as collective punishment. We don't have an ID. Hence, we call him the driver," said Hunter.

The head of GCHQ asked, "How did you obtain this information?"

"Same as you," said Hunter, unsure where he stood legally.

The Home Secretary read his hesitation and said, "These are extraordinary times, Mr Hunter, please continue."

"We repurposed AI software developed by your MI5 IT specialist. Sadly, the two coding experts from MI5 were betrayed by their supervisor, Alan James, a Russian sleeper spy. A ZL kill team murdered the two MI5 agents and torched Thames House," said Hunter.

Estelle Davis said, "And a forensic officer at a shopping centre car park."

Hunter said, "Correct. A ZL team member entered the Thames House basement car lot using the pass cards of one of the MI5 IT guys. You know the rest."

Sir Brian Jackson leaned in and asked, "What are your thoughts on the bomber and Catterick Garrison and why collective punishment? Why that target?"

"We believe the driver is from Bagdad. He intentionally decapitated all law enforcement agencies at that meeting to draw the military onto the streets, empty the barracks, and then bombed the families at Catterick Garrison. We suspect the UK military in Iraq may have killed his family or friends, and he performed collective punishment as revenge," said Hunter.

Estelle Davis was shocked, "Collective punishment, rather out of proportion."

Hunter said, "Correct."

Sir Brian Jackson asked, "And the second 'Red Banner?'"

Hunter said, "We don't know. Joyce, the MI5 AI software, is searching for clues as we speak. Joyce found the flying and parachuting lessons the driver took years back, and we have a truck registration number, but no truck," replied Hunter.

Brian Jackson said, "So, this was all about revenge?" Hunter paused, and Lapel saw the hesitation.

Lapel stared at Hunter, saying, "If you have more intelligence but are weighing up, how much to tell us? I want to warn you right now. I started as a journalist assigned to Paris. I caught the shooting at the Bataclan concert hall. Black-clothed gunmen calmly fired their AK-47s into the crowd, shouting, 'Allah Akbar.' Then shooters and bombers attacked busy restaurants and bars. Jihadists injured three hundred fifty and murdered one hundred and twenty. I felt scared that night, Mr Hunter, but today I am angry. This group, working together, will do everything to stop this from happening again. So, if you have anything we can use to stop this madness. And if you are withholding anything, I swear...." She stopped talking, walked over to the window to get her emotions back under control, then returned and sat down. All heads turned to Hunter.

Chastised, Hunter said, "Liv Wei from the Joint Staff Department Intelligence Bureau of China and Wang Li Jun from JSD Intelligence Bureau stole approximately USD 75 million from a US bank. It was wired worldwide using shell companies, finishing up as cash in Bagdad to finance the theft and placement of the 'Red Banners.' The

Chinese spies told the driver to place a 'Red Banner' in the spire of St Mary's-Le-Strand. The plan was to detonate it when the Royal family passed by to attend some function. A King's College student informed the two Chinese spies that a 'Red Banner' wasn't in the church spire. The Chinese agents came to London to sort out the problem," said Hunter.

Estelle Davis asked herself, "Why would China be behind the bombings?"

"We need to find out if China is or isn't or if these two were under instructions. All this information we have has come from ASIS in Australia. They've been tracking and watching both of these men."

The officer from Vauxhall Cross asked, "Where are they now, these two Chinese chaps?"

"They're dead and are tucked away about 100 meters north of the platform in the tunnel of Strand Station or Aldwych Station. They had suicide pills. They were surprised the 'Red Banner' was not in place. We don't know if somebody ordered them to do this or if they acted alone."

Brian Jackson said, "Even if the Communist Party were behind this, they would still deny it, so there is no point."

"I assume you're all aware of several ZL Russian kill teams in the UK chasing after the 'Red Banners' to retrieve them, regardless of cost and life?" said Hunter.

Estelle Davis, "President Driminov has denied the existence of the Red Banners."

Jackson ran his fingers through his grey hair. "That will not hold for long. The rumour is someone will topple him when the second 'Red Banner' surfaces."

"He normally gets rid of any contenders for his job," added Carol.

Jackson asked, "Hunter, do you know of any connection between the Chinese spies and some Russians?"

"Not yet. I have only two more things, if I may. Based on a house in the suburbs of Bagdad and an embedded ASIS agent, we believe two people are involved. One we call the 'Driver' and the other Abu Sarek. In Amsterdam, the driver laundered USD 35 million through several cash businesses through a company with a sole director, Abu Sarek.

That company paid for the theft of the 'Red Banners.' The Russian Mafia did the job. The driver murdered them, tying up all loose ends. The name of Abu Sarek keeps coming up everywhere we investigate. But Sarek died in a drone strike in Bagdad."

Sir Brian Jackson said, "I assume the flyboys verified his death?"

"They held to it when we asked." Hunter turned to Carol Lapel and asked, "Home Secretary, I assume there are no details yet coming out, Catterick Garrison?"

"No," said Carol Lapel.

"Finally, when is the next Royal Family public event," asked Hunter.

"You're thinking the second 'Red Banner'?" asked Sir Jackson.

"Yes," said Hunter.

"Memorial Sunday," said Carol Lapel. The Home Secretary thanked Hunter. She informed everybody about taking a 10-minute break, and they would resume. Hunter was free to go.

Brian Jackson came over and gave Hunter his card. "Well done, son. I have spoken to a few experts who informed me that it exploded at height. It was most likely a plane of some sort."

"A plane?" replied Hunter. "Interesting."

"Maximum damage, old boy, maximum damage. Your driver is a smart one. I was wondering if you'd be open to a chat in two hours. This meeting should be over by then. Shall I pick you and your team up from the Embassy? Yes? It's just marvellous.

"By the way, old boy, I expect you'll get the shove by all these plodders soon," said Sir Jackson.

"Lovely," replied Hunter.

CHAPTER 100

MEMORIAL SUNDAY
Brian Jackson parked his Bentley Mulsanne in the middle of Parliament Street beside the Cenotaph. Emma whispered to John, "This is a very nice ride." They all got out of the vehicle. Traffic was whizzing past on both sides.

"This site is a National UK war memorial and remembrance site," said Sir Jackson. Everybody, including the royal family, will be here on November 11th, Armistice Day. This site commemorates the end of World War One. Since 1918, once a year, at 11 am in November, people have gathered to show their respect."

"They close down the street?" asked Emma.

"Yes. On your left is Downing Street, the new PM's digs. Looking further along the road, we have the Women of World War II statue. Further still is the Earl Haig Memorial, then the George Duke of Cambridge Stature."

"You love your statures," said John.

"What happens here at 11 am?" asked Emma.

"It's not a public holiday but an observance," replied Sir Jackson. "At 11 am, there are two minutes of silence. There are wreath-laying ceremonies at memorials across the UK, including here. Most businesses pause. The BBC does a closeup of the Big Ben clock chiming 11 and then portrays people observing silence."

"Sir Jackson?" asked Emma.

"Please, Brian."

"Brian, if I recall, I thought the Latin word 'Armistice' meant a truce, a cessation of hostilities?" asked Emma.

"Yes. Put your guns down while we attempt to negotiate a lasting peace," replied Sir Jackson. "There can also be the firing of a ceremonial canon to start and end the silence, or sometimes it ends with a bugler sounding the 'Rouse,'" said Sir Jackson.

Emma looked up and read the inscription, "The Glorious Dead."

"Who will be here?" asked Hunter.

"The armed forces and local civic leaders, ex-servicemen and women, Scouts, Guides, Salvation Army, and the Royal family will lay wreaths. It is no longer called Armistice Sunday but Remembrance Sunday, held on Sunday nearest November 11th," said Sir Jackson.

"Remembrance Sunday," said Emma. If the driver detonates the second 'Red Banner' here at 11 am, is it a slap in the face of the Armistice?" Everybody waited for his opinion.

"Yes," replied Hunter. He was examining the surrounding buildings.

"Where are the nearest tube stations, Brian?" asked John.

"Charing Cross is a three-minute walk. Embarkment underground is four minutes, and Westminster tube station is seven minutes," said Sir Jackson, pointing toward each station entrance.

Emma was staring at the Cenotaph and asked, "Is this structure the original?"

Sir Jackson replied, "No. It replaced a stone one."

Emma asked, "How different is this one from the stone structure?"

"It represented the absent dead rather than a tomb structure," said Sir Jackson. "The stone structure was immediately popular with the public, with over a million paying their respects. The public presented petitions to the House of Commons to build a permanent replacement. Some wanted it in Parliament Square away from the traffic while others demanded it stay in the same place."

Hunter was looking at the base, "Are there any original drawings?"

Jackson got out his phone and spoke for several minutes. "The Government of the day awarded the construction contracts to Holland, Hannen and Cubitts. The drawings are in the National Library. Shall we go?" asked Sir Robert.

The librarian pointed out that the company of Holland, Hannen and Cubitts had constructed many important buildings, including West London Air Terminal and Trawsfynydd nuclear power station, and has since been acquired several times. "I have the original drawings of the stone, Cenotaph, and the replacement reconstruction drawing. Last week, some confused young people sprayed painted it and tried to burn the Union Flag," said the librarian.

"Some people today believe their morals are far superior to yesterday's pioneers or slave traders," replied John.

Jackson smiled at John's wit and asked, "Madam, would you be so kind as to run us off several copies?"

"Not a problem, Sir Jackson," said the librarian.

Emma turned and said, "Sir Jackson, you are well known." She returned with A3 copies of all the plans and manuscripts on the minutes of meetings and notes.

"Might I suggest a good pub with good food and a private room to read through everything?" said Sir Jackson.

John smiled, and Emma said, "I could eat a horse!"

Hunter turned back to the librarian. "Thank you for your help. Might I ask a special request?"

"Anything for those who work for Sir Jackson," replied the librarian. Everybody gave a slight smile for that line.

"I'm asking on behalf of Sir Jackson: You know, National security is all hush, hush?" said Hunter.

She smiled and whispered, "Yes."

"I'm asking for you to break confidentially for Sir Jackson. Has anybody else asked for a copy recently?" Hunter indirectly pointed to the CCTVs.

The librarian went to her computer. "Just a moment. I have it now. Two years ago, a mail-ordered arrived, with a cheque asking for copies of the original drawing," said the librarian.

"You have a good memory. Do you have a name?" asked Hunter,

"Abu Sarek," replied the librarian.

CHAPTER 101

S T GILES HOTEL LONDON
Laura Ruby phoned Milton to ask whether they should reopen the office tomorrow. "Laura, I think that would be a good idea," said Milton. "Can you contact the site managers and find out if all our workers and their families are safe? I would like to know if any extended families have become victims of this tragedy."

"I'll get onto it immediately," replied Laura.

"Laura, are you okay, your family?" asked Milton.

"The media are saying there is a second nuclear device. That's what worries me," replied Laura.

"If you prefer to stay home, that would be okay," said Milton.

"No. I want to come in. I'm going crazy at home. Tonight, I'm going to a memorial vigil at the London bombing site. It's like a show of support," said Laura.

"Is it safe?" asked Milton.

"The police will be there. I'm going with a friend. Candles and flowers to remember people" replied Laura.

"Okay. See you tomorrow. Bye." He put the phone down on the balcony table. Milton drank a cup of tea. He still had the business card from the police detective who visited him in the hospital, Detective

Carol Ian, Albany Street Police. He turned the card over and over in his hands. 'I've called their Crime Stoppers twice,' thought Milton. He gazed at the busy streets below from his unit balcony, 'My brother murdered mothers and babies.' Milton finished his tea and then placed the cup back on the saucer.

"Is it possible to have what that pastor has, your past wiped, your guilt forgiven?" Milton asked himself.

Milton made his decision. "I want life."

CHAPTER 102

MANCHESTER UK
The two-burner phones.
"Where are you?"
"Manchester."
"Do you have the second RB?"
"Yes."
"Functional?"
"Yes."
"Agreed time and date."
"Yes."
"Will you proceed?"
"Yes."
End of text messages.

CHAPTER 103

AUSTRALIAN EMBASSY, LONDON.

"Karen, I asked Lucas to give me some Geo-mapping before the bomb exploded. Do you know where that is at?" asked Hunter.

"Yes, he found the plane. It was an authorized halo jump. Lucas thinks the height of the twin-engine Cessna matches the scenario," replied Karen.

"A halo jumps with the plane on autopilot," replied Hunter. "So if he survived, he landed somewhere."

"The Cessna flew west and turned around above a town called Otterburn. He would have reset the auto-pilot and then jumped," replied Karen.

"I wonder if he survived. It would be good if he didn't. The bombing of Catterick Garrison was revenge and a deviation from the plan. The Chinese spies were surprised that a 'Red Banner' was not in the spire of St. Mary-Le-Strand," said Hunter.

"Does the driver know the Chinese spies are dead?" asked Karen.

"I doubt it," asked Hunter. The driver has no family, and I think he has been putting his plan together for years. I see no reason for him to stop. We're working with Sir Jackson, ex-MI6, out of retirement."

"Okay," replied Karen.

"Yesterday, at the London Historical Library, we discovered that Abu Sarek purchased photocopies of the London World War I Cenotaph construction," said Hunter. "He did this two years ago."

"The Cenotaph, the Glorious Dead," replied Karen.

"The next event where the armed forces and the Royal family will be in attendance is Memorial Sunday at the Cenotaph near Downing Street," replied Hunter. "We have our copy of the original construction plans."

"So the 'Red Banner' is already in place?" Karen wondered more to herself than to Hunter.

"I think it has already been in place for several years," replied Hunter.

"Our HQJOC, IT guy, made an error regarding the stolen money?" said Karen. "The money originated from Belarus but could be a false flag.

CHAPTER 104

DOG & RED LION PUB UK

Later that day, Sir Brian Jackson Hunter and his team were in a small private room at a local pub. "There are no menus here. Pub grub consists of steak, kidney pudding, shepherd's pie, fish and chips, or bangers and mash. What's your fancy?" asked Sir Jackson.

Emma replied, "I don't know what you just said!"

Sir Jackson laughed. "Okay, no takers? Let me order a group of dishes."

John stared at Hunter. "Bangers and mash?" Brian returned with jugs of real ale or British beer. "Let me fill those glasses while you folk get out the paperwork. The food will be here in ten minutes."

John had already looked for secret doors or removable stone pieces leading to a cavity. But when he checked some of the hand notes, he said, "What is interesting in these technical notes is that somebody removed the first Cenotaph. They dug down 30 feet. That's what it says here. 'Reinforced foundation depth 30 feet.' That's too deep a foundation.

"You're thinking of a room," asked Hunter.

"Maybe," replied John. "I'm just saying 30 feet is a foundation for a bridge, not a Cenotaph."

Sir Jackson said, "If a room exists, there is an entrance. Perhaps some people wanted to personally honour the soldiers with a marble coffin."

"This is a nice beer," said Emma. "Are we thinking like an Egyptian? A secret tunnel, a stone slab like Jesus' tomb and gold and silver treasure?"

"More like a secret tunnel and a bomb," said Hunter.

They were all looking at her. "The beer is nice," repeated Emma. "What?"

Sir Jackson said, "Let's enjoy our meal. Then I will try to whip up some ground-penetrating radar to see what is below."

CHAPTER 105

OWNING STREET, LONDON

At 2 am, the Police had blocked off one-half of the road and were redirecting traffic. Some post-doctoral and doctoral students from a university who usually work in archaeological digs pushed a machine backwards and forwards through a tight grid. Sir Jackson had bribed them with a free round of beer. The doctoral student returned with a laptop and told Sir Jackson, "There is an anomaly here leading in this direction." The student looked away from the computer, and she pointed out the direction of the anomaly. "It starts here and goes over there. It was hard and precise. There is also a shadow under the anomaly," said the student.

Hunter said, "Over there, you mean that house there? You think, the PM's house to here?"

"Yes. I would think the lines are straight and at a depth of 27 feet. It is a tunnel," said the student, looking up and smiling. Is that what you're looking for?"

Hunter smiled and then asked, "Can we check to see if the tunnel changes direction and ends on the other side of Downing Street, even up to Horse Guard Road?"

"Not a problem," said the student as she wandered off with new instructions.

"Hunter, this is public knowledge we have a crisis management centre beneath Whitehall here and the Ministry of Defence over there," said Sir Jackson. "It is hard and precise."

"Are they connected?" asked John.

"Yes, one large operational room with large connecting tunnels," said Sir Jackson.

"But nothing goes near the Cenotaph?" asked Emma.

"In the 1990s, we built a bunker for communication and military purposes. It took years to build, and there are servers and a medical centre. It is a military citadel. The teams below talk with the joint headquarters in Northwood," said Sir Jackson.

"I'm interested in the shadow," replied Hunter.

The doctoral student-supervisor returned. "It goes under the Statue of Earl Mountbatten, then proceeds under the road and finishes under the tree on the other side of Horse Guards Road," replied the student. The entire group walked across the road and looked under the trees.

"You think it ends here? Where?" asked Emma.

"The radar shows an ending right here," replied the student. Nothing appeared out of the ordinary, with manicured grass, tree roots, and a path.

"The grass doesn't look disturbed. The concrete footpath looks normal," said Sir Jackson.

"That piece of footpath looks slightly different from that piece there; the grain differs," said John.

Sir Jackson looked at his watch and said, "Thank you for your time. Please express our thanks to your fellow students. The University of London Union has my name, and please enjoy a meal and drinks. Thanks again, my dear."

"Will do," said the student with a smile.

Sir Jackson turned to Hunter, "That manhole over there needs checking."

John looked at the PM's residence, then back to the park. "I guess we go back to the library and find the drawings for 10 Downing Street?"

Hunter looked at Sir Jackson and said, "I doubt the library will help us this time. I assume this shadow tunnel may not be on any drawing."

John kept examining Downing Street. "So if it is below the citadel tunnel at thirty feet. I agree it won't be on any drawings. Would there be an entrance under the Cabinet Office?"

"Good question," said Sir Jackson.

"If some WW1 Field Marshall wanted a special place to honour the 'Glorious Dead' for himself and his General mates, then it will have been forgotten by now," said Emma. "The secret society, with special handshake and all that jazz. They most likely tore up the plans and lit a sacrificial fire followed by an oath of secrecy." John smiled.

"Downing Street may have always had a tunnel to the park here," said John. "Perhaps somebody blocked it off years ago, but the driver came upon it, unsealed it, inserted the RB, and resealed it. Though a bit obvious, people are watching here, out in the open. No, this is not it."

"When Harris, Harrods and Hilary built the Cenotaph, they may have connected their tunnel to that old tunnel, John," said Emma. "We should look first at Downing Street. No? Is it plausible?"

"Holland, Hannen and Cubitts," said John with a grin.

That's what I said, "Harris, Harrods and Hilary."

Sir Jackson pointed out the features of the street. "Downing Street is ancient. British Prime Ministers have lived there since 1735." He pointed to the houses on either side of number 10. "Number 10 has consumed 11 and 12 Downing Street. Underneath it is an ancient Roman, Anglo-Saxon, and Norman settlement."

Really, in the same spot," asked Emma.

"That stayed the same for 1,000 years. The Saxons then built a structure on top of the Roman buildings. Mind you, the Axe brewery stood here until the 1500s," said Sir Jackson.

"A pub? Sorry, a brewery, really?" asked John.

"Yes, Sir Thomas Hynot built the first house right here in 1851. Mr Hynot arrested Guy Fawkes. It's rather symbolic, I would think," replied Sir Jackson.

Emma asked him, "How come you know so much about this house?"

"Somebody named the street after George Downing," said Sir Jackson. He was a horrible man but a good diplomat and administrator who traded in secrets, often changed political sides, and was knighted. He bought all the land around and got the lease on what was then Hampden House. Somebody knocked it down, and Christopher Wren designed the new houses. Having said all that, I am related to that ugly chap, Mr George Downing, through his wife."

"You're not an ugly person, Sir Jackson Downing!" said Emma with a smile. Sir Jackson laughed and then explained the military citadel built in the 1990s. "The doctoral students may have picked up some old leftover renovation structures on their ground-penetrating radar."

John replied confidently, "We know the builders of the Cenotaph went thirty feet down. This implies a tunnel system to access it. Or they built a special room and sealed it forever. I like the idea of a secret handshake, a drink, and a ritual."

"I really can't see the driver knocking on the door of 10 Downing Street," said Hunter. "I have a 'Red Banner' on my trolley, and I need to throw it down a 30-foot staircase. I can see a digging machine and fake warning signs of a gas leak, plus a blind fence."

"Well, this is what I see. The Field Marshall and his mates finish their moment of respect, climb a staircase, sit in a room drinking rum and tea, and tell stories of victory, heroism and defeat. They did it once a year, a closed club, now passed away and completely forgotten," said Emma. "The entrance is at 10."

"So, there are two tunnel entrances under Number 10. One brand new and the other hidden forgotten inside a closet, like that UK movie," said John.

"The Lion, the Witch and the Wardrobe," said Sir Jackson.

"Shall we go and ask? Who has a hammer?" asked Emma with a smile.

"I will need to talk with several people first, dear friends," said Sir Jackson.

"We have four days until November the 11th," replied Hunter.

CHAPTER 106

OTTERBURN UNITED KINGDOM
Her first experience as a passenger in the AS365Z3 Dauphin helicopter called Blue Thunder was exhilarating for Emma.

It was customary for Hunter to sit beside elite SAS officers dressed in black body armour—elite SAS officers from counterterrorism. They wore Kevlar vests with ceramic plates covering the heart region, knee pads, and polymer tactical gloves. Hunter countered the advanced firearms, including high-powered M4 machine guns with silencers, carbine automatic weapons, RPGs, speciality ammunition, and black Kevlar helmets. Hunter suspected they had other weapons hidden out of sight.

The noise from the twin turboshafts made conversation difficult. "This is the best unit in the UK, Hunter," shouted Sir Jackson.

"I believe you," said Hunter, smiling. The briefing was outside the mobile Police Command Centre. Sir Jackson then introduced the team to Chief Inspector Kwon, who was responsible for the search. Originally from South Korea, Kwon was educated and trained in the UK.

"We have groups of police and dogs searching these properties," said Kwon.

Kwon pointed to consecutive pieces of land on the map, forming a circle. "We estimate the pilot turned the plane around near Otterburn and then engaged the autopilot. The pilot then performed a halo jump landing in this circle."

Somebody asked politely, "What exactly are we looking for?"

"A dead body or evidence of a chute," replied Chief Inspector Kwon.

"Do you think he hit a tree and died?" asked Emma.

"That is a real possibility," replied Kwon. "A halo jump is dangerous and requires specialized training, and we have only one record of a practice halo training jump up north made by Mr Abu Sarek."

All four mumbled, "Abu Sarek." Chief Inspector Kwon looked at them, waiting for an explanation.

Hunter said, "It is not his name."

"Any pictures or driver's license presented at the training school?" asked Emma.

"No, Sarek just used a credit card to ID himself, and Sarek paid all the standard jumps with that same card and signed an insurance disclaimer form. He was wearing driving gloves when he signed," replied Chief Inspector Kwon.

"The trainer noticed that?" asked Hunter.

"Yes, but only during our interview with him. He thought it was for health reasons," said Chief Inspector Kwon. It was skin problems."

Hunter asked, "Any CCTV at the school?

"No. But we have a Police digital artist working with the trainer," replied Kwon.

"When training for halo jumps, don't they do dual jumps and take photographs?" asked John.

"There are no records of Sarek performing a dual halo jump in training," replied Kwon. "Do you have any other questions? We are concentrating our search in this area because Sarek abandoned a truck near a farm." They were all looking at the map. The truck was tested and showed minute evidence that a 'Red Banner' had at some point been inside.

"He parked the truck where he estimated he would land," said Hunter. "How did he get back to the airport?"

"He stole a car from the pub in town," replied Kwon. "The car has no prints except the owners."

Hunter's phone chirped. "Hunter, Lucas. Our HQJOC, IT guy, has managed to track the money back to a Russian Bank."

"The USD 75 million. Name?" asked Hunter.

"Franz Zhukov. This guy has about USD 80 billion in his bank," replied Lucas.

"Never heard of him," said Hunter.

"Zhukov uses three stock brokers. This morning, Zhukov borrowed and sold 40B USD in shares at market price. He will repurchase them Monday morning at a lower price after Memorial Sunday," said Lucas. "Wayne is a good hacker."

There was a commotion behind Hunter. He turned and saw people pouring out of the Command Centre, joining the group. "What's happening?" Hunter asked Emma.

"They found a body," said Emma.

"Lucas, I will phone you back," replied Hunter. He shouted to Chief Inspector Kwon, "Tell them not to touch the body and to step back. It might be booby-trapped."

Sir Jackson's vehicle was following the Police vehicles, "Why do you think it's a trap?"

Hunter didn't respond; he thought about what Lucas had told him. "Sir Jackson, get the commander on the phone and ask if they have a bomb squad nearby."

Jackson's car had Bluetooth and several other communications systems. They all heard the commander respond, 'Manchester bomb squad is two hours out.' Then Sir Jackson's office called with permission to enter 10 Downing Street and the Military Citadel tomorrow morning, Memorial Sunday. Police had already spent time checking the Citadel tunnels for the 'Red Banner' but had found nothing.

Police and emergency vehicles clogged the road. Everybody had to walk through a paddock and down a hill, then up to a rise of trees. Towards the edge of the trees lay the body. The Police had stood back as requested. Forensics had set up a tent away from the body, and everybody was waiting for the Bomb Squad to arrive. Hunter observed the SWAT team's disappointment.

"I think they would have preferred a live target," whispered Hunter. Emma turned and observed them. Hunter knew these guys were tough and rarely took advice from an outsider. He approached the SWAT leader and said, "If that body is not the driver, would you consider he or a ZL bloke may be watching us and has planted...."

The SWAT leader acknowledged the possibility, and his hand went to his radio; Hunter put his hand onto the radio first, saying, "The forest may have ears." The SWAT team formed a circle around the site.

"Chief Inspector Kwon? Did the search team withdraw when they saw the body? They didn't go near him," asked Hunter. "Okay, can we switch off all radio and digital phones?"

Kwon gave the order. "You're thinking a ZL kill team arrived before us and planted a device?"

'Yes, based on the Hotel explosions and the ZL idiots," said Hunter. Before Kwon could order everybody back 100 meters, Hunter heard multiple thuds in the grass with a small dirt spray near the body. Hunter shouted, "Sniper!" The bullets kept coming, left then right. It was all over after 30 seconds. SWAT had returned fire until they exhausted their bullets.

"It's automatic, no shooter. We tripped a sensor," said Hunter to Jackson.

"Anybody hurt?" shouted Kwon. There were injuries but no deaths. SWAT approached the clump of trees to find a van with its rear door open. A remote-operated, rapid-firing, large-calibre machine gun was bolted to the van floor. SWAT return fire damaged the firearm, the van and a camera. "All clear," shouted the SWAT leader.

Everybody stood again and turned as they heard the bomb squad 4x4 turbo diesel truck growling, making its way up through the cow paddock to their position. The truck parked 30 meters away from the crowd. One man in a Police uniform went to the rear of the 4X4 truck and began to unpack equipment. The other officer approached Chief Inspector Kwon. "I'm Snapper Rocks. What have we got?" he asked.

"Halo jumper possibly booby-trapped," replied Kwon.

"Where is the EOD?" asked Rocks.

"It could be anywhere or near the dead body. SWAT just killed an automatic machine gun up on the hill," replied Kwon.

"I will switch on a jamming device. No radio triggers or signals will work, including your phone," replied Rocks—Snapper Rocks dressed in the EOD or bomb suit. Rocks examined the body and, holding a small mirror, checked under it. He stood and walked back to the group.

"It is a Russian PMN-4 blast mine. There are two under the body. The PMNs are in good condition. I suspect this might also be an MC-3 version," said Rocks.

Kwon looked confused, then Hunter said, "Anti-handling device designed to kill de-miners. There are no devices underneath?"

"Not that I can see. Afghanistan?" Hunter gave a slight nod.

"Chief, what do you want to do? We can't move him. Our standard render-safe procedure is to destroy these in situ using a small charge," said Rocks.

"Can you lift the mask and take a photo, maybe of finger-prints?" asked Hunter. He gave Rocks his tablet. "That button for a photo. For fingerprints, remove his glove and allow his hand to rest on the tablet. The screen will be red and then turn green when completed. It will take two seconds."

"Done," said Snapper Rocks, returning the tablet to Hunter. He would need to wait for Rocks to switch off the jamming device before sending the fingerprints and image to Lucas.

Rocks brought out a plastic demountable frame and placed it gently over the body. It had a weighted plunger system in the middle. He then gently put a four-inch-thick, heavy blanket around the plastic frame. He twisted the timer and then stepped back to the group. The plunger dropped, detonating the mines. Rocks cleaned up and switched off the jamming device.

"You are not going to believe this? I recognize that face," said Hunter. It's Ivan Bely, a Russian SVR/RF foreign intelligence officer."

Sir Jackson asked Hunter, "Really? How do you know him?"

"Medkov sent Bely to throw us out of Murmansk. They didn't want ASIS on their turf. Bely saw through my cover, but we worked together to track the 'Red Banners,'" replied Hunter.

John needed clarification. "Has Bely been the driver all along?"

"No. We worked together," said Hunter. "Bely's boss knew we were there and told Bely to throw us out of Russia. Bely said he would keep in contact, and he did. He informed me in Stockholm of the ZL kill teams. The driver wanted us to believe Bely did the Halo jump and died. We were to conclude the driver was Bely."

"I'm dead, so you can all go home now. The crisis is over," said Emma.

"The mines were a mistake," said Hunter.

"In what way?" asked Emma.

"Land mines under bodies was a technique used around Bagdad," replied Hunter.

"Bely worked out the driver halo jumped here," said Emma. "He confronted him and was killed. The driver put him in his halo suit, putting the fireworks underneath him to stop us. Who put the gun on the hill?"

"Either ZL or the driver," replied Hunter. "The driver is still alive."

Sir Jackson interrupted, saying, "We must get down to those tunnels. If we find nothing, then every rooftop within a circular mile of that memorial site must be searched before tomorrow, November 11th."

Emma asked Sir Jackson, "Would they cancel the event?"

"The Glorious Dead must live on," replied Sir Jackson

CHAPTER 107

NOV 9THLONDON

He was almost in a trance, standing in line at a fast-food store. He paid and thanked the teenager who served him. He sat on a park bench, blew over his hot coffee, sipped it a little, and then put it down. Then he ate his chicken sandwich. He was thankful for his family and the people he loved. He watched as a couple walked through the park. The woman was carrying her baby in a pouch. He thought of love, family, and children.

"Children, Ahmed, children."

The sun shone through the trees, and the inner-city park was deep green, manicured, clean and silent, a glorious retreat.

Milton read Detective Carol Ian—Albany Street Police Station business car. He wrote Ahmed's full name and plan on the fast food napkin. He approached the Royal Mail Street Penfold pillar box on the park corner.

"My dear brother. I have loved you all my life. But I must stop you. May the Christian God forgive me for the evil I have done. Heavenly Father, stop my brother, Amen."

He looked at the tissue with overwhelming sadness and relief as he placed it inside the pillar box.

CHAPTER 108

NOV 11. 10 DOWNING ST. LONDON

Sir Jackson introduced the team to the senior engineer of the military citadel. They followed him into the PM's home and were escorted down a set of carpeted stairs into the basement, which was more like a personal library with reading chairs and reading lamps. A deep red carpet covered the room, giving the room an executive feel. The subdued lighting made the space warm and inviting. The bookcases reached from the floor to the ceiling, filled with books and journals.

Emma whispered to John, "I was expecting a pile of old furniture stacked high and covered in dust, like my basement."

"Why are you whispering?" asked John.

Emma gave him a dirty look, turned, and read some book titles. At the far end of the room was a foot-thick steel door. The door had a digital lock, leading to a short corridor, then down a long set of stairs leading to the sub-basement. The sub-basement was a square room. On the left was a commercial electric lift used by the PM and Cabinet. On the right were distribution boards, and in front was a steel door. It had a fingerprint and touchscreen keyless lock. The engineer explained in detail how a building company constructed the military citadel.

John asked the engineer, "Was the citadel a new construction and not an extension of something older or attached to some previously built room?"

"Sir Jackson informed me that you are searching for an older set of tunnels and rooms. I don't believe they exist. Our construction here is entirely new, and we didn't break into any other pre-constructed rooms or tunnels. I am sorry to disappoint. They do not exist," replied the engineer.

"Those three doors, what are they?" asked Hunter.

"Two go to Government buildings and double as emergency exits, and the third is the server room."

Hunter thanked him. "Where did you dig from?"

"From the Government Building to here," replied the engineer.

"I assume these walls are several feet thick, and we are in some type of Faraday cage?" asked Hunter.

"Yes. These walls and floors are four feet thick, and the ceiling is six feet," replied the engineer.

"How far down are we?" asked Emma.

"23 feet." Hunter thanked the engineer, and they returned to the library.

The library was a more pleasant room than the sub-basement; there was no woody or earthy aroma. Hunter noted the room temperature was cool and dry and guessed the humidity was 35% with no intense light. It was a room where you could relax, read, drink, and talk. Hunter ran his finger over the top of a closed book. No dust. He smiled to himself. There were two tables, several high-back lounge chairs in a rich burgundy colour, a drink cabinet and an ornate but disused fireplace. The warm room invited you to sit, read and talk.

Hunter turned to the engineer and asked, "Why did you choose this room to be the entrance to the citadel?"

"The PM only uses this room when he desires to have a private conversation or some time out, from upstairs or downstairs," said the engineer.

"The only changes you made were that steel door and the stairs, correct?" asked Hunter.

"Yes, everything here is original and has been here for decades," replied the engineer. Hunter instructed everyone to look for something odd.

"Odd?" asked Emma. "Apart from those standing in the room." John smiled. He liked her humour.

"Something that shouldn't be here, wrong place, wrong size, just odd," repeated Hunter. They found nothing. The room refused to give up any of its secrets. Hunter looked at the ceiling, searched for the air conditioner's return vent, saw it, and moved the library ladder over. Hunter climbed the ladder.

"Does anybody have a coin?" Hunter asked. Emma, would you please close that door to the upstairs?"

"Here you go!" said John. "A copper one pence or 1p, I think."

Hunter used the coin to open the vent lock, placed his jacket between the vent and the filter, closed it, and locked it, blocking the return airflow. Hunter found a box of Cuban cigars beside the drink tray and gave everybody one. Looking at the engineer, then to Sir Jackson, "I do hope your PM will forgive me?"

The engineer was now nervous. "What are you going to do?"

"Let me light your cigars; we need lots of smoke," said Hunter.

The engineer objected, "The fire alarms will go off."

"I doubt that very much," replied Hunter with a sneaky smile. The air-conditioner did its job by pressurizing the room, seeking an exit. The smoke slowly drifted to one bookcase. "Here we go." Emma was smoking like a pro, then started coughing. Hunter and John watched the smoke sail to the top of the bookcase.

Sir Jackson poured a drink for Emma, "Here you go, my dear."

Hunter looked up at a book on the top shelf on the left. The bookcases stretched four metres from the floor to the ceiling. "John, would you please bring that library ladder over here?" Hunter climbed to the top. The spine on that book says Bleak House by John Jarndyce. Charles Dickens wrote Bleak House, and Jarndyce is a character in the book?"

Emma told John, "So Hunter is not just a gunslinger."

John smiled and said, "He's a novel critic and gunslinger."

Hunter positioned the ladder closer to the book and reclimbed it. "Definitely, 'Bleak House.' This is interesting," said Hunter.

Emma added, "Dear mystery novel gunslinger, what hath thou found?"

He removed the Charles Dickens book. "Words have been carved into the back of the bookcase. Polish and paint have filled the letters, but it is still visible." He turned his head sideways to read: 'De Oppresso Liber.'"

"Free from the oppressed one," replied Sir Jackson.

"There is a small hole in the back of the bookcase." Hunter took out his phone and turned on the torchlight. He focused the light into the hole.

"What can you see?" asked John.

"It is the tip of a steel rod, a hexagon; no, an octagon," replied Hunter. He turned away from the bookcase and examined the room. There was nothing on top of each bookcase. He scanned the room, stopping on the disused fireplace.

"John, see the ornate fireplace," said Hunter. Would you put your hand inside the exhaust brickwork and feel for a steel rod?" John removed a steel crank with an octagon head from the fireplace chimney.

"Someone welded words onto the crank," said John as he brushed off some dust.

Emma got in first and said, "De Oppresso Liber?"

"Exactly!" replied John. He passed the crank to Hunter, who inserted it and started twisting anti-clockwise.

Sir Jackson said, "This bookcase is moving. The one to your left." Hunter turned his head to look, then kept turning the crank, revealing an open doorway.

"I expected a different aroma for a room that has opened in 120 years," said Emma.

"Let me get some LED torches," suggested the engineer.

Sir Jackson said, "No cracking of paint or polish. A splendid design."

The engineer returned with LED torches for everyone. Hunter went first. "It is a circular shaft dropping down; I would guess 40 feet. The staircase is a decorative spiral design made of antique iron. It looks ornate Victorian. I suggest one person descends the staircase at a time, considering its age."

Hunter kept talking as he descended. "The circular walls are concrete, covered with green-coloured tiles." Everybody gathered near the base of the steps. "There are no dust footsteps on the tiled ground floor. The driver never came this way," said Hunter. They looked at another steel door. Hunter put his ear to the door. "I can hear a slight water movement."

"Well, that would make sense," said the engineer. "At this depth, we are below the water table."

John looked for another door, "There is no rising damp on these walls, no evidence of salt."

The engineer said, "They made a built-in drain with an exit. The amount of water will be minimal but constant. Shall we open the door?" The engineer was correct. There was a gently sloping underground channel to transport rising water to the left. The tunnel was two meters high with a curved ceiling and one meter wide, with a small drain cut out in the middle of the floor. The stream of water heading left was in the direction of the Duck Island Cottage or Guards Road.

"That water would empty into an underground well," said the engineer. The group turned right and started to walk uphill. The path became horizontal and then declined into the dark.

"This is like an ancient qanat. It acts as an underground aqueduct and stops this tunnel from filling with water. Follow that water flow, and I suspect it will end at the Thames," said the engineer. "That's your entrance."

Their LED torches lit up a steel door ornately designed with vines, guns, and poppies. Sir Jackson rubbed a hand across the door. 'De Oppresso Liber,' said Sir Jackson. "We appear to be in the right spot."

Hunter shone his LED torch on the floor tunnel, "Tyre marks. The 'Red Banner' came in on a trolley, perhaps from a boat. We should not open those steel doors. The driver likes setting traps."

"Does the Bomb Squad handle nuclear devices?" asked Emma.

"They will drill a hole, put a camera inside, and look around," replied Hunter.

"Memorial Sunday observance starts in three hours," said John.

Sir Jackson shone his LED light down the tunnel, "I will go back up the stairs and get the Bomb Squad here, then come back down. I will call to see if we can get a nuclear specialist. I would prefer if they could enter through the exit of this tunnel rather than Downing Street. There will be too many cameras and journalists. Hunter and John, can you stay? Emma, the engineer, and I will find the Thames exit. When we reach the tunnel exit, I will give the bomb squad the location. Is that okay with everybody? I'll be back in a moment, chaps. Don't blow anything up."

Emma rolled her eyes. "Just smashing, don't blow anything up."

Sir Jackson's voice carried down from halfway up the stairs, "Emma, your British accent is coming along rather nicely, my dear."

To that, she rolled her eyes again.

The area around the Cenotaph was ready. Preparations for the 11 am observation ceremony are complete. The event organizers were in place, with barriers, banners, Police, and TV cameras on scaffolding stands.

"I assume nobody above knows what is below?" asked John.

"Sir Jackson said they would never cancel," replied Emma.

"But shouldn't we at least stop people from coming?" said John. The engineer was turning white, realizing the current predicament.

Hunter said, "Nobody dies today."

Everybody heard Sir Jackson descending the stairs. "Okay, I have made contact. I will lead; let's go now!" said Sir Jackson. Hunter watched the three LED lights moving until they went around a bend, and the tunnel went black again. Then Hunter and John heard a familiar sound. It was slight but recognizable, a silenced gun.

Hunter whispered to John, "Turn your light off." "Okay, take your shoes off. No sound, okay?" John and Hunter both moved silently through the dark. Hunter almost tripped over the engineer. The engineer's torch was still under his body, providing a glimmer of light.

'No pulse,' said John. Hunter listened to any sounds.

John whispered, "Did the shooter follow Emma and Sir Jackson?" Running at full speed, even with his torch on, was dangerous, as you had to straddle the slimy drain. Hunter had to stop any more deaths, so he ran at full pace. Almost a mile later, he came to the exit, which ended in a two-meter drop into the Thames.

Hunter thought, 'I didn't hear a splash.' He turned around and retraced his steps, running fast. He was shining the torch everywhere. 'Nothing, how can that be?' thought Hunter. When Hunter ran, he focused on the tunnel path, not wanting to break or twist an ankle. As he retraced his steps, Hunter was scanning the walls and ceiling with the torch.

Ahmed hid in a ceiling cavity facing towards the Cenotaph room. He could hear Hunter's footsteps.

Hunter saw a glimmer of green light. It was only for a split second, and then it was gone. Ahmed switched off his digital night vision binoculars and placed them inside his backpack. He started to close the zip but stopped.

Ahmed made a fatal error. Hunter heard the sound of a zip. Ahmed closed his eyes and waited for his night vision to return. He would wait until he heard Hunter was directly below him, then fire his silenced Glock straight down and then leave.

Sir Jackson took off his jacket and tried to squeeze the water out. They were both saturated. Emma was also soaked but could do very little about it. They both stood on the path, waiting. She asked Sir Jackson, "Is that a real Egyptian obelisk? Is that the right word?"

"Yes, that is the correct word," said Sir Jackson. "What's interesting is that part of the pedestal inside is a time capsule from 1878." He kept patting his wet clothing.

Emma was curious. "Do you know what is in the capsule?"

"This whole thing is called Cleopatra's Needle. I believe there are pictures of beautiful women of the day," replied Sir Jackson.

"Miss Cleo was a stunner?" said Emma, raising her eyebrows at Sir Jackson.

"More or less, my dear. For the men, there are cigars, children's toys, some coins and a painting; I think of Queen Victoria, even a Bible and some other books," said Sir Jackson.

Emma said, "The capsule better be airtight." They walked over to the Egyptian sphinxes. Jackson scanned the road, checking and then glancing back at the sphinxes.

"I suppose you can read these hieroglyphic inscriptions?" asked Emma.

"Netjer nefer men-kheper-re di ankh," said Sir Jackson. "The good god, Tuthmosis III, has given life," said Sir Jackson.

"That is very kind of Tuthmosis. I laugh every time I see the inscription on the Rome Pantheon. Marcus built this or something to that effect," said Emma. "Sir Jackson, I'm sorry. I talk a lot, a whole lot when I am nervous."

Sir Jackson said, "I am nervous also, my dear." Jackson's phone chirped. "The Bomb Squad is five minutes out."

Emma asked, "Is that shrapnel damage on that sphinx?"

"World War I, a German air raid. The bomb landed rather too close," said Sir Jackson. Two trucks drove up onto the wide footpath. The Bomb squad teams exited their vehicles and approached Sir Jackson. Some of the group were unloading a miniature version of the Wheelbarrow Mk8d, a remotely controlled bomb disposal unit with a jet.

"Sir Jackson, I'm Noel Eric. I am in charge of the team tonight. Is this the Red Banner, sir?"

"Noel, perhaps we can gather the team around for a moment," said Sir Jackson.

"Gentlemen, this is a delicate and time-sensitive operation. You may be dealing with the second 'Red Banner.' We believe it is inside a large room underneath the Cenotaph. It's most likely nuclear. The timer should be set for 11 am11 am this morning, Memorial Sunday. There is a steel door to the room. We have not opened it as it may be a rigged trap. The tunnel starts at 10 Downing Street, passes by the steel door room, then under the Cenotaph, and exits under the Needle into the Thames."

Sir Jackson turned and pointed to Cleopatra's Needle. "The tunnel exit is under the Needle. Sorry, chaps, but you will need to get into the river, go inside, and look directly up. You'll see the entrance. Thanks, and good luck," said Sir Jackson.

The Bomb Squad team returned to their trucks and unloaded all needed equipment. Sir Jackson turned to Emma. "Are you okay?"

"It's a bit cold," she replied. Her body started to shake. Noel brought some towels over to them to keep them warm.

"When you get to the door, you will find three chaps, Hunter, Moody and an engineer," said Emma.

Hunter changed tactics when he heard the zip sound. The green light was a night vision goggle, switched off and placed into a zip pocket.

Hunter shouted, "UK Bomb Squad approaching. Hold your fire." Hunter didn't have a weapon, so he used his height and crawled towards the engineer. Hunter lay flat on the bottom of the tunnel with no torch shining, closed his eyes to regain complete night vision, and waited. When he opened his eyes, he thought he saw a glimmer of light, something on the roof, 20 feet away. But in the dark, it was hard to tell the distance.

'An overhead recess, a corner, a vent. It was the driver. He is up there,' thought Hunter. He calculated the number of steps and slowly crept forward, counting the distance in complete darkness.

The shooter fired in the general direction of the engineer. The muzzle flash destroyed both their night vision. Hunter lunged forward, seeking to tackle the shooter, only to grab an arm and crash into the side of the tunnel.

Hunter pulled hard, drawing a body down on himself with a grunt. Punches started to fly.

He punched the concrete instead of the driver. Hunter groaned but then started using his legs, guessing where the man's torso was, and starting punching with his opposite hand. Some of the punches hit nothing, and several made contact. Hunter's opponent got three solid blows into Hunter's head, with the third hitting the concrete wall. The Bomb Squad was now shouting, and the tunnel lit up with their powerful torches. Two squad members were running at full speed, and one officer fell over the engineer's body, causing a traffic jam.

Hunter was lying on his back, unconscious.

The driver whiplashed him with his Glock and left. Emma arrived.

"Hunter, are you okay?" She stopped talking and looked up. A small exit tunnel leading to two steel plates was open. Emma and Sir Jackson climbed up the hole using rusted steel hoops built into the wall. They looked around and saw a man running towards Victoria Embankment Gardens. He was almost 200 meters up the road and would pass under the Golden Jubilee Bridge in seconds. John was heading in a different direction. Jackson put his head in the hole and shouted, "We need help now. We need this guy before he gets away!" Emma had started running and was now 100 metres from Jackson. A bomb squad guy emerged from the tunnel. Turning around, he saw Sir Jackson pointing and taking off at the speed of a 100-metre Olympic runner, and Emma shouted the man's description as he ran past her. Ahmed turned right into Northumberland Avenue, heading towards the roundabout of Trafalgar Square.

John Moody had badged into the Cabinet House, ran up the internal stairs, and exited the roof. He held his badge as two army snipers turned towards him.

"My name is John Moody, and we're chasing the driver, the Red Banner guy."

"I'm listening to a bomb squad guy reporting in now; he's chasing the guy up Northumberland."

Both snipers were looking through their scopes up to the square.

"It is too narrow, no leaves but too many trees." said one sniper. John looked at the stationary flags, then the chimney behind him.

"Help me up." They both pushed John by the feet. They passed the rifle up. "It's narrow. What's the distance to Trafalgar?"

"Two thousand five hundred feet?" shouted the army sniper. John rechecked the flags in the square and then rechecked the flags in the field.

"One army sniper yelled, "Three thousand two hundred ninety-six feet."

John yelled, "Runners report?"

"I am Entering the roundabout in four seconds. The driver is crossing Whitehall Road, this side of Charles I stature."

John counted down, took the silenced shot and hit Ahmed in the arm, passing through muscle and then ploughing into the statue. Ahmed was knocked over, stood and started running again.

"I got his arm. Bullet went into the statue." He locked the trigger mechanism, dropped the gun, and slid down the chimney.

"Good shot!" said the army guy, "1004 meters, balancing on a tower, bloody hell!"

"The runner confirmed the shot, and the driver is still running," replied the SAS sniper.

"Got to go, boys, thanks," shouted John.

The crowds were now settling in, waiting for the ceremony to commence. There was very little talking. The sun was bright, and there was no breeze. The Police blocked Whitehall on both ends. People were not pushing or trying to get into a better position behind the barriers. Some children were sitting on their parents' shoulders. The parade of both former and current armed forces had finished. The time was 10:45 am.

The ceremony organizers draped the area surrounding the Cenotaph with a sea of red poppies and a glorious carpet of red flowers, invoking memories for those long gone but not forgotten. People wore red paper poppies. These flowers bloomed in Belgium's former battlefields and, in Northern France, made famous in a poem called "In Flanders Field" by John McCrae. Wreaths were now being laid against the Cenotaph by members of the Royal family. It was a solemn moment. The flags were at half-mast and refused to flutter when the breeze stopped.

The time was approaching 10:46 am10:46 am.

Exiting Charing Cross Station, Milton Kahnt and his fiancé Laura Ruby held hands as they walked along the Strand, following the crowd down Whitehall. Ahmed stopped running, wrapped his jacket around his arm, and walked towards Charing Cross Station.

Ahmed turned slightly and saw his pursuer stationary, 100 meters behind him on his far left, scanning the crowd. 'One hundred meters was enough,' thought Ahmed. He cut through the oncoming mob and headed towards the Tube station. Milton heard a person say, "Excuse me." He recognized the voice, the tone turned and saw Ahmed pass by, blood dripping from his arm.

Milton was stunned. He thought Ahmed would have been arrested by now. Milton thought about why Ahmed was here. He looked at his watch, understanding what would happen next. Milton breathed a simple, silent prayer. 'God, I don't know how to pray, but may this not happen. Protect these people from my brother's revenge.'

The time was 10:47 am10:47 am. Ahmed saw the express to Scotland leaving in one minute, bought his ticket, boarded, and hid in the restroom after stealing a carry-on case from the platform. He changed shirts and wrapped his injured arm.

CHAPTER 109

C ENOTAPH 10:48 am

Emma slapped Hunter's face several times. "Hunter! Wake up!" He opened his eyes and saw Emma and Sir Jackson.

"Don't shine the light in my eyes, please. I'm okay. Can you help me up?" asked Hunter.

Sir Jackson leaned down, "Emma, let me, please."

"What happened to your face?" asked Emma.

"The driver whiplashed me with his Glock. I think I punched the wall several times instead of the driver," replied Hunter. John came down the hole, "The driver took a bullet in the arm but then disappeared."

Sir Jackson said, "Can you walk? Let's join the Bomb Squad." Noel Eric saw them approaching. Portable lights were illuminating that section of the tunnel. "You guys, okay? My young bloke gave chase. Did he get him? Radio doesn't work down here."

John said, "The driver took a bullet in the arm. He's in the wind."

Hunter asked, "What's the time?"

Sir Jackson looked at his wrist. His watch must have slipped off in the Thames. Eric said, "We have exactly 12 minutes until 11 am. We drilled a hole through the steel door. Our little snake camera saw the small charge attached that would have blown outward, killing anybody opening the door. The guys are now working on disarming the nuclear device."

Portable LED lights had been placed around the room, facing the centre. The room was shaped like an octagon made of black granite panels. Each panel of black granite stretched from the floor to the ceiling. Carved out from the vertical slabs of granite were soldiers, standing tall with their heads bowed, the muzzle of their rifles resting on the soldier's left foot, "Reverse arms," said Sir Jackson. Hunter thought it was a rather sobering and haunting sight.

Emma whispered, "Each soldier had slightly different uniforms and weapons." Hunter leaned against a wall, "What's the time?" Before Emma could answer, they could hear a bugle playing the "Last Post.'

"That's the last post. It will last for three minutes, then two minutes of silence?" said Hunter.

Eric spoke to his men. "You have less than 5 minutes!"

Sir Jackson bowed his head and whispered to himself, "God help us."

Hunter was thinking of the crowds above and the millions of people who lived, laughed, and worked in the city of London, now standing silent, remembering the end of a brutal war and would, in a few minutes, be the first victims of a new war. But hope was not yet lost.

"Hold onto hope, people," whispered Hunter.

Tears rolled down Emma's face. She was thinking of her dad. She argued with him, left home, and never sought reconciliation—her one foolish regret.

Noel Eric knew his family was directly above, standing in the crowds. He thought of each of them and his new baby girl, now 18 months old. Then the bugle stopped.

Then there was silence.

CHAPTER 110

PARIS, FRANCE

Ahmed had flown from Edinburgh, Scotland, to Paris Charles de Gaulle Airport late on Memorial Sunday, using his last fake passport.

He bought new clothes at Edinburgh airport, dumping the clothes in the men's toilet bin. He caught the train from Paris CDG Airport to Menilmontant Station, where five years ago, he purchased a two-bedroom unit. Like many wealthy Parisians in his community, he lived alone, in the city of love. As he walked his dog every morning, he wondered how he would spend 45 million euros.

CHAPTER 111

MOSCOW, RUSSIA

Russian President Denya Driminov received a phone message from an unknown caller on his private cell in the middle of the night.

"Hey Deny, this is Wayne from Australia, mate. Sorry to call you so late. I work in IT at HQJOC. How are things going in Russia? Mate, I'm calling to let you know your mate Franz Zhukov organized the theft of the Red Banners and a few of his mates intending to short the UK stock market after your Red Banners go 'kaboom' on Memorial Day. But it didn't go kaboom. They wanted to make a stack of money and throw you out on your ear, mate! I thought you would like to know. See you later!"

The president got the message translated. Zhukov had his fortune removed and redistributed. He now lives in Norilsk, Siberia, beside the Putoran Mountains.

CHAPTER 112

THE SAVOY LONDON
Sir Jackson shouted Emma, John and Hunter to a 'High Tea.'

"I thought we should celebrate. Please enjoy carrot cake, vanilla slice, black tea, clotted cream, English muffin, pancakes, tea pastries, some quiche, roasted quail and Champaign," said Sir Jackson.

Hunter turned to John. "What did he just say?"

Emma turned to Hunter with a smile and asked, "Would you like some cucumber sandwiches or asparagus quiche?"

"Could you translate what you just said?" asked Hunter, smiling.

Milton Kahnt married Laura Ruby in St. Mary's Le Strand, London. Their first daughter was named Grace, and their second was called Faith.

OTHER BOOKS BY PAUL ALLEN

Hunter saves a helpless accountant in a failed Mafia assassination attempt in Milan, Italy. Competing Italian mafia families pursue the accountant and the information he is carrying. Hunter helps the accountant disappear as his ASIS Gulfstream diverts from Sydney to the Marshall Islands in the Pacific.

A mystery ghost cocaine boat may hold the remains of an undercover AFP officer. Hunter and the accountant attempt to retrieve his remains but run foul of drug-smuggling MP's group while, at the same time, a rogue Chinese spy intentionally launches a Ronald Reagan missile. An ASIS team joins Hunter to fly to Hainan Island in China to find a Swiss missile engineer.

With an Australian traitor, Chinese double agents, and a devastating undisclosed mission, all hell breaks loose on the island.

Working alongside a group of skilled agents, John Moody and Emma Smirnov, and the accountant Paolo, Hunter makes an impossible choice to shut down a potentially devastating military attack by a rogue Chinese General.

When Detective Dido Belle teams up with Detective Inspector

Barker, they face a daunting task-hunting down the killer of a painting forger who amassed a fortune swindling international art auction houses. The killer, adept at hiding in plain sight, complicates their investigation with professional forgeries and Gold Coast politics.

In this gripping psychological thriller, the story unfolds with a shattering revelation. Detective Inspector Barker, haunted by a secret from his past, stumbles upon a serial killer. Will his guilt-stricken conscience hinder his pursuit of the killer, adding a layer of psychological depth to the narrative?

Prepare for a heart-pounding ride filled with murder and mystery in this high-octane double crime whodunnit. Set against the breathtaking backdrop of the Gold Coast of Australia, the fast-paced plot will keep you guessing until the very end.

www.ingramcontent.com/pod-product-compliance
Lightning Source LLC
Chambersburg PA
CBHW070836260626
47170CB00007B/2394